Praise for Margaret Truman

"Truman 'knows the forks' in the nation's capital and how to pitchfork her readers into a web of murder and detection."

—*The Christian Science Monitor*

"She's up-to-the-minute. And she's good."

—Associated Press

"[Truman is] a first-rate mystery writer."

—*Los Angeles Times Book Review*

"A dazzling series."

—*The Atlanta Journal-Constitution*

"Former first daughter Truman probably knows Washington as well as anyone and offers it to readers with equal dollops of affection and cynicism."

—*The Plain Dealer*

"Truman can write suspense with the best of them."

—LARRY KING

BY MARGARET TRUMAN

First Ladies
Bess W. Truman
Souvenir
Women of Courage
Harry S Truman
Letters from Father:
The Truman Family's Personal Correspondences
Where the Buck Stops
White House Pets
The President's House

IN THE CAPITAL CRIMES SERIES
Murder in Foggy Bottom
Murder at the Library of Congress
Murder at the Watergate
Murder in the House
Murder at the National Gallery
Murder on the Potomac
Murder at the Pentagon
Murder in the Smithsonian
Murder at the National Cathedral
Murder at the Kennedy Center
Murder in the CIA
Murder in Georgetown
Murder at the FBI
Murder on Embassy Row
Murder in the Supreme Court
Murder on Capitol Hill
Murder in the White House
Murder in Havana
Murder at Ford's Theater
Murder at Union Station
Murder at The Washington Tribune
Murder at the Opera
Murder on K Street
Murder Inside the Beltway

Murder Inside the Beltway

A CAPITAL CRIMES NOVEL

BALLANTINE BOOKS • NEW YORK

2010 Ballantine Books Mass Market Edition

Published in the United States by Ballantine Books, an imprint of The Random House Publishing Group, a division of Random House, Inc., New York.

BALLANTINE and colophon are registered trademarks of Random House, Inc.

Originally published in hardcover in the United States by Ballantine Books, an imprint of The Random House Publishing Group, a division of Random House, Inc., in 2008.

ISBN 978-0-345-49889-2

Cover design: Jerry Pfeifer
Cover photograph: glowimages

Printed in the United States of America

www.ballantinebooks.com

9 8 7 6 5 4 3 2 1

Dedicated, with love, to our mother, Margaret Truman Daniel. For more than thirty years, she liked nothing better than to sit at home in New York, murdering people in Washington, D.C., one at a time.

Clifton Truman Daniel, Harrison Gates Daniel, Thomas Washington Daniel

Chapter 1

"What a waste."

Matthew Jackson went to where Walter Hatcher stood holding a framed eight-by-ten color photograph he'd pulled from a bookshelf. "She's a knockout," Hatcher said. "I wouldn't have minded getting some of that myself."

Jackson ignored Hatch's comment—it wasn't unexpected from the senior detective—and simply agreed that she was, indeed, beautiful.

The woman in the picture was posed the way photographers liked to shoot glamour girls of yesteryear, provocatively positioned on a white divan. She wore a bloodred kimono, left open enough to display plenty of leg and cleavage. Jackson tried to discern her lineage; probably Mediterranean a few generations back judging from her inky black hair and large, almond eyes. Her expression was inviting, slightly parted full crimson lips hinting at a mischievous smile, teasing whoever viewed the photograph.

Hatcher put the picture back on the shelf facedown and turned to look at the body sprawled in the center of the bedroom floor. "Looks like some john figured he didn't get his money's worth."

"She's a hooker?" Jackson said.

Hatcher looked at the young detective as though he'd mispronounced a simple word. "What do you *figure* she was, Jackson?" he asked. "Your mother decorate her bedroom like this?"

Jackson drew a breath. "Yeah, you're right," he said. He'd almost gotten used to his partner's put-downs. Almost.

The room to which Hatch referred was a large bedroom on the second floor of an apartment in the Adams Morgan section of Washington. If a set designer had been charged with creating the quintessential bordello, he might have used the same approach. There was the requisite mirror on the ceiling over the king-sized bed, which was suspended by four gold chains. A few feet from it was a mirrored ball that, when rotated, caught the light from tiny red and blue pin-spots. The bedding was golden and silk-like. Animal-print rugs (leopards and zebras) and upholstery created a cross between Animal Planet and *Vegas*. Dimmers controlled the lights. A fully stocked minibar occupied one corner. Soft rock music that had been playing when the detectives arrived continued to sound from small speakers high up in the room's four corners.

Whoever killed her hadn't attempted to maintain the room's décor. It was a mess. Bottles and glasses from the bar were strewn on the floor. The bedding was bunched up; one corner of the duvet was smeared with her blood. A red barrel chair had been overturned, as had a wrought-iron stand, its furry-leafed plant resting in the middle of a dark water stain on the carpeting.

She'd obviously put up the good fight.

The cops knew her name. The building's super, who sat in the apartment's living room with two other residents of the building, had provided it: Rosalie Curzon. She'd been a tenant for two years: "Always paid her rent on time," the super had told the cops. "Nice lady."

Hatcher called headquarters to run the name. Her history was brief. Ms. Curzon had twice been arrested for prostitution four years ago when she worked for one of D.C.'s myriad escort services. She'd paid a fine—or someone did—and she walked.

Matt Jackson turned his attention to the floor-to-ceiling bookshelves from which Hatch had lifted the photograph. The deceased's reading selection was eclectic—leather-bound editions of classics, potboiler fiction, and a dozen erotic novels lined up next to six volumes on sexual practices. Jackson smiled as he read the spine of one in the latter grouping, *Kosher Sex*. He pulled it down, saw that it had been written by a rabbi, and returned it to its place on the shelf.

Sections were reserved for home decorating books, murder mysteries by big name authors, and for biographies of a variety of famous names in business, politics, the military, and religion.

"The well-read hooker, huh, Matt?" Hatcher said, joining his young colleague in perusing the books. His eyes eventually went to the top shelf, twelve inches below the crown molding that separated the wall from the ceiling, where ten videotape boxes stood nestled in slots provided by a blue, faux-leather slipcase designed for that purpose. They were too high up to reach. "Grab that desk chair," Hatcher instructed. Jackson dragged it over, stood on it, and handed the slipcase down to Hatcher.

"Hey, wait a minute," Jackson said, pointing to a small video camera that had been partially concealed by the tapes, its lens tilted down in the direction of the bed.

"Grab that, too," Hatcher ordered.

Jackson gave the camera to Hatcher, jumped down from the chair, and joined him in reviewing what was written on the spines of the tapes.

Hatcher looked at Jackson and grinned. "Look'ee here," he said, referring to the neatly handwritten notations on the videos. Each indicated a span between two dates, followed by initials.

"You don't figure the lady was a movie producer, too, do you, Jackson?"

Jackson's thought matched Hatcher's. Had the deceased prostitute videotaped her trysts with paying customers? If so, was it possible that she'd captured her own murder on tape?

Hatcher's laugh was a mirthless low rumble. "Maybe we got lucky."

"It would be nice."

"It would be better than nice. It would be a home run."

"Two are missing," Jackson offered, referring to empty slots in the slipcase that was designed to hold twelve tapes.

"Maybe business was slow," Hatcher said. He opened the compartment of the camera and retrieved a tape. A quick examination showed that approximately half of it had been used.

They turned as the third member of their team, Mary Hall, entered, followed by crime scene techs and a D.C. medical examiner.

"Took you long enough," Hatcher said to the young, prematurely balding ME in the white coat.

The ME ignored him and went directly to the body. One of the techs began making a video recording, circling the body to capture it from a variety of angles.

"What do we know?" the ME asked Jackson.

"One of her neighbors called nine-one-one, said she heard noises from the apartment. She got hold of the super and he used his key to get in."

"How long ago?"

"We got the call forty-five minutes ago."

The ME knelt next to the victim and leaned close to examine the injuries to the back of her head, and to the one side of her face that was visible. "This is the way you found her?" he asked no one in particular.

"If you mean did anybody move the body," Hatcher said, "the answer is no."

The ME moved to the other side of the deceased.

"Somebody beat her up pretty good," Jackson said to Mary Hall, who'd come to his side.

"And strangled her," said the ME, pointing to bruising on her neck. He stood and surveyed the room's disorder. "She didn't go down easily."

"Where are the super and the other tenants?" Hatcher asked Hall.

"In the living room."

"You get statements from them?"

"Preliminary ones."

"And you leave them alone in there to get their formal stories straight?"

"Hatch, I—"

"Get back in there!"

Jackson avoided Hall's exasperated look as she left the room.

"The nine-one-one call came in at ten thirty-seven," Jackson said. "Somebody in the building said she heard noises in here, like a fight. That pins down time-of-death."

"She's warm but starting to cool," said the ME. "It didn't just happen. I'd say two, two-and-a-half hours ago."

"Maybe the lady waited a while to make the call. Go ask her, Jackson."

Jackson returned minutes later. "You were right, Hatch," he said. "She says she heard the fight going on around seven, seven-fifteen, but her husband didn't want to get involved."

"So what made her change her mind at ten thirty-seven?"

"She says she knew she'd never get to sleep without doing something."

"Her husband with her?"

Jackson nodded.

"Tell Mary to take them back to their apartment to get their statements." He called over one of the crime scene techs who'd started to mark blood spatter on the carpet with small tent cards. "Where's your evidence bag?" he asked.

The tech went to where he'd dropped it on a chair and brought it to Hatcher. The veteran detective led Jackson to a corner where they wouldn't be overheard. He placed the camera, the tape it contained, and the ten marked videos into the bag and handed it to Jackson. "Take this back to headquarters and wait for me there. Don't let it out of your sight. Understand? You show it to nobody until I get there."

"You don't want me to log it in?"

"You catch on quick, Jackson. Go on, move."

Hatcher went to the living room, where Mary Hall was about to escort the husband and wife back to their apartment. He waited until they were gone before addressing the only other person in the room, the building's superintendent, a beefy Hispanic man with pockmarked cheeks and a tic in his left eye.

"Tell me about the lady in there," Hatcher said, nodding toward the bedroom.

"Miss Curzon? What about her?" His English was good.

"How long has she been here?"

"Must be two years now."

"She sign a lease?"

"*Sí.* Everybody does."

"Don't *sí* me, José. You're in America, so speak American. English."

The super's expression mirrored his confusion, and fear.

"How much she pay you on the side?"

He stared blankly at the detective.

"Come on, José, don't give me that dumb look. You

knew she was turning tricks. She's a *puta,* right? A whore. How much she pay you to look the other way?"

"Oh, no, no, sir, you are wrong. I do not care what the tenants do as long as they don't bother nobody else. I say live and let live." He forced a smile in the hope it would indicate sincerity.

"How much every month? A couple of bills? Five?"

"I told you that—"

Hatcher closed the gap between them, his face now inches from the super's. "You're lying to me, scumbag. That's a crime, pal. I'm going to look into every corner of your life, and when I come up with what I know I'll find, you're going to be dead meat. Tax fraud. Obstructing justice. Lying to a cop. In the meantime, we'll go to MPD and have a nice, long chat."

"Sir, I—"

"You stay in this room until I'm through in there. You hear me?"

The super nodded.

Hatcher returned to the bedroom, where the ME was finishing up his initial examination. "Blunt force trauma," he told Hatcher, "and apparent strangulation. Can't tell which one killed her until we autopsy."

"No weapon?" Hatcher asked.

"That's your department, Hatch. From what I can see of her wounds, whoever did it used his hands. I'd say he was pretty pissed off."

One of two uniformed officers who'd been first to arrive at the scene entered the room. Since the arrival of the detectives, he'd been stationed in the hallway to keep the curious at bay. His partner had taken up a position downstairs at the building entrance. Hatcher ordered them to remain at the scene and to make sure no one entered the apartment. "There'll be reinforcements soon to canvas the neighborhood and the rest of the tenants."

He rejoined the super and told him to take him to

where Detective Hall was questioning the husband and wife.

The door to the apartment directly beneath Rosalie Curzon's was open when they arrived. Hatcher told the super to wait in the hall and joined Hall in the couple's living room.

"You about finished?" Hatcher asked.

"I think so, Hatch."

Hatcher returned to the open door and ran his fingers over its peephole. "You must see a lot of what goes on here, huh?" he said to the wife.

"I mind my own business," she said, looking nervously at her husband, a thin, tense man wearing glasses with thick, clouded lenses.

"I tell her all the time to mind her own business," the husband said, "but she won't listen. She never listens."

Hatcher ignored him and asked the wife if she'd seen anyone coming or going that evening.

"I don't pay attention to who comes and goes," she said.

"That's all she does," countered the husband. "She's always standing at that damn peephole to see who's coming in and going out."

"And who'd you see tonight?" Hatcher repeated.

"No one," she said, vigorously shaking her head.

"Let's go," Hatcher said. Mary Hall snapped her notebook shut, thanked the couple for their time, and left the apartment with Hatcher. On his way out of the building he locked eyes with the super, who looked as though he might cry at any minute. "I'm going to give you overnight to decide to be straight with me, José. I'll be back tomorrow. You got twenty-four hours to take some memory pills. Got it?"

"*Sí,* yes, *gracias.* Thank you."

Hatcher pressed his index finger against the super's

fleshy lips. "Twenty-four hours, my friend. Don't disappoint me."

The detectives walked to where Hatcher's car was parked crookedly at the curb. Hall and Jackson had arrived together in Jackson's car, which he'd taken back to headquarters.

"Damn, I'm hungry," Hatcher complained as he and Hall headed for MPD on Indiana Avenue.

"Stop and get something," she suggested. "We going back to headquarters?"

"Yeah. You ever watch porn movies, Mary?"

"I've seen a few."

"Feel like watching some tonight?"

"Oh, Jesus, Hatch, what the hell are you doing, entering your dirty old man phase?"

He laughed. "Jackson's back in the office with a batch of amateur porn for us to watch."

"Great. You and Matt get your jollies. I'm off-duty."

"No you're not, Mary. We've got a long night ahead of us. I think I will grab something to bring back. Chinese?"

"Whatever turns you on, Hatch."

Chapter 2

Matt Jackson anticipated what Hatcher would want when he arrived at MPD headquarters. He secured a seldom-used interrogation room that contained a TV set and video/DVD player. Once inside with the doors closed, he drew drapes across the one-way mirror, and turned off the harsh overhead fluorescents, leaving on only a small lamp. The evidence bag containing the tapes and camera from Rosalie Curzon's apartment sat between his feet underneath the scarred table. He hoped no one would come in and ask what he was doing there. Hatcher had made it clear that the tapes were to remain within his possession, at least until Hatcher had a chance to view them.

Could it possibly be that the prostitute's killer *was* caught on tape? Obviously, the tapes cataloged and stored in the slipcase couldn't contain such material. But there was that half-used tape in the camera. Had the camera been running during the attack? If so, Rosalie Curzon's case might possibly avoid joining the ranks of MPD's burgeoning file of unsolved murders.

His mind wandered as he sat alone in the room. He was tempted, of course, to pop a tape into the player, but knew that Hatcher would be angry if he did. Barely a year ago, when he'd been promoted to the rank of detective after four years as a uniformed patrolman and assigned to Walter Hatcher's squad after a brief stint with another team, it seemed a golden opportunity to learn from one of the force's most decorated cops. He didn't harbor any illusions that working with Hatcher would be easy. The man defined hardnosed, impatient, and unforgiving. There were rumors that he had taken the law into his own hands on more than one occasion, but as far as Jackson knew, the senior detective had never been brought up on departmental charges. Or, if he had, nothing had ever come of it.

Working side by side with Hatcher had been the learning experience Jackson had expected. He knew he had a lot to absorb and excused Hatcher's tendency to berate him for every mistake. Jackson wasn't thin-skinned and didn't take Hatcher's sarcastic comments and bombastic eruptions personally. What *did* bother him also had to do with his skin—its color.

He was the product of a mixed marriage, his father a black man, his mother white. Fair-skinned, he sometimes passed for white, although he never tried to conceal his African-American roots. Hatcher used slang for every minority—blacks, Hispanics, Muslims, Jews, and women, an equal-opportunity bigot. That provided some solace for Jackson. At the same time, he sensed a deeper, darker disdain that Hatcher had for him because of his mixed parentage, and because he was a college graduate, his major sociology. As far as Hatcher was concerned, college was a waste of time and money for anyone seeking a career in law enforcement, and he never hesitated to say so. Too, Hatcher often said that Jackson didn't *look* like a cop, whatever that meant. True, Jackson was reed thin and not tall, and leaned toward tweed jackets with leather elbow patches, button-down shirts, knit ties and desert boots, not a cop out of central casting. But this wasn't Hollywood. This was Washington, D.C., with a police force of almost four thousand, two-thirds of them African American, twenty-five percent female. What did a typical cop look like? Like Walter Hatcher, big and rawboned, thick-necked, red-faced, and with a perpetual nasty scowl?

Jackson often considered confronting his boss about his feelings, but hadn't, deciding instead to ride out his apprenticeship and hope for a transfer when it was over. He wasn't especially proud of his willingness to allow Hatcher to verbally abuse him, but rationalized that discretion was the better part of valor, at least in the short term. He was determined to get through this initial phase of his training without incident. He wanted to be a cop, the best cop he could be, and allowing Hatcher to derail that dream was anathema to him.

He was deep into these thoughts when Hatcher and Mary Hall arrived. Mary carried a large take-out bag from a nearby Chinese restaurant that stayed open late. "I got you General Tso's chicken, and brown rice," she told Matt.

"Great." He wasn't hungry, but it was nice of her to think of him.

"Where're the tapes?" Hatcher asked.

"Right here," Jackson said, pulling the bag from beneath the table.

"Let's get started," Hatcher said. "Gimme the one that was in the camera."

Hatcher turned on the TV monitor, slid the tape into the video recorder, and pushed REWIND. Mary opened food containers and distributed them.

Once the tape had rewound, Hatcher pushed PLAY.

"What are these?" Mary asked. She'd posed that same question to Hatcher during the drive to the Met, as headquarters was called, but never received an answer.

"We found them in the apartment," Jackson said. "The victim had a video camera up on one of the bookshelves. Hatch figures that—"

"Shut up," Hatcher said as the screen came alive, and sound hissed through the speaker.

They watched in silence as a very much alive Rosalie Curzon was seen walking into the frame, followed by a man. She wore the red kimono she'd worn in her still photo. The man was dressed in a suit.

"Long time, no see," Curzon said.

"I haven't been back to D.C. in a while," he said.

Jackson was surprised at how good the picture and sound were.

"Got something for Rosie?" she asked.

"Sure." He reached into his inside jacket pocket and pulled out an undetermined number of bills that he'd obviously counted out beforehand. He handed them to her, and she disappeared.

"Let's get rid of these clothes," she said when she came back, reaching for his tie.

They moved out of camera range. When they reappeared, both were naked.

"Look at that," Hatcher said. "She's turning the john so that he's facing the camera. The bitch knows what she's doing."

She led him to the bed, where their gyrations were captured on the tape. When they were finished, she complimented him on his lovemaking. She slipped back into her kimono, and he dressed. She kissed his cheek. "Don't be such a stranger," she cooed. The screen went black.

"Do we have to watch this stuff?" Mary Hall asked.

"Turn you on?" Hatcher said.

"Turns me off."

Hatcher used chopsticks to shovel beef and broccoli into his mouth. Images and sound appeared again on the screen. The same scenario was played out, but with a different man. When that segment had run its course, the screen went blank again, and stayed that way.

Hatcher muttered an obscenity.

"Looks like she didn't have it rolling when she was killed," Jackson offered.

"Another brilliant observation from Detective Jackson," Hatcher said. "Let me have another tape."

"Do we have to watch more?" Mary asked.

"Yeah, we do," said Hatcher.

Neither Jackson nor Hall ate while sitting through scene after scene of Rosalie Curzon entertaining her paying male customers. For Jackson, the initial scenes had been sexually arousing, but numbness soon set in, the sameness of the act becoming anything but erotic, sometimes even silly. But after the third tape started to play, everyone's attention perked up. The john's face was all too familiar, a six-term pol with a penchant for publicity. There was no mistaking him—Congressman Slade Morrison of Arizona.

"What'a you know," Hatcher muttered, writing down the name.

On the fourth tape, Hatcher recognized another john, although neither Jackson nor Hall did. "The guy's name is Joe Yankavich," Hatcher said. "Runs a bar in Adams Morgan, Joe's, bad food and watered drinks."

Hatcher rewound and again played the portion where Rosalie Curzon had turned the naked man toward the camera.

"I recognize him now," Jackson said. "I've been there a few times. It's a couple of blocks from my apartment."

Hatcher noted Yankavich's name on the pad.

In the middle of the final tape—it was now almost six in the morning—Mary, who'd had to fight falling asleep and had nodded off on a few occasions, let out an involuntary gasp.

Hatcher stopped the tape. "You recognize him, Mary?" he asked.

"Ah, no. Forget it."

"Hey, Mary, this is a murder investigation," Hatcher said. "If you know the guy, speak up."

"He's a cop."

"Yeah?" Hatcher said.

"An instructor at the academy. Defensive tactics, baton training," she said glumly.

"What's his name?"

"I don't know."

"Get it for me."

"Okay," she said.

After the final scene had played, Hatcher stretched, yawned, and turned on the overheads. He looked at Jackson, who rubbed his eyes.

"So, we've got us three live ones to talk to," Hatcher said.

"What are you going to do with the tapes?" Jackson asked.

"Take 'em upstairs and let 'em know what we've got. I can see political fallout written all over this."

Hatcher placed the tapes in the evidence bag and opened the door. He looked back at Jackson and Hall, who remained in their chairs. "Coming?" he asked. "Go grab a couple of hours. I want to get back on this at noon."

Jackson and Hall wearily pushed themselves up from their chairs and followed Hatcher through the door. "Funny," Jackson muttered.

"What's funny?" Mary asked.

"Every time the victim is seen on the tapes, she's wearing that red bathrobe."

"It's a kimono," Mary corrected.

"Okay, a kimono. But she's wearing it every time."

"So what?" Hatcher said.

"So, she wasn't wearing it tonight when she was murdered."

"Sooo?" Hatcher said.

"She was wearing a sweat suit," Jackson said, "like

runners wear. Maybe whoever killed her wasn't there for sex, hadn't made an appointment or anything."

Mary looked at Hatcher. "Good point," she said.

Hatcher grimaced and said, "See you back here at noon. We got some horny johns to talk to."

Chapter 3

Jackson and Hall drove in his car from the Met to Adams Morgan. After finding and securing a rare parking spot on the street, they went to the diner on 18th where they had bacon and eggs before walking in the opposite direction, to Jackson's apartment building. It was eight o'clock. They were due back on duty in four hours.

He'd lived in the apartment for the five years since leaving Chicago to join the Washington MPD, and had immediately felt comfortable in the ethnically mixed, lively Adams Morgan community, Washington's only truly integrated neighborhood. Originally, it had attracted primarily a large influx of Hispanics, but they were soon joined by Ethiopians and Asians, as well as middle-class blacks looking for a community in which skin color meant little, and enlightened whites looking for the same thing.

Jackson's apartment was on the top floor of a six-floor building that had been built in the 1950s. It lacked certain modern updates, but was in overall well-kept shape. Directly across from his apartment was a door leading to a roof garden that he made good use of when off-duty.

The first time Mary had been there, six months before, she'd commented on how neat he was.

"Yeah, I'm a real Felix Unger," he'd said with a laugh.

"No, I mean it. You put me to shame. Remind me to

never invite you to my place. It looks like Baghdad on a bad day."

It was on that first visit to his apartment that they'd made love. All the signs had been there that they would eventually end up in bed, the furtive flirtations, provocative comments, and their growing need to spend off-duty time together, coffee dates, the movies, and dinners at some of Adams Morgan's ethnic restaurants. But as their relationship deepened, they both knew one thing: they had to keep it sub-rosa, secret, quiet, under the covers as it were. Bad enough they were both MPD detectives; department regulations discouraged romantic relationships within the MPD. But they also worked together on the same squad, with Walt Hatcher as their boss. If anyone was capable of screwing up a budding relationship, it was Hatcher.

Entering into a personal relationship with Matt hadn't been easy for Mary. She'd developed a hard shell as a defense against the cruelty of her father, who when not slapping her around, substituted verbal abuse: "You're no beauty, that's for sure," he often said. "Better hope you meet some blind guy who won't know how ugly you are."

The shell that she wrapped herself in had been off-putting for many men and had worked to shield her from further hurt. But there was something compelling about Matt Jackson's calm and gentleness, and intelligence, that worked to lower the barrier little by little, that allowed her to believe him when he said he thought she was very attractive, and enabled her to drop her guard and let him into her life. He'd meant what he'd said about her looks. He liked her slender figure and full breasts, and the way her lip curled into a sly smile when she didn't buy what someone said. He found her especially sexy when she removed her contact lenses and donned reading glasses, and told her so. Neither talked about anything long-term, which served them both well. One day at a time, one shoe before the other.

They slept until eleven. She kept some clothing at the apartment, and changed into another outfit before they headed back to work on that overcast day.

Walt Hatcher also slept until eleven when his wife of many years, Mae, woke him as she'd been instructed to do when he'd arrived home that morning.

"Time to get up, sleepyhead," she said softly, sitting next to him on the bed and touching his thinning hair.

He groaned and turned away from her.

"You said you had to get up," she said.

He struggled to prop himself against the headboard and squeezed his eyes open and shut.

"Do you really have to go in?" she asked. "You worked all night. You deserve a day off."

"Yeah, I gotta go in. We caught a homicide last night in Adams Morgan. People to interview today."

"I'm sorry you missed dinner. I made lasagna the way you like it."

He swung his legs off the bed and scratched his belly. "Sorry about that. By the time I got off last night I figured I missed dinner." He laughed. "Hell, I knew I missed it. I stopped in at Tommy G's place for a drink and something to eat, got involved talking to Tommy and some others. I got the call there. We brought in some Chink food after we came back from the scene."

"I'll make you some eggs."

"That'd be nice, Mae. Thanks."

He took an abbreviated shower, put on fresh shorts, socks, and T-shirt, got back into the wrinkled, stained, gray pin-striped suit, white shirt, and tie he'd worn the night before, and went to the kitchen. He came up behind his wife and kissed her neck.

"Thank you, sir," she said, continuing to scramble eggs in a frying pan.

He sat in the breakfast nook and turned on a small TV. The local news was being reported—two drive-by shootings in Southeast, a major drug bust in Alexandria, a homosexual knifed to death by a jealous partner in a DuPont Circle apartment. He clicked off the set.

"Nothing but bad news," Mae said as the toaster oven dinged.

"So what else is new?" he grumbled. "It's a rotten world, Mae, with too many rotten people."

"You see the worst of it," she said, taking two halves of an English muffin from the toaster oven and buttering them. She delivered his breakfast and joined him. "I spoke with Christina today about all of us getting together at the Florida house. She loved the idea."

"Yeah, that'd be okay," he managed between bites of egg and muffin. He finished what was on the plate, wiped his mouth, and sat back. "You know what I think, Mae?"

"What?"

"You've been after me to pack it in at MPD for a long time now. I—"

"Only because I worry about you, Walt. You're getting older and—"

"Just me?"

"You know what I mean."

"Yeah, I do. Anyway, I've pretty much had it. This city's being turned over to the scum—the whole country is, for that matter. You can't find a store clerk who speaks English anymore. The government's run by a bunch of morons who only care whether they get reelected, big money from lobbyists buying their votes, and I end up playing nursemaid to a rookie detective who can't find his own rear end with both hands. Maybe it's time I turned in the gold badge and we headed for Florida, like you've been wanting to."

She beamed. "You mean that?"

He patted her leg and nodded. "Yeah, I mean it. It's not going to happen tomorrow, but maybe we should start planning for it, huh? I might even drag out the golf clubs, if I can find them, and become—" He gestured broadly and intoned, "A man of leisure."

She giggled and squeezed his hand. That was one of the things that had attracted him to her twenty-five years ago, her fresh-scrubbed naiveté, and the fact that she found almost everything he said to be funny.

"Gotta run," he said. "I'll see if I can leave today at a decent hour, maybe grab something out tonight. Okay?"

"Okay, boss," she said, tossing him a snappy salute.

As she watched him drive away, her sunny face turned cloudy. She hoped he was serious about planning to retire and move to the Florida house they owned. Their three children were in different parts of the country—two sons, one in San Francisco, the other in Colorado, and a daughter living and working in Atlanta. And there were the precious grandchildren, four of them, living too far away. Planning a family reunion in Florida had been a dream of hers for the past few years. Maybe now that Walt seemed serious about considering a change, it would become a reality.

She didn't harbor any delusions about her cop-husband. He was a difficult man by any standard, crusty, cranky, and opinionated, incapable of accepting any views that didn't mesh with his—a true my-way-or-the-highway personality. And he was cheap, too, although she preferred to think of him as being frugal and responsible. There were times when she wished he wasn't quite as tight-fisted with their money. He often criticized her for having spent too much at the market for foods he didn't feel they needed, or for failing to make better use of coupons and not seeking out bargains. Buying the house in Florida had been a wrenching decision for him, and it took more than a year of cajoling, coupled with her making the case that it was a good investment, before he budged and agreed. She knew he'd come from a family in which money was always tight, and felt she understood his frugality. He was obsessed with saving every possible dollar from his paycheck, as though he expected the bottom to fall out of their financial lives at any moment. Aside from an occasional dinner out at the local Italian restaurant, or a hot dog at a mall, little was spent on anything but the necessities. He was a responsible man and husband when it came to their money and family, and she respected that. Still . . .

Mae knew how to handle him, however, or at least felt she did on most occasions. It was all a matter of tapping into his gentle, caring side, a side few knew he possessed. Sure, they'd argued on many occasions, and there were times that she'd felt belittled. But those times never lasted long. She'd wait for him to say something he considered clever and amusing and laugh heartily, which seldom failed to defuse the situation. Walter Hatcher was, as she often told her kids and friends, a good man in a lousy job, seeing the underbelly of society, responding to grisly murders and brutal rapes, young punks killing one another over a marijuana cigarette or a pair of sneakers. He tried to pass off those experiences as simply part of the job: "If it got to me, I wouldn't do it."

She knew better. It affected him deeply; how could it not? There were times when he came home with the smell of death on his clothing, even spots of blood. No one, she knew, could spend his or her day in those circumstances without it leaving its mark.

She wished he'd stayed with Vice and not transferred to Homicide two years ago. Not that the vice squad spent its days with a better class of people. Far from it. He would tell her of arresting pimps and prostitutes whose lives were, as far as she was concerned, dredging the bottom of the human condition, spreading disease and destroying families. Gambling rings took money from men and women who couldn't afford to lose it, their rents and food money tossed down the drain while their families suffered. All of it, her husband told her, fed the coffers of organized crime, funding its drug trade and the thousands of addicts whose lives were ruined. "Victimless crime?" he would say, snorting at the mere suggestion. "Nothing *but* victims."

Would he follow through on what he'd said that morning and leave his job behind, walk away in one piece and with his head held high for having made Washington a better, safer city? She closed her eyes and said a silent prayer that he would, before a stroke or heart attack or cancer dashed that dream.

Chapter 4

When Jackson and Hall arrived at headquarters on Indiana Avenue a little after noon, they were told that Hatcher was in a meeting upstairs with the white shirts. They passed the time talking with other detectives until Hatcher walked into the room at twelve-thirty.

"What's up?" Hall asked.

"Nice outfit," Hatcher said to Hall, referring to the black slacks and sweater she wore. "Goes nice with your black hair."

"Thanks."

Hatcher looked at Jackson. "You ever wear anything besides that jacket with the patches on the sleeves?"

"No," Jackson replied, tempted to say that Hatcher's suit looked like he'd slept in it.

"Here's the drill," Hatcher said. "Our esteemed leaders looked at the tapes, at least the portions I flagged for them. That cop at the academy, Mary, is Al Manfredi. There's somebody else we didn't recognize." He consulted a note he'd written. "Lewis Archer. He's a well-connected lobbyist with hooks into the White House. So, it looks like we've got a few jerks to interview."

"Where do we start?" Jackson asked.

"With Congressman Slade Morrison, champion of the people of Arizona. I want you to call his office, Mary, and set up an appointment."

"Why me?"

"A woman's less threatening."

Jackson saw the wisdom of having Mary make the call, but doubted that it had been Hatcher's idea. More likely it came from one of the chiefs with whom Hatcher had been conferring. Approaching Congressman Morrison was sensitive; sensitivity wasn't Hatcher's strong suit.

"Here's the number, Mary," Hatcher said. "See if you can set up something for later today. In the meantime, the three of us will pay a visit to this Lewis Archer character. Depending on what happens with the congressman, you two get hold of Manfredi, maybe swing by the academy, remind him that you were a student, Mary, get him in a chatty mood, catch him with his pants down, too." He chuckled at his witticism. "I'll take care of Joe Yankavich. I know the creep. We on the same page?"

Hatcher and Jackson waited, and watched, while Mary made her call to Congressman Morrison's office in the Cannon House Office Building.

"This is MPD Detective Mary Hall," she told the staffer who answered. "Is the congressman available?"

There was a pause as Mary listened to the response. "It's a police matter," she said.

Another long pause. "Congressman Morrison? This is MPD Detective Mary Hall. We'd like to speak with you about a homicide last night in Adams Morgan. . . . That's right. The victim was a Rosalie Curzon. She was a prostitute and . . . Oh, yes, sir, I am serious. We have reason to believe that . . . What? . . . Sir, all I'm asking is that we have the opportunity to sit down with you and ask a few questions. . . . Sir, I'm not accusing you of anything. If you'd prefer, we can just stop at your office and . . . No, sir, I'm not threatening anything. . . . What? Yes, I think sometime tomorrow would be acceptable. . . . What? You'll pick the place?" (She glanced over at Hatcher, who nodded.) "Yes, sir, that will be fine. . . .

You'll call? Here's my cell number, Congressman. I'll expect to hear from you by the end of today. Thank you, sir."

"Smooth, honey," Hatcher said when Mary hung up.

"He sounded nervous," Mary said.

"Good," said Hatcher. "Make him squirm." He laughed. "I hope it's him, you know? I'd love to take down one of those arrogant congressional bastards."

Before heading for Archer's office on K Street—Washington lobbyists' street of dreams—they Googled the name. Prior to joining a lobbying firm with six names, including his own, he'd been a two-term congressman from California. Defeated in a bid for a third term, he ended up with a cushy job in the Defense Department's procurement branch. After eleven years buying $12,000 ashtrays and $14,000 toilet seats, he jumped to what had become known as the "fourth branch of government," lobbying his former employer on behalf of defense-contractor clients. A photo of him prompted Hall to ask, "Do you figure those are his own teeth?"

"Bright, huh?" Hatcher said. "Break out the sunglasses."

A receptionist told them that Mr. Archer was in a meeting.

"Get him out of it," Hatcher said. "He'll be meeting with us."

His tone told the receptionist that to argue wasn't prudent, nor would it accomplish anything. She left her desk and disappeared into the recesses of the firm. A few minutes later, Archer accompanied her to the reception area. The smile he flashed was as white as the monogrammed shirt he wore. "I understand you want to see me," he said. "Is something wrong?"

"We just need a few minutes with you," Jackson said, extending his hand and introducing Hatcher and Hall. "You have a conference room that's not being used?"

"This won't take long, will it?"

No one replied.

"This way," he said, and led them to a large conference room, where they sat at a huge oblong cherry table. "What's this about?" he asked once they'd settled in the guest chairs.

"We're investigating a murder that happened last night," Hatcher said. "In Adams Morgan."

"A murder?" Archer said, brow furrowed. "That's terrible. But what does it have to do with me?"

"The victim was a prostitute," Jackson said. "Her name was Rosalie Curzon."

The three detectives sat silently and waited for him to respond verbally, although anything he might say was negated by the knowing expression on his deeply tanned face.

"Are you suggesting that I knew this woman?" he finally said.

Hatcher offered what passed for a smile. "Are you suggesting that you *didn't* know her, Mr. Archer?"

"What if I did? I mean, I had nothing to do with her murder, if that's what you're getting at."

"When did you last see her?" Jackson asked.

Archer pressed his eyes shut as though that would help jog his memory. When he opened them he said, "Months ago. At least two months ago."

"Sure about that?" Mary Hall asked.

"I can't be sure about a date," he said, "but I know it was a long time ago. How did you know I knew her?"

"You starred in one of her movies," Hatcher said.

"Her movies?" He slapped the side of his head. "Oh, no, don't tell me she made tapes of her . . ."

"Johns," Hatcher filled in for him.

"Jesus," he muttered, and laughed. "I can't believe this."

"Where were you last night?" Hall asked.

"Last night?"

"That's what the lady said," Hatcher growled.

"I was . . . let me see . . . I was with my wife. Hey, there's no need to drag my family into this . . . is there?"

"Where were you and your wife last night?" Hall followed up.

"We went out to dinner. I worked late and—"

"How late?"

"I don't know, eight, eight-thirty."

"Anybody here testify to that?" Jackson asked.

"Sure. No. I mean, the place cleared out around seven. I was here alone after that."

"Sure you didn't decide to drop in on Ms. Curzon before having dinner with your wife?" Hatcher said. "You know, get a piece before hooking up with the missus."

"I resent that," Archer said, not sounding as though he did. It seemed the thing to say.

"*She* resented getting her head bashed in," Hatcher said. "How'd you end up with her, Mr. Archer? You look up hookers in the Yellow Pages?"

"I don't think I should be talking to you," Archer said. "I don't like the way this is sounding."

"Please answer Detective Hatcher's question," Jackson said. "How did you first become a client of Ms. Curzon's?"

"A friend of mine told me about her."

"Who was that?" Hall followed up.

"I don't want to involve other people."

"Suit yourself," said Hatcher. "Maybe your wife will remember the names of your friends."

"This is harassment," Archer said.

They stared at him.

"All right, a friend of mine named Jimmy told me about Rosalie."

"Jimmy have a last name?"

"Patmos. Jimmy Patmos. He's Senator Barrett's chief-of-staff."

Hall noted the name on her pad.

"Look, if you talk to him, don't say that I gave you his name, okay? I do a lot of business with him and the senator."

"Know of anyone else who availed themselves of Ms. Curzon's services?" Jackson asked.

"No."

Hatcher stood and tossed his card on the table. "Give me a call if you think of anything else that might help us. By the way, where did you and the missus have dinner last night?"

"Charlie Palmer's."

"Expense account, huh?" Hatcher said.

"It is expensive," Archer agreed.

"Have a good day, Mr. Archer," Jackson said as they left the room.

"What'a you think?" Hatcher asked as they climbed into their car.

"I don't think he killed her," Hall offered.

"Based on what?" Hatcher asked as he pulled away.

"Gut feeling."

"A woman's instinct?" Hatcher said. "Not worth a damn."

"If she feels that way," Jackson said, "I think she's entitled to it."

"Right, and present that to a jury." He added dramatically: " 'My instincts tell me, Your Honor, that the accused did it.' Beautiful."

The two younger detectives fell silent. Hall smiled. Jackson clenched his fists and looked out the window.

Jackson and Hall checked out an unmarked car at headquarters and headed for the Maurice T. Turner, Jr., Metropolitan Police Academy in Southwest.

"You okay?" Hall asked from the driver's seat.

"Yeah, I'm okay."

"He really gets to you, doesn't he?"

"Hatch? I try not to let him."

She laughed. "You should try a little harder, Matt."

"He's a racist."

"That's pretty harsh. He's just old-school."

"What's that mean, lynching's okay?"

"You know I don't mean that."

"Williams and Shrank are considering filing a bias complaint against him."

"I didn't know that."

"He evidently got into it with them the other day, called them stupid, said there's proof that blacks' IQs are lower than whites', the usual garbage from him."

"Do you think they'll follow through?"

"All I know is that I can't wait to get transferred to another unit."

"You won't miss me?"

"Why? You planning on staying with him?"

"Hey, Matt, I'm no fan of Hatch either, but the job's the thing. He's a good cop."

"A good old-school cop, as you say. That's a whitewash, Mary."

She fell silent. They'd had few conversations about their racial difference since becoming intimately involved. She knew and respected his sensitivity about the subject and avoided that topic.

He shifted gears. "How do we approach Manfredi?" he asked.

"I think Hatch is right. I'll mention that I was one of his students, sort of like we're just stopping in to say hello. I'll keep it light and then you bring up the homicide."

"Good cop, bad cop," he muttered.

"If you have a better suggestion I'll—"

"No, no, that's the way to go. Sure, you set him up and I'll hit him with the real reason we're there."

* * *

After splitting off from Hall and Jackson, Hatcher drove to Adams Morgan and parked in front of Joe's Bar and Grille. Its owner, Joe Yankavich, was behind the bar when Hatcher entered. He had the place to himself. The detective grabbed a stool at the far end of the bar. "Hello, Joe," he said.

"Hello, Hatcher. You on duty? What, a Diet Coke or a Shirley Temple?"

"A Bloody Mary, Joe, and a burger. You got any chopped meat that hasn't been in the freezer for a month?"

The burly owner ignored the comment and shouted through an opening to the kitchen.

"With fried onions," Hatcher said.

"Fried onions on that burger," Yankavich instructed.

Hatcher watched as Yankavich mixed his Bloody Mary and wondered what it would be liked to tangle with the bar owner. He was a bear of a man, with a barrel chest, shaved head, and massive arms that strained against the sleeves of the red shirt he wore. A bush of chest hair protruded through the open upper buttons. He plopped Hatcher's drink down in front of him.

"Hey, Joe . . ." Hatcher said.

Yankavich turned and glared. "You here to break my chops today, Hatcher?"

Hatcher grinned. "Why would you say that, Joe? I never break chops."

"And Congress isn't on the take," Yankavich snorted.

Hatcher waited until his burger had been served before saying anything else to Yankavich. He ate enthusiastically, having poured on plenty of ketchup. A few locals arrived and took tables to the rear of the place. Hatcher finished eating and summoned the owner.

"You want dessert, Hatcher?"

Hatcher shook his head.

"Good to see you," said Yankavich. "The burger's on me." He pulled an envelope from the rear pocket of his pants and slid it across the bar. Hatcher picked it up and put it in his inside jacket pocket.

"We need to talk," Hatcher said.

"About what?"

"In the back."

Yankavich left the bar and retreated into a closet-sized back room that functioned as an office and storeroom. Hatcher followed. He closed the door behind him and leaned against it, arms folded.

"You know a pretty lady named Rosalie, Joe?" Hatcher asked.

Yankavich looked up from his chair behind the desk. "Huh?"

"Rosalie Curzon," Hatcher said. "She lived in the neighborhood."

Yankavich exhaled loudly and sat back. "I heard," he said. "It's all over the street. Somebody whacked her last night, as I understand it."

"You know her, Joe? She was a customer?"

"No. She never came in here."

"So, you knew her."

"I didn't say that."

"If you didn't know her, Joe, how could you be sure she never came in here?"

"I don't know. Maybe I met her once or twice."

"You send her customers?"

"I don't know what you're talking about, Hatcher."

"Come on, now, Joe. We both know you run broads out of here, and some of that white stuff that goes up the nose. I mean, not you personally, but you—how shall I say it?—condone it. Right?"

"That's what you want to talk about, Hatcher?"

"What'd she charge, Joe?"

"Huh?"

"Her fee for a trip to heaven. How much?"

"You're blowing smoke, Hatcher."

"You visit the lovely Ms. Curzon last night?"

"Hey, wait a minute, Hatcher. What the hell are you getting at?"

"We know you were a customer of hers, Joe. It's on tape."

"What?"

"Where were you last night?"

"Right here."

"I suppose there's an army who'll testify to that."

Yankavich's grin was crooked, his large lips moist. "That's right," he said.

"What'd she do, Joe, call you Godzilla or something?"

Yankavich stood. "Unless you got somebody who puts me at her place last night, I've got customers to take care of," he said. He moved toward the door, but Hatcher stood his ground. They were a foot from each other.

"I'm just doing my job, Joe, that's all. Somebody gets murdered, I go find who did it. I believe you when you say you weren't with her last night, but if I find out different, I'll do my job."

Hatcher stepped aside to allow Yankavich to open the door and leave the tiny room. He extracted the envelope from his pocket, opened it, counted the bills it contained, returned it to his pocket, and stepped back into the restaurant. He went to where he'd been sitting and laid money on the bar. "Good burger, Joe. There's a tip there, too. Thanks for the offer, but freebies are against the rules."

Officer Al Manfredi was on a training field teaching a class in defensive maneuvers when Jackson and Hall arrived. He noticed them standing just outside the door but didn't acknowledge them.

After ten minutes, he dismissed the class and fell in line with his students as they headed for the door.

"Officer Manfredi," Mary Hall said as he approached.

"Yeah?"

"I'm Mary Hall. I was in your class a few years ago."

"Oh, sure, Mary Hall. Hail Mary." He laughed. "That's what they used to call you."

She, too, laughed. "I remember it well. This is my partner, Detective Jackson."

Jackson and Manfredi shook hands. Jackson's immediate thought was that up close, Manfredi looked like the comedian Don Rickles. A stiff wind over the open area sent the few strands of hair Manfredi possessed into action.

"So, what brings you back to the old stomping ground? Refresher course or just hanging out?"

"Actually," Mary said, "we need to talk with you."

His pleasant façade abruptly changed to stone. "About what?" he asked.

"It's about a homicide we caught last night," Jackson said.

"Yeah?"

"Yeah," Jackson said. "A prostitute in Adams Morgan, name Rosalie Curzon."

This time, Manfredi's smile was forced. "Looks like you were in the wrong place, wrong time, huh? I'm glad I don't catch cases any more; keep me up all night. Sorry, but I've got a ton of paperwork to do."

They followed him inside.

"Officer Manfredi," Jackson said as they walked closely behind him down a long hallway, "we have reason to believe that you were acquainted with the victim."

Manfredi slowed his pace like a mechanical figure whose batteries have run out, stopped, turned, and said, "What the hell are you two, IA?"

"No, we're not from Internal Affairs," Jackson said. "Look, can we sit down someplace alone and go over this?"

"Get lost," the academy instructor said, resuming his march up the hallway, with Jackson and Hall in close pursuit.

"We know you were one of the victim's customers," Jackson said loud enough to be heard over the sound of their shoes on the hard floor.

Manfredi never broke stride as he walked through an open doorway and slammed the door shut. Hall and Jackson looked through the window and saw him disappear into another room.

"I don't think he wants to talk to us," Jackson said.

"Looks that way."

"Do we keep after him?"

She shook her head. "We report back what transpired here and let the department handle it."

Her cell phone rang. She walked away from Jackson and spoke with the caller out of earshot. When she'd finished, she returned and said, "Congressman Morrison's office. We're on for eleven tomorrow, the Crystal City Marriott."

"A hotel?"

"I suppose the congressman doesn't want to be seen with us in the District. I'll call Hatcher."

"He wants us to go back to Adams Morgan and help a team that's canvassing the neighborhood," she reported after talking to Hatcher. "We meet up with him in the morning, eight sharp. Come on, let's get it over with. Dinner's on me."

Chapter 5

That morning, Deborah Colgate was escorted onto the Boeing 757 jet ahead of other passengers. She occupied the window seat in the front row of first class. The aisle seat had also been booked for her and would remain vacant for the duration of the flight from San Francisco to Washington Dulles International Airport. The two Secret Service agents assigned to her for this trip took up positions in the aisle seat across from her, and on the aisle in the row behind.

The senior flight attendant who'd gotten her settled asked if she wanted something to drink.

"Orange juice would be fine," Deborah replied.

She put on a set of earphones attached to her iPod, sipped her juice, placed the empty glass on her tray, and closed her eyes. It had been a hectic week; but then again, every week was hectic since her husband, Robert, had won his party's primary and was now running for president against the incumbent.

Deciding to run against Burton Pyle had come easily to Bob Colgate. He'd had his eye on the White House since first entering politics as a Maryland state legislator, advancing through the ranks to become the majority leader of the state senate, and then going on to the governorship. When his four-year term expired, he declined to seek reelection, instead quietly focusing on an eventual run for the White House, putting together a formidable team and calling in his chips, along with filling his campaign coffers with plenty of cash before tossing his hat into the crowded primary.

He placed second in the Iowa caucuses and rolled to wins in New Hampshire and South Carolina. With those victories under his belt, the Colgate steamroller dominated the field in subsequent primaries, culminating in a rousing acceptance speech at his party's convention that filled the faithful with confidence that "Handsome Bob" would crush the sitting president, whose administration was rife with scandal, military misadventures, diplomatic gaffes, and fiscal irresponsibility. That Colgate had chosen a woman as his running mate, Ohio Senator Maureen McDowell, only added to the ticket's appeal, a melding of north and south, male and female, experience in managing a state and navigating Congress.

What a team!

Couldn't miss!

Or could it?

The campaign had become ugly. Deborah Colgate's husband's reputation as a ladies' man and serial adulterer had been kept front-and-center by Pyle's people. The Pyle reelection team was headed by the president's longtime political guru, Kevin Ziegler. Ziegler had masterminded Pyle's political climb from his earliest days as the son of a wealthy Florida businessman who'd made his fortunes in shipbuilding, an international food trading company, and as owner of two professional sports franchises. Burton had shown little interest in following in his father's business footsteps, and dabbled in various pursuits until someone suggested he run for state office. He won handily, outspending his opponent tenfold, and by following the instructions at every turn offered by his campaign manager, Ziegler, with whom he'd become friendly.

Ziegler had been enthralled by politics since his teen years, and graduated at the top of his class as an undergraduate in political science at the University of Miami. He achieved the same ranking when earning his MBA and Ph.D in the same discipline at the University of Chicago. He lived and breathed politics, although his interest was not in holding elected office. For him, the power didn't rest with elected officials. The power, the *real* power, was vested in those behind the throne who pulled the strings and achieved their goals through officeholders. It seemed to Ziegler that he had in Pyle the perfect specimen—and he viewed him in those terms—to put into play what had become by now his keenly honed views of how the nation, and the world, should be, and could be reshaped. Pyle was personable and easygoing, a comfortable glad-hander, the sort of candidate voters might enjoy having a beer with, or joining in a friendly softball game. He wasn't stupid, but lacked intellectual curiosity, disinterested in delving beneath the surface of any issue. In a word, he was malleable, the most important trait from Ziegler's point of view. Too, there was the Pyle family money to draw upon. Old man Pyle was impressed when Ziegler first broached the subject with him of his son seeking higher office, perhaps reaching for something as lofty as president. While he had always been disdainful of the way Joe Kennedy had used his wealth and power to help his sons achieve high political office, his view of that family had more to do with Kennedy politics than the process. This was different. Ziegler espoused a political viewpoint that matched that of the elder Pyle, and he eagerly signed on to the packaging and nurturing of his son, Burton Pyle, who sometimes seemed bewildered by it but who happily went along.

It worked. Through Ziegler's careful attention to every detail, every speech, every position paper, every aspect of fundraising, he built an organization that propelled his "specimen" to the pinnacle of politics in America, the presidency of the United States.

That the first Pyle administration had botched things at almost every turn meant little to Ziegler as the drive for a second term commenced. The administration's failures weren't the issue, not as long as you had a candidate like Robert Colgate, whose politics were anathema to Ziegler, and whose personal life was ripe for picking, for slandering, for raising doubts about the sort of moral leadership, or lack of it, he would bring to the highest office in the land. Keeping the ineffectual Pyle in the White House for a second term had become an obsession for the obsessive Ziegler.

His surrogates had leaked reports by "knowledgeable sources within the Colgate campaign" that Colgate and his wife were close to splitting. These same "knowledgeable sources" reported late-night screaming matches between the couple, thrown objects, vile language. No matter how much Colgate denied the rumors, they had legs. One columnist, on Ziegler's payroll, went so far as to say that a Colgate presidency would turn 1600 Pennsylvania Avenue into a house of ill-repute.

Accusations by women from Colgate's days as governor of Maryland only fanned the flames. There were times when Deborah considered giving credence to the rumors by bailing out of both the campaign and the marriage. But to give in to personal considerations at this juncture would derail the other dimension of her partnership with Bob Colgate. She'd been as seduced by the lure of political power as he'd been, from the earliest days of their courtship and then marriage and throughout the rigors of elected office. You didn't just walk away from being within months of occupying the White House, the wife of the most powerful leader in the world.

The flight was uneventful, as most flights are, aside from a fellow passenger wanting to engage her in conversation. He was gently, but firmly, dissuaded by the agents. At times like this, the decision to fly commercially was brought into question. She would have been justified in using one of the campaign's two leased 737s. After all, her trip to San Francisco was to address a woman's fundraising dinner, which she'd done successfully—the event raised three-quarters of a million dollars, not bad for a night's work. But it had been decided that making judicious use of commercial flights would add a needed common touch to the campaign, the future first lady rubbing elbows with the masses. Of course, "the masses" sat in the rear of the aircraft, their knees crushed by the seatbacks in front of them, their so-called snack lunch barely edible.

As they began their descent, the flight attendant leaned across the vacant seat and said, "I probably shouldn't be saying this, Mrs. Colgate, but you will be the prettiest first lady ever."

Deborah smiled and extended her hand. "Thank you so much. That's very kind of you."

The flight attendant beamed. "Not only that," she said, "I'm rooting for your husband." She lowered her voice and leaned closer. "I don't think President Pyle has been a very good president."

"I'll pass that along to my husband," Deborah said. "Thank you."

Two cars were at Dulles to meet her and the agents. They were driven into the District, where she was dropped off at the imposing townhouse she and her husband had purchased three years earlier. Although they maintained their home in suburban Bethesda, most of their time since the campaign started was spent in the more central Georgetown residence, one floor of which was used as an unofficial campaign strategy center.

That evening, at a little before six, Deborah joined her husband in a private office off their bedroom.

"I hear it went well," he said.

"Better than well," she said, kicking off her shoes and settling in a large leather wing chair, feet drawn up beneath her. "They asked the right questions. The advance people did their job."

"The teachers' union endorsement is tomorrow."

"Pyle's record on education is abysmal."

"Did you catch up with Jerry while you were out there?"

"Briefly. We crossed paths this morning."

Jerry Rollins, an inside-the-Beltway veteran of many political wars, was Colgate's closest friend and advisor. Their relationship went back to Colgate's earliest days in the Maryland senate. Rollins's role in Colgate's run for the presidency was unofficial, but everyone in the campaign knew that each important decision had to be cleared through him. Colleagues called Colgate and Rollins the "policy twins," although their differences were obvious aside from parallel political beliefs. Colgate was movie star handsome, tall and trim and with a full head of sandy hair, penetrating blue eyes, and a boyish smile. He was also one of the best public speakers politics had seen in decades, someone who connected almost instantly with his audiences and who made each person in the audience feel he was talking directly to them. His grasp of the issues and their subtleties was impressive, as was his ability to turn every question, friendly or combative, into a positive for him.

Rollins, considerably shorter than Colgate and reed thin, was quiet and introspective; no one ever applied the term "gregarious" to him. A lawyer, he'd forged a career in D.C. as a smooth negotiator and confidant, someone who kept secrets but who knew how to use them if necessary to advance a client's agenda.

"He's due back anytime now," Colgate said. "We're meeting with people from the Congressional Black Caucus."

Deborah, who'd picked up a copy of the *Washington Post* from a table next to her chair, glanced up and said, "Good."

Colgate had been dressing for the evening. He finished adjusting his tie in the mirror and said, "You've got the night off. Lucky you." He came to where she sat and leaned over to kiss her. She turned her head so that his lips only grazed her cheek. He started to say something, thought better of it, said he'd be late, and left the room.

She sat staring at the newspaper, its words a blur as tears welled up. Soon, those tears rolled freely down her expertly made-up face. She got to her feet, threw the newspaper to the floor, went to the bedroom, where she stripped off her clothes, and got in the shower, the water as hot as she could stand it.

Chapter 6

The meeting with six members of the Congressional Black Caucus was held at the home of one of Washington's most influential African-American business leaders. Jerry Rollins was a half hour late and apologized. He'd come directly from the airport, with his luggage.

They met for almost two hours. When it broke up, Colgate invited Rollins back to the house for a nightcap.

"Another time, Bob. I need to get home and wash away the flight." He smiled. "Ah, for the good old days before deregulation, when the airlines didn't treat you like cattle, or worse. It's disgraceful, an issue you might consider attacking. Deborah got back okay?"

"Yeah. She said you two crossed paths this morning in San Francisco."

"She did? That's right. In the hotel lobby."

"How did it go out there?"

"Fine. Looks like things will run smoothly when you arrive next week. Everything's in place."

"Good. Thanks, Jerry. If I pull this off, it'll be because of you."

"I think you might have had something to do with it," Rollins said. "Let's go. I still haven't been home."

Colgate's limo, followed by a car containing two Secret Service agents, dropped Rollins in front of his home in Foggy Bottom before depositing the presidential candidate at his townhouse.

"Is Mrs. Colgate still awake?" Bob asked one of the household staff.

"No, sir. She said she was dog-tired from the trip and was going to bed early. Can I get you anything, sir?"

"I'd love bourbon in a snifter," he said. "I'll be in the library."

Jerry Rollins unpacked in his bedroom, showered, dressed in pajamas and robe, and padded downstairs to the kitchen, where his wife, Sue, sat drinking decaf tea and reading that day's *Washington Post.*

"How was the trip?" she asked.

"Successful but tiring. How was your day?"

"The usual. Busy. I spent most of it chauffeuring Sammy from one activity to another, and a party, too, of course."

Rollins laughed as he came around behind and massaged her shoulders through her robe.

He'd married later in life than most of his friends; Sue was twelve years his junior. Their daughter, Samantha, "Sammy" to friends and family, was a precocious seven. There were times, many of them, when Rollins found it hard to believe that the beautiful, bright, delightful little creature was actually his daughter, wide-eyed and trusting in his love and that of her mother. She'd never have to doubt their love and devotion. It was total and unconditional. The world, however, was another story. He sometimes wondered how any child grew up, considering the threats out there, illness, accidents, bad deeds. If he could, he would wrap her in an impenetrable sheath and never allow the world to touch her. If only that were an option.

After downing his nightly ration of vitamin pills, he said he was going to bed. He stopped in front of Samantha's bedroom and peered into the darkened room, the only illumination a clown night-light. He quietly stepped into the room and sat on the edge of her bed, observed her steady breathing and the small, sweet smile on her lips. Sensing his presence, she opened her eyes and said sleepily, "Daddy's home."

"That's right, sweetheart, Daddy's home."

"Did you bring me something?"

"Of course I did." He hadn't. "I left it at the office. I'll bring it home tomorrow."

"Okay."

"You go back to sleep now. I'll see you at breakfast before you go to school."

"All right."

She turned over and buried her face in the pillow. He adjusted her covers and sat for a few minutes before going to the master bedroom and climbing into bed next to Sue. "Good night, hon," he said.

"Good night. Was Deborah there with you in San Francisco?"

"Yes, but I only saw her briefly this morning."

"Good night," she repeated. "I'm glad you're home."

Chapter 7

Before meeting Mae for dinner at Amalfi's, a family-owned restaurant not far from their home, Hatcher made a few stops after leaving Joe's Bar and Grille.

The first was the apartment building where Rosalie Curzon had been murdered. He was about to enter when Jackson and Hall approached. They'd been questioning residents of nearby buildings and were about to call it a day.

"Pick up anything?" Hatcher asked.

"No," Mary Hall said, "except that the victim's profession wasn't a secret to some people."

"They knew she was turning tricks?"

"Those willing to admit it," said Jackson. "She evidently had a favorite hangout, The Silver Veil, around the corner."

"You checked with them?"

"Yes. The owner—maybe he's the manager—he says that she used to come in pretty regularly with a friend."

"Male?"

"Female. He gave us her name."

Jackson fished a slip of paper from his pocket and read from it: "Micki Simmons."

"Mickey?"

"The female version. M-i-c-k-i."

"You get an address for this female Mouse?"

"No. We just left the place."

"I'll follow up on it," Hatcher said, taking the paper from Jackson. "What happened with Manfredi? You get to talk to him?"

They filled him in on their brief, abrasive encounter with the instructor.

"I'll take it from here," Hatcher said.

"We were about to call it quits for the night," Hall said. "That okay with you?"

"Half a day, huh?" They stared at him. "Lots to do. See you at eight sharp."

Hatcher watched them walk away and wondered if there might be more to their relationship than being cops. He'd had that suspicion before, but always dismissed it as implausible. They had nothing in common. They weren't even the same color.

He went inside and found the Hispanic superintendent, whose expression at seeing the big, menacing Hatcher again was less than welcoming.

"You decide to be straight with me now, José?" Hatcher asked.

"I know nothing," the super responded. "I swear it. She was a nice lady, that's all I know. No money from her. I get no money."

Hatcher grinned and patted the super on his shoulder. "Okay, amigo, relax. But what about the men who visited her, her customers? You must have seen lots of them."

The super shrugged. "They come, they go, like everybody in the building."

"You wouldn't remember what any of them looked like if I showed you some pictures?"

He shook his head.

"You're sure about that?"

"*Sí.* Yes."

"All right, buddy," Hatcher said, adding an additional slap on the shoulder, harder. "I'll be back. We'll talk again."

Hatcher next drove to Constitution Avenue on Capitol Hill, where he pulled up in front of Charlie Palmer Steak House. He went inside and asked to see the manager, who happened to be the man he'd approached.

"Walt Hatcher, MPD," Hatcher said, showing his gold badge.

"Yes, sir, what can I do for you?"

"I need to know if a certain person had dinner here last night."

"Who is that?"

"Lewis Archer. He's a lobbyist. I understand a lot of them come here."

The manager smiled. "Oh, yes, of course. Mr. Archer is a regular customer. He was here last night with his wife. Is something wrong?"

"No, nothing's wrong. I'm just touching all the bases. You remember what time he and his wife showed up?"

The manager frowned. "Let me check." He returned a few minutes later holding a computer printout. "He got here at quarter of nine. They sat right over there. He likes that particular table."

"They arrive together?"

"Ah, no, as a matter of fact. She got here first, but that's not unusual. Mr. Archer tends to run late." He laughed. "He has a very understanding wife."

"I guess he does. Thanks for the info."

"Anytime. I hope Mr. Archer isn't in some sort of trouble."

"Not at all. Just routine checking. Have a good night, pal."

He preceded Mae to Amalfi's and enjoyed a drink with one of the owners while waiting for her. She arrived on time and they were shown to a table.

"How was your day?" she asked.

"Nothing new and exciting. I'm glad I left early. Calamari to start?"

They ordered a bottle of Chianti with the calamari. A waiter poured the shimmering red wine into their glasses, and they touched rims. Mae observed him across the small corner table. Her husband of many years seemed to have aged unreasonably over the past year, gray bags beneath his eyes more pronounced now, the sparkle in his green eyes muted. He'd been taking medicine for an enlarged heart since his last physical, which was three years ago, and a nagging pain in his lower back, along with a knee that the orthopedist said needed replacing, caused him to walk differently. Hatcher was a stubborn man when it came to medicine—when it came to most things—and he seldom complained about his physical ailments. Of course, Mae reasoned, she was getting older, too, and undoubtedly didn't look the same to him either.

But she didn't suffer the strain and tensions of his job. She'd read many articles about how police work, particularly in large cities, took its toll on cops, and on their families, too. The divorce and suicide rates for cops were far above the average. To spend each day going to gruesome murder scenes was bound to change a man, she knew, and not for the better. The few friends they had through Hatch's work were bitter and cynical, men hardened by their daily routines, their women cautious in the way they approached them.

"Florida's looking better every day," he said.

"I spoke with Christina today," Mae said, pleased that the topic had come up. "I told her that you might retire and that we'd move to the house in Florida and—" He was frowning. "That's okay, isn't it, that I told her?"

"What? Yeah, sure. I stopped at Charlie Palmer Steak House on my way here, had to ask about some lobbyist who had dinner there last night. You know what they get for a steak there, a porterhouse? A zillion bucks, Mae. A lot of fat-cats eat there, dropping a bill or two on a meal." He shook his head. "I got in the wrong business."

She was sorry that the conversation had now veered in this direction without provocation. It was something he tended to dwell on when his spirits were low, the disparity in pay between people like cops and firemen, who actually did something good for the community, and those who became rich by simply pushing money around, or using it to buy influence.

She placed her hand on his. "I think you got into the *right* business, Walter. It's something you always wanted to be, a detective helping people, putting the bad guys away so they can't hurt anyone else. As for money, you've been a wonderful provider for me and our three children. The mortgage is paid off on both houses, the kids all graduated from college, and we can go out for dinner like this anytime we want. What more could we ask for?"

A grin crossed Hatcher's broad face. "You always see the bright side, don't you, Mae?"

"Only because—"

"No, I mean that as a compliment. For you, the glass is always half-full, and that's a good thing. Maybe if I turn in the badge and soak up some of that Florida sun, I'll see things the way you do."

"That would be great," she said, beaming. "Are you having the usual, osso buco?"

"Yeah. You, shrimp scampi?"

"Yes. We know each other pretty well, don't we, Walt?"

"After all these years, we'd better," he said, not stating his second thought, that he was lucky to have her as his wife.

Chapter 8

Like every other step in the campaign, the announcement of Colgate's endorsement by the nation's teachers was smoothly choreographed. It was held on the steps of an inner-city public school, in a predominately black neighborhood. The school had recently been cited for the excellence of its teaching staff, and many of them were on hand at eleven o'clock that morning, along with a select group of students turned out in their Sunday best. With a half-dozen American flags flapping in the background, the association's president took to a portable podium and welcomed the assembled. Bob and Deborah Colgate stood to the side, the kids grouped in front of them, allowing Colgate to banter with them and to occasionally run a hand over a head, all of which was dutifully captured by video and still photographers. Deborah wore a stunning beige suit, white blouse, and an equally stunning perpetual smile.

"Where's Jerry?" Colgate whispered to his wife. "I thought he was supposed to be here."

"I wouldn't know," she replied.

The association president was winding up his comments.

". . . and so, my friends, after four years of neglect of our crucially important education system, it is with considerable pleasure that I am able to deliver to the next president of the United States the enthusiastic endorsement of more than three million dedicated men and women in whose classrooms the future leaders of this great nation are taught and nurtured." His voice rose to a shout. "Robert Colgate!"

A Dixieland band broke into a spirited tune as Colgate and his wife came to the podium. He raised his hands high, his campaign smile ensuring that all was well and that there would be happy times ahead for the nation's education system. After allowing the applause to ebb and the music to trail off, he launched into a fifteen-minute speech that sounded off-the-cuff, but that had been carefully crafted well in advance. He was good at sounding spontaneous. He ended by thanking the teacher's union for its faith in him and the vision he had for the nation, particularly in its classrooms. He placed his arm around Deborah's waist and gave a final wave before being led away to the waiting limousine.

Their Secret Service detail piled into two nearby cars. The chief agent assigned to the Colgate campaign had lobbied to have at least one agent in vehicles with the candidate and his wife at all times, but Colgate adamantly disagreed. "I need some private time," he'd said, "and the backseat of a car provides it. No agents with us in cars!" He prevailed.

"Went well," he commented after he and Deborah were in the secure confines of the limo.

"Did you expect it *not* to go well?" Deborah asked, her eyes fixed on the scene outside as the vehicle inched through the crowd.

"You never know," he said, grabbing her hand. "Loosen up, Deb. We're on a roll."

She slid her hand from beneath his and said absently, her attention still focused on the passing scene, "I have a luncheon to get to. What's next for you?"

"Interview at the *Post.*"

"They'll ask about us."

His laugh was forced. "They always do, and the answer is always the same."

"Yes, it always is, isn't it?"

He dialed Jerry Rollins's number on his cell phone. "I thought you were planning to be at the teachers' endorsement," Colgate said sharply.

"I had a meeting come up at the last minute. Sorry. I saw some of it on TV. Looked like a home run, Bob."

"I need to talk to you."

They arranged to meet at Colgate's Georgetown home at four.

Deborah was dropped off at the Ritz-Carlton in Georgetown, while her husband proceeded to the *Washington Post*'s offices on 15th Street, NW, where his press secretary, Linda Chu, waited with others. The interview lasted an hour. As expected, the question of whether there was a serious, potentially terminal rift in the Colgate marriage came up.

Colgate responded through a smile: "Deborah and I love each other and are totally committed to our marriage. She'll make a terrific first lady, and I'm looking forward to enjoying the White House *together* for the next eight years."

He returned to the house, went to the library, draped his jacket over a chair, kicked off his shoes, and dove into a new set of briefing papers and talking points provided by members of his staff. He was due to leave the following day for a two-day campaign swing through the Midwest. After an hour of digesting the material, he turned to the *New York Times* and *Washington Post*. A speech on the economy delivered by President Pyle received front page coverage in both publications, with the *Post* devoting two full columns. The reporters covering the speech pointed to inconsistencies in some of Pyle's claims, which pleased Colgate and led him to a moment of introspection.

Colgate couldn't imagine a weaker opponent to run against than the incumbent, Pyle, whose administration was viewed as perhaps the worst in modern history. The president's approval numbers were in the mid-twenties, and there recently had been calls for his impeachment. While Pyle's vulnerability was pleasing to Colgate from a pragmatic view—he'd have to stumble badly to lose to Pyle—it also served to reinforce his belief that he was the best person to lead the country and to undo the series of blunders made by the Pyle administration. There were no moments of self-doubt in the middle of the night, no questioning whether he was up to the job of president of the United States. As many voters and pundits said, anything—anyone—would do a better job of setting America back on course than Burton Pyle, a paranoid man whose visions were, at best, shortsighted and whose brain was putty in the hands of advisors.

He'd just started to peruse the inside pages when a personal assistant came into the library to tell his boss that he'd almost finished packing for the Midwest trip but had a few questions. He started to ask them when the housekeeper interrupted: "Mr. Rollins is here, Governor."

Rollins replaced the assistant in the room, closing the door behind him.

"Good day, huh, Bob?" Rollins said, shedding his jacket.

"Yes, it was. But I'm concerned about the debate next week."

Rollins frowned and shifted in his chair. "Anything in particular?"

"The constant focus on Deborah and me, the rumors about our marriage."

"I can understand your frustration," Rollins said, "but I don't believe it will be raised in the debate."

"Maybe not by the moderators, but Pyle will find a

way to work it into the conversation. I can hear him now, saying how important it is to have a strong and loving first lady in the White House. Hell, his wife's numbers are a lot better than his."

Rollins was a man who took long pauses before responding to comments or questions, a calculated indication of a thoughtful nature. When he didn't immediately respond, Colgate added, "It's Deborah, Jerry. She refuses to address the issue."

"She feels that it's better to remain above the fray on issues like this, Bob. I agree with her."

"I did. I don't anymore. I sometimes wonder if she's out to sabotage the campaign."

"That's ridiculous, Bob! She's out there working hard for you."

"I know that. She's all business, but like an automaton. These rumors can become cumulative, corrosive."

"Have you spoken with her?" Rollins asked.

"Sure. She refuses to discuss it, takes that so-called high road, not lowering herself to rumormongers."

"Are you asking me to do something?"

"Talk to her."

"Why do you think she'll listen to me if she won't discuss it with you? You're her husband." His easy laugh softened the comment.

Colgate looked at him but said nothing.

"I'll mention it to her, Bob, at an opportune time."

"Good."

They spent the next hour going over the position papers Colgate had been reading. Rollins agreed with most, but took issue with some, which convinced Colgate to discard those. As Rollins slipped into his jacket in preparation for leaving, he asked casually, "You couldn't convince Deborah to accompany you tomorrow?"

"She prefers the events in Virginia and Maryland. Closer to home."

And less awkward, Rollins thought.

"Did you catch Maureen's talk at the Press Club today?" Rollins asked, referring to Colgate's running mate, Senator Maureen McDowell.

"No, but the club is sending a DVD."

"She was wonderful, Bob, very strong and on-message."

"Glad to hear it. Do you get a sense, Jerry, that Pyle has something, or someone, waiting in the wings to spring on us?"

"Not that I know of," Rollins replied, "although you never know."

"That's my point, Jerry. If he does, I'd like to know."

Rollins nodded. "Anything else?"

"No. Thanks for coming by. Sue and Samantha okay?"

"They're fine. Thanks for asking." He slipped on his jacket. "I'd better be going. Travel safe."

"I'll stay in touch."

Rollins went directly to his downtown law office, where a pile of phone messages awaited him. He shuffled through them, creating piles based upon relative importance, and returned those calls that he considered most urgent. His secretary joined him and asked whether she could leave. It was her husband's birthday and they were meeting friends for dinner.

"Sure, go on, Helen. My best to Jim. Tell him the only reason he stays youthful is because he married you."

She laughed and promised to convey the message.

She left as one of Rollins's young associates, Brian Massie, poked his head in the door. "Got a second?" he asked.

Rollins had hired Massie a year ago after the young attorney had put in a stint in the civil rights division at Justice. His education had been top-notch, head of his graduating class at Harvard Law and editor of the *Law Review.* That he'd grown disillusioned at Justice was no surprise to Rollins. President Pyle had stacked the agency with cronies and supporters; it was the most politicized Justice Department in history. Political concerns ran rampant over the law at every turn. The decision to hire Massie had been a good one. He'd quickly proved himself able to grasp the most complex of legal issues, and had forged a close relationship with his boss.

"Okay, Brian, but make it quick."

They spent ten minutes going over a brief Massie was due to file the following morning.

"Looks good," Rollins said. "Nice job."

"Thanks, Jerry. Anything else for me?"

"No. Have a good evening."

Now alone, Rollins went to a James Vann neo-cubist painting of a jazz musician hanging on the wall—*Smoke Gets in Your Eyes;* Rollins was a devoted jazz lover. He took it down and opened the wall safe behind it. He reached beneath dozens of envelopes and assorted documents and withdrew a smaller sealed envelope, which he took to his desk. He sat quietly, the envelope in his hand, staring at it as though he might be able to see through the heavy paper. His fingers traced the contours of the flat, four-inch by seven-inch item contained inside.

He'd retrieved the envelope that morning from where he'd been instructed it would be. As he turned it over in his hands, he was stricken with a rare sort of inertia. He was known as a decisive man, someone who quickly summed up a situation and made the right decision.

But this was different. The impotency of his inability to act stabbed him in the gut.

He put off the decision he knew must be made, placed the envelope in the safe, locked it, and returned the painting to its place on the wall. Then, turning out the lights, he slowly left the building.

Chapter 9

That same morning, a blinding headache had been Hatcher's sunrise. He'd been suffering more such headaches lately but refused to see a doctor. To Mae, "Doctors only make people sicker and then send a bill. Besides," he said, hauling himself out of bed, "it was the wine last night. Red wine always gives me a headache."

Her creased face reflected her concern as she watched him disappear into the bathroom, losing his balance as he went and bumping against the doorjamb.

She threw on a robe and slippers and went downstairs to prepare breakfast. When he appeared a half hour later, showered and dressed, he smiled and said, "Feeling better, Mae. Damn wine always does it to me."

She didn't buy it but didn't say anything except, "That's good, Walt. I'm glad your headache is better."

Mae went to shower, leaving her husband to enjoy his breakfast. He consulted a slip of paper on which he'd listed things to be accomplished that day. Heading the list was the eleven o'clock meeting at the Crystal City Marriott with Congressman Slade Morrison. The contemplation of grilling the congressman was pleasing. Hatcher had little use for elected officials: "Whores whose only interest is in preserving their power, the nation be damned." Whether Morrison had murdered Rosalie Curzon was almost irrelevant; Hatcher's pleasure would come from seeing the Arizona congressman squirm.

He decided to bring Mary Hall with him. She'd made the initial contact, and her presence at the meeting would add an interesting dimension. Matt Jackson would not accompany them, Hatcher further decided. The rookie detective had demonstrated an annoying softness during the questioning of suspects, rounding off the rough edges that Hatcher preferred. The kid would never make a good detective, from Hatcher's perspective, any more than most of the new breed coming into MPD. They were all book-learning and theory, or knee-jerk do-gooders without the necessary street smarts to work the city.

Also on the list was the name of Curzon's friend, Micki Simmons. Hatcher had intended to follow up on her personally, but changed his mind. Jackson could chase her down while Hatcher and Mary met with the congressman.

He also intended to revisit the lobbyist, Lewis Archer, and make contact with the man who'd recommended Archer to the dead hooker, Jimmy Patmos, chief-of-staff to Utah Senior Senator William Barrett.

And there was the question of what to do about Al Manfredi. He'd need to think that through before going upstairs with what Jackson and Hall had reported to him about their run-in with the police instructor.

The list ended with Manfredi, but Hatcher knew they'd have to widen the circle of suspects and do it fast. Had Rosalie Curzon's client list not included men like Archer, Congressman Morrison, a top senatorial staffer, and the cop Manfredi, her killing would soon be relegated to the bottom of unsolved D.C. murders. But once he'd shared the juicy portions of the tapes with his bosses, the Curzon file rose to the top of the pile and would stay there until there was a resolution.

Mae returned to the kitchen and cleared the table.

"Home for dinner?" she asked while walking him out to his car.

"Hard to say. I'll give you a call."

"How's your headache?"

"Fine. Better." It had abated slightly, but was now back with a vengeance. He put on dark glasses to shield his eyes from the sunlight.

"That's good." She kissed his cheek and watched him drive off to spend another day experiencing Washington, D.C.'s underbelly. Retirement and Florida couldn't come fast enough.

Matt Jackson also woke with a headache that morning, although it was minor compared to Hatcher's. Wine had, indeed, contributed, along with a lack of sleep.

After leaving Hatcher, he and Mary had gone to dinner at the Reef on 18th Street, known for its organic and free-range foods. From there they walked to Columbia Road to catch a local blues band at Chief Ike's Mambo Room. That's where the argument ensued.

Like most of their spats—and there hadn't been many—he couldn't remember the following day what had triggered it, although he knew it had to do with their racial differences. He splashed water on his face, made a cup of instant coffee, and sat by a window that overlooked the street. Looking down into the cup, he remembered that a previous argument had erupted over his using instant coffee, rather than brewing fresh. Mary refused to drink his instant concoction. To add insult to injury, she accused him of not having taste buds, or standards. He found that to be an unnecessary assault on his character and told her so, which sent her from his apartment back to her place, near Dupont Circle. Silly, they both knew, and they were back together the following day, sipping coffee he'd brewed in a coffeemaker she'd delivered that morning, along with herself. But, alone at the moment, instant would do just fine.

As he pondered the previous night at Chief Ike's, he realized why MPD had a policy of cops not becoming intimately involved. It would be one thing if they'd had a fight and went off the following morning to their different jobs. But that wasn't the case. They'd both have to arrive at headquarters on Indiana Avenue and spend the day together, much of it in the close confines of a car, tempted to bring up the previous night but knowing they couldn't, or shouldn't, especially not with Hatcher around.

The genesis of the argument came to him as he stepped into the shower and stood beneath the streaming water.

He'd fallen into a sour mood as the evening progressed, nothing to do with Mary, all having to do with Walter Hatcher. The senior detective's persistent jibes at Matt, especially those with racial overtones, gnawed at him.

It wasn't as though Matt was obsessed with race. While aware that prejudice existed despite advances made by African-Americans, he'd suffered little of it growing up in an affluent, multi-racial area of Chicago. His parents were professionals—his father was an optometrist, his mother a high school teacher, a thesis away from her Ph.D. Yes, there had been schoolyard incidents, but his slight stature had invited more taunts than his color. He was aware that there was plenty of racism in Washington, and within the MPD, but most of it was veiled, certainly less overt than forty or fifty years ago. Jackson witnessed those subtle messages but usually dismissed them.

But there was something about Hatcher as the messenger of bias that particularly irked him, which was very much on his mind last night. The bottle of wine at dinner, and drinks at Chief Ike's, did a good job of allowing his feelings to surface and his tongue to loosen. As the Mose Allison lyrics went: "Your mind is on vacation, your mouth is working overtime." Mary was usually effective at changing the subject whenever he fell into a funk about it, but she'd failed this time.

She'd indulged his obsession for most of the evening, which didn't mean always agreeing with him. At one point at Chief Ike's, she said that it distressed her as a white woman without prejudice to be viewed with suspicion by blacks simply because she was white.

He came back with, "Maybe your prejudice shows in other ways."

Now, hackles up, she challenged him to explain.

He tried to deliver his message casually so as to not fan the flames. "Maybe you think I'm with you because I want to be with a white woman. You know the old cliché—"

Her angry eyes and tight lips stopped him in mid-sentence. There was a moment when she considered throwing her drink in his face. Instead, she left the club, leaving him to extend his hand and call after her.

He came out of the shower and dialed her number. "Mary, are you there? Are you there? Please pick up if you're there. It's Matt. Look, I'm sorry about last night. I said things I shouldn't have and I apologize. I never should have had that last drink and . . . and I'm sorry. See you at work."

She was cold to him when they met up at MPD, but not terminally, and Hatcher's arrival curtailed any further discussion.

"Here's the drill," Hatcher said, still wearing his sunglasses. The headache hadn't gone despite the glasses and a mouthful of Tylenol. "Mary and I will talk to the congressman at eleven. Matt, I want you to run down this Mickey Mouse broad and see what you can get from her." He glanced at Mary. "You've got a dirty mind, kid," he said. "I didn't mean what you think I meant."

She rolled her eyes and shook her head.

"We'll meet back here at four," Hatcher said. "The deceased's father is arriving this afternoon. Got it?"

On the way to the parking lot where they'd checked out two unmarked vehicles, Matt whispered to Mary, "I called this morning and left a message. I'm sorry about last night and—"

"What the hell are you two doing?" Hatcher growled. "Making a date?"

Mary and Matt's eyes met as they prepared to climb into different cars. Her tiny smile buoyed him.

Before leaving headquarters, Matt ran a computer check on Micki Simmons. Like Rosalie Curzon, she lived in Adams Morgan. He drove to her apartment building and called her number on his cell. A sweet, sexy, southern-tinged recorded voice said, "I'm not available at the moment, but I do want to talk to you. Please call again soon."

He left a message saying who he was, and included a phone number at which he could be reached.

Matt sat in his car and watched people come and go from the apartment building. After a half hour, boredom set in. He pulled the printout he'd run at headquarters. Micki Simmons: According to the sheet, she was thirty-one years old, although a photograph taken when she'd been booked a few years earlier showed what appeared to be a woman older than that. But that was a booking photograph, usually less flattering than even driver's license and passport photos. Natural redhead? Hard to tell, but probably not. Nice features, a little swollen from crying. Getting booked often brought out the tears.

She was born in South Carolina and came to D.C. six years ago. Aside from a few busts for prostitution, one as a result of a sting while working for an escort service, she had no further criminal record, not even a parking ticket. As he studied her photo, he read into it a vulnerable woman, her eyes sad and looking for something in her life that she'd probably never find. Hatcher would consider such an analysis to be naïve, even stupid.

He forced Hatcher from his mind, got out of the car, and walked to the building's entrance, where he scanned the tenant list next to call buttons. Her apartment was number 9-C. He pressed the button and heard it sound in the apartment. No voice responded through the small speaker.

An older woman pushed through the door.

"Excuse me," Jackson said.

She eyed him suspiciously.

"I'm looking for Ms. Simmons."

The way she said, "I don't know her," coupled with the disgusted look on her face, told him that she did.

"Do you know if she's away?" he asked.

"I hope so," the woman said, and left.

He was about to return to the car and go back to headquarters when the door to the building opened and Micki Simmons exited. She wore a scarf over her head, and carried a suitcase.

"Ms. Simmons?" Jackson said.

She stopped and glared at him.

"Can we talk for a minute? I'm—"

She walked away.

"Whoa," he said, catching up with her and blocking her path. He fumbled for his detective's badge and displayed it. "I'm Matt Jackson, detective, MPD. I'd like to speak with you."

She cocked her head and sneered, "Yeah, I'm sure you would. Maybe another time."

He shifted his position to prevent her from advancing toward the curb, where a taxi had pulled up.

"Get out of my way," she said.

"Look," Jackson said, "either you agree to talk with

me now, or I slap cuffs on you and we do it at headquarters. Your call. It's about your friend Rosalie Curzon."

"I never would have guessed," she said. "That's my cab waiting."

"After we talk, I'll drop you wherever you want. But first we talk."

Until this point she'd been all toughness and challenge, not a hint of any southern accent or charm. Then, as though she'd received an instant Dixie transplant, she sighed, lowered her suitcase to the pavement, and said in a softer voice, "Ah suppose ah don't have any choice, do ah?"

Jackson smiled. "No, ma'am, I suppose you don't."

She looked around. A middle-aged couple came from the building and didn't try to hide their interest in what was going on.

"Can we go somewhere?" she asked.

"Your apartment?"

"No, ah don't think that's a good idea."

"My apartment?" Jackson said.

It was her first hint of a smile. "Are you sure you're a cop?"

"Want to see the badge again? Look, tell you what, we'll go to my apartment. It's in Adams Morgan, only a couple of blocks from here." He pointed to his car. "That's mine. I make good coffee, the real thing. When we're through, I'll drive you wherever it is you want to go."

She chewed her cheek.

"By the way, where *were* you going?"

"Home. All right. But if I answer your questions, I'm free to go?"

"That's right, unless you confess to killing your friend. Then—"

"Don't even joke about that."

They dismissed the taxi, whose driver was visibly

miffed, placed her suitcase in the trunk of Jackson's car, and drove the short distance to his apartment.

"You live here alone?" she asked.

"Yeah. I mean, sometimes my girlfriend stays but—"

"It's so neat."

He laughed. "I like order around me. Must mean I have a disorderly brain. At least that's what a professor of mine claimed about externally neat people."

"You went to college?" she said, going to a window and looking down at the street. In her experience, cops weren't college-educated.

"Uh-huh," he said from the kitchen, where he readied the coffeemaker. When he returned to the living room, she'd removed her raincoat and settled on the couch, her shoes on the floor in front of her. She wore a white sleeveless sweater that was too tight across her sizable bosom, and jeans that were also too tight. This was a woman who would fight a weight problem as she aged, he thought. But that was in the future. Right now, she was a tall, solidly built woman who looked as though she spent considerable time in a gym, maybe even lifting weights. The most striking thing about her was a mane of copper hair.

"Coffee will be ready in a minute," he said, pulling up a yellow director's chair.

She spread her arms. "So, go ahead and ask your questions."

He pulled a slender notebook and pen from his inside jacket pocket, removed the jacket, hung it over a matching chair, and resumed his seat. "I suppose I can start by asking why you were leaving D.C. and going home. Home is South Carolina?"

"How did you know that?"

"Your, ah, your sheet."

She winced. "Pretty sad, huh, a nice southern girl like me having a rap sheet?"

"We all make mistakes."

"It wasn't a mistake. It's what I chose to do with my life, at least for part of it."

"Prostitution."

She nodded.

"I'm not judging you, Ms. Simmons."

"Good. You can call me Micki."

"Okay, Micki, and I'm Matt."

"Micki and Matt," she said with a laugh. "Sounds like a TV sitcom."

"It does, doesn't it?"

An expression crossed her face. "I can't believe Rosalie is dead."

"Tell me about her, Micki."

She shrugged and wiped a single teardrop from her cheek. "We were friends, that's all."

"How'd you meet her?"

"The agency."

"Which agency?"

"Beltway Escorts. I'm sure that's on my rap sheet, too."

"Yeah, it is. You both worked there for a while?"

"We both worked there for too long. More than one day is too long as far as I'm concerned."

"Why do you say that?"

"The slob that runs it."

His raised eyebrows said that he wanted the name.

"Billy McMahon," she said. Jackson noted it. "He's a low-class bastard."

"He why you were leaving D.C.?"

"It's time I left," she said. Her laugh was sardonic. "Ah came here because I thought living in the city would be neat, you know? Small-town girl makes it big. Jesus, what a dope I was."

"Did you have any jobs here besides turning tricks?"

"Sure. Lousy ones, low pay, long hours. That's why . . ."

"That's why turning tricks appealed. Money."

"Why else do it?"

"I don't know. Tell me about Rosalie."

"She was great. Man, she had a sense of what was going on and how things went down. She made me look like the naïve jerk that I am."

"Did she like the life?" Micki's expression was quizzical. "Prostitution," Jackson clarified.

She sat back and blew a stream of air at a red strand of hair that had fallen over her forehead. "She hated it as much as I did," she said, "only she knew how to make it work. How do I say it?—She was worldly. I guess that's the way to say it. She knew how to make the most out of a bad situation."

His immediate thought was of the video recorder and tapes found in Rosalie Curzon's apartment. Was that what the woman seated across from him was referring to, her dead friend's ability to "make the most out of a bad situation"? He almost brought it up but thought better of it. Instead, he said, "Tell me more about the escort service and this guy McMahon."

Her expression was worth a hundred words. "Billy McMahon is a creep. Maybe you should talk to him about Rosalie's murder."

"Oh?"

"Yeah. When Rosalie decided to leave the agency and go solo, she encouraged me to go with her. I did. Billy never forgave her. Not only did I walk away along with her, he accused her of taking clients with her, lots of them. He said she promised them better service at lower prices if they'd come directly to her instead of booking through the agency. He threatened to kill her."

"Literally?"

"That's right." She leaned forward, a sense of urgency in her voice. "Hey, look, don't tell him I told you this. Right? I mean, I think the guy is capable of anything."

"Including murder."

She sat back, closed her eyes, and nodded.

He dropped the pad on the table and stood. "I forgot about the coffee," he said, and went to the kitchen. He returned carrying two steaming mugs on a tray, along with sugar and a pint container of half-and-half. He placed it on the table.

"Do you have Sweet'n Low?" she asked.

He brought it from the kitchen.

"You won't tell Billy what I told you," she repeated.

"No need to. Did you and Rosalie share clients? I mean, did you pass them back and forth between you?"

"Sometimes. If Rosalie was away, or I was, we'd suggest that one of our clients see the other if they were upset or didn't have much time. But we didn't do that much, just now and then."

"We're looking for Rosalie's killer," Jackson said. "Chances are that it was one of her johns. Can you give me some names of men you sent to her when you were away?"

She shook her head with conviction. "I would never do that," she said solemnly.

"Even if it might help solve the murder of your friend?"

She looked down and thought before responding. "Ah don't think it's right to just name a bunch'a names and have them dragged through the dirt. If you know somebody who you think did it, and if I know that person, then I might talk about it. But ah don't want to be sending you on some wild-goose chase that'll hurt people for no good reason."

He silently agreed with her, although he knew he shouldn't. Hatcher certainly wouldn't have bought her rationale. So what if a bunch of men were embarrassed at having bought the services of a prostitute? Chances were, they had those who would be deeply hurt by knowing of the infidelity. Was it more unsavory to have paid for sex rather than having fallen into an affair with a neighbor or office colleague? It didn't really matter. Hurt was hurt, regardless of its genesis.

"Where in Carolina did you grow up?" he asked.

"A little town outside of Sumter. You have any more questions?" she asked, slipping her feet into her shoes.

"I'm sure I'll have more, Micki, but none at the moment."

"That's good." She stood and picked up her raincoat. "Hey, how did you know about me?"

"Somebody in the neighborhood told me that you and Rosalie were friends."

"Who?"

"It doesn't matter."

"You get to ask questions but I can't?"

"Yeah, that's the way it works. Sorry."

"Stinks."

He slipped into his jacket and held the raincoat for her. "How are you traveling to South Carolina?" he asked.

"Train."

"Okay. I'll drop you at the station. I need to know how to reach you in South Carolina. We may want to have you come back to D.C."

She pouted, but wrote down an address and phone number in Sumter.

"What will you do about your apartment?" he asked as they left his place and went to where he'd parked the car.

"Keep it for a while, I guess."

"That's probably smart," he said, holding open the car's door. "You'll have to come back to D.C. at some point."

As she got out of the car in front of Union Station, and Jackson had retrieved her suitcase from the trunk, she smiled at him and took his extended hand. "You're okay," she said.

"For a cop?"

"No," she said. "Just okay."

He watched her disappear into a crowd of people, and for the first time allowed his concern about Hatcher's reaction to allowing her to leave town—to have *helped* her leave—to surface. He'd be furious and demeaning. No doubt about that.

Jackson used the radio in his car to ask headquarters for information about Beltway Escorts. Its phone number was cross-referenced to a street address, and Jackson headed in that direction. He'd deal with Hatcher when he had to, and the senior detective faded from Jackson's thoughts as they shifted to the pimp, Billy McMahon.

Chapter 10

Deborah Colgate was picked up at the Georgetown house for the short trip across the Potomac to her scheduled appearance at a fundraiser in the Crystal City Marriott. She was accompanied this morning by her personal assistant, her press secretary, and her best friend, Connie Bennett. Roommates at the University of Maryland, Deb and Connie had hit it off almost immediately and became inseparable during their undergraduate years. Their friendship carried over into their post-university lives—maid of honor at each other's weddings, godmothers to their children, and most important, close confidants. Connie didn't often accompany Deborah to her campaign appearances, but was always available following them to hear her friend's analysis of how things went.

"Bob's in the Midwest?" Connie asked as the limo crossed Memorial Bridge.

"Yes."

"Getting the teacher's union endorsement was wonderful."

"Not unexpected. Pyle's record on education is dismal."

"Like his record on almost everything else."

"He scares me," Deborah said.

"Scares you?" Connie replied, adding a quizzical laugh. "Oh, you mean what he's doing to the country."

"No," Deborah said. "I mean he's capable of anything. He's been running the dirtiest campaign in history. I wake up every morning and wonder what new trash he's had his people spread overnight."

"We're way ahead in the latest polls," Deborah's assistant weighed in. "Every one of them."

Deborah ignored her and said to Connie, "I just have this feeling that a second shoe is about to drop."

Connie knew what her friend was talking about. They'd spent many hours discussing the impact of Bob Colgate's alleged extracurricular romantic life on the campaign—more important, on Deborah, and the scrutiny to which she was subjected on a daily basis. It wasn't so much a matter of people asking her directly about the myriad rumors. The press tended to give her a pass on having to comment on what obviously was a painful personal subject. But there was the unstated, visceral atmosphere that caused Deborah to feel, real or not, that people were looking at her with a sense of pity. She hated the feeling. Connie Bennett was the only person to whom she openly expressed it.

As Deborah and her entourage, flanked by Secret Service agents, entered the Crystal City Hotel, among those observing them were Detectives Walt Hatcher and Mary Hall. They'd arrived early for their meeting with Congressman Morrison and occupied chairs in the recently renovated lobby.

"That's Mrs. Colgate," Mary commented.

Hatcher removed his sunglasses and looked in the direction of the Colgate group. "Big deal," he muttered.

"You don't like her?" Mary asked.

He shrugged. "You?"

"Yeah, I like her. I like her husband, too."

Hatcher guffawed. "He's not worth a damn," he said.

"He's a lot better than Pyle," Mary said, aware that she was moving into dangerous conversational territory.

Hatcher's views of politicians, particularly those who leaned left, were well known within MPD.

"Like the rest of them," Hatcher said. "You know what I think?"

Mary sighed. "What?"

"I think he's a whore, and I think his wife is a dyke."

"That's—that's ridiculous. Why do you say that?"

"I've got a sense about things like that. You spend enough time on the streets, kid, and you get to know people, can size 'em up in ten seconds. Trust me."

She knew dissent would be both futile and inflammatory.

Ten minutes later, they left the lobby and went to Restaurant Mez where they were to meet Morrison. They asked for and were given a table in a far corner of the restaurant. They ordered coffee and waited. At fifteen minutes past eleven, Hatcher said, "Looks like the son-of-a-bitch decided not to show."

"Looks that way," Hall agreed.

"Big mistake on the congressman's part," Hatcher said. "Very big mistake." He pulled a small bottle of Tylenol from his pocket and downed two gels with water.

At twenty after eleven, Hatcher said it was time to leave. As he motioned for a check, Congressman Morrison burst through the door, surveyed the room, and came to them. "Sorry I'm late," he said, "but some pressing business came up. I'm on the House Commerce Committee and—"

"Sit down," Hatcher said, indicating the chair they'd pulled over from an adjacent table.

Morrison was shorter than he appeared to be on TV, at least from Mary Hall's perspective. His wide face was deeply tanned, which highlighted the whiteness of his teeth. His brown hair had obviously been dyed, albeit tastefully done, and was combed over his bald pate from just above one ear. He wore a navy double-breasted blazer, gray slacks with a razor crease, a pale blue shirt, and a solid burgundy tie. His smile seemed perpetual.

"You didn't tell me what the two of you looked like," he said, "so I took a guess." He fixed on Mary. "You're the lovely young lady who called. The police obviously have good taste when it comes to hiring female officers."

A waitress took Morrison's coffee order.

Hatcher observed the look exchanged between Morrison and Mary with a sour expression on his mottled face. He'd removed his sunglasses and placed them on the table. The headache, which came and went, hung on, and his grimace confirmed it. He put on the glasses. "You finished?" he said to Morrison.

The congressman looked at him quizzically.

"With the patter. Let's get to why you're here."

"All right," Morrison said. "Why *am* I here? The young lady said something about a prostitute being murdered. What does that have to do with me?"

"Her name was Rosalie Curzon," Hatcher said.

"And?"

"And, Congressman, we know that you and she were friends."

"That's nonsense."

Hatcher gave him a counterfeit smile.

"Look," said Morrison, "I—"

Hatcher's smile disappeared. He leaned forward and pointed an index finger at Morrison. "No, Congressman, *you* look. If you want to sit here and BS us, that'll make me pretty damned mad, and when I get mad, I do things people don't like, like cuffing you and dragging you out of here. Plenty of cameras around, too."

"Go ahead," a deflated Morrison said. "I'm listening."

Hatcher leaned even closer and lowered his voice. "We know that you and the dead hooker used to get it on."

"That's a lie."

"You want to come with us to headquarters and we'll

roll the videotape? You know, like a football game replay."

"Videotape?"

"Uh-huh."

"In color," Mary said.

Hatcher glared at her for interrupting.

"How can that be?" Morrison asked, weakly.

"She made tapes of her customers," Mary explained.

"Ain't this a great technical age we live in?" Hatcher said. "Imagine that, you and Ms. Curzon live and in living color."

Morrison sat back, his eyes darting between Hatcher and Hall. The two detectives said nothing, allowing the congressman to process the fix in which he'd found himself. Finally, he said to Hatcher, "Could you and I talk privately?"

Hatcher screwed up his face into a question mark.

"Just you and me, man-to-man," Morrison clarified.

"No," Hatcher said, "Detective Hall is—"

"Please?"

"It's okay," Mary said, standing. "I'll be right over there."

She left the table and Morrison's smile returned. He shook his head and said, "I think it's great how many women are in law enforcement. Pilots with the airlines, too. I had a female pilot just the other day."

"Is that so?"

Morrison moistened his lips before continuing. "Let's be honest, Detective," he said. "You look like a sensible man, someone who's been around and knows something about human nature. Let's say I did spend some time with this woman. Frankly, I don't remember her, but I'll take your word for it. You say there's a tape?"

A blank stare from Hatcher.

"I may be an elected official, Detective, but I'm also a

human being, like any other man who occasionally has certain needs."

"You married?" Hatcher asked.

"Yes. I have a wonderful wife, a wonderful family. But what man doesn't now and then seek out the companionship of another, maybe a younger woman? I'm sure you've done it yourself."

Hatcher looked around the restaurant before fixing on Morrison. "If I wanted to blow my pension, Congressman, I'd bust your jaw right here and now. I'd really enjoy doing that."

Morrison started to protest but Hatcher cut him off. "Because you're a sleazebag, Congressman, doesn't mean everybody is. I've got a wonderful wife and family, too, and I don't go around buying hookers."

"I didn't mean to offend you, Detective. All I meant was that as two worldly men, we could see eye to eye."

"You were wrong."

Morrison's posture and expression suddenly changed. Until that moment he'd been all smiles, a model of pleasantness, his tone smacking of easy camaraderie, the way Hatcher assumed he schmoozed with potential voters in his hometown of Phoenix. Now his voice was firm, his expression matching it. "I don't intend to be insulted by someone like you," he said. "You're dealing with an eight-term U.S. congressman."

"And maybe a murderer," Hatcher said flatly.

Hatcher's comment pierced Morrison's newfound bravado. "Murderer?" he said. "That's absurd."

"Tell you what, Mr. Eight-Term U.S. Congressman, I suggest you get off your high horse and answer what questions we have for you." He waved for Mary to rejoin them. "We're investigating the murder of a high-priced hooker, and we know that you were one of her customers. That makes you a suspect."

"I did not kill anyone."

"That remains to be seen. When did you last spend time with the victim, Rosalie Curzon?"

"I have no idea. It must have been years ago."

"You're failing the test, Congressman. The tape has the time and date on it. You were taped two weeks ago."

Hatcher could see the wheels spinning in Morrison's head. *Is this a bluff? Does the video recording actually indicate when I was there?* He evidently decided not to fight such evidence. "All right," he said. "I was there a couple weeks ago. What does that have to do with her death? She had many clients, dozens of them. Why pick on me?"

"Why not?"

Mary Hall interjected herself. "Maybe you could give us the names of some of her other clients, Congressman."

"How would I know who else saw her? It's not like we were some sort of club or anything."

Hatcher cited the evening she was killed, and asked Morrison where he'd been that night.

The congressman shrugged and shook his head. "I'll have to check my calendar."

"Yeah, that's a good idea, Congressman," said Hatcher. "You check your calendar and let us know what it says."

They asked him a series of questions that lasted fifteen minutes. When they were through, Hatcher handed him his card, and Hall passed over hers. "I expect a call no later than tomorrow morning, Congressman, with the information we need. And I'd like to see that calendar of yours."

Morrison ignored Hatcher as he shook Mary Hall's hand. "I'll be back to you tomorrow, Detective Hall," he said. He cast a final hateful glance at Hatcher and walked from the room.

"What'a you think?" Hatcher asked Hall.

"I don't know. It's hard for me to conceive of a U.S. congressman murdering someone, but I suppose it has happened."

"Bet on it. Did you see the weasel squirm?"

She said nothing.

"These guys think they're holier than thou, but they're nothing more than a bunch of lowlifes." He laughed. "I think he was putting the make on you, kid."

"Let's go," she said, wanting to leave the restaurant, get in the car, and return to headquarters. Most of all, she wanted to find time to talk to Matt about last night. She'd decided that she'd overreacted and had been insensitive to his feelings. Who was she to judge the pressures an African-American man felt in what was still a white, racist society?

On their way back to headquarters, Hatcher continued his rant against politicians, particularly those like Morrison who lived hypocritical lives, standing tall in public for so-called family values, but living a private life very different from their public proclamations. Mary had heard it from him before, plenty of times, and had developed an internal filter through which the words passed without evoking a reaction.

As they stopped at a light, Hatcher moaned and massaged his temples.

"You okay?" Mary asked.

"What? Yeah, I'm okay. Guys like that always give me a headache."

They progressed another block before Hatcher abruptly pulled to the curb, opened his door, leaned out, and vomited. When he'd finished and had wiped his mouth with a handkerchief, Mary said, "You look like hell, Hatch. Maybe we should go to the emergency room."

"Ah, don't be silly," he said, using the back of his hand to wipe his lips again. "Just some damn bug that's going around. I'm fine."

Matt Jackson was at headquarters when they arrived. "How'd it go with the congressman?" he asked.

"Good. How about you? You run down Mrs. Mouse?"

Matt looked at Mary, who suppressed a smile.

"I found her," Jackson said. "I interviewed her."

"Yeah? What'd she have to say?"

"I'm writing up the report now," Jackson said, not anxious to deliver it verbally.

"Good."

"I also tried to interview the guy who runs the escort service where the deceased and Ms. Simmons once worked. He wasn't there. I'll give it another stab tomorrow."

"All right. Look, we have to make contact with this senate aide. What's his name? Patmos? You take care of that, Mary. The hooker's father is due here this afternoon. Finish up your report, Matt, and Mary, you get hold of Patmos. Talk to the father when he gets here. I've got some stuff to do this afternoon. Catch you in the morning."

They watched him walk from the office.

"I think he's sick," Mary said.

Matt laughed.

"I don't mean *that* kind of sick," she said. "He threw up on our way back here from Crystal City."

"Where? I mean—"

"He stopped the car. Matt, about last night—"

"I'm sorry," he said.

"I am, too."

"Dinner when we get off?"

"Sure. Dinner sounds great. Glad our leader is otherwise occupied."

Chapter 11

Jackson and Hall did paperwork while waiting for Rosalie Curzon's father to arrive.

Matt paid particular attention to how he worded his report about interviewing Micki Simmons, leaving out that the meeting took place at his apartment, and that he'd driven her to Union Station to catch her train to South Carolina. Mary's report was necessarily incomplete; she hadn't been party to the entire interview with Congressman Morrison, although Hatcher had told her enough during the ride to headquarters to help fill in some of the blanks.

They were summoned to the front desk, where Rosalie's father waited. He was a short, compact man, no more than five feet, six inches, with a chiseled face, his posture erect, his gaze steady. He wore a crisp white shirt and a wrinkle-free tan safari jacket. His salt-and-pepper hair was in a buzz cut, the sides of his head shaved close. Neither Jackson nor Hall was surprised when he announced that he was career military, army, retired; his final rank, master sergeant.

They escorted him to an interview room and asked if he wanted coffee or a soft drink.

"Just water, thank you," he said.

He sat straight up in the wooden chair, hands folded on the table. His expression hadn't changed since their initial introduction to him, a man used to taking orders—and giving them—and who accepted whatever was thrown at him without flinching. A good soldier.

"We're sorry about your daughter," Mary said.

His response was a curt nod.

"I know this is difficult for you," she said, "but we have to ask some questions that might help lead us to your daughter's killer."

"I understand," he said. "I'm sure you're doing everything you can."

"We're trying," Matt said.

"When was the last time you saw or spoke with your daughter?" Mary asked.

He lowered his eyes and stared at his folded hands before looking up and saying, "It's been a very long time."

"Can you be more specific?" Matt said.

"At least five years."

"You were estranged," Mary said.

"That's correct."

"I hesitate asking this," Mary said, "but were you aware of what your daughter did for a living here in Washington?"

For the first time, his stoic expression cracked. He squeezed closed his eyes and his lips tightened.

"I'm sorry, sir," Mary said.

His eyes snapped open. "No, it's all right. I'm just glad that her mother never knew."

"She . . . ?"

"She died when Rosie was in high school."

"I see," said Mary. She turned to Matt.

"Even though you hadn't had contact with your daughter in quite a while," Matt said, "it's possible that you know someone who might have been close to your daughter during your period of estrangement."

"Only Craig."

"Who's Craig?" Matt asked.

It seemed as though he'd been holding his breath.

Now, he exhaled, and shifted his posture in the chair. "Craig was a man she'd been dating here in Washington. At least that's what he told me."

"You knew him?" Mary asked.

"Yes. He—"

"How did you come to know him if you hadn't been in contact with your daughter?"

"He came to see me a few years ago. He found where I was living and came to see me. I'm retired, you know, twenty-six years in the U.S. Army. I live in West Virginia."

"Yes, sir," said Matt, feeling the need to be respectful to this man who was obviously proud of his service to the country.

"It wasn't the best life for my family," Curzon said. "We moved a lot, too many times for my wife and Rosalie. It was hard on them, especially Rosie. We were never in one place long enough for her to put down roots and make real friends."

"Not easy," Mary said.

"No, not easy," he agreed.

"About this fellow Craig," Matt said. "You say he was seeing your daughter here in D.C.?"

A nod from Curzon. "He said they'd been dating for more than a year. He said he wanted to marry her."

Both Matt and Mary's eyebrows went up slightly in unison, and their thoughts were in sync, too. The daughter's life as a prostitute was obviously the reason for her boyfriend's visit to her father.

"Craig wanted me to do something about Rosalie, about the way she was living her life."

"Were you able to?" Mary asked.

"No. I didn't even try. The last time Rosalie and I were in contact, I'd come to Washington to visit with her. I didn't know that she was a prostitute, had no idea. She'd told me that she was working as a hostess in a fancy restaurant, and was taking acting lessons. It was all a lie."

"Understandable," Mary offered. "She didn't want to hurt you."

"It was worse finding out the way I did."

"Through this Craig?"

"No. I knew before that. I sensed things weren't the way she said they were. She never allowed me to visit where she lived in—what is it, the Morgan section of the city? Every time I suggested I'd come by there, she had some excuse. She used a post office box, no home address. The same when I wanted to have lunch or dinner in the restaurant she said she was working at. Always a reason not to go there. I knew something was wrong. One day when we were having lunch in a cafeteria in one of the museums, she left her purse when she went to the restroom. A letter was sticking out that had her home address on it. She'd said we couldn't get together that night because she had other plans, so I drove to the address on the letter and parked across the street. I saw her leave the building dressed like a whore. Later, she came back and a few men arrived. I didn't know whether they were there to see her, but I had a feeling that was the case. The second or third man—I don't remember which—eventually came out of the building, and she was with him. They walked down the street and disappeared around the corner. I knew then what she was up to."

"Did you confront her about it?" Mary asked.

"No, I couldn't bear to do that. I went back to my hotel, checked out, and drove to West Virginia that same night."

"Didn't she wonder why you did that?" asked Matt. "Didn't she contact you?"

"No. I sent a letter to her address at the apartment building and said in it what I now knew about her. She never replied."

"But then Craig arrived," Matt said.

"That's right. He seemed a nice sort of fellow. He told

me that he was in love with Rosie and wanted them to get married, but first she would have to give up what she did for a living. He wanted my help."

"And you couldn't help," Mary said.

"I wouldn't help, I told him."

Neither Jackson nor Hall pressed him as to why he refused to come to the aid of his daughter. Instead, Matt asked, "Did Craig indicate that your daughter wanted to give up her life as a . . . as a call girl?" It seemed the gentlest of terms to describe his daughter's occupation.

"I don't recall whether he said that or not," Curzon replied.

"What was Craig's reaction when you refused to help?"

"Oh, he was angry. He said he was disappointed in me. I suppose he had reason to be. Don't think it was an easy decision to make. I thought about it for days after he left. But I've lived my whole life under a set of rules and beliefs. To me, life is nothing more than a series of decisions. You make good ones and things go pretty well, barring a calamity over which you have no control, you know, an earthquake or a plane crash. You make bad ones, well, things don't go so well. Rosalie made a bad decision, one she had to live with. It was up to her to straighten out her life. No one could do it for her, including me. I suppose I was still angry at being lied to all that time."

While both Matt and Mary didn't agree with his thinking—how could he *not* have tried to help his daughter escape a life of degradation and, as it turned out, danger?—it wasn't their role, nor was it the place to air their feelings.

"Tell me more about Craig," Matt said. "What was his last name?"

"Thompson."

"Did he say what he did for a living here in Washington?"

"He said he was a consultant."

"For whom?"

"He didn't tell me that."

"Did he give you an address or phone number where you could reach him?"

"No."

There didn't seem to be anything else to gain from him, and Matt stood. "Thank you for coming in, sir," he said, "and for being candid with us at what must be a very difficult time for you. We'll get back in touch if we make any progress in finding Rosalie's killer."

Curzon, too, stood, erect, as though awaiting his next order. "Can you tell me how I can arrange the release of Rosalie's body?"

Mary answered. "I'm afraid it will be a little while before that can be done, Mr. Curzon. Murder victims are held longer than others."

"I want to bury her next to her mother, in Oklahoma. We bought a family plot when I was stationed there."

"I'll check for you," Mary said. "You're staying in Washington for a few days?"

"Yes, at Andrews Air Force Base. I have rooming privileges there as a retired soldier."

After eliciting further contact information, they walked him to the front reception area and shook hands. As Jackson did, he said what he always heard politicians say when speaking to someone from the military: "Thank you for your service to the country, sir."

Curzon nodded and left. Hall and Jackson returned to the room in which the interview had taken place.

"Breaks your heart," she said.

"Tough for a man like that to find out his kid is turning tricks.

"What about this guy Craig Thompson? He falls in love with a hooker."

"Maybe he wanted to save her from prostitution. Lots

of books written about shining white knights coming to the rescue," Mary said.

"For a hooker with a heart of gold," Matt said.

"He must have been serious, going to West Virginia to ask her father for help.

"Let's find him and ask what it was all about," Mary suggested.

"And where he was the night she was killed," Matt added.

"Yes, that, too."

Chapter 12

Hatcher left headquarters and went directly to Tommy G's restaurant and bar, a hangout for the city's cops, politicians, and wiseguys. Telling them apart wasn't always easy.

Tommy Gillette had arrived in Washington ten years before with a stash of cash from various projects in his native New Jersey, some of them legal. He'd left New Jersey when a new governor waged war on "businessmen" of Tommy's ilk. The heat was turned up; the Garden State was no longer fertile ground, and so Tommy went south, to D.C., where an older brother had settled and opened a succession of restaurants, none of which lasted very long. He convinced Tommy that together they could make a killing in D.C.

Their first partnership was the Gillette Grill, a shot-and-beer joint in the non-trendy, non-gentrified Southwest quadrant. It wasn't long before more than bad food was being served along with the whiskey. A pusher cut a deal with them and used the place as a cover. There were women, too, who were kept busy making outcalls to hotels where male clients awaited their arrival.

Within a year, the Gillette brothers were arguing daily. Tommy, who'd been accustomed to rubbing elbows with fat-cat Jersey politicos and show-business types from Atlantic City, considered the restaurant's clientele to be beneath him: "They're all a bunch'a losers," he constantly told his brother. Two years into their partnership, his brother dropped dead of a heart attack while hauling a beer keg up a flight of stairs, which left Tommy as the sole owner. He sold the place to the drug dealer and headed for downtown, where he found a location for a new, more upscale restaurant and bar—Tommy G's, Fine Spirits and Quality Cuisine. It was a large space consisting of two rooms, the bigger devoted to a long bar manned by wisecracking bartenders, the smaller, the dining room in which a simple menu was served—shrimp cocktail, steak, salmon, and a few other items that didn't tax the kitchen.

Although the Prohibition era was long gone, Tommy ran the place as though it were a speakeasy, palling around with customers, doing favors, slapping backs, and making everyone feel like a high roller in a posh casino—D.C.'s answer to Toots Shor. The décor was an eclectic mix of Paris and the Old West, huge prints of nudes and scenes from the Folies Bergère sharing the walls with black-and-white and sepia photos of mining towns, saloons, and roundups.

It worked. Business was usually brisk, especially later at night when other places were winding down. Tommy worked the crowd wearing expensive, custom double-breasted suits that slenderized his bulked-up body. He was in his element.

"Hey, Detective Hatch," Tommy said as Hatcher walked through the door. "Long time, no see."

"Been busy keeping the city safe," Hatcher said. "Things good with you?"

"Everything's cool, man. What'll you have? First one's on Tommy."

"I need a snooze, Tommy."

"Hey, no problem, pal. You know how to get there."

Hatcher crossed the barroom and went through a door leading to Tommy's office, and to an adjacent room in which two single beds were made up and waiting for occupants. Tommy maintained the room for moments like this, for a cop to crash after coming off a long shift, or a politician needing to sleep off too much booze before heading home. It was known to insiders as "Tommy's Motel."

As Hatcher tossed his suit jacket on one of the beds, he saw that perspiration had left dark rings in the armpits. He pulled down his tie and fell heavily on the second bed, letting out a prolonged sigh. He felt like hell. Once, on the ride from headquarters, he'd had to pull over when an excruciating stab of pain in his head caused momentary blindness. It lasted only a few seconds, but long enough to concern him.

He closed his eyes and sleep came almost immediately, but didn't last long. A series of dreams kept waking him. He tried to grab hold of them but their fragments vanished as quickly and suddenly as they'd materialized. But not all. Once, he awoke suddenly, sat up, and let out a moan as he saw his daughter, Christina, as a small girl, standing on the edge of a building. "Don't," he said, reaching for her. But she fell, face-first, her arms outstretched as though in a swan dive, leaving Hatcher looking over the precipice and seeing her small body smash to the sidewalk many floors below.

He wiped sweat from his face with his hand and tried to nod off again, but a succession of similar dreams made that impossible. In one, tethered to a long rope attached somewhere high in the sky, he spun out of control in a vast void, around and around, until the rope broke and he disappeared.

After a half hour, he slowly got to his feet and looked in a small mirror on the wall. "What the hell is going on?" he asked aloud. He knew he should go home, but Mae would see that he wasn't well and insist he see a doctor.

He went to the men's room, where he splashed cold

water on his face, returned to fetch his jacket, and rejoined Gillette in the barroom. Virtually empty when he'd arrived, the bar now had a dozen customers. Hatcher went to a small bistro table out of the mainstream and ordered a double bourbon from the waitress, Jill, who'd worked at Tommy G's since it opened. He recognized some of the people at the bar; a few waved to him.

"Something to eat, Hatch?" Jill asked when she delivered his drink.

"Yeah, thanks. Baked stuffed clams and some bread, huh?" *Maybe that's what I need,* he thought, *some food in my belly.*

Tommy G. joined him. "You okay?" he asked. "You don't look good."

"Ah, I've got some kind'a bug, some kind'a flu."

"It's goin' around. Too many germs, you know?"

"Yeah, I know."

"You still working that hooker murder?" Tommy asked.

"Yup."

Tommy lowered his voice. "I did a little asking around of my own, Hatch. You know, we get some working girls come in later at night. I don't mind as long as they don't flaunt it. Anyway, I asked a few whether they knew this gal—what was her name?"

"Curzon. Rosalie Curzon."

"Right. Rosie Curzon. I asked whether they knew her." He grinned. "These types hang around together, you know. Anyway, one of them says she met her a few times but it was a while ago."

Jill delivered Hatch's food.

"No tab," Tommy told her. There never was a tab for Hatcher, but he always tipped big.

"I bet there's a few guys around town looking over their shoulders, huh?" Tommy said.

Hatcher agreed through his first mouthful of bread and clams.

"I know a couple of regulars here are hoping she didn't keep a little black book."

Hatcher said nothing.

"Did she, Hatch? Keep a book with her johns' names in it?"

"I don't think so, Tommy. No, she didn't."

Tommy's expression said he didn't buy it, but he didn't press. "Anyway," he said, "you should take a couple'a days off, stay in bed, get rid'a the flu. Best thing is to stay in bed, plenty'a liquids."

"I'll do that, Tommy," Hatcher said, breaking off a piece of crunchy Italian bread and using it to mop up garlic sauce. "Thanks."

"Hey, pal, for you, anytime. Ciao." He joined a knot of customers at the bar, leaving Hatcher with his half-filled glass of bourbon, and his thoughts.

At headquarters, Matt Jackson was busy writing up the interview they'd done with Rosalie Curzon's father, while Mary Hall ran through a database of names in the D.C. area. She came up with dozens of Thompsons, but only two with the first name "Craig": one married and employed by the Department of Agriculture, the other single and living in the District. His occupation was listed as "Consultant." Although they wouldn't rule out either man, chances were that it was the bachelor who'd been involved with the victim. He'd be first on their list.

Mary, instructed by Hatcher to reach the senatorial aide, James Patmos, who'd allegedly introduced the lobbyist Lewis Archer to Rosalie Curzon, called Senator William Barrett's office in the Russell Building at First and C Streets, NE, and asked for Jim Patmos.

"He's not here," she was told.

"Do you expect him back today?"

The woman laughed. "One never knows," she said. "Can I take a message?"

"No, that's all right. I'll try him again tomorrow."

"No luck?" Matt said after she'd hung up.

"He wasn't there. I didn't want to leave my name."

"Why not?"

"I'd rather he not have time to come up with a story."

"We didn't worry about that when you called the congressman."

"*Hatcher* didn't worry about it, Matt, but I do."

Deborah Colgate's limo driver dropped her and Connie Bennett in front of the Colgates' Georgetown townhouse. The events at which she'd spoken had gone well, plenty of checks written, and even more money pledged to the Colgate campaign for president. Deborah hated the fundraising aspect of running for elected office, found it demeaning and even fraudulent in what it promised to donors. Why did they contribute, she wondered, especially those whose checks were for small amounts? Did they expect something in return besides the psychic payoff of having put their money where their beliefs lie? The big donors certainly expected a bang for their bucks—access to the candidate once he or she was in office, and clout when it came to legislation that would affect their lives, especially their bottom lines. Politicians, she decided, were like televangelists, promising miraculous improvements in the lives of those who sent their money, salvation and freedom from disease and pain—or in the case of politicians, better jobs, lower taxes, and a sunny future.

She and Connie went to the kitchen, where a housekeeper was preparing snacks in anticipation of their arrival, salmon with a dollop of horseradish sauce on crackers, and Deborah's favorite, hummus on toast points.

"We'll be in the study," Deborah told the housekeeper.

"Cognac?" she asked Connie once they'd kicked off

their shoes and were settled in the book-lined room at the front of the house.

"Love one."

"Me too."

"You knocked them out today," Connie said after they'd touched the rims of their snifters.

"I'm getting better at it."

"You've always been good at it, Deb, going back to college. Remember when you rallied support for that professor who'd been let go? You not only fired up the students, you got the administration on your side."

Deborah laughed. "Silly student stuff," she said.

"It wasn't silly at all. The guy might have been odd in his thinking, but he was a good teacher. He deserved to stay—and he did, thanks in part to you."

"He was a pervert."

"He was not. Besides, if he was a pervert, why did you champion his cause?"

"I guess I was into perversion at the time."

Connie smiled. "I miss those days, Deb."

"So do I, although lately I feel as if I'm back there."

"How so?"

"Back when perversion was on my mind."

Connie's expression said she didn't understand.

"My whole life these days is perverted, Connie."

"What do you mean?"

"I'm living a life of lies."

"That's not true, Deb."

"Yes it is. My marriage to Bob has been a lie for a very long time. Isn't that one definition of perversion, living a life of lies?"

"Maybe. I wouldn't know. What I *do* know is that you and Bob have forged a remarkable life together. You're about to become the first family of this country, Deb. First Lady of the land."

"At what price?" She sighed deeply and drank.

Connie didn't respond, and Deborah continued. "Connie, I've made a decision."

Her friend's laugh was forced. "Any decision is better than no decision," she said, lightly, a smile on her face. "Isn't that what the shrinks say?" Her expression now turned serious. "You aren't saying . . . ?"

"I'm afraid I am. I can't do this anymore, Connie. I can't keep putting on this campaign face, pretending as though everything is wonderful between Bob and me, asking people for money to fund what is, in reality, one great big sham. I'm dropping out of the marriage *and* the campaign."

Connie's glass slipped from her hand as she suddenly got up and stood over her friend. "Don't say that, Deb," she said. She picked up the glass from the floor and ran her foot over the cognac that had stained the beige carpet. "Sorry," she said.

"Don't worry about the carpet," Deborah said.

Connie used a small napkin the housekeeper had provided with the snacks.

"I said, don't worry about it!" Deborah said sharply, causing Connie to look up, surprised at her friend's icy tone.

"I intend to tell Bob of my decision when he gets back from his Midwest swing," Deborah said. "Frankly, I don't care what his reaction is. Oh, I can certainly anticipate it. He'll talk about how the pressures of campaigning have me on edge, and how once the campaign is over, we'll be able to settle back into the life we once had, how we can't do this to the kids—kids? they're all grown—and how the country needs us to undo the damage Pyle has done to the nation. It's all bullshit, Connie. I've had it."

"I need a refill," Connie said, going to a leather-fronted freestanding bar and refreshing her drink. "Deb?"

"What? No, nothing more for me."

Connie resumed her chair opposite her friend. "I can't

believe I'm hearing this," she said, "or that you mean it. You'll absolutely destroy Bob's run for the White House, and no matter how angry you are about what's going on inside your marriage, there's a nation to think about."

Deborah guffawed. "You sound like one of his speech-writers or strategists, Connie. The hell with the good of the country. What I've come to care about is what's good for me, and staying married and continuing to campaign isn't. You haven't had to live it, the rumors about Bob's affairs, the pitiful looks at me as a woman who stands by her man either because she's too weak to leave, or because she's power-hungry and sticks with him to get to the White House." She energetically shook her head, sending her blond hair in motion. "I can't do it anymore, Connie. I just can't."

The tears flowed. Connie wrapped her arms around Deborah as though to provide a shield against the hurt her friend was suffering. "You're exhausted," she said softly. "You need some time off." She pulled back and her voice stiffened. "But don't jump ship now, Deb. Please, go away for a day or two, a spa, New York and a few Broad-way musicals, anything to change the dynamic. If you want to go through with it after that, there's nothing I can do to stop you. But please, Deb, sleep on it."

"All right," Deborah said.

"Have you discussed this with anyone else?" Connie asked. "Anyone in the campaign?"

"No." Deborah managed a smile. "You're stuck with being my only sounding board."

"And proud to be," Connie said. "I have to run."

"And so do I. I'm having dinner with a couple of sen-ators who're backing Bob. The show must go on, huh?"

"And so it must. Remember what I said. Find a break of a day or two and get away. It'll do you wonders."

Deborah walked Connie to the front door and watched her cross the street to her car. She returned their glasses and plates to the kitchen, went back to the library, pulled her cell phone from her purse, and dialed.

Jerry Rollins answered. "Hello?"

"It's Deborah."

"Hi."

"Can you talk?"

"No. I'm in a meeting."

"When can we talk, Jerry?"

"I don't know, I—"

"Jerry, we have to talk."

Chapter 13

With Matt Jackson still at her side, Mary called the first Craig Thompson on her list, the bachelor-consultant.

"Mr. Thompson, this is Detective Mary Hall with the MPD. I'm trying to reach a Craig Thompson who was a friend of Rosalie Curzon. Ms. Curzon was a murder victim and—"

"You're calling about Rosalie?" he said quickly, his voice slightly distorted through the speakerphone.

"That's right, Mr. Thompson."

He cleared his throat. "I read about it in the papers, just a small piece. How did you know to call *me*?"

"Ms. Curzon's father was here at police headquarters this afternoon. He mentioned you."

Silence on Thompson's end.

"We understand that you and Ms. Curzon were romantically involved at one time."

Another silence, followed by, "We were engaged to be married."

"Engaged? Her father said you'd wanted to marry her, but I didn't realize that you were formally engaged."

"I don't know whether it was a formal engagement," he corrected. "I suppose what I meant to say was that we were serious about it."

"You knew that she worked as a prostitute," Mary said.

"Unfortunately."

"That was why you sought out her father and asked him for help in persuading her to give up that life."

"That's right. He wasn't helpful."

"So he admitted. Mr. Thompson. How long ago did you and Rosalie break off your relationship?"

"A few years ago, not long after I returned from seeing her father. She was furious at me for doing that. I'd given her an ultimatum, but it was a waste of time. The minute she learned that I'd talked to her father, she ended the relationship. She felt I'd betrayed her."

As Mary thought of the next question to ask, Jackson jumped in. "Mr. Thompson, I'm Detective Jackson, Detective Hall's partner in the investigation. Have you had any contact with Ms. Curzon since the breakup of the relationship?"

"No," was his quick, emphatic answer.

Jackson looked at Hall, whose eyebrows went up.

"No contact at all, sir?" Matt asked.

"None. Absolutely none."

"Are you married, sir?" Mary asked.

"Why are you asking me that?"

"Just to get a more complete picture of whom I'm speaking with," she replied.

"Well, I haven't married, and I haven't seen Rosalie. Any other questions?"

"Not at the moment," Jackson said, "but we know where to find you if we do."

The line went dead.

"What do you think?" Mary asked Matt.

"I think I don't especially like the guy. Let's find out more about him."

They pulled up every file they could on Craig Thompson, including three photographs—on his driver's license; a mug shot from his only arrest, for disturbing the peace outside a D.C. nightclub; and a picture from the

Washington Post of Thompson with two other men, following a meeting at the Pentagon. Thompson was identified in the caption as having attended the meeting to discuss the progress of a new weapon being developed for the military.

They studied the photos. Thompson was a chubby, middle-aged man, his face fleshy, his mouth weak.

"So, how does he end up proposing marriage to a hooker?" Matt mused, placing the printed downloads in his briefcase. "He must have spent a lot of time with her, gotten to know her pretty well."

"More questions for him," Mary said.

"Yeah, more questions for him."

They were about to leave when a white shirt from upstairs came to where they sat. "Where's Hatcher?" he asked.

"He wasn't feeling well," Matt said.

"He really looked lousy," Mary added. "He threw up this afternoon and—"

"I don't need the gory details. You two interviewed Officer Manfredi at the school?"

"Right."

"Hatcher mentioned it was you two. It's stayed here, right?"

"Stayed here?" Jackson said. "If you mean did we tell anyone about it, the answer is no."

"Good. Keep it that way. When you talk to Hatcher, tell him the chief wants to see him ASAP."

"Okay."

Matt and Mary left headquarters and went to where they'd parked their cars.

"Where for dinner?" he asked.

"Mind if I beg off, Matt? I don't feel great. Maybe I'm catching what Hatcher has."

"As long as you're not catching his personality."

"Sure you don't mind if I bail out? I know we should talk about what happened last night but—"

After a quick glance about, he silenced her with a kiss on the lips. "We'll talk another time. You go on home, drink some hot tea, and get in bed. I'll see you back here in the morning."

As he turned to leave, she grabbed him and returned the kiss, harder and longer than his had been. "Take care, Matt. Enjoy an early night."

He got in his car and headed for Adams Morgan and his apartment. As he went, the comment by one of his superiors about Officer Al Manfredi stuck with him. Did the brass intend to cover up Manfredi's involvement with the slain prostitute? Would they sweep it under the rug, turn their eyes away, for fear of tainting the department? It was a possibility. He'd seen it happen before when a cop, especially one higher in rank, got into some sort of trouble. Sure, there were departmental sanctions and punishments for misdeeds that embarrassed MPD, but that's usually as far as it went. As the former FBI head J. Edgar Hoover famously said repeatedly, "Don't embarrass the Bureau." That was Hoover's mantra, and God help any agent who violated it.

But would MPD go that far if Manfredi was Rosalie Curzon's killer? Matt couldn't conceive of that, but if it happened, it would mark Matt Jackson's last day as a cop.

He decided on his way home to stop for something to eat. Chinese takeout was an option, but he preferred to eat a meal where it had been cooked. He settled on the Silver Veil, the restaurant and club around the corner from Rosalie Curzon's apartment, where he'd first learned about Micki Simmons. Word around the neighborhood was that it served decent Lebanese food, which appealed to him.

Evidently, he was the only Washingtonian in the mood

for Middle Eastern food that night. He had the place to himself. He was shown to a table and ordered a white wine. A middle-aged waitress brought him a menu. "Suggest something for me," he said. She did, and he approved the choices—hummus b'tahini, rolled grape leaves, hot pita bread, and lamb kabobs.

As he sipped his wine and nibbled at the bread, he saw the manager—or was he the owner?—eyeing him from where he stood near the entrance. The man came to the table. "Is everything all right?" he asked.

"Yes, everything's fine."

"You're the detective who was here the other night."

"That's right."

"Did you . . . ?"

Matt waited for him to finish.

"Did you find Ms. Simmons?"

"Oh. Yes, I did."

"I hope you didn't tell her where you heard about her."

Matt smiled and shook his head. "No, I didn't mention you. I wouldn't do that—unless it was absolutely necessary." Matt took in the empty restaurant. "Care to join me?" he asked. "Looks like you have time on your hands."

The man surveyed the empty dining room. He shrugged. "Yes, thank you."

He was obviously of Middle Eastern origins, complexion swarthy, eyes almost black, and with a heavy beard line. There was no hint of an accent.

He looked worried.

"Everything okay?" Matt asked. "Business okay?"

"It's been slow lately. I appreciate that you didn't tell her about me. I wouldn't want to cause her any trouble, or cause myself trouble with the police."

"Why would you have trouble with the police?" Matt questioned. "All you did was help us."

The man looked around before saying, "It isn't easy running a restaurant."

Matt laughed. "From what I've seen, it's got to be one of the toughest businesses in the world."

The man nodded.

"You own this place?" Matt asked.

"Yes."

The waitress brought a course to the table, and the owner started to leave.

"No, wait," Matt said. "Keep me company."

"Thank you, but I wouldn't want to intrude. There is no charge for your dinner."

Matt waved his hands over the table in denial. "Sorry," he said, "but that's against the rules."

The owner's laugh was dismissive.

"I mean it," Matt reiterated. "It's against the rules for a police officer to accept free meals—free anything."

It was obvious to Jackson that the owner wanted to stay and talk, but was torn, and Matt doubted whether it had to do with other business to take care of. He said, "Do other officers come in here and expect free meals?"

The owner looked down at Jackson, his expression a cross between compassion, and surprise at the young detective's naiveté. "You're a nice young man," he said. "You haven't been a policeman long enough to understand how it is done."

The owner turned to walk away. Jackson sprung to his feet and grabbed the man's arm. "Wait," he said. "I want to talk to you about this."

The owner shook his head. "Please," he said, "I don't want trouble."

"And I won't cause you any. Maybe you can help me understand. Maybe you can help me—grow up."

His comment brought a smile to the owner's face. He looked down at the floor, as though the answer to whether he should rejoin Jackson at the table could be found there. He looked up. His smile widened, and he took his chair again.

"Look," Jackson said, "I assure you that nothing you say to me will leave this table. I promise you that. Understood?"

The owner nodded.

"By the way," Jackson said, "I'm Matthew Jackson. I don't remember your name."

"Kahil."

"All right, Kahil, you said that cops come in here and expect free meals. Do they expect more than that?"

"I don't understand."

"Money. Do they ask you for money?"

Kahil thought for what seemed a very long time before saying, "It's the cost of doing business."

"Your cost?"

"It's expected."

"It's expected of the mafia," Jackson retorted angrily. "Not the police."

Kahil shrugged.

"If someone is shaking you down, Kahil, you should file a complaint with the police. We have an Internal Affairs division that—"

"Detective," Kahil said, placing his hand on Jackson's arm, "you are obviously an honorable man. I admire that. But honorable men don't always see the reality of things."

"The reality I see is that you're the victim of a crime."

"I appreciate your concern, Detective, but I have already said too much. Enjoy your dinner."

Jackson had arrived hungry, but he no longer was. The conversation had been unsettling. It was obvious that Kahil had wanted to talk about whatever squeeze he found himself in, but was unwilling to go beyond using Jackson as a sounding board. That there were members of the MPD that wielded their positions of authority to shake down honest businessmen wasn't news to Matt.

He'd heard the locker-room jokes about it among senior officers, and was offended at their easy, open acceptance of the practice. He sometimes wondered whether he would eventually become that jaded as he progressed in his career. He was sure he wouldn't—he would quit first—but could you ever be certain of how you would behave as you grew older, as you got closer to retirement and were concerned that there wouldn't be enough money to support you in your dotage? He'd witnessed changes in his mother and father—nothing dramatic, but representing a shifting set of worries that caused them to adjust some of their views of the world.

He forced himself to eat a portion of his dinner, but what Kahil had said gnawed at his stomach.

"You didn't like it?" the waitress asked, eyeing his half-consumed meal.

"No, no, it was fine. I just wasn't as hungry as I thought I was."

"Take it home?"

"Sure. That would be good. And I will have coffee."

While waiting for his coffee, he pulled papers from his briefcase and perused them, looking for nothing in particular but occupying himself while alone. The photos they'd uploaded of Craig Thompson captured his attention and he leaned closer to better examine the face in them. He realized he was doing what he abhorred in people, making snap judgments based upon a person's appearance. Stereotyping! How wrong. But he couldn't shake his reaction to Thompson in the photographs. He looked like a man not to be trusted, easily swayed, willing to say or do anything to reach a goal, like too many politicians.

He was immersed in studying the pictures when Kahil came to him with the check. "I would be happy to buy you dinner, Detective," he said.

"I appreciate that," Matt said, "but it's really out of the question."

As Matt fumbled in his wallet for his credit card, Kahil leaned over to see the photos on the table. Matt looked up at him. "Just some pictures of someone we're talking to," he said.

"You know him?" Kahil asked.

"We've spoken on the phone. Do *you* know him?"

"Yes. He used to come in with the woman who was killed. Ms. Curzon."

"They knew each other at one time," Matt said, sliding the photos back into his briefcase.

"They used to come in together maybe two years ago. I remember because they fought sometimes, were angry with each other."

"Really?"

"Then he no longer was with her, until maybe two weeks ago."

Jackson had taken a swallow of coffee, which he almost spit out. "Two weeks ago?"

"Yes. Only once. And then he came alone a week or so ago. He sat at the bar and had too much to drink. I was worried about him driving, but he called for a taxi."

Jackson quickly paid the bill. On his way out, he thanked Kahil. "If you ever decide to put a stop to whatever certain cops are doing to you, let me know." He handed Kahil his card. "Remember that."

Kahil said nothing as Jackson left the restaurant. When he got in his car, he pulled out his cell phone and called Mary Hall.

"Wake you?"

"No. I'm watching *Law and Order.* They really get it right."

"I know. Lennie Briscoe was my idol. Look, Mary, I just left the Silver Veil, that restaurant around the corner from Curzon's apartment. Ready? Catch this. Mr. Craig Thompson . . ."

Chapter 14

Billy McMahon lived a charmed life, considering how many times he'd broken the law.

He'd started getting in trouble as a twelve-year-old in Oakland, California. His offenses were considered by the police and the judges as more public nuisances than serious crimes, and he'd been able to get away with stern warnings from the bench—and a smack from his father—rather than ending up in a facility for troubled, disruptive youths. As he progressed into adulthood, he learned two things: only chumps worked hard, and the key to success was to be charming, especially when the heat was on.

"Charming Billy Boy."

Billy loved that tune from an unknown Welch songwriter, and sang it often. But its final line, "She cannot leave her mother" didn't apply to him. He'd gotten away from his mother at the first chance, leaving home when he was sixteen, lining his pockets with money stolen from his mother's "retirement fund," a wad of cash she kept in a bag in the freezer. His father had cut out two years earlier.

Billy never looked back, and had no further contact with "the old hag" until the day she died. He told friends that he was hurt that she hadn't provided for him in her will, and they sympathized with him. How could a mother be that cruel? "She was an evil woman," was Billy's explanation. Poor Billy. Charming Billy.

He bounced around the country doing odd jobs, stealing when he thought he could get away with it, conning a few old ladies with his boyish, freckled face, curly red hair, and engaging grin. *What a nice young man*, these older women believed until they realized that their bank account was bare and Charming Billy was gone. They never knew his real name; he had an array of aliases, and forged documents to support them. He ran afoul of the law on a few occasions, but wasn't punished for his misdeeds aside from a two-month stint in a small town Oklahoma jail, where the jailer's wife was so taken with him that she saw to it that he was well fed.

His break into the "big time" came one day in Baltimore, where he'd ended up selling chimney repairs to senior citizens whose chimneys worked just fine. He'd been on that job for only a week when he befriended Augie, a fellow salesman with big ideas. Augie had recently come out of prison, where he'd served a sentence for running an escort service in Baltimore. He'd been caught in a sting. He'd sent two of his girls to hotels to meet with clients who'd phoned for their services. The problem was that the men were undercover vice squad cops, who arrested the women for solicitation. One of them turned state's evidence against Augie as the brothel's owner in exchange for probation.

"It's a good business, Billy," Augie told him over beers one night, "only you've gotta be smart and clever, figure out ways to beat the cops."

"Maybe I'd like to take a crack at something like that," Billy said.

"Not in this town," Augie counseled. "This new mayor's on his high horse, man. He's some kind of evangelist or something. D.C. is better. I got a friend there who runs a service, rakes it in. A cash cow. The cops look the other way; like, you pay them off and they're cool about it."

"So, how come you don't go there and hook up with your friend?" Billy asked.

"Him and me had a falling out, so I stay clear. Besides, I don't need the aggravation. The biggest problem ain't the cops, Billy. It's the girls. They can drive you nuts."

Billy smiled. "I never have any problems with women," he said.

"Yeah? Maybe you should take a shot at it, then. Hell, you make a go of it in D.C. and I'll come see you, maybe hook up with you someday."

"Maybe so," Billy said. "How do I get hold of this friend?"

A few weeks later, Billy presented himself at the office of Beltway Entertainment and Escort Service, located in a one-story yellow building with peeling paint, and weeds growing in a bed where flowers once flourished.

Augie's former friend, Luke Gardner, sat behind a scarred desk, a phone pressed to his ear. Billy was surprised at how old he was; had to be damn near seventy, was Billy's guess. He wore a large cowboy hat and a silver-tipped string tie over a plaid shirt. "Believe me," he said into the mouthpiece, "we're not like other services, no extra charges, no games. . . . Sure . . . How do you spell that? . . . She'll be there in a couple of hours."

He looked up at Billy. "What can I do for you?"

"My name's Billy McMahon. An old friend of yours, Augie, told me to look you up."

The man guffawed. "That lowlife? Why'd he tell you to look *me* up?"

"Augie's a jerk," Billy said with a wide grin, taking the room's only other chair. "Forget him. I ran some escort services other places, Oklahoma City, Chicago, Baltimore, and figured you might be looking for some help. Believe me, I know how rough this business can be, keeping the broads in line, handling the phone, stuff like that."

"Tell me about it. What'd you say your name was?"

"Billy. Billy McMahon." He stood and extended his hand across the desk. "What do you say, Mr. Gardner? Give me a try. You won't be sorry."

Gardner sat back and clasped his hands behind his head. "Yeah, I could use an extra hand. You from around here?"

"Just arrived in D.C. The heat was on in Oklahoma City, so I figured I'd head east. From what I hear, D.C. is wide open, everything's cool with the cops."

"We get along."

Their conversation was constantly interrupted by the ringing phone, and the man's calls to his stable of women, assigning them to various hotels, offices, and homes. Billy was impressed. If this afternoon was any indication, Beltway Entertainment and Escorts was a thriving business.

During a momentary lull, Gardner said, "Maybe it was good you stopped in. I've been thinking about hiring someone to take the pressure off me, and you having experience in this business is good. Sometimes I think I'm getting too old for this. When can you start?"

"Right now," Billy replied. "No time like this time."

After a hurried briefing on the way things were run at Beltway—the johns pay $250 an hour, sixty percent to the company, forty percent to the girls—Gardner gave Billy a trial run at taking incoming calls and arranging for the callers' "dates." He passed muster. Gardner offered him a salary of $600 a week, and told him he would work the slower day shift. "Not too slow, though," Gardner said, shaking his head. "These high rollers got needs any time of day."

Things went well over the next year. Billy was in his element. Gardner taught him everything he needed to know about running an escort service, including which members of MPD's vice squad were on the take in return for looking the other way. Gardner started spending less time in the office and rewarded Billy's longer hours with raises, enabling him to buy a used silver-gray Audi, and to move from the rooming house in which he'd been staying into a downtown apartment. Although the job didn't provide perks such as health insurance or a 401K plan, there was the added-value attraction of Beltway's working women, who provided Billy, albeit reluctantly, with plenty of sex to supplement what he enjoyed from a girlfriend or two.

But Augie had been right. Keeping the "girls" in line was the hardest part of the job, and Billy soon found himself having to get tough with anyone who strayed from the party line. That included an occasional beating, which he enjoyed administering. One escort who'd tried to increase her forty percent take from the tricks she turned ended up with a bloody lip and broken nose, compliments of Billy's fists. She got his message. Once healed, she never tried to rip them off again.

Gardner suggested to Billy that his tactics might have become too harsh, and that he should try to cajole the women into playing by Beltway's rules. Billy said he would. But he quietly dismissed the older man's protestations as a sign of weakness, and used an iron hand from time to time to keep everything running smoothly.

As months went by, the day-to-day running of the business fell more heavily on Billy's shoulders, and he began to resent his salaried status. He broached the subject of becoming a partner with Gardner, one night over dinner at a local restaurant. To Billy's surprise, Gardner wasn't averse to the notion.

"I've been thinking that very same thing," Gardner said. He'd been drinking more lately, and his speech and gait testified to it. Still, Billy knew he was a tough old bird, with leathery skin, a broad chest, and muscled arms. “You know, Billy, I sometimes think of you as a son.”

Billy beamed. “And I’ve been thinking about you, Luke, like the father I never had.”

“What happened to your dad?” Gardner asked.

“The law. He spent practically his whole damn life in prison. He died there.”

Billy McMahon had been lying for so long about so many things that the truth was forever blurred.

“That must have been tough on you, Billy.”

“Yeah, it was. On my mom, too. She was a saint, raising me and my sisters and brothers alone,” Billy, an only child, said.

“You’ve been doing a good job, Billy.”

“Thanks. That means a lot coming from an old pro like you.”

“You know, Billy, I’ve never lost a night’s sleep doing what I’m doing. The government’s got no business telling grown men and women what to do when it comes to sex.”

“I agree with that, Luke, one hundred percent.”

“So here’s what I’m thinking, Billy. I’d like to take more time off, get down to Florida, where I’ve got a house, spend more time with my two daughters there and the grandkids. I’m ready to make you a partner in Beltway.”

“I’d be real flattered, Luke. Real flattered, and grateful.”

“Of course, I wouldn’t want to go too fast. What I’m suggesting is that as my partner, you take a fair share of the profits. Say, twenty percent.”

Billy didn’t allow his disappointment to surface. He’d kept a close eye on the profits. Twenty percent wouldn’t give him much more than he was currently making in salary. He forced a smile and said, “That’s real generous, Luke.”

“Of course,” Luke said, “once I’m gone, the business

will be yours." He laughed. "I can't leave it to my daughters, now, can I?"

"No, I suppose you can't, Luke."

Three weeks later, after the attorney for Beltway had drawn up partnership papers between Billy and Luke Gardner, Luke was run down and killed by what a witness thought was a silver-gray sedan.

The driver was never found.

Beltway Entertainment and Escorts now belonged to Billy McMahon.

Chapter 15

Beltway. You'd like to book a date?"

"No. I'm looking for Billy McMahon."

Billy paused. *He smelled trouble. He usually could.*

"Are you Mr. McMahon?"

"Who's calling?"

"Detective Jackson, Washington MPD."

"Uh-huh."

"I'm speaking with Mr. McMahon?"

"That's right."

"We'd like to meet with you, Mr. McMahon."

"What about?"

Billy went through a fast mental calculation. *The pay-offs to the vice squad cops are up-to-date.*

"About the murder of Rosalie Curzon. When's a good time for us to get together?"

"I don't know. I run a busy business and—"

"We can dispatch officers to bring you here to headquarters," Jackson said. "Or we can talk to you at your place of business. Your choice."

"I don't know anything about a murder."

"Ms. Curzon worked for you as an escort."

"She did? I don't remember her."

"Shall I send officers to pick you up, Mr. McMahon? Or—?"

"All right, all right, you can come here. How about tomorrow?"

"How about in an hour?" Jackson said.

"An hour? Jesus, I—"

"A half hour," Jackson said.

"You're breakin' my chops over nothing. Yeah, all right, an hour."

Hatcher walked into headquarters as Jackson and Hall were winding up their conversation with McMahon. They filled in the senior detective on what had transpired, and also told him of their telephone conversation with Craig Thompson, and of Jackson's chance meeting with the owner of the Silver Veil, which revealed that Thompson had lied about when he'd last seen Rosalie Curzon.

"We're heading over to interview McMahon," Mary said.

"Okay," Hatcher said. "Give me the contact info on Thompson. I'll take a shot at him."

"How're you feeling, Hatch?" Mary asked.

"Good. I feel good."

Which was true in a relative sense. His headache's severity had lessened, but was still there, and waves of nausea came and went, like the tide.

"What about Patmos, Senator Barrett's chief-of-graft?" he asked.

"I couldn't reach him yesterday," Mary said, "but I'll try again later."

After another fifteen minutes of conferring, Jackson and Hall checked out an unmarked vehicle and headed for the offices of Beltway Entertainment and Escorts.

"The fact that Curzon worked there doesn't mean much," she offered as they sat in a traffic jam created by a disabled truck.

"Except that Micki Simmons told me that the owner was furious with Curzon for leaving the agency and taking clients with her. She claims he threatened to kill her."

"We all make angry threats once in a while," Mary said.

"I never have."

"You've never been mad enough at someone to say you wanted to kill them?"

He shook his head.

"Well," she said, "I have, but I didn't mean it literally. It was just a figure of speech."

"Yeah, but the way Micki Simmons put it to me, this McMahon character wasn't into figures of speech. He meant it."

"We'll see," she said.

Billy McMahon sat behind a desk, wearing a wireless telephone headset. Next to him was a middle-aged woman logging in calls as they were received. Ordinarily, Billy wore jeans, sandals, and a T-shirt of various bright colors to work. But knowing he would be receiving a visit from cops, he changed into a dark blue suit, white shirt with an open collar, and black tasseled loafers he kept in a locker. He was in the midst of a call when Jackson and Hall entered. They waited patiently just inside the door for him to acknowledge their presence. He mumbled something to the woman to his right, indicated with a finger that he would be with them in a moment, removed the headset, handed it to the woman, and stood.

"Welcome to Beltway Entertainment," he said.

"Mr. McMahon?"

"That's right, William McMahon." He came around the desk and extended his hand, first to Mary, then with some reluctance to Jackson. "You must be the detective who called. Like some coffee, soda pop, maybe something stronger?"

"Where can we sit down and talk?" Jackson asked.

"How about my conference room?" Billy suggested, leading them through a door into a small office that contained a rickety card table and four chairs. "Pardon the mess," he said, "but I'm just in the process of moving the offices downtown, a nice high-rise, as high as you can be in this town." He laughed. "They have a law that says no building can be taller than twenty feet higher than the width of the street it's on. Bet you didn't know that."

"It's a 1910 law," Jackson said. "Before that, no building could be taller than the Capitol Building."

Mary smiled and looked to McMahon for a response.

"Looks like you're a history buff," McMahon said to Matt. "So am I. I love history."

Jackson and Hall sat and stared at him. He, too, took a chair.

"Now, what can I do for you gentlemen?" he said. "Oops, ladies and gentlemen." He gave them a toothy smile.

"We're here investigating the murder of Rosalie Curzon," Hall said.

"So you said, so you said," Billy replied. "Terrible thing, all the murders that happen in this city. A bunch'a animals out there."

"She worked for you as an escort," Jackson said.

"That's right," Billy said. "When you mentioned her name on the phone, it didn't ring a bell. But I took the trouble of going back through our employee records, and sure enough, she *did* work here, but only for a very short time."

"How long a time?"

"Oh, let me see . . . maybe a week or two."

"We'd like to see those records," Mary said.

Billy curled his mouth into an O, as though about to blow a smoke ring. He exhaled loudly. "Those are private records," he said. "Privileged, like between lawyers and clients."

"No they're not," Jackson said. "If you'd prefer, I'll make a call and have a subpoena for them here within the hour. Might as well make it a subpoena for all your records. Everything."

Billy's expression said he'd been insulted.

"Look, Mr. McMahon," Mary said, leaning a little closer to him, "we know you run a prostitution business here. The last time I heard, that's illegal."

"What are you saying?" Billy said, pressing his palms against his heart. "Beltway Entertainment is a legit business. Besides, prostitution isn't illegal in D.C."

"You left out the 'escort' part of the name," Jackson said. "*Besides,* solicitation is illegal, ninety days, big fines."

"Yeah, whatever. But we don't provide sex as part of our services. We offer high-class female companionship for gentlemen who'd like an attractive female on their arm. Strictly legit, aboveboard, no sex allowed. If I catch one of my escorts breaking that rule, she's gone—man, gone, out the door with my footprint on her rear end."

"The employment records for Rosalie Curzon," Jackson said, pulling his cell phone from where it was clipped to his belt.

"All right, all right, but there's really not much in the way of records." He glanced at the phone in Jackson's hand. "I'll be right back."

"What a creep," Mary said after McMahon had left the room.

"Hey, like the man said, he runs a legitimate business here. Maybe you could moonlight for him, you know, be that attractive woman on the arm of some fat cat."

"There's gay escort services, too," she said, lightly. "Maybe you could—"

McMahon returned, carrying a single sheet of paper, which he placed on the table in front of Matt. It contained handwritten scribble—Curzon's name a few times with dates next to mentions of her.

"This is it?" Jackson said.

"The girls come and go, a revolving door. No need to keep more than this."

"According to the dates on this sheet," said Jackson, "she worked here for more than a year."

"Yeah? Lemme see." He frowned as he read the handwriting. "Looks like she did. I guess she didn't make much of an impression on me. Don't remember her at all, not at all!"

Jackson sat back and sighed. "I'm getting tired of this BS," he said. "How about you, Detective Hall?"

Her sigh matched his.

Jackson pointed his index finger at McMahon. "We know that when Ms. Curzon quit working for you, McMahon, you threatened to kill her."

"That's a lie."

"You were pissed at her because she took clients away from you, cost you money. Am I right?"

McMahon shook his head.

"Like I said, McMahon, I'm getting tired of this BS from you. You knew her a lot better than you claim, and you had a motive to kill her. Where were you the night she was murdered?" He provided a date.

"Jesus, how am I supposed to remember that?"

"Do yourself a favor and try."

"I'll check my calendar," he said.

"When's the last time you saw Rosalie Curzon?" Hall asked.

He shrugged. "I guess when she left."

"Not since?"

"No. Hey, look, so maybe we did have some words when she quit on me, but that doesn't mean I'd kill her, ferchristsake." His face lit up, like a cartoon character with a balloon over his head signifying a sudden brilliant idea. "You want a lead in this case? Maybe you should check her girlfriend Micki. Her and Rosalie left the same day. Micki was a real problem, a really big problem. Vicious type. Man, sometimes she scared me."

"What's Micki's last name?" Jackson asked, pretending to write it down.

"Simmons. She'd kill her own mother for a buck."

Matt and Mary ended the interview by asking for his driver's license and other ID. "You live at this address?" she asked.

"Yeah. Nice pad, really nice."

"We'll be back, Mr. McMahon. You wouldn't think of going anywhere, would you?"

"You mean I can't?"

"You're very astute," said Mary. "You're not to leave the city."

"So what am I, a suspect?"

"You might say that."

As they returned to the main office, the woman who'd taken over phone duty was cooing into the headset: "Beltway Escorts and Entertainment. Would you like a date with one of our lovely ladies?" She looked up at the detectives, smiled, and continued taking the order.

As they drove away, Jackson said, "I don't care whether he killed her or not, I'm going to break his chops, pull his tax returns for the last hundred years, get vice on his case, the works."

"You know who you sound like, Matt?"

"Who?"

"Hatch."

"I'll forget you ever said that, Mary, and don't ever say it again."

Chapter 16

Jerry Rollins, respected Washington attorney and confidant to the presumptive next president of the United States, was, among many things, a methodical man, perhaps even obsessive-compulsive. His days were structured by a strict set of personal rules, every move anticipated and planned for in advance, little left to chance. Of course, unexpected occurrences did crop up now and then. He disliked it when they did, and had trouble shifting gears to compensate for them.

Deborah Colgate's phone call the previous evening was one of those intrusions into his ordered life. Not that he wouldn't want to talk with her. They spoke often, and spent considerable time together in the normal course of events, going back to Colgate's days as Maryland's governor, and especially since Deborah's husband launched his bid for the White House.

But during this brief phone call her voice had been tinged with palpable desperation, a tone foreign to him. To not respond quickly was out of the question.

His wife usually slept later than he did, leaving to him the routine of getting Samantha ready for school, and driving her on most days. He enjoyed that time with his daughter and didn't resent Sue's habit of sleeping in. He was surprised this morning when she joined him and their daughter in the kitchen.

"Busy day?" she asked casually.

"Very. Between the practice and the election, there never seem to be enough hours."

"I saw Bob's new commercial last night. He's getting tougher on Pyle and his record."

"Against my advice. He's way ahead in the polls. No need to leave the high road and get down to Pyle's level."

"I thought he always listened to you," she said as she pulled a Greek yogurt from the fridge.

"He usually does. He didn't this time."

"Maybe Deborah could get through to him."

Was there a hint of sarcasm in her voice?

"I'm meeting with Karl Scraggs today about representing his book," Rollins said, bluntly changing the subject. Scraggs was a former member of the Pyle cabinet who'd resigned, and was now shopping his memoir to publishers. Rollins had recently begun representing high-profile D.C. types in their book deals, a slice of business that he found refreshing compared to others.

"How can you represent someone like that?" she asked.

Rollins laughed. "You could ask that about many of my clients, Sue, and you have."

"And you never give me a reasonable answer," she said. To Samantha: "Cereal, sweetheart? And toast with jam? I bought your favorite, blueberry."

"Yum," Samantha said. She turned to her father. "Are we going to take a vacation like you said we would?"

"You bet, honey," he said. "As soon as the election is over and Uncle Bob is in the White House, we are getting on a plane and flying to Hawaii. How's that sound?"

"That's far away."

"Yes, it is, far away from Washington. You'll love it there. You can learn how to do the hula dance."

"What's that?" she asked.

"You'll see."

"Have you made reservations?" his wife asked.

"Not yet, but I will." He stood. "Excuse me. I have to shower and dress."

"You're having lunch with Scraggs?" Sue asked as he came down later.

"Ah, yes. Lunch."

"I don't know how you stay so slim," she commented, "with all your fancy lunches."

"It's in the genes." He kissed the back of her head, gave Samantha a peck on her nose, and headed for the garage.

Besides being methodical, Jerry Rollins believed in moderation in almost all things—except when it came to his car, a red 2003 Porsche 911 GT3, 380 horsepower, 0-to-60 in 4.3 seconds, with a top speed of 190 mph. The car provided him with a sense of being alive as he manually slipped through the six gears with precision and ease, secure in its wraparound cockpit, reveling in the air swirling about his head. Sue hated the car. She would say after watching him lavish tender loving care on it that it was his mistress, and refused to drive in it with him, which didn't bother him in the least. It had cost almost $100,000 back in '03, money well spent. A mistress would have cost more.

There was, of course, the expense of keeping it in pristine running condition, and the occasional speeding ticket he'd earned over the past five years, but that was part of the appeal. Besides, three days a week on a shrink's couch wouldn't be cheap, either, and not nearly as much fun. Actually, he'd been ticketed only a few times. On two occasions, the officers who pulled him over were so admiring of the growling beast that they let him go on his way with only a warning.

He pulled into the underground parking garage in his office building, glided into his reserved parking slot, and rode the elevator up to his suite, where four younger lawyers, and four administrative staff, were already busy. He went directly into his private office and reviewed a lengthy brief prepared by one of his underlings while he awaited the arrival of Karl Scraggs.

Scraggs had been Secretary of the Interior for the first three years of the Pyle administration. He'd resigned, delivering the canard that he wanted to spend more time with his family. Everyone knew better. Scraggs had gotten himself some unfavorable press after being caught in a compromising position with a woman who wasn't Mrs. Scraggs. He denied any wrongdoing, of course, and his staunch wife stood by his side when he gave his pro forma press conference. But for Pyle, whose last remaining supporters were evangelicals and wealthy developers, Scraggs's unappreciated notoriety was politically intolerable.

"I consider Karl Scraggs to be a public servant of the first order," Pyle had said following Scraggs's resignation, "a man of honor who has worked tirelessly at my side for the good of the American people. I shall miss him as a colleague and as a friend. Godspeed, Karl!"

Scraggs was best described as a roly-poly man, fond of wide, garishly colored ties, and a signature straw hat in summer. He seemed to laugh at anything and everything, a pleasant fellow to be around, unless you were negotiating something, in which case a venal vein replaced the laughter; the counting of fingers was recommended.

Scraggs arrived at eleven carrying a twenty-page proposal for his book.

"Who's writing this with you?" Rollins asked as he flipped through the pages.

"A sweet little thing from back home. Got a nice way with words. She's had some things published. She's quite a poet."

Rollins cleared his throat before saying, "A major publisher probably won't accept her as your collaborator,

Karl. They'll want to assign a writer with whom they've worked before, a writer with a track record."

"Well, then, that's the way it'll have to be. She'll be disappointed, I'm sure of that. I sort of told her she'd have first crack at it, but I'll get her to understand. How much money do you think these publishers in New York will come up with for my book?"

Rollins grappled for a reply, but Scraggs continued. "I'll set the record straight about those rumors of me and that woman." He shifted forward in his chair. "And I've got some pretty juicy tales to tell, Jerry Rollins." He winked, and laughed.

Rollins put up with Scraggs for another half hour. Finally, after assuring Scraggs that he would read the pages and get back to him, Scraggs asked, "How much of a cut will you be taking?"

"I don't take a cut, Karl. I'm not an agent. I charge my usual hourly legal fee. If the book generates considerable money, you'll come out ahead that way."

"And what's your hourly fee, Jerry?"

"Five-fifty. But let's not worry about that now. You'll hear from me soon."

Again alone in his office, Rollins sat back and sighed. He was sorry he'd agreed to represent Scraggs. Not only did he find the man's politics and personality anathema, he held out little hope that he could interest a mainstream publisher in the book, at least not for the sort of money Scraggs was expecting. But maybe he was wrong, he reasoned as he turned to other matters before leaving for lunch. It never failed to amaze him the sort of books that were produced by Washington insiders, and the amount of money publishers were willing to throw at even a fairly recognizable name with a promise to tell tales out of school.

At noon, he informed his secretary that he'd be gone for a few hours.

"You have that one o'clock with Congressman Stamm," she said.

"It'll have to be rescheduled," he told her. "Call his office and set up another date."

"Where can you be reached?"

"I'll have my cell on," he said, slipping into his suit jacket and heading out the door, leaving her perplexed. Rarely had he left the office without providing a detailed schedule of his movements.

He drove from the garage and navigated traffic to I-95, careful to keep his speed below that which would attract police attention. He headed north into Maryland until the turnoff onto Route 32, toward Columbia. Fifteen minutes later he pulled into the parking lot of a Federal period mansion, once a stately home that had been rebuilt in 1890 after a fire, more recently a popular restaurant, the Kings Contrivance. He took note of other cars in the lot. One, he knew, belonged to Deborah Colgate. Another contained two young Secret Service agents, who'd been told to wait outside.

He entered the old house and told the hostess that he was meeting someone in the Columbia Room, one of several small, intimate spaces that could be reserved for private meetings. Deborah sat alone at a large, circular table set for two. Rollins nodded to the hostess, who smiled and closed the door behind him.

Seeing that the drapes were drawn over the room's only window, he kissed her cheek.

"Thanks for coming," she said.

He sat next to her. "You sounded . . . well, you sounded upset," he said.

"I was. I am."

Her hands were splayed on the crisp white linen tablecloth. He covered one with his own. "What's going on, Deb? What's the problem?"

She withdrew her hand and stiffened her spine against

the chair's back. "I can't do this anymore, Jerry. That's what's going on."

"The campaign," he said flatly. "It's getting to you."

"It's gotten to me ever since it started," she said. "There comes a point when no one should have to be subjected to what I've had to endure."

He drank from his water glass. "You aren't considering dropping out, are you?"

A laugh burst from her. "Considering it? Come on, Jerry, you know I've been *considering it* from day one."

"Considering is one thing, Deb. Acting upon it is another." He wasn't sure of the next thing to say, so he suggested they order lunch.

"Drink?" he asked.

"No."

He summoned a waitress: he considered having a single malt scotch—the restaurant was noted for its collection of single malts—but thought better of it and seconded her iced tea order. Each opted for rockfish filets stuffed with crabmeat over bok choy.

They said little until drinks and salads arrived.

"Bob spoke with me a few days ago about the situation," Rollins told her.

"What situation?"

"The rumors about his alleged adulteries, and your refusal to address them."

"God, you *are* a lawyer, aren't you," she said. "'Alleged'? You know as well as I do that he's been sleeping around for our entire marriage."

Rollins knew she was right, of course, but didn't confirm what she'd said. There was nothing to be gained, and he had become adroit over the years at withholding comments that didn't promise a benefit, just as he'd honed his ability to lie when an occasion suggested or demanded it—usually small white lies, lies of omission, mostly in a professional context, but sometimes personal, too. He didn't consider having told Sue that morning that he was having lunch with Scraggs to be a lie. It was simply pragmatic. To have said that he was driving to a romantic inn in Maryland to have lunch with Deborah Colgate would have created an awkward moment. Awkward moments with Sue were best avoided.

Rollins considered his next words. "Let's say that's true, Deb. I would never, could never, condone that. But if it's been going on for as long as you say—and you've been aware of it for all those years—then why choose this pivotal moment to take action? I know you've never been a fan of politics, and you know that I haven't been either. But to bail out on Bob now seems to me to be—"

"To be what, Jerry? Unpatriotic? Disloyal?"

"Those are your words, not mine."

The serving of their lunch interrupted the conversation. With the waitress gone, Deborah said, "I'm afraid, Jerry."

"Of what?"

"Of everything blowing up in my face, a revelation from the Pyle people, a bombshell of some kind, photos, another bimbo rising out of the gutter . . ."

He cocked his head waiting for her next words.

"A revelation about us."

They'd discovered that their feelings for each other ran deeper than close friends shortly after Bob Colgate announced his run for the presidency. Of course, they weren't strangers meeting on a train, or falling into each other's arms on a business trip. They'd known each other for a long time, from her husband's days in the Maryland senate.

Back then, Rollins was an up-and-coming D.C. attorney who'd been recommended to Colgate's recently formed special task force on a banking scandal that had rocked the state's financial institutions. The governor and Rollins quickly forged a close working relationship that morphed into a personal friendship despite their obvious differences.

Colgate was as gregarious and impetuous as Rollins was reserved and calculating. Physically, they were opposites, too. Governor Colgate was a tall, solidly built man who was forever dieting to thwart a tendency to pack on weight. He had a mane of sandy hair with just the right tinge of gray at the temples, and a ruddy complexion. Rollins was slender, and shorter than his powerful friend. His complexion was as gray as his outlook, his silky dark hair thinning, off-the-rack clothing drab in comparison to Colgate's custom-made suits and shirts from Savile Row.

It was their differences that brought them increasingly close.

Rollins's thoughtful nature, honed by his law training, balanced Colgate's penchant for shooting from the hip and the trouble to which it occasionally led. And Colgate's loose style provided Rollins with, by extension, the excitement lacking in his day-to-day life.

As their working relationship solidified, their families grew closer, too. Sue, Deborah, and Deb's college roommate, Connie Bennett, became a threesome, although Deborah's duties as Maryland's first lady often limited her availability to socialize with them. Still, there were plenty of occasions when they hooked up for a shopping spree, a girls' night out, or a lengthy gabfest during which they exchanged views of virtually everything, including their love lives.

At parties enjoyed by the couples, spirits were high and laughter reigned. Spirits of the other kind flowed freely at those soirees, loosening tongues and lowering inhibitions, although never to the point of waking up in the morning embarrassed at what had transpired the previous evening. But after Bob Colgate left the governor's mansion and started laying plans for his run at the White House, the tenor of the parties changed, at least for Deborah and Rollins. They would find a quiet corner away from the festivities and engage in long, private conversations. At first, their spouses made jokes about it: "Hey, you two, what the hell are you plotting over there? Come on, join the crowd."

They would mingle as prompted, but after participating in the gaiety, would gravitate back to that more secluded space, where they would pick up their conversation.

Sue Rollins was the first to question her husband about those moments.

"What do you and Deb talk about?" she asked, easing into what was really on her mind.

"Talk about? Politics, how the Redskins are doing, Washington gossip. The usual."

"I'd almost think you were planning an affair."

"Oh, come on, Sue, that's absurd."

"No it's not. People are talking."

"Who's talking?"

"Others at the parties. Marcia Davis wondered whether you were bored with our friends."

"Hardly, but you know I'm not much for social chitchat. I love our friends. It's just that after a while, I like to find some quiet."

"With Deb."

"I suppose she's looking for quiet space, too."

"I just don't want to see a nasty rumor start, that's all, with Bob running for president and—"

They were sitting next to each other on a glider on their screened porch when Sue raised the topic. Rollins put his arm over her shoulders and pulled her close. "Sue, my darling, Washington, D.C., is the capital of nasty rumors. You know that. The last thing I would ever want is to end up on the receiving end of one of those rumors. Tell you what, at the next party I'll wear a lamp shade and—"

"That's not funny, Jerry."

"No, I guess it isn't. What I mean is that Deb and I both enjoy finding some space at the gatherings, that's all. But if you think it's inappropriate, that's the end of it. Okay?"

"Okay."

But it wasn't the end of it.

They began finding that "quiet space" away from the parties, away from everyone, including their spouses. Their growing infatuation with each other moved slowly, and involved only spasmodic meetings, on a park bench on a sunny day, or lunch outside the Beltway at a nondescript, sparsely populated restaurant. There was no physical intimacy during these initial days, aside from kisses on the cheek, and hugs when leaving. It was all talk, a sharing of views, and the recounting of stories from their pasts. She was taken with his quiet, thoughtful demeanor and clearheaded take on issues large and small, while he responded to what he perceived as her innate decency, and easy acceptance of ideas other than her own.

At times, of course, the topic turned to their respective married lives and spouses. Neither was harshly critical of their mates, although an undercurrent of dissatisfaction was usually present. For Deborah, of course, the allegations of Bob's infidelities were at the root of her disenchantment with her marriage, and Rollins's ear was forever sympathetic to her obvious pain. His discontent had nothing to do with Sue. Had he a complaint about her, it was that she tended to be jealous, the irony of which wasn't lost on him as he sat holding hands with one of Sue's best friends. For him, it was more a matter of a vague restlessness that butted heads with his buttoned-down, pedantic approach to life. He was, he told Deborah, a classic Apollonian personality, a person who acted upon what his head told him, rather than his heart. "I sometimes wonder what it would be like on the other side," he told her.

"The other side of what?" she asked.

"The Dionysian side," he explained, "the side where the heart rules and you're free to be naked and ride bareback through a field at night, like the character from *Equus.*" They'd seen a revival at the Kennedy Center, and their reaction to the play and its message had dominated much of their conversation in the days following.

Rollins got his chance to taste the "other side" a few weeks later. Bob Colgate was preparing for his first primary debate, with four other candidates, and had dispatched Deborah as his surrogate to Philadelphia for a meeting of Pennsylvania campaign strategists. Jerry decided to drive the Porsche, and invited her to join him. Bob Colgate kidded with them before they left: "Keep that thing under ninety," he said, "and get the future first lady back here in one piece."

"Not to worry," Rollins said.

His departure from his home hadn't been quite as sanguine. Sue expressed her displeasure at both his driving there in the Porsche and his taking Deborah with him. "She should be traveling on her own," Sue offered, "and have Secret Service protection."

"It's too early in the primary for protection of spouses," he explained. "Besides, it's a chance for me to open up the Porsche a little. Since I'm driving there anyway, it just makes sense for Deb to go along."

Sue didn't pursue her objection. After all, there had never been any tangible evidence to support concerns about her husband having an affair with anyone, much less the wife of his best friend and one of her closest chums. Still. . . .

Rollins's jump to the other side occurred during that

trip to Philadelphia. He and Deborah had adjacent rooms in the hotel. Late the first night, after an all-day round of meetings, they relaxed in his room with a drink. Ending up in bed just seemed to happen, no pre-planning (although both obviously knew that it was in the offing), no seductive choreographing, no losing decorum because of too much liquor (a single drink each), no excuses.

It just happened.

And would happen again over the coming years, not often, always circumspect, the secret theirs, too much at stake, families to be destroyed, reputations to be upheld—and a future president of the United States being cuckolded.

Was there guilt?

Lots of it for Jerry Rollins. Less so for Deborah Colgate. At one point, she told him that she considered their affair to be retribution of a sort for all the cheating her husband had done over the years. For the logical Rollins, that smacked of illogic. It also caused him to wonder whether she'd used him to extract revenge on her husband, hardly the sort of stuff Dionysian dreams are made of. He considered breaking off the relationship many times, usually the day after they'd ended up in a tangle of hotel sheets after meetings to advance Bob Colgate's presidential aspirations. There was something wrong with it, he felt.

But it was too sweet to end it, the smell and feel of her, and the roar of his Porsche's mighty engine, his lifelines to the other side.

They left the King's Contrivance separately, she first, he following fifteen minutes later. Nothing had been accomplished. Their lunches sat barely touched, appetites suppressed by more pressing needs. Nothing had been decided. Like Connie Bennett, he'd persuaded her to step back and disengage from the day-to-day rigors of the campaign, to get away for a few days, take a deep breath, and clear the turmoil assaulting her mind.

But he knew she wouldn't follow that advice, and the contemplation of having her running loose, her nerves frayed and reasoning powers compromised, sent a shiver up his spine. More than anyone, he knew what that could mean.

Chapter 17

Hatcher reviewed Jackson's notes on Craig Thompson, paying particular attention to the apparent lies Thompson had told about when he'd last seen his former girlfriend, Rosalie Curzon. Nothing gave Hatcher more pleasure, gave *any* detective more pleasure, than catching a potential suspect in a lie. Liars were stupid, like trying to cover up a crime was stupid. Hatcher had worked hundreds of cases over his career in which the cover-ups and lies were more damaging to the suspect than the crime itself. Politicians were the dumbest, as far as he was concerned. Nixon, Reagan, Bush, Clinton. You'd think they'd learn.

He decided to bring Thompson into headquarters to make a formal statement, rather than questioning him elsewhere. His gut told him that Thompson could be a hot lead. Why else would he lie about having recently seen the victim? He skimmed the information Jackson and Hall had downloaded about Thompson and studied the photo on his license. Thompson looked to Hatcher like the sort of guy who would take money from his church's poor-box, or denounce his mother if it would benefit him. The info indicated that he was a consultant. What did that mean, that he didn't have a job? That's the way Hatcher viewed all consultants, out-of-work types trying to inflate their egos. Jackson had claimed that Thompson was belligerent on the phone. Another reason for Hatcher to look forward to the confrontation. He loved belligerent suspects. The more belligerent they were, the easier it was to take them down, make them sweat, reduce them to pleading for mercy.

All of these thoughts were pleasing enough to mitigate the pain in Hatcher's head, at least for the moment. But a particularly nasty, searing flash caused him to squeeze his eyes shut against it, and to clench his fists. Maybe Mae was right. Maybe it was time to see a doctor—an unpleasant contemplation.

The pain subsided as a white shirt from upstairs walked into the room.

"Chief Carter wants to see you, Hatch."

"Yeah? About what?"

A shrug. "Didn't Jackson and Hall tell you he was looking for you?"

"No. Were they supposed to?"

"He's waiting."

"Okay, only I was about to pick up a suspect in the happy hooker case."

"Later."

MPD's chief of detectives, Willis Carter, was a tall, slim, forty-something African American who'd come up through the ranks. Those who resented what they considered to be an unreasonably rapid series of promotions chalked it up to his smooth style—"slick" was the term generally used—and his political savvy within the sprawling department. From Hatcher's perspective, being black hadn't hurt. Carter was a strikingly handsome man, his face a series of small, finely chiseled granite blocks covered by a coal-black membrane pulled tight. He was on the phone when Hatcher arrived, and pointed to a chair.

"You wanted to see me?" Hatcher said when Carter ended his call.

"Yes, I did. Thanks for coming in."

Thanks for coming in? What choice did I have?

"Two things, Hatch," Carter said. "First, this Curzon murder."

"What about it?"

"What's the status?"

"We're working it hard. I was about to pick up a solid suspect when they told me you wanted to see me."

"That's good. What happened with Congressman Morrison?"

Hatcher looked at him blankly.

"The congressman has lodged a complaint with us."

Hatcher guffawed. "Based on what?"

"Based on what he claims was harassment by you. He said you threatened him."

"The hell I did."

"He claims you threatened to cuff him in a public restaurant to humiliate him."

"Morrison is slime, Chief. He gave me a hard time. Hell, we—Detective Hall was with me—accommodated the bastard by meeting him across the river, and then he gives me this talk about how we're both men and men have needs and . . ." He waved away the need to continue.

"Do you have any evidence linking him to the murder?"

"He was one of the hooker's clients. He's on tape. You saw it yourself."

"And he's a respected member of Congress, Hatch. He's not your everyday, run-of-the-mill john. Have you checked his whereabouts the night of the murder?"

"He said he had to consult his calendar. He's supposed to call us today about it. We gave him a break. He's probably doctoring his calendar as we speak."

"That may be," said Carter, "but lay off him unless you have tangible reasons to label him a suspect."

Hatcher's grunt was noncommittal.

"Are you hearing me, Detective?"

"Yeah, I'm hearing you."

"I met earlier this morning with Detectives Williams and Shrank."

The mention of their names prompted a promise of nausea. It passed.

"They're willing to drop their charges against you."

"That's really nice of them," Hatcher said.

"I wouldn't be sarcastic if I were you."

Hatcher leaned forward in his chair. "They had no business phonying up a charge against me. They said I'm a racist." A forced laugh. "Hell, you know me better than that, Chief. So I kid around with them now and then, just for fun, goofing back and forth."

"Using racist slang."

"Just words, for christsake."

"Words are tough, Hatch. Words can kill."

"What words ever killed anybody?"

"Words that came out of Hitler's mouth rallied millions of Germans to kill Jews." Carter was known for seldom raising his voice. It had gone up a notch now. "Words send people to wars to kill and die. Words are powerful, Hatch."

"I hear you people use them all the time, you know, slang about your people."

" 'My people,' " Carter said, sighing. "I thought we were in this together. 'My people.' 'Your people.' Hatch, if *we* use slang, it's okay because it's between us. It's not all right for someone who isn't one of—'our people.' Understood? At any rate, Williams and Shrank are willing to drop their charges if you'll agree to knock off the racial comments and apologize."

Hatcher said nothing.

"Otherwise," Carter continued, "they'll go forward with the charges. Your call, Detective."

"Apologize?"

Carter nodded.

"Yeah, all right, I'll say something."

"Good. Now, let's get back to the Curzon case. PA tells me *City Paper* is doing a piece on it. They're claiming many members of Congress are nervous about whether the victim kept a black book with the names of her tricks."

"If she did, we didn't find it," Hatcher said.

"But you found the tapes."

"Right. I brought them to you right after we looked at them."

"The guy who's writing the piece knows about them, Hatch."

"The tapes?"

"Yes. Who leaked it?"

"Beats me, Chief."

"What about . . . ?" He consulted papers on his desk. "What about Jackson or Hall?"

"I don't know. I mean, maybe one of them did. Jackson's a little bit of a loose cannon, you know?"

"I didn't know. Find out for me."

"I'll try. It wasn't me, that's for sure. We done? I want to pick up this suspect I told you about."

"We're almost finished, Hatch. The reporter at *City Paper* is claiming that one of the suspects in the case is a police officer." He stared intently at Hatcher.

"Manfredi," Hatcher said flatly.

"Who leaked *that*?"

Hatcher shrugged.

"Detective Hall was the one who recognized him from the tapes."

"Right. She and Jackson went out to the academy and confronted him. He blew them off."

"From now on we'll handle him internally. Understood? No one approaches him again from your squad."

Hatcher was tempted to say what he was thinking,

that it had the odor of a police cover-up. Instead, he said, "Yeah, I understand." He winced.

"You all right, Hatch?" Carter asked.

"Me? Yeah, I'm fine."

The chief broke out a paternal smile. "You're pretty close to packing it in, aren't you, Hatch?"

"That's right, pretty close."

"There comes a time when retirement makes sense. It's one of the passages of life. You devote most of your working life to a job, and then it's time to pass the torch and enjoy the fruits of your labors."

Hatcher didn't know how to respond, so he said nothing.

"Thanks for coming in," Carter said. "Try to wrap up this Curzon case as quickly as possible. If you need more manpower, I'll see what I can do."

Hatcher went downstairs, where he bought a candy bar from a vending machine. He walked outside and drew in gulps of air as he devoured the candy. His anger had pushed the headache to the sidelines.

While sitting with Carter, he'd felt like a schoolboy being admonished by a teacher. *How dare he treat me that way? I've forgotten more about being a detective than he'll ever know. Uppity bastard, sitting behind his desk in his white shirt and telling me, Walter Hatcher, how to conduct an investigation.* Carter's caving in to that dirtbag congressman was typical. The world—and the Washington MPD—had sunk to a new low. What did the congressman expect, tea and crumpets and a pat on the head? Morrison was known in Congress as a staunch conservative who championed family values at every turn. Typical. Say one thing to get elected and then do the opposite. Had he killed the hooker? Would he get away with her murder? Hatcher knew that he didn't have any tangible evidence linking Morrison to the killing, but that shouldn't preclude badgering the creep until he slips up, contradicts himself, or spills a damaging comment.

And what of Manfredi? Sure, if he'd killed Curzon and it could be proved, that would be too big an issue to sweep under the rug to preserve MPD's reputation. But the guy had broken the law by soliciting a prostitute. He'd get a lecture from some higher-up, maybe be given a week off without pay, and be right back teaching recruits how to be good, law-abiding cops.

His zeal for pursuing Craig Thompson had abated, but he knew he had to do it. He called the home number and was greeted by a sleepy-sounding Thompson.

"This is Detective Hatcher, Mr. Thompson," he said in as pleasant a voice as he could muster.

"Oh? Yes?"

"I need to get a statement from you regarding a homicide I'm investigating."

"I've already given one." Hatcher heard Thompson blow his nose.

"Yeah, I know you spoke with my two partners, but I need a formal statement from you."

"A *formal* statement?"

"Right. Look, I hate to bother you like this, but it's my job. My partners told me that you cooperated and were open with them, that you hadn't seen the victim for a couple of years, so this is just a formality. We're doing it with everyone who'd had some connection with her."

"I don't know, I—"

"It'll only take a half hour or so. I can pick you up if you need a ride."

"You want me to come to where you are?"

"Right. All formal statements are taken here at Metro. We're on Indiana. Want me to swing by and pick you up?"

"No, that's not necessary. Look, Detective, do I need an attorney with me?"

"Hey, Mr. Thompson, that's up to you, but I suggest you save your money. We're not charging you with anything. We know you had nothing to do with the girl after you broke up. That was years ago. Right?"

"Yes, that's correct."

"Just want to get down on paper what you told my partners when they called."

There was a long pause before Thompson said, "All right. I can come this morning."

"That'd be perfect, Mr. Thompson. Like I said, I hate bothering you. But that's what I'm paid for, bothering good people."

Thompson said he would be there in an hour. Hatcher hung up and grinned. Usually, he would have played the tough, no-nonsense detective. But he'd decided to be nice with Thompson, lull him into cooperating. It had worked. As far as Thompson knew, they'd bought his story that he hadn't seen Rosalie Curzon in two years. He'd find out differently in an hour, and it would all be on tape.

Jackson and Hall stopped for coffee after leaving Beltway Entertainment and Escorts.

"What do you think?" Jackson asked as he stirred in sugar. They stood at a small bar at the front window of the Dunkin' Donuts.

"He is a creep," Mary replied. "Ooh, that's hot," she said as the black coffee burned her lips. "What about his comment about the woman you met with, Micki Simmons? She seem like the sort of woman who'd kill a female friend?"

Jackson smiled. "No, but what I think doesn't mean much."

"Judging from the way Rosalie Curzon was killed, I'd say it had to be a man."

"Not necessarily. Ms. Simmons is a solidly built

young lady. She's capable of it." Another sip. "But nah, I think McMahon threw us her name to get the light off him."

"You're probably right. Still, Matt, we've got to follow up on her."

"I know."

"You said she went home. South Carolina?"

"I have her number there."

"Let's get back and call her. And I have to try Mr. Patmos at Senator Barrett's office again."

On the drive back to Metro, Mary brought up Hatcher's health. "I think he's sick, Matt," she said.

"Maybe."

"He doesn't look good, and there was the vomiting the day we interviewed Congressman Morrison."

"He'll be all right," Jackson said. "Guys like that live to be a hundred."

When she didn't respond, he added, "And become grouchy old men, snarling at kids and puppies and making life miserable for everyone around them."

She laughed. "Is that what you'll become in your old age?"

"God, I hope not."

Hatcher didn't wait for his dotage to snarl at his two junior detectives when they walked into headquarters. "Where've you two been?"

"Interviewing McMahon, the guy from Beltway Escorts," Jackson said.

"Anything there?"

"Maybe. The guy's a lowlife, and he had a grudge against the victim. We'll keep on him."

"He suggested that the victim's girlfriend, another hooker, was—"

"I'll write up the report," Jackson said quickly, cutting Mary off in mid-sentence. She looked quizzically at him. He replied with a small shake of the head. He didn't want Micki Simmons brought up with Hatcher, not after he'd willingly allowed her to leave town, and even drove her to the station.

"I've got this Thompson guy coming in," Hatcher said. "Should be here any minute."

"You want us with you?" Mary asked.

"No. This one's mine. Tell me again what he said when you called him."

Ten minutes later, Thompson arrived and was escorted to an interview room fitted out with video- and audio-recording equipment. He was seated in a hard wooden chair at the scarred table and was told that Detective Hatcher would be with him momentarily. Hatcher stood in an adjacent room and observed him through the two-way mirrored wall. With him was a uniformed officer.

"Let's let him marinate a little," Hatcher said.

"He's a suspect in that hooker's murder?" the officer asked.

"Yeah, and he's a live one. Used to be her boyfriend."

"How can a guy have a hooker for a girlfriend," the young, pink-cheeked officer said.

"Beats me," Hatcher said. "Here's what I want you to do. After I'm with him for fifteen, twenty minutes, I'll give you some sort of sign. You come in and say I've got a phone call or something. Then, when I leave, you stay in the room with him. Stand over him. No conversation."

"Okay, Hatch."

Hatcher hitched up his pants over his belly and entered the room. His arrival startled Thompson, who jerked in his chair.

"Mr. Thompson, Detective Hatcher," Hatch said, using his most soothing voice.

"Right," Thompson said, standing and offering his hand. Hatcher shook it and took the chair across from him.

"Thanks for coming in," Hatcher said, recalling Chief

Carter's similar words. "I'm taping your statement, Mr. Thompson. Just want you to be aware of it."

"All right."

"Before we get to it, please spell your name for our records."

Thompson did.

"And what is it you do for a living?"

"I'm a consultant on national security issues."

"Oh. That's a pretty important job, national security."

"Yes, it is."

"Where do you consult? I mean, I don't get a chance to talk to too many consultants."

"Homeland Security, the Pentagon."

"Impressive. Keeping the country safe. Can't imagine a more worthwhile thing to do."

"It is important."

"Damned important. So, Mr. Thompson, let's go over your relationship with Ms. Rosalie Curzon. I understand that you and she were sort of a couple."

Thompson thought before answering. "I suppose you think it's strange that I'd be involved with a prostitute."

"Hey," Hatcher said with a shrug, "different strokes for different folks. Live and let live. So, how did you meet her?"

Thompson looked down at the table. "I was a customer."

"Oh."

He looked up at Hatcher. "I knew right away that she was much more than a prostitute, Detective. She had a very sweet side to her that I knew I could bring out."

Hatcher smiled despite the pain in his temples. "That's nice," he said. "So, what happened? You couldn't convince her to go straight, get out of the life?"

"That's right. We split up because she wouldn't give up what she did. I pleaded with her, even went to her father to ask him to talk to her. He refused. Some father."

"Doesn't sound like much of a father to me," Hatcher said as if agreeing. "When's the last time you and Rosalie got together, Mr. Thompson."

Here comes the lie. Hatcher could see it in Thompson's eyes, mouth, and body language.

"I'll try to be as accurate as possible," Thompson said, looking to earn points for effort. "It will be two years this coming November. I believe I told your colleagues that it was two years since I'd last seen her. I'd like to correct that. It's just shy of two years."

"I appreciate your honesty, Mr. Thompson." Hatcher now slowly stood and leaned over the table. Gone was his pleasant, I'm-just-a-regular-guy-in-your-corner smile. Replacing it were angry eyes, compressed lips, and a voice that was more a raspy growl. "You're a liar, Thompson," he said.

Thompson recoiled back against the chair as though struck physically. His eyes opened wide, and his lips quavered.

"You hear me, Mr. Consultant? You're a liar."

"What are you saying. I haven't lied. I—"

Hatcher turned to the two-way glass and signaled to the uniformed cop, who'd been watching the scene in the room. The cop entered and said, "Phone call for you, Detective Hatcher."

"Please," Thompson said, "there's a misunderstanding here. The last time I saw Rosalie was—"

Hatcher slammed the door behind him. He stood where the officer had been standing and watched, and listened, as Thompson tried to get the officer to listen to him. His words were wasted. The young cop, as he'd been instructed, stood behind Thompson with his arms folded across his chest, a stern look on his face.

Hatcher was about to reenter the room when Thompson suddenly got to his feet, came to the door, and opened it. He and Hatcher were face-to-face.

"Going someplace?" Hatcher said.

"I want a lawyer," Thompson said weakly.

"Yeah, I think you're going to need one," Hatcher said. "But I'll tell you this, Mr. Thompson, you already lied to the other detectives, and now you're lying to me. We have witnesses who saw you with her as recently as two weeks ago."

Thompson's lips were doing a jig now; he was on the verge of tears.

"Let's go back inside and continue our little talk," Hatcher said, back to his pleasant, reassuring voice, a solo performance of good cop–bad cop. "When we're done, you can call a lawyer. How's that sound?"

Hatcher had him pegged right. Thompson melted, fighting back tears, and followed Hatcher back into the room.

"Now," Hatcher said, "let's go back over things, Mr. Thompson, starting from the beginning and right up until last Tuesday."

The video- and audiotapes ran silently as Craig Thompson began to tell the truth.

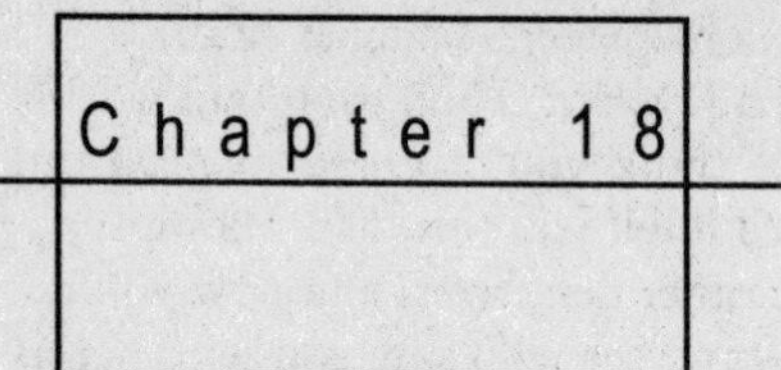

Chapter 18

A woman with a molasses accent answered Matt Jackson's call.

"May I speak with Micki Simmons," Jackson said.

"Who might ah say is callin'?"

"Ah, Mr. Jackson. Matt Jackson. I'm calling from Washington."

"May I tell her what this is in reference to?"

"Oh, she'll know. We're friends."

The woman called to Micki. The sounds of loud children played in the background, and a dog barked, evidently a large one. Its bark was deep. Did it bark with a southern accent? Jackson couldn't be sure.

"Hello," Micki said.

"Hi. It's Matt Jackson, Washington MPD."

She spoke in a harsh whisper. "Why did you have to call me here?"

"It's the number you gave me."

"I didn't think you'd be actually *callin'* me here."

"We need to talk to you again," he said.

"I don't know," she said after a long pause.

"You promised you'd make yourself available if we needed to speak with you, Micki."

"But not here. That was my mother who answered the phone." She placed her hand over the mouthpiece, but Jackson heard her yell, "It's nothing, Momma. Just a friend."

"Micki?" Jackson said.

"What do you want to talk about?"

"We want to ask some more questions about Rosalie Curzon, and your relationship with her."

"I told you everything I know."

"That may be true," Jackson said, "but I'm afraid you're going to have to come back to Washington for a day or two." She started to protest, but he added, "There's no argument, Micki. I was nice enough to let you leave town, but now you have to return. Sorry."

"I was planning on stayin' here, calling the apartment manager and telling him to get rid of my stuff."

"You can do that while you're here."

Mary Hall smiled at the exasperation on Jackson's face.

"Look, Micki," Jackson said, adding steel to his voice, "either you come back within the next few days or I send a couple of South Carolina cops to slap cuffs on you and drag you up here. Your choice." He wasn't sure he could do that with someone who hadn't been labeled a suspect—or as the prosecutors preferred, person-of-interest—but it sounded like a reasonable threat.

"I'll try," she said.

"Try hard, Micki. When can I expect to see you?"

"There's things I have to do here and—"

"Take a train tomorrow," Jackson said. "You have my cell number. I'll expect to hear from you by five o'clock."

He clicked off his phone in the midst of her protest.

"She's coming?" Mary asked.

"She'd better," he said, the steel not quite gone.

Their conversation was interrupted by Hatcher, who appeared with Craig Thompson. The two men said nothing to each other as Thompson, who looked like someone who'd just been given a death sentence by a doctor, left the room, his head low, his eyes averting others.

"How'd it go?" Mary asked Hatcher.

"He's scum. He admits seeing her a few weeks ago, claims he wanted to try again to convince her to stop turning tricks." A crooked smile formed on Hatcher's lips. "He'll have to get that suit cleaned. He sweated buckets."

"But he denies seeing her the night she was killed?" Jackson asked.

Hatcher shook his head and frowned. "No, he gave me a play-by-play of how he did it, drew me a picture. Get real, Jackson."

They went to an unoccupied office, where Jackson and Hall filled in their boss on their trip to Beltway Entertainment, and their conversation with Billy McMahon. Jackson decided to include Micki Simmons in the discussion, and did.

"How come you let her skip town without getting a formal statement?" Hatcher asked, overtly displeased.

"She was on her way home to South Carolina. I didn't see any need to—"

"Did you tape it?" Hatcher asked.

"No, I—"

"Where'd you interview her?"

Jackson drew a breath before answering, "In my apartment."

"Oh, that's cozy," said Hatcher. "What'd you do, get a freebie?"

"Hatch!" Mary said.

"No written statement, no tapes," Hatcher said, sneering. "Jesus! You bleeding-heart types make me laugh."

"I did what I thought was right at the time," Jackson said. "Anyway, she's coming back to D.C."

"When?"

"Tomorrow, I think."

Hatcher turned to Mary. "He thinks! What about Patmos, over at the Senate?"

"I was about to call when you and Thompson arrived."

"Do it. Don't take any excuses from him. I want him interviewed this afternoon. Understood?"

They nodded, and he walked away.

Mary saw the anger on Jackson's face. She touched his arm and said, "Don't let him get to you, Matt."

"I notice he doesn't talk to you that way."

"Sure he does."

"Well, I haven't seen it much. You calling Patmos?"

"Yes."

"I need a walk. Be back in a half hour."

He left the building, crossed the street, and ordered an iced tea from a fast-food place on the other side of Indiana Avenue. He took his drink outside and sat in a wobbly plastic chair at a wobbly plastic table. From there he could see the imposing building that housed the Washington MPD, his home away from home since joining the force five years ago.

His initial assignments, while arduous, had been fulfilling. As a uniformed cop he'd soon encountered the breadth of the human condition, drug dealers and users, irate tenants in public housing, domestic situations in which murder was on the mind of a husband who'd been cuckolded, or a wife whose addiction had drained every cent out of the family budget. The most wrenching were cases in which a child was involved, beaten or starved, neglected like a discarded teddy bear. Of course, there were more uplifting experiences, too, mediating a dispute between two otherwise friends, greetings from shop owners who appreciated his uniformed presence on their block, helping find a youngster who'd strayed from his mother's side in a park, even directing traffic at a busy intersection after a power failure had knocked out the lights.

He thought about these things as he sat and sipped his drink, and realized he'd grown misty.

Hatcher!

Jackson had been paired up with a variety of cops before joining Hatcher's squad, men and women of seemingly every color, religion, and political persuasion. They'd all gotten along, knew they'd better if they were to survive on D.C.'s mean streets. He'd met plenty of detectives, including white men and women who, while quick to point out his mistakes, had treated him with respect. They didn't see him as a black cop. They simply saw a young *cop* learning the ropes and aspiring to join their ranks.

Hatcher!

Jackson had stayed up late the night before pondering whether to ask for reassignment to another squad, or quitting the force altogether. He'd spoken with his father earlier that evening. He loved his parents, and he knew they loved him. His father was a large, gentle man with a low, rolling laugh and eyes that opened wide when listening to people, his patients as well as his many friends. Matt knew that his parents wanted more children but his mother had almost died following his birth; a complete hysterectomy had to be performed to save her life. Matt sometimes wished he'd had brothers and sisters, but also benefited from being the only child. He had his parents' undivided attention, although it stopped short of outright spoiling him.

"How goes it, son?" his father asked during their phone call.

"Pretty good, Dad."

His father laughed. "You don't sound convinced."

"No, I'm fine. But I've just about had it with my boss."

"Detective Hatcher."

"Yes, Detective Hatcher."

"You said the last time we talked that he's a bigot."

"He sure is."

"You've met and dealt with bigots before, Matt."

"I know, but I never had to spend every day working with them, being that close."

There was a pause on his father's end. "Sure you're not mistaking his take-no-prisoners personality with bigotry?"

"Dad," Matt said, "Hatcher is a bull-headed, close-minded, nasty bastard. On top of it, he's a bigot. Other than that, he's a prince of a guy."

"I don't doubt you for a moment, son. I get the impression that you're thinking of resigning."

Matt hesitated. "That's right," he said. "Maybe you and Mom were right, being a cop was a dumb idea."

"We never said it was dumb, Matt. We respected your desire to get out and do something tangible for people. That's admirable."

"But I don't think I can take much more of Hatcher's browbeating. He treats everything I say or do as though I was a—" Matt grinned. "As though I was a dumb kid, and a black one, at that."

"Know what I think, Matt?" his father said. "I think you'd never forgive yourself if you gave up because of this man, tucked your tail in and ran. That's not what you're made of. Remember when we'd come home from parents' night at your school? You'd complain about one teacher or another, that she 'rots,' as you liked to say, wasn't fair, that sort of thing. And what would we tell you? We'd say that you'll have to learn to get along with a lot of difficult people in your life, authority figures you don't like, people who don't think or act the way you want them to."

"You don't know Walter Hatcher."

"Oh, I think I do," said his father with a chuckle. "You've told me he's a good cop."

"That's what they say."

"So, you're learning to be a good cop from him. Ignore his bullying side and look for the good things about him."

Matt said nothing.

"I'm not saying that you aren't right, Matt, and if you decide to quit, you have our blessing. But be sure you'll be able to live with yourself if you allow this fellow to force you out—which is exactly what he wants to do. Sure you want to give him that satisfaction?"

"I'm not sure of anything anymore."

"A good night's sleep and you'll come to the right decision. When will you be coming home again? We miss you."

"Maybe sooner than you think. Thanks for the pep talk. You always make so much damn sense."

"That's what fathers are for, son. Take care. Mom is at her book club but told me to send her love when I called."

The conversation with his father had initially put a few things into focus for Jackson, but it didn't last long. He'd found himself pacing the apartment and having conversations with himself, and with Hatcher, vacillating between trying to reason with the older detective and telling him off in no uncertain language. He tried calling Mary a few times, but only reached her answering machine. He finally went to bed, but tossed and turned for what seemed the entire night. When he awoke that morning, he was tired and more confused than when the evening had started. By the time he arrived at work his mood was almost as sour as his stomach.

He looked across at the MPD building from outside the fast-food restaurant and thought of what his father had said, that Hatcher would love to see him fold and slink away, the half-black college nerd with a degree in sociology unable to take the heat.

No! He wouldn't allow that to happen.

As he stared at the building, he saw Mary come through the doors and stand on the steps, shielding her eyes against the sun as she peered in his direction. She navigated the busy avenue and came to where he sat, his Styrofoam cup empty. She pulled up a plastic chair. "Taking the day off?" she said, playfully.

"Not a bad idea. What's up?"

"I got hold of Patmos in Senator Barrett's office. He's meeting us in an hour at a coffee shop in Georgetown."

"These pols sure don't want us coming to their offices, do they?"

"Can't blame them. Come on. I reserved a car."

"Yeah, okay."

As they prepared to retrace their steps to Metro, Matt asked, "Has Hatch said anything about that other guy on the tape, Yankavich, who owns that joint in Adams Morgan?"

"No, I don't think so. He was following up on him."

"I never saw a report. Did you?"

"No. We can ask."

"Yeah. Let's do that."

James Patmos, Senator Charles Barrett's chief-of-staff, had told Mary that he'd be wearing a tan suit, blue shirt, and green tie. They spotted him the minute they walked into the coffee shop. He was seated at a table he'd obviously chosen because it was relatively distant from the others. He stood as they approached, smiled, and extended his hand. "Jim Patmos," he said as though campaigning. "Pleased to meet you."

A waitress took their order, coffees all around.

"Now," said Patmos, "I understand you want to speak with me concerning the murder of a woman in Adams Morgan."

"Rosalie Curzon," Mary said.

"Yes. I knew her. We dated at one time. Not for long. Nothing serious."

"Dated?" Jackson said.

An expansive smile came across Patmos's tanned face. "Yes. Does that strike you as unusual?"

"Well, I guess it does," Jackson said. "Ms. Curzon was a prostitute."

Patmos's expression went serious, as though he wore the twin masks of comedy and tragedy, each there to be called upon when needed. "Prostitute?" he said. "I'm sorry, but I can't believe that."

"Believe it or not, sir," Jackson said, "that's what she was. You had no knowledge of it?"

"None whatsoever. I will tell you what turned me off, though."

"Yes?"

"Turns out she went both ways."

"Meaning?" Mary asked, knowing the answer.

"Men, women. She was really turned on, but the lesbian thing turned me off once I heard about it."

Mary surveyed their surroundings. It was not the sort of conversation to be shared with others. Confident that their words stayed between them, she leaned closer to Patmos and said, "Sir, we have tapes from her apartment. Her customers are on them."

"Are you saying that I'm on a tape with her?"

Jackson was tempted to lie, to say that Patmos had, indeed, been photographed by Rosalie's video camera. But he didn't. Hatcher probably would have, but he wasn't Hatcher. "No, sir," he said, "but a friend of yours was. He gave us your name as the person who'd introduced him to Ms. Curzon."

Patmos laughed. "Maybe I did," he said. "Who told you that?"

"I'm not at liberty to divulge that, sir," Jackson replied. "But it's our understanding that you sent this friend to her because she was a prostitute."

Patmos thought for a moment, then said, "Which would make me a pimp."

Jackson was glad Patmos had said it, not him.

"Look, Mr. Patmos," Mary said, "we're not interested in everyone's sex life. We're investigating the murder of a woman. We're following up every lead we have, every person we know to have had contact with the victim. I personally don't care whether you engaged the services of a hooker or not, or whether you passed her number along to a friend. What we *are* interested in is when you last saw the victim, and what you were doing the night of her murder."

He said nothing. Mary's thought at the moment was that he was a very handsome young man, well dressed and with a powerful job in a city of powerful jobs. He undoubtedly had attractive young women falling all over him. Then again, she reasoned, he might be one of those men who doesn't have time to date women, preferring to get his sex by paying for it rather than having to wine and dine a woman into bed, which was time consuming, and probably more expensive.

"When was she killed?"

They gave him the date and approximate time of her death.

He smiled. "I know exactly where I was and what I was doing," he said. "I was with Senator Barrett at a fundraiser at the Mayflower Hotel."

"All night?"

"A good portion of it."

"I'm sure there are people who were with you who can vouch for your presence there," Jackson said.

"Of course. But I wouldn't want you approaching

them. That would be embarrassing for me—and for Senator Barrett if it got back to him."

"We'll be as discreet as possible," Mary said. "Could you give us some names?"

"You know," Patmos said, "I find this to be a form of harassment."

"It isn't meant to be," Jackson said. "Names?"

"There were so many people there," the chief-of-staff said. "Hundreds."

Easy to get lost in the crowd, slip out, and spend an hour with Rosalie Curzon, Jackson thought.

"Just give us the names of a few who were with you all night," Mary said.

"I'll have to think about that," Patmos said.

Mary took a sip of her now-cold coffee. "We're in no rush," she said sweetly.

Jackson and Hall left the coffee shop with two male names, who Patmos said would vouch for his attendance at the fund-raiser. He'd turned on the charm at the end of their meeting, apologizing for anything he might have said that could be construed as arrogant or combative. "Anything I can do to help, please call," he said.

They stood on Wisconsin Avenue and watched him disappear into a crowd of window-shopping tourists.

"What do you think?" Mary asked.

"I'm thinking that all we have to go on are the few people caught on those tapes. She must have had dozens of other clients we'll never know about. Shame she didn't keep a little black book like they're supposed to."

She laughed. "I didn't know that was a rule with hookers, Matt."

"It should be," he said.

As they drove back to Metro, Mary said, "I was thinking in the coffee shop about something you said the morning after the murder."

"What's that?"

"That she wasn't wearing that red kimono she wore on the tapes. Sweatpants and sweatshirt. Maybe whoever did her in wasn't a john, wasn't there for sex."

Chapter 19

The Colgate campaign for president was picking up steam every day, which meant increased involvement for Jerry Rollins. He wasn't happy about that. Colgate was calling upon him for advice at all hours of the day and night, asking that they get together to discuss strategy, or to mediate spats between members of his staff. While Rollins's displeasure had much to do with the time it took from his law practice, to say nothing of eating into his fragmented domesticity with Sue and Samantha, he also had to admit to himself that he was trying to avoid Deborah.

He'd never imagined he would end up in a quandary like this, not the trap-minded, focused, clearheaded, insightful attorney that he'd always been. Along with the guilt, it was anger at having succumbed to such a basic instinct, cognition overruled by sheer passion and lust.

He'd cheated on Sue. That was bad. He'd slept with one of his wife's best friends. That was worse. And the woman with whom he'd been arranging sexual trysts was poised to become the nation's first lady. Certainly that transcended mundane adultery.

His furtive lunch with Deb had been unsettling, at best.

He'd known for some time, certainly for the past few months, that she was close to unraveling. During recent assignations, there had been more talk than sex. That didn't disappoint Rollins. A chill had set in between them that was hardly conducive to steamy, naked romps. He was actually relieved that their occasional meetings involved no more than a cursory kiss, maybe a squeeze or two, and long and occasionally intellectual conversations of the sort that had drawn them to each other in the first place.

He sat in his office pondering the situation. He'd been doing a lot of that lately, trying to codify his thoughts and feelings, attempting to cram sense and inject order into what were, damn it, jumbled thoughts. He knew that were he and Deborah no more than a married man and married woman who'd lapsed into an affair, the ramifications would be purely moral, with the possibility of something legal injecting itself should their affair be discovered and result in divorce. He and Sue had friends for whom that scenario had played out, creating domestic turmoil, accusations and guilt, damaged children, and hefty counseling and attorneys' fees.

But this was different, as any third-party observer would certainly agree. He'd found himself sucked into the cortex of a presidential campaign. His friend of many years, Robert Colgate, former governor of Maryland and poll leader in the presidential race, depended on him to offer sage counsel, and to always do the right thing, say the right words, do nothing to derail what had become Colgate's freight train to the White House. That the man himself had acted recklessly countless times wasn't the issue, at least not for Rollins. He'd always prided himself on the ability to compartmentalize and to detach himself from a situation in which he'd been fully attached. Take Colgate's marital transgressions, as an example. Rollins was not only aware of some of them, he'd played the beard at times, booking a hotel room for his politically ascending friend, knowing all too well what would transpire in that room. But here was detachment at its finest. Booking the room, and forgetting that he had if asked, had nothing to do with who was in that room, or what he did there. Don't ask, don't tell. Ignorance is bliss. My hands are clean.

If only he'd been able to do that with Deborah Colgate. There was no ignorance of what he'd done, nor was there bliss beyond the purely physical type. His hands were dirty.

He fielded a call from the insufferable Karl Scraggs, who asked what Rollins had thought of his book proposal.

"Very interesting," Rollins said, as he told friends who'd performed poorly in a community theater production and awaited his evaluation backstage. *A very interesting performance.* That seemed to placate them, although God knew what a cliché it was. We hear what we want to hear.

"I thought you might have a check for me for a half-million bucks," Scraggs said, laughing. Always laughing.

"I want to give it some more thought, Karl," Rollins said. "I'll need a few more days."

"You take all the time you need, Jerry Boy. I'm not going anywhere."

No, you're not, was Rollins's thought as he hung up the receiver.

His secretary appeared at the door. "Jerry, there's a reporter on line two."

"A reporter. From where?"

"*City Paper.* His name is Langdon."

"What does he want?"

"He wants to talk to you."

"About what?"

She shook her head and bunched her lips together.

He sighed, swung around in his swivel desk chair, stared at the phone for a few seconds, and picked it up. "Rollins here."

"Hi, Mr. Rollins. I'm Josh Langdon. With *City Paper.*"

"Hello." It occurred to Rollins at that moment that he knew the name of the reporter, not from *City Paper,* but from a blog the reporter ran that purported to expose corruption in Washington, sort of a poor man's Drudge Report. *Watch what you say,* Rollins silently told himself.

"What can I do for you, Mr. Langdon?"

"I'm wrapping up a story on the murder of that prostitute in Adams Morgan, Rosalie Curzon."

"Yes?"

"I understand that videotapes found in her apartment included some of her clients on them."

"That's interesting. But why call me about it?"

"My sources tell me that your friend Governor Colgate might have a . . . well, a tangential connection with the victim."

"Is that so?"

"I thought you might be able to help me shed some light on this."

"I have no idea what you're talking about, Mr. Langdon."

"No comment on it?"

"It sounds to me that you're chasing after some politically motivated rumor that's nothing but trash."

"Okay, Mr. Rollins. I appreciate you taking the time to talk with me."

"You mention your 'sources.' Who might they be?"

Langdon's laugh was dismissive, and nasty. "Can't say, Mr. Rollins. But I will say that they're pretty reliable. Nothing like a good story about sex and politicians. Craig, Vitter, Spitzer. Who's next? There are all those rumors about Governor Colgate and other women that—"

"Anything else?" Rollins asked.

"Not unless you have something to offer, Mr. Rollins."

"I don't. Good-bye."

Rollins realized he'd begun to sweat, and wiped his brow with a tissue. His secretary called on the intercom: "Your wife's on the phone."

"Tell her to hold on," he said, getting up, going to the wall safe, and laying fingertips on the dial. He snapped out of the momentary trance he'd lapsed into, returned to the desk, and greeted Sue on the phone. "Hi," he said.

"I don't know how your weekend is shaping up," she said, "but I thought that if you could get free on Saturday we could attend the Smithsonian folk music festival on the Mall. Samantha would enjoy it, so would I, and we haven't done a family thing in too long. Can you shake free on Saturday?"

He glanced down at his large desk calendar. He was scheduled to meet with Colgate at noon to go over speeches he was scheduled to give on the economy and health care.

"Sure," he said, pleased that he hadn't hesitated to make the decision. "I was supposed to meet with Bob, but I'll cancel. You're right. We need some time together as a family."

He could see the smile on her face.

"Yeah, let's do it."

Chapter 20

When Jackson and Hall returned from their Patmos interview, they sat with Hatcher to go over reports of their questioning of those captured on Rosalie Curzon's tapes. Jackson gave a brief oral recap of what Patmos had said; Hall provided the two names Patmos had given them to confirm his whereabouts the night of the murder.

"Follow up on them," Hatcher said.

"Shall do," said Hall.

"I also want you two to go back to the building where the murder took place and reinterview everybody."

"Everybody?" Jackson said.

"Oh, I'm sorry, Detective Jackson. Will that be too much of a burden for you?"

"Not at all, Detective Hatcher."

"Don't cop an attitude on me, Jackson," Hatcher said.

Jackson turned away, visibly ignoring him.

As they were about to break up the meeting, Mary asked Hatcher, "Did you ever write up a report on that guy who owns the restaurant in Adams Morgan, Yankavich?"

"No," Hatcher said. "Haven't gotten around to it yet. Doesn't matter. He's not at the top of the list. I interviewed him. His alibi is tight."

Jackson and Hall said nothing, although their thoughts

were similar: It wasn't like Hatcher to summarily dismiss a suspect, or to ignore writing a report of his interview.

"Where will you be later on today, Hatch?" Mary asked.

Hatcher's hesitation spoke loudly. He grimaced and closed his eyes, opened them and stared at Jackson. "Among other things, I'm meeting with Amos and Andy."

Jackson looked at him quizzically.

"Williams and Shrank. Your buddies."

Jackson's jaw tightened.

"They say I'm a racist. You think I'm a racist, Jackson?"

Mary looked back and forth between them.

Jackson didn't respond.

"I have to tell them I'm not a racist, tell them I shouldn't have said some of the things they claim I said. That make you happy, Jackson?"

"We'll interview people at the building," Jackson said, and left the room.

"He's got a thin skin, kid, too thin to be a good cop," Hatcher told Mary.

"Why don't you lay off him, Hatch?"

His grin was crooked. "I just want him to be a good cop, like the way I want you to be. That's what I'm supposed to do, turn the two of you into good cops. Anything wrong with that?"

"No, Hatch, nothing wrong with it."

She'd seen him slip into this combative mood plenty of times since being assigned to his squad and had learned that it was best to get away as quickly as possible.

"You know, Mary, I'm really not a bad guy. I just care too damn much."

She nodded and was gone.

Hatcher prepared to leave, too, but his wife called.

"Hey, babe, what's up?"

"I'm just making sure you don't miss the doctor's appointment I made for you this afternoon."

"Yeah, yeah, I'll go."

"It's important, Hatch."

"I know it is. Don't worry. He'll tell me to take a couple of aspirin and forget about it."

"You're probably right, but better safe than sorry. That's my motto."

"You got a lot of mottos, Mae."

She giggled. "I guess I do. Don't be late for your appointment, Hatch. Promise?"

"I'll probably have to sit there for an hour. You know how these damn doctors are. But I'll be on time. Gotta run. Things to do."

He'd agreed to see their family physician to stop Mae from nagging him, although he'd finally, albeit reluctantly, admitted to himself that the severe headaches he'd been suffering, and the occasional nausea, had worried even him. Actually, their "family" physician pretty much had Mae as his only patient. The kids were gone, and Hatcher hadn't been seen by him since a physical three or four years ago that pronounced him in relatively good health aside from high cholesterol, high blood pressure, swelling in his legs, nagging lower back pain, almost constant acid reflux, and assorted other ailments that made it sound to Hatcher as though he was about to keel over. The doctor urged him to have further tests, and Hatcher assured him that he would. He never did. Nor did he tell Mae what the doctor had said. All that would have accomplished was to initiate a new round of badgering. He didn't need that.

For Mae, that he'd agreed to see their physician that afternoon represented a major breakthrough. Men could be so stubborn, she was fond of telling her female friends at their weekly gathering to play cards and swap stories about their husbands.

Hatcher had a few hours to kill before his doctor's appointment. There was paperwork to catch up on, including writing the report of his "interview" with Yankavich, but he wasn't in the mood for it. He decided to go to Joe's Bar and Grille for lunch, and maybe a vodka or two to steady his nerves. Wouldn't do to breathe high-octane bourbon fumes on the doc, would it?

As cavalier as he was with Mae about his health, the thought of actually seeing a doctor had set him on edge. The worst possible scenarios filled his thoughts: "*You have a month to live, Mr. Hatcher. I suggest you go home and put your things in order.*" Or "*You have a very aggressive form of cancer, Mr. Hatcher. Our only hope is an equally aggressive form of chemotherapy that will wipe you out for at least six months. And oh, by the way, there's no guarantee it will work.*"

He was all bravado on the outside, somewhere inside a frightened little boy.

Hatch was on his way out of the building when fellow detectives Shrank and Williams arrived.

"Hello, Hatch," Williams said, gruffly.

"Yeah, hello," Hatcher said. "You two got a minute?"

"Just a minute," Shrank said.

They stood outside. "I understand you two heard me wrong," Hatcher said. He shifted from one foot to the other.

"That so?"

"Yeah. It seems you guys were filing some sort of complaint against me, like for not being politically correct." He gave them a toothy grin.

"You've got a big mouth, Hatch," said Shrank. He was even taller and heavier than the white detective.

"Yeah, well, sometimes I like to kid around, you know? That's all it was, kidding around."

"You've got a different sense of humor," Williams said. He was shorter and older, with cotton patches of white hair at his temples.

"You've gotta have a sense of humor in this job, huh?" Hatcher said. Another smile. "Anyway, no hard feelings. You misunderstood me, that's all."

"You got anything else to say, Hatch?"

"No, that's it, except if what I said got your noses outta joint, I—I apologize. All right?"

"All right, Hatch," Williams said, leading his partner through the doors.

"Screw you," Hatcher muttered. "What'a you want from me, blood?"

He needed that vodka more than ever.

Yankavich wasn't in the restaurant when Hatcher arrived. He took his usual spot at the end of the bar and ordered a Bloody Mary from a waitress doing double duty as barmaid. "Where's Joe?" he asked.

"At the bank. He'll be back in a couple'a minutes."

A pile of that week's edition of *City Paper* rested on the bar. Hatcher absently took one and started skimming it. He wasn't a fan of the paper, didn't particularly like any newspaper, especially the *Post* and the *New York Times* and all the other media he considered knee-jerk liberal. He often called the *Times* "Pravda," which brought a laugh from like-minded friends. *City Paper* was termed an alternative weekly, focusing on local news and the arts. It had been around since the early '80s. Its stated circulation figure was more than eighty thousand readers. It was one of the most prestigious and influential of the nation's alternative weeklies, a must-read for everyone in D.C. wanting a different take on D.C. politics.

The Josh Langdon article on the Rosalie Curzon murder took up all of page three, and it caused Hatcher to stop scanning and to read more closely. The article's thrust was that the call girl's murder had politicians scurrying for cover. The writer relied on a few "unnamed but credible sources," including the possibility raised by someone "high up in political circles" that presidential front-runner Robert Colgate *might* have had a connection with the victim. Langdon had referred to his call to Colgate friend and senior campaign advisor Jerrold Rollins, quoting Rollins as saying ". . . you're chasing after some politically motivated rumor that's nothing but trash."

Langdon went on to mention the possibility that the murdered call girl had videotaped some of her trysts with prominent politicians, and that a source within the Metropolitan Police Department indicated to the reporter that cops in that agency might, too, have bought sexual favors from the deceased and been caught on tape.

Hatcher angrily closed the paper and cursed the leaks alluded to in the story. You couldn't keep anything under wraps in Washington, D.C., leak city. Reporters were worse whores than Curzon ever was. Hatcher had once heard on a cable news show that the Constitution protected only two classes of people, two specific professions: lobbyists and journalists. Between them there wasn't an ounce of honor, as far as Hatcher was concerned. He was stewing in that thought, his glass half-empty, when Yankavich walked through the door. Seeing the hulking detective prompted a sour expression on the owner's face. He tried to ignore him, but Hatcher motioned for the owner to join him.

"How's things, Joe?"

"Things are fine. You?"

"Fine. I need to talk to you again about the hooker murder around the corner."

"What for?"

"To go over your alibi."

Yankavich snorted. "I don't need no alibi." He whispered into Hatcher's ear. "So I got me a piece now and then. That makes me a normal guy, right? It don't make me a murderer."

"You never told me how much she charges, Joe."

"What's it matter?"

"Tell me."

"We worked out a deal."

Hatcher's face brightened. "Like a barter deal?"

The waitress answered a phone call and told Joe it was for him. "I got things to do," he told Hatcher, walking to where the waitress waited, the phone in her outstretched hand.

When Yankavich hung up, he returned to Hatcher. "I've got to go someplace, Hatcher. Enjoy your drink. It's on me."

"Keep your drink, Joe," Hatcher said, tossing bills on the bar. "I'll be back. We've got more to talk about."

Yankavich watched Hatcher exit into the sunlight. He noticed that the detective was walking funny, a little unsteady on his feet. He mumbled curses under his breath. He'd shed no tears if Hatcher dropped dead on the sidewalk, as long as his body didn't prevent customers from coming through the door.

Hatcher arrived at the doctor's building early and sat in his car until it was time for his appointment. The receptionist greeted him and asked that he fill out some forms.

"I already did that," Hatcher protested.

"I see that that was almost four years ago, Mr. Hatcher. You'll have to fill them out again."

Hatcher did as instructed and returned them to her desk. Fifteen minutes later, fifteen minutes past his appointment, a nurse ushered him into an examining room and told him to strip to the waist and to slip on a skimpy hospital gown that tied at the back. After taking his blood pressure, temperature, and an EKG, she left him sitting on the edge of an examination table. Another fifteen minutes passed before the doctor appeared.

"Well, Mr. Hatcher, where have you been?"

"What'a you mean?"

"It's been a long time since I last saw you."

"Yeah, well, I've been busy."

"How've you been feeling?"

"Pretty good, except I have this damn headache, and sometimes I get nauseous."

"Every day?"

"Pretty much."

"Your blood pressure is elevated. It's quite high."

"It's the job."

"You're a detective."

"Right, but not for much longer. I'm getting ready to pack it in and take the pension."

The doctor ignored him as he listened to Hatcher's chest and back through a stethoscope, and looked down his throat. "Your EKG shows some abnormalities, Mr. Hatcher."

"But it's nothing, right?" Hatcher said.

"We won't know until we do a battery of tests, a CAT scan, MRI, an echocardiogram and a carotid artery test. I'll also order an angiogram."

"What do you do, Doc, get paid by the test?"

The doctor flipped through Hatcher's chart again. "I see that I ordered tests four years ago. You never followed up."

"Yeah, I know."

"But you *will* follow up this time."

"Sure. If you say so, Doc."

As Hatcher was about to leave, the doctor, whose years of intense medical training had left him personality-challenged, said gravely, "I don't like what I see, Mr. Hatcher. It's vitally important that you have these tests."

He handed him a prescription, on which he'd written the ones he'd recommended. "Please schedule these as soon as possible. My assistant at the desk will help you book the appointments."

Hatcher went to the desk and showed the assistant the paper. "The problem is," he said, "I don't have my calendar with me. I'm pretty tied up these days. I'll call you when I get home this afternoon."

"All right," she said, eyeing him suspiciously and handing him a card with phone numbers on it.

After Hatcher was gone, the doctor came to the desk and said, "Make a note to call Mr. Hatcher in a week to schedule tests. The man's a walking time bomb."

Chapter 21

Hall contacted Patmos's two alibi witnesses, both of whom confirmed that he'd been at the fundraiser.

"Was he there all night?" Hall asked each.

One of them laughed. "How should I know?" he said. "There were hundreds of people milling around. I saw Jimmy at the start of the evening. I think I saw him at the end when he left with Senator Barrett."

"And in between?"

"I'm sure he was there."

"Because you saw him there all evening?"

"No. I mean, why would he leave? Hey, what's this all about? Is Jimmy in some kind of trouble?"

"No, not at all," Hall said. "Just a routine inquiry. Thanks for your time."

"He doesn't have an alibi," she told Jackson after ending the second call. "He could have skipped out of the event for hours without anybody noticing."

"He's like the rest of the men who we only know were involved with her because they showed up on tape. Buying her services as a hooker is one thing, coming up with evidence that they were involved in her murder is another. Know what I think? I think that the Curzon murder is never going to be solved, not unless one of her johns has a burst of conscience and strolls into Metro pleading to be locked up."

"That'd be nice," Mary said.

"I suppose we might as well go back to Curzon's apartment building," Jackson said through a yawn.

"Late night?" she asked as they walked to their car.

"Yeah. Couldn't sleep. I tried you and—"

"I heard your messages. I caught dinner and a movie with Betty. I thought I told you I was planning to do that."

"Maybe you did. I must have forgotten."

"You sounded agitated. Right word?"

He smiled. "As good a word as any to describe how I felt. I had a long talk with my father."

"About the job?"

"Uh-huh. I told him I was thinking of quitting."

"And he said?"

"He told me not to let Hatcher drive me away."

"Good advice."

"My dad always has good advice, but I don't always listen."

"Sounds like you're listening this time."

"Maybe I'm growing up."

They spent the rest of the day canvassing residents of Rosalie's building again, including the elderly couple who lived downstairs from the victim.

"Sorry to bother you," Jackson told the wife when she finally let them in after spending what seemed an eternity at the peephole, and asking questions of him through the closed door.

"We thought you and your husband might have remembered something about the night your neighbor was killed that you didn't recall the first time we questioned you," Mary said.

She shook her head. "Like I told you the last time, I mind my own business."

A cynical grunt came from her husband, who sat in a chair and continued to read a newspaper.

"I know this is a difficult question, ma'am," Jackson

said, "but were you and your husband aware of what Ms. Curzon did for a living?"

She energetically worked her mouth as though having inadvertently chewed a hot pepper at a Chinese restaurant.

"She was a whore," the husband said. "Nice looking, too."

"Harry!"

"Well," he said, dropping the newspaper to the floor, standing with difficulty, and coming to where they stood in the open doorway, "that's what she was, wasn't she? Either that or she had a hundred boyfriends."

"You never saw any of the men who came to her apartment?" Jackson asked the wife.

An emphatic shake of her head.

"I've seen some of them," the husband said.

Jackson and Hall looked at each other, then Jackson said, "Why didn't you mention that when we were here the night she was killed?"

"Nobody asked me, that's why."

"Well," said Jackson, "can you describe any of them?"

"Harry, I don't think that—"

"Hush," he told his wife. He said to Jackson, "Don't get me wrong. I didn't see many of them, just one now and then when I'd be coming into the building and he'd be coming out, or vice versa. Can I remember what they looked like? No. Just men. Mostly middle-aged, I'd say, and pretty well-dressed, as I recall. No bums or anything like that. Some of them looked like politicians."

Jackson's eyes opened a little wider. "Politicians? Anyone in particular?"

"No. They just had that look about them. Seems like from what I read, they're all pretty much the same when it comes to having women on the side. Not one of them you can trust."

"What about the night of her murder?" Hall asked. "Did you see any of them coming or going that night?"

The old man shook his head. "I didn't go out that night, but we did hear the racket upstairs."

More questioning failed to turn up anything more. The detectives thanked them again for their time and left. The wife followed them into the hallway. "He's getting senile," she said. "You shouldn't pay any attention to what he says."

"Yes, ma'am," Jackson said, smiling and patting her arm.

The super nervously answered their questions and had nothing new to offer when it came to knowing what Rosalie did for a living, or the men who might have visited her apartment. Jackson tried another tack: "What about women friends?" he asked. "Did you meet any of her girlfriends? Señoritas or señoras?"

His lowered eyes said that he had.

"It's okay," Jackson said. "Nobody will get in trouble. We just need to know."

"One woman. Nice woman." He pointed to his hair. "Very *rojo,* very red."

"Her name Micki?"

"*Sí.* Miss Micki."

"Well, thanks for your time. We'll try not to bother you again."

"Speaking of Micki Simmons," Jackson said once they were outside, "I hope she's on her way here. I'm starving. Think we can pack it in for the day?" It was a little after six.

"I'll call Hatch."

She reached him at home on his cell phone. "Yeah," he growled, "knock off. See you Sunday." The following day, Saturday, was a day off for the Hatcher team.

"Feel like Middle Eastern food?" Jackson asked Mary.

"Always in the mood for that."

"The Silver Veil's around the corner."

"Where we first learned about Micki Simmons."

"And where the owner told me about seeing the guy who used to date her, Craig Thompson. We know Thompson lied based upon what the owner told me after seeing his picture. By the way, I learned more than that from the owner," Jackson said.

"What else did you learn in here?" Mary asked after the owner, Kahil, had seated them and taken drink orders.

"A couple of MPD types have been shaking him down," Jackson said in a low voice, nodding toward Kahil.

"Who?"

"Don't know. He wouldn't say. Can't blame him, I suppose."

They perused the menu and decided to share dishes—baked falafel, macaroni béchamel, and lamb chops. After a second round of drinks had been served, and they'd ordered their dinner, Jackson's cell phone sounded.

"Hello?"

"It's me, Micki Simmons."

"Hey, Micki. Are you in D.C.?"

"I'm at Union Station." She didn't sound happy.

"Ah—my partner and I just ordered dinner. We're at a place you know, the Silver Veil."

"That dump?"

Jackson's head jerked as though her comment had stung. "I kind of like it," he said. "Join us?"

Mary looked at him quizzically. He held up his fingers to indicate he knew what he was doing.

"No thanks," she said.

"Well, then, how about we catch up after dinner? Your apartment?"

"Let's just get it over with, okay?" she said.

"We'll be as brief as possible. Sure you don't want dinner? My treat."

"I'll be at my apartment," she said flatly.

"Matt," Mary said after he'd ended the conversation, "don't you think we should take her to Metro for a formal statement, get it on tape?"

"Let's see how it goes at her apartment. We'll take notes. If she gives us a hard time, we'll take her down for further questioning. Besides, I don't want to show up at Metro with these drinks under our belt."

On the way out, the owner took Jackson aside. "No need for you to pay," he said.

"I told you last time that it's against the law for me to accept free food."

"I know, but—you didn't say anything about what I told you, did you?"

"No, but I wish you'd file a complaint. I can show you how to do it."

He shook his head vehemently. "I don't want trouble."

"Suit yourself," Jackson said. "If you change your mind, you have my number."

Jackson rang Micki Simmons's bell in the vestibule of her building. She didn't bother answering through the speaker, just activated the latch to allow them to enter. They rode the elevator to her floor, where she stood in her doorway.

"Micki, this is Detective Hall," Jackson said. "We work together."

"Hello," Micki said, no hand extended.

Jackson and Hall took in the apartment as Micki led them to the living room. Unlike Rosalie Curzon's apartment, it didn't scream "prostitute." Of course, Curzon had been murdered in her bedroom, where she plied her trade. The detectives noticed that a door, presumably leading to a bedroom—Micki's place of business—was closed. What it looked like in there was anybody's guess.

"Mind if we sit down?" Jackson asked.

"Go ahead." She lit a cigarette and dropped the match

into an ashtray already overflowing with butts and matches.

"Okay," Jackson said, "let's get this over with. First of all, I appreciate you coming back on short notice."

"I didn't have a choice, did I?"

"No, I suppose you didn't. The reason we wanted you back here, Micki, was to learn more about your relationship with Rosalie."

"I already told you we were friends."

"Good friends, as I understand it," Jackson said.

"We were close. We were in the same rotten business."

"Both working for Beltway Escorts."

"That's where we met."

"And the two of you decided to go freelance."

She leaned forward on the couch to emphasize what she was about to say. "We decided to get away from that creep McMahon. Have you talked to him? He's the one you ought to take a close look at."

"Yes, we did interview him, Micki. Did you and Rosalie ever have any problems between the two of you?"

"Like what?"

"Oh, I don't know, get into a hassle over money or johns and anything else?"

"No."

"You know a man named Craig Thompson?"

She guffawed. "Poor Craig," she said. "He's pathetic. He followed Rosalie around like a puppy dog, begging her to marry him. He was—how should I put it?—he was one of those jerks who decided he'd save a hooker." Another dismissive sound from her. "Jesus, spare me those types."

"Think he might have killed Rosalie?"

"No. He's too weak."

"When was the last time you saw Rosalie alive?" Jackson asked. He glanced over at Hall, who was quietly making notes in a slender steno pad.

"The night she got it."

"Oh? You didn't mention that before."

Of course she hadn't. He hadn't asked. Maybe he wasn't cut out to be a detective after all.

"Tell us about it," he said.

"We had dinner together in that place you just left, the Silver Veil. Rosalie liked that kind of food, why I don't know."

"Did she seem upset?" Mary asked, her first question since they'd arrived.

"Sure."

"Sure? You make it sound as though we should know why she was upset."

"A couple of things. One, I'd decided to pack it in and go home. She wasn't happy with that. She liked having me around."

"Because you were a friend."

"Of course."

"What was the other reason she was upset?"

"She was tired of being shaken down, that's why."

Shakedowns certainly weren't unknown in MPD. There were always cops who used their positions of authority to make an extra buck from businesses who paid for protection, especially those whose activities were less than honest. Cops who traveled that route were in a minority, of course, usually older ones brought up in that tradition. They didn't consider it illegal or unethical. For them, they rationalized that it represented being adequately compensated for doing a thankless job and putting their lives on the line to protect the city's citizens—a rationalization, to be sure, but adequate to salve what was left of their consciences.

"Who was shaking her down?" Mary asked.

"Oh, come on," Micki said. "You know damn well who."

Jackson laughed and held out his hands. "Hey, I don't know. Tell me."

"You. Cops. Vice squad. You either want money, or a piece of what I'm selling. Man, can you really be that naïve? It's bad enough making a living the way we do, catering to rich fat cats with big bellies and body odor and telling them what great lovers they are. On top of that we have to pay off cops who're supposed to protect us, not rip us off."

Jackson's immediate reaction was to not feel sorry for Micki, or any other woman who *chose* to become a prostitute. She wasn't like those young women, even kids, who are sold into sexual slavery, or streetwalkers being beaten by their pimps every night and given just enough money to support their drug habits. Micki Simmons, Rosalie Curzon, and others like them—Washington, D.C., had more prostitutes per capita than any other city in the country, according to a report he'd recently read—weren't disadvantaged women. They'd chosen to become hookers because it was easier money than doing an honest day's work in an office or factory.

On the other hand, she was right. Cops who preyed on them were part of the problem, abettors of their illicit lives.

"Who were these cops, Micki?" Mary asked.

"They don't matter to me anymore," Micki answered. "I'm giving up my apartment here—and the life. I want out of D.C. as fast as possible, away from all the phonies and users. I've had it with all these guys puffed up with their importance, as though working for the government makes them special—full of talk, nice suits, lying through their teeth every time they open their mouths."

"Tell us who the cops were, Micki," Mary repeated. "We'll try and do something about it."

"Sure you will. You're going to change the system? Christ, you sound like that jerk, Craig Thompson, who was going to set Rosalie on the straight-and-narrow. Forget about it, lady. You or anybody else isn't going to make one damn bit of difference. But if you have to know, they were working vice. Nice deal they had. They arrest us for prostitution, then tell us they can keep it from happening again as long as we pay up. "

"And you paid them," Mary said.

"Every month, like clockwork. I will say this, they kept their part of the bargain. No busts once the payments started."

Now Jackson got up and went to the window. It overlooked an alley. Across it was another apartment building, with a restaurant on the ground floor, its sidewalk café bustling with customers.

"Are we through here?" Micki asked.

Jackson turned. "Did you know that Rosalie videotaped some of her johns?" he asked.

"Oh," Micki said, "let's not get into that."

"Why not?" Jackson asked, retaking his seat.

"I told her she was playing with fire, but she wouldn't listen. She said those tapes would be her ticket out of here someday."

"She intended to blackmail her johns?" Mary said.

"Sure. That's why she did it."

"Had she?" Mary asked. "Used them to blackmail anyone?"

"Not that I know of."

"Who else knew about the tapes?" Jackson asked.

Micki shrugged. "Nobody."

"Just you? You really think you're the only person she would have confided in?"

"Maybe."

"What about you? Who did *you* tell about the tapes?"

"Nobody."

"Oh, come on, Micki," Jackson said. "I may be young, but I wasn't born yesterday."

"All right. Maybe I mentioned it to a couple of people."

"The cops who were shaking you down?"

"I don't remember. Yeah, one of them anyway."

"And that same cop was shaking down Rosalie?"

She nodded. "Look, I really have things to do and—"

"Was Rosalie bisexual?" Jackson asked.

"Why ask me that?"

"Because we've been told that she was."

Micki lit another cigarette—she'd gone through four or five since their arrival—and drew deeply on it. "Rosalie bisexual?" she said absently. "No, Rosalie wasn't bisexual," she said, "but she serviced a few women."

"Really?" Mary said. "Women came to her as a prostitute? I've heard of women paying male prostitutes but—"

"I never got into that," Micki said, proudly. "But Rosalie—hell, she's not the only one—she had a few lesbian clients. I guess you can't call them johns." She laughed at her joke. "Janes maybe, huh?"

"Yeah, janes maybe," Jackson said.

"We finished?" Micki asked.

"I want to know the names of the vice squad cops who were shaking you and Rosalie down," Jackson said.

"It doesn't matter," she protested.

Jackson slammed his palm on the coffee table. "It matters to us, Micki," he said in a voice louder than he'd intended. "Your friend, Rosalie, was murdered, damn it, beaten and strangled to death. We need help solving it."

"Sorry, but I don't remember any names. Besides, it's all behind me. If you're finished, I want to—"

"Don't leave town, Micki," Jackson said.

"I'm going home."

"You're going home when I say you're going home. Want to come with us as a material witness and spend a few nights in a cell? You've been in a cell before."

"You bastards are all the same."

"No we're not, Micki. Don't play games. You leave D.C. and you'll have cops knocking on your mother's door in South Carolina." To Mary: "Let's go."

As they opened the door, Jackson turned and said, "Did you kill Rosalie, Micki?"

"No."

They left. Once back on the street, Jackson drew deep breaths to calm down. His annoyance at Micki's lack of cooperation had surprised him. He seldom experienced anger, sometimes wondering whether it represented some sort of inadequacy in him.

"I like her," Mary said.

"You do?"

"I think she's gone through a tough time and is trying to maintain some dignity. She's entitled to that."

"Stay at my place tonight?" Matt asked.

"Yes."

It was after they'd both changed into pajamas and were sitting in front of the TV that she asked, "There's something really bothering you, isn't there, Matt. What is it?"

"Those cops who were shaking down Micki and Rosalie."

"What about them?"

"Hatcher worked vice before he switched over to homicide. Maybe he knows the guys who were hitting them up."

"If he does, he'll never rat them out."

"You're probably right. But we can ask."

Chapter 22

It was a sparkling Saturday on the Mall and all of Washington seemed to have decided to take the day off and enjoy it. Frisbees caught the sun as they flew lazily overhead, lovers blissfully strolled hand in hand, as though men and women weren't dying in Iraq and Afghanistan, and families poured onto the vast expanse of lawn that is the Nation's Backyard. Stretching between 3rd and 14th Streets, with the Washington Monument at one end and the Capitol Building at the other, the Mall was the vision of Washington's city planner Pierre L'Enfant, although he saw it more as a wide boulevard lined with mansions. It wasn't until 1901 that this sprawling expanse of grass and pebbled pedestrian pathways was transformed into the city's main gathering place and tourist attraction. Ringed by the Smithsonian's many museums (the National Air and Space Museum is the world's most popular museum, attracting more than ten million visitors each year), it is equally as famous as the scene of protest marches and demonstrations, and is the setting for concerts and festivals. It also features the city's most utilized jogging track and the softball field on which congressional leagues vie.

Matt and Mary had slept late, enjoyed breakfast at the Diner, and decided to spend the afternoon at the National Museum of African Art, where an exhibit of works by the artist El Anatsui had opened earlier in the week. Matt had begun collecting African musical instruments and recordings, a modest collection, to be sure, but one in which he took increasing pride. He didn't play the instruments but enjoyed the visual flair they provided his apartment.

For Walt Hatcher, not having to go into work meant time to get to a chore he'd been meaning to do for weeks, clean out the garage. He, too, had slept late, unusual for him, and lingered over breakfast with Mae. "I'm glad you got a good report from the doctor," she said. "I've been so worried about you."

"I told you it was nothing. Speaking of which, when are *you* due to see the doc again, Mae?"

"Not for six months."

It was what he wanted to hear.

The Rollins household was up and active by seven that morning. Rollins was pleased that he'd decided to cancel his meeting with Bob Colgate to spend the day with Sue and Samantha. He'd been feeling increasingly guilty over the past few months as his unofficial role in the Colgate campaign ate up more and more of his time. His law practice had suffered, but not terminally. It was the time away from family that bothered him, and he made a silent pledge to rectify that situation once Colgate was elected, a foregone conclusion based upon every poll, and the legions of TV pundits who breathlessly reported them as if fact on a daily basis.

Sue packed a lunch, which Jerry put in a small cooler housed in a canvas bag with a shoulder strap. He loaded it into their family vehicle, a silver Volvo station wagon, along with two lightweight folding chairs and a small blanket. He wasn't especially looking forward to a day of folk music. His musical passion was jazz, especially artists from the BeBop era—Miles, Dizzy, Charlie Parker, and other innovators—and he took pride in the large collection of LPs and CDs he'd amassed over the years.

He'd played drums with a rock-'n'-roll garage band while in high school, and while listening to his idols on his car's CD player often pictured himself grooving behind a drum set.

But the music genre wasn't that day's draw. It was enjoying leisure time with his wife and daughter that appealed. Although he wasn't a sentimental man, there were times when the sheer beauty of the two women in his life, and the fact that they loved him, were overwhelming. He suffered that exquisite feeling that morning as he watched mother and daughter work together in the kitchen, and had to leave the room lest the tear in his eye prompted a question.

He and Sue often joked that they had a patron saint of parking spaces looking over them. They seemed always to find a spot even in the most crowded of situations, and that morning was no exception. A car pulled away from the curb just as they were approaching, and Jerry deftly backed into the vacant space. They gave each other a high-five, and Samantha, giggling, included her hand in the celebration. The day was off to a good start.

They spent most of the morning strolling through the myriad performing areas and concessions scattered across the Mall. A few folk groups captured their attention, and they set up their chairs and took in the music, feet tapping, Samantha breaking into a charming dance on occasion.

"This is wonderful," Sue said into the air, leaning back in her chair, closing her eyes, and allowing the sun to play over her face. Jerry looked at her and smiled at the vision. She was as beautiful as the first day they'd met on the campus of the U of Maryland, where she was a freshman and he was in his last year of law school. She'd majored in English, had gone on to earn a Masters in library science, and still worked three days a week at the Cleveland Park Public Library. She was a voracious reader with eclectic interests, from literary fiction to biographies, politics to historical romance novels. Her passion for books had rubbed off on Samantha, who fell asleep each night with an open book beside her on the bed. *My two beautiful women,* Rollins mused, as the trio onstage sang of shattered dreams.

By noon, they were hungry and set up their mini-picnic beneath a tree alongside one of the performing sites. Samantha happily played hostess, carefully removing items from the cooler and positioning them on the blanket, alongside plastic knives and forks, plates and cups. She poured lemonade from a thermos, taking care not to allow any to drip on the blanket, and unwrapped cheese-and-tomato sandwiches.

"This is awesome," she announced as she plopped down on the blanket, removed her sandals, and joined her parents in a toast to a good day, touching rims of the cups.

After they'd eaten, Samantha wandered to the front of the stage to watch and listen to a new group that had taken the microphone.

"She's going to be a knockout when she grows up," Sue said to Jerry.

"She already is," he countered. "That's what worries me."

Sue laughed. "Spoken like a true and loving father. I pity the young men who date her, having to pass your muster."

"Aside from the metal detector and X-ray machine at the front door, and the FBI background check, they'll be welcome."

Her smiling face turned serious. "It always is a worry, isn't it?" she said absently.

"Unfortunately."

"Was Bob disappointed that you canceled with him today?"

"Angry is more like it. He's acting lately as though his campaign is in trouble. As far as I can see, unless he . . ."

"Unless he's caught in bed with someone other than Deb."

"Yeah, that would not be good. Remember what Huey Long said: 'The worst thing that can happen to a politician is to be caught in bed with a dead woman, or a live boy.' "

Their laughter at the Kingfish's wit and wisdom trailed off, along with the final notes of the folk group's song.

"Have you seen Deborah lately?" Sue asked nonchalantly.

"No. Why do you ask?"

"No reason. She's been keeping pretty much to herself these days."

"Probably just as well. The press is all over her whenever she makes an appearance, always bringing up the rumors."

"Are they? Just rumors?"

"I wouldn't know."

"Come on, Jerry. You two are close. Surely he's confided in you."

"Confided in me? Yeah, he does, about many things. But his sex life is off-limits. Don't buy into that myth that sex is all buddies talk about. Not true."

"We talk about sex," Sue said. "My friends and I."

"About your own sex lives?"

"Sometimes. Of course, I have nothing to offer those conversations." She looked left and right before leaning toward him and saying, "One of our little circle has had affairs."

He held up his hand and laughed. "Don't tell me."

"I didn't intend to. Incredible how many politicians are brought down by their extracurricular sex lives."

"More today with a no-holds-barred attitude by the media. Politicians used to get a free pass from the press when it came to their dalliances. Those days are gone forever."

"Gary Hart might have been president."

"Might have."

"He might have been a good president."

"We'll never know."

Their conversation was interrupted by Samantha. "Let's go over there," she said, pointing to another area of the Mall, close to where they'd parked the car. "There's an awesome band playing, not old folksy music like this, really cool."

Sue and Jerry smiled. "Okay, princess," he said, starting to put things back into the cooler, and emptying trash into a nearby pail. The cleanup completed, they folded the chairs and headed in the direction of a large crowd gathered in another performing space. Samantha was right; the music was more of the rock-'n'-roll variety, the band's large amps pumping the dissonance out to the audience. As they walked, Jerry turned suddenly when he sensed that someone was watching them. It was a nondescript man, middle-aged, wearing jeans, a maroon sweatshirt, and with a baseball cap with a large bill pulled down low over his forehead. He didn't look familiar. As Rollins turned, the man swiveled his head to look in another direction.

"Someone you know?" Sue asked.

"No."

"Hey, Jerry."

"But this guy I know," Rollins said, shaking hands with an attorney and his wife with whom he and Sue had been friends for years.

"Dad," Samantha said, pulling him by the hand in the direction of the group onstage.

"You go ahead, sweetheart," Rollins said, "but don't go far."

After a few minutes of banter, the Rollinses went to where Samantha had secured a spot from which she could see the performers. "Isn't it cool?" she asked, beaming.

"Yes, it certainly is," Rollins replied, wincing against the audio assault and wishing it had been jazz instead of folk and rock. He took comfort that there would be a jazz fest later that month at Wolf Trap; he'd already gotten tickets for it.

They'd tired by mid-afternoon and decided to call it a day. Rollins was pleased that they were relatively close to their parked car.

They'd almost reached it when they were approached by another set of friends.

"Give me the keys, Daddy," Samantha said. "I'll open the car."

"Enjoy the music?" one of their friends asked.

"What?" Rollins said. "Oh, yes, very much, but you know—"

Samantha poked his arm.

"Oh, sure, honey, here," he said, handing her the keys.

Their conversation with friends lasted only a few minutes more.

"Great seeing you," Rollins said. The women pressed their cheeks to each other and the men shook hands. Rollins and Sue took steps toward the car.

"Samantha?" he called.

Sue turned. "Samantha?" she said.

"Where the hell—?"

Sue came to his side. "Where is she?"

"Look," Rollins said, pointing to the ground near the rear of the car. The keys he'd given his daughter rested in a clump of grass.

"Samantha!" he shouted, and repeated it two more times.

Sue pushed through a crowd of tourists on the sidewalk, frantically looking for their daughter. Her voice carried over the din of the music and car horns and chattering people—"S-A-M-A-N-T-H-A!"

Chapter 23

It had gone easier than expected.

They'd pulled the car, a nondescript tan four-door sedan, up next to the Rollinses wagon. The man and woman got out through the rear doors. The driver stayed behind the wheel, the engine running. The man and woman noticed that Samantha's parents were preoccupied with another couple, saw the girl run to the car, keys outstretched, and observed that there was no one else at that moment in the immediate vicinity. It helped, too, that she came around to the rear of the station wagon and started to open the tailgate, keeping her out of the path of anyone who might stroll by. It took only an instant for the man to sweep the girl up, a hand over her mouth, and toss her into the backseat. The driver pulled away, easily, slowly, so as not to arouse attention. As far as they could tell, no one had even noticed the abduction. If someone had, they hadn't started to make a fuss about it.

The man wearing the maroon sweatshirt and baseball cap had one hand on Samantha's throat; the woman pressed a handkerchief into her mouth. She struggled.

"Cut it out, kid," he growled.

"Calm down," the woman told the child. "Take it easy. We don't want to hurt you. Just stop kicking."

"Watch your speed," the maroon sweatshirt told the

driver, a younger man, wearing a suit and tie on this leisurely Saturday. "Don't get us stopped."

They crossed the Potomac on the George Mason Memorial Bridge into Virginia, and continued on I-395, passing the Pentagon and proceeding to exit seven, where they turned onto Route 120, taking them in a northwesterly direction. At Ballston, they turned left on Wilson Boulevard and proceeded through Arlington until reaching Seven Corners, their final destination, a well-kept small one-story gray stucco house set far back from the road. A row of seven-feet-high hedges close to the house spanned the front, shielding it from street view.

By now, Samantha had stopped struggling, reduced to whimpering and occasional outbursts of full-fledged wailing. During the trip, the man had secured her hands and ankles with black duct tape and affixed a large, clean, powder-blue handkerchief across her eyes. They quickly carried her from the car to the house, entering through the front door and locking it behind them. The driver, who'd remained in the car, turned it around and drove away.

Once inside, the woman placed Samantha on a single bed in a rear bedroom. The only window was locked and nailed shut, and covered with a heavy red drape sealed at the edges with tape. The man in the sweatshirt went to the kitchen, where he turned on a police scanner and listened to a rapid succession of messages concerning the event: "*Child abduction reported on the Mall, Independence Avenue, all available units report to scene.*" He smiled. Nothing about the car or their identities. Smooth as silk.

He went to the bedroom where the woman, whom he now called Greta, had removed the gag from Samantha's mouth and loosened the tape from her hands. The little girl sat up against the bed's headboard and cried.

"Now, look," said Greta, "I know you're scared out of your wits, and I don't blame you. I would be, too. But here's the deal. You seem like a smart kid, so I'm sure that we'll get along just fine—provided you do what I tell you to do." She reached for a homemade ski mask sewn from a multi-colored piece of fabric and slipped it over her head. She indicated that the man, Paul, was to leave the room. With the mask over her face, Greta undid the handkerchief from Samantha's eyes.

"That better?" Greta asked.

"Who are you?" Samantha managed.

"That's not important. We don't want to hurt you, and we won't. You just have to stay here a little while until we make some business arrangements. Once that's done, you'll be back home with your family. How's that sound?"

"I want to go home now."

"Well, that can't be, my dear. That just can't be."

Greta was a stocky, solidly built woman in her late thirties or early forties. Her voice didn't match her frame. It was a deep, soothing, sexy voice of the sort heard on all-night big city radio stations from female disc jockeys cooing into microphones and spinning romantic music for the nocturnal lonely. The tone had its intended effect on Samantha. She visibly relaxed and brought her sobbing under control.

"Now," Greta said happily, "how about some macaroni and cheese, and a soda? I bought some things especially for you that I think you'll like. Most girls your age like mac and cheese and soda. Sound good?"

"Yes."

"Good. Now, I'm going to lock the door behind me. There's nothing in this room that can get you in trouble, and don't even think of trying the window. It won't open. And don't start yelling or anything silly like that. There're no other houses near us, not a soul to hear you. Understood, Samantha?"

She nodded.

"That a girl," Greta said, patting Samantha's hand. "Back in a jiffy."

She went to the kitchen, where Paul had put on coffee. "Sweet kid," she said.

The idyllic Saturday at D.C.'s famed Mall was now chaotic. A half-dozen marked police cruisers, lights flashing, radios blaring, had shut down Independence Avenue where the abduction had taken place. A legion of uniformed cops created a wide circle around Jerry and Sue Rollins, who stood by their Volvo, their faces testifying to the trauma they were experiencing. Other MPD vehicles continued to arrive, their plainclothes occupants spilling from them. Matt Jackson and Mary Hall also showed up. They'd been contacted at the museum on Matt's cell phone and took off at a run.

"She's gone," Sue said to anyone and everyone close enough to hear. "My God, somebody has taken my baby!"

A tall, lean detective dressed in jeans, a tan safari jacket, and sneakers established himself as the person to whom Jerry and Sue Rollins should direct their comments. "I'm Detective Kloss," he said. "You're the parents?"

"Yes," Jerry replied. "I'm Jerry Rollins. My wife, Sue."

No handshakes were exchanged. The detective recognized Rollins as being part of the Robert Colgate campaign, which told him this would be more than a simple child abduction, if ever there could be such a thing.

"Give it to me fast, Mr. Rollins," Kloss said. "From the top."

Rollins tried to pace his retelling of events, but the words tumbled out as though every second counted, which it did.

". . . afternoon on the Mall . . . getting ready to go home . . . stopped to talk with friends, gave the keys to

Samantha . . . that's our daughter . . . she's seven . . . we left our friends and Samantha was gone. . . . Gone! . . . It all happened in a second."

"Are you sure she didn't run off somewhere, Mr. Rollins?" Kloss asked. "I have a kid that age and—"

"No, of course not," Rollins snapped. "She wouldn't do that." He extended his hand in which he held the car keys. "These were over there," he said, pointing to where he'd found them on the ground.

Kloss turned to the crowd, which was by now substantial—men, women, and children, teenagers and young couples, tourists with funny hats and T-shirts, some capturing the scene on their video and still cameras. "Anybody see anything?" he barked.

Some shouted comments based upon what they'd heard had happened. There were no eyewitnesses. A ruddy-faced man said loudly, "Let's go looking for the kid. Come on, she's got to be around here somewhere."

Kloss took a description of Samantha and the clothes she was wearing, and instructed officers to isolate the area around the car with crime scene tape, and to post guards to keep it from being violated. He dispatched other officers to begin a search of the Mall, and called for backups, including the Park Police. He suggested to the Rollinses that they get in his car, away from the madness. Sue balked: "I have to find her," she said, turning toward the crowd. But her husband grabbed her arm. "No, Sue," he said. "Let's do what he says."

As they pushed through a knot of gawkers, Rollins heard a woman say, "People should keep their eyes on their kids."

He spun around to say something, but didn't.

When they reached Kloss's unmarked vehicle, the detective spotted Jackson and Hall interviewing bystanders. He told the Rollinses to get in, and went to the two young detectives. "Hey, Matt, you heard?"

"Yeah. I got a call. We were here at the Mall and—"

"I can use you two," Kloss said. "Stay close."

When Jackson had been promoted to detective, he'd initially been assigned to Kloss's squad. Kloss was a skilled hostage negotiator who'd worked a number of difficult cases, and had been lead on a kidnapping in Southwest only three months earlier that had turned out badly. A four-year-old boy had been abducted by a recently released sexual predator and murdered.

Jackson liked and respected Kloss, a soft-spoken man with a hint of a southern accent and a reasoned view of things, professional and personal. The senior detective had been high on Jackson, too, and welcomed having him assigned to his unit. But a month later, another of what seemed like a never-ending series of personnel shake-ups occurred, and Jackson was transferred to Walter Hatcher's group. Not a good day.

Kloss joined the Rollinses in the car. "Look," he said, "I'll have every available cop in the city scouring the Mall for your daughter. If she's anywhere near, we'll find her. Did either of you notice anyone suspicious when you were walking around, especially after you came out to get your car?"

"No," Rollins said. "Well . . ."

"Yes, sir?"

"There was a man who was looking at me funny. I can't be sure. It might have been my imagination."

"Description?"

"He had a sweatshirt on, a red one. No, more maroon. And a baseball cap."

"Team logo?"

"Not that I noticed."

"What about a car?"

"Car?" Jerry and Sue said in unison.

"In the event whoever took her used a car."

"Oh, my God," Sue said.

"I didn't see any car," Jerry said. "Did you, Sue?"

"No." She began to sob into her hands. Her husband put his arm around her and uttered words meant to comfort.

"We'll get out an Amber Alert. Tough without a vehicle to ID, but someone might see her and respond. I want you two to drive back to your house. We need a picture of your daughter as soon as possible. Do you have one?"

"Of course."

"Multiple pictures, if possible. Are you okay to drive?"

"Yes," Jerry said.

"I want detectives with you."

"Is that really necessary?" Rollins asked.

"I prefer it, sir."

"Okay. Ready, Sue?"

"What will happen to her?" she asked.

"We'll do everything we can to get her home safe," Kloss said.

He looked through the open door to where Jackson and Hall stood, got out of the car, and approached them. "Matt, I'd like you to go with Mr. and Mrs. Rollins in their car. They're driving home."

"Right," Matt said. "By the way, this is my partner, Detective Hall. Mary Hall."

"Okay, Mary," Kloss said. "Since you two work together, how about you go with Matt? Wouldn't hurt to have a woman with the mother." He noted her concerned expression.

"Problem?"

"No, sir. It's just that we're assigned to Walt Hatcher's unit and—"

"Don't worry about Hatcher," Kloss said. "I'll square it with him. Right now, I need help and I need it fast. When you get to their house, keep them calm, drapes closed. I'll get a tech unit there to monitor the phones.

See what you can get from any callers, people who might have it in for the family. You know who we're dealing with?"

"It's Jerry Rollins," Jackson said.

"One and the same."

"High profile," Mary said.

"With plenty of people who might have it in for him. Come on, I'll introduce you."

The ride to the Rollins home in Foggy Bottom took only minutes. Jackson had offered to drive, but Rollins wouldn't hear of it. Silence reigned throughout the short trip and until they'd entered the house. Mary immediately went to the front windows and drew down olive-green duvet shades. Sue asked why she'd done that. "Orders," Mary said. "It's better." She gave the street a quick scan before drawing the final shade.

Sue Rollins gathered up a selection of photographs of Samantha and handed them to an officer, who quickly left the house to put them into circulation. Jerry Rollins headed for his first-floor study: "I need to make some calls," he announced.

"I wouldn't, sir," Jackson said, "not until Detective Kloss gets here. He'll manage the case. They're sending a tech unit to put taps on your phones."

"Your mother," Rollins said to his wife. "She'll hear it on the radio or TV and—"

"No, Jerry. Please."

"Did you see any press before we left?" Rollins asked Sue.

She nodded. "A WTOP car was pulling up."

"Damn!" Rollins said.

"Sir," Jackson said, "any chance of getting a cup of coffee?"

The Rollinses looked quizzically at him. So did Mary.

Jackson smiled. "I think we should all sit down, have

a cup of coffee, and wait calmly. Maybe we can use the time for you to fill me in on anyone who might have had a grudge against you or your daughter, someone with a motive to have taken her."

"Motive?" Rollins blurted. "What sick bastard could have a motive for taking a beautiful, precious, innocent little seven-year-old girl?"

Neither Jackson nor Hall gave a response. Everyone's thoughts were the same. *A pervert. A child molester. A deranged monster to whom the life of a child meant little, if anything.*

The silence was broken by a ringing phone.

Rollins moved toward the kitchen.

"Extension?" Jackson asked.

"Here," Sue said, leading him to a small cordless one on a table in the living room. Jackson rested his hand on it and looked through to the kitchen, where Rollins was about to pick up. Jackson nodded. Both phones were raised simultaneously.

"Jerry? It's Bob. What the hell is this I'm hearing? Samantha kidnapped?"

Jackson recognized the distinctive gravelly voice of the presidential candidate.

"I'll come over," Colgate said. "I can't believe this. I—"

"Sir," Jackson said into the phone. "Governor Colgate. This is Detective Matthew Jackson, MPD, sir." He glanced at Mary, whose open mouth said it all. "Sir, I would advise that no one come here, that no action be taken until our special units are in place and a plan has been put into motion."

"What's he saying?" Colgate asked Rollins.

"He's a detective, Bob. I think we should do what he suggests."

"Jesus! How's Sue?"

"Upset, of course. No. Frantic."

A knock on the door caused Rollins to say, "I have to go, Bob. I'll be in touch as soon as it's the right time."

Mary Hall opened the door to allow Kloss and other detectives to enter. She looked across the street, where an MPD van had parked. Two men exited the vehicle and came to the house carrying black cases of the sort used by airline pilots to carry aeronautical charts. They removed digital tape recorders; a central tap to trace calls had been installed through C&P Telephone.

Sue Rollins busied herself in the kitchen filling a coffeepot, and pulling an assortment of cookies from a cupboard. The younger detective's suggestion that there be coffee made sense to her, gave her a purpose, and helped distract her from the terrible thoughts that flooded her mind. Mary's offer to help was accepted, and she joined Sue in the kitchen.

Kloss and his next in command, a middle-aged Hispanic detective, sat with Jerry Rollins at the dining room table. Jackson was invited to join them. "All right," Kloss said, "let's start from the beginning, from the moment you got up this morning. Who knew you planned to spend the day at the Mall?"

The question left a blank expression on Rollins's face. "I don't know," he eventually said. "I might have told friends we had these plans. I canceled an appointment today so we could do it."

"An appointment with who?"

"Ah . . . with, ah, Governor Colgate. I work with him on his campaign."

"He called before you got here," Jackson said.

"He knew?" Kloss said.

"Yes," Rollins said.

"Quick."

"Not surprising," Rollins said.

"What did he have to say?"

"Nothing. He was shocked, that's all. He asked how my wife was. Your detective here—"

"Matthew Jackson, sir," Jackson helped.

"Yes. Detective Jackson here was on the extension when I spoke with the governor. He was going to come but Detective Jackson dissuaded him until you'd arrived."

Kloss nodded at Jackson.

"What is the plan?" Rollins asked as Sue and Mary delivered the coffee and cookies.

"I'd like you to join us, Mrs. Rollins," Kloss said. "I was asking your husband who knew that you intended to go to the Mall today."

She looked at Jerry. "I told a few people, I'm sure. Friends. I was happy that we could find family time."

"Did your daughter know of your plans?" Kloss asked.

"Of course," Sue replied. "She was tickled pink. I'm sure she told her friends at school about it."

Kloss made notes in a pad before saying, "Okay, let's talk about your daughter's friends. She have run-ins with any of them lately?"

"Not that we know of," Sue said.

"How about you, Mr. Rollins? You're a pretty familiar face around Washington—lawyer, clients who maybe felt they got the short end of the stick in a case you handled for them."

"That's always possible, but . . ."

And on it went for the next hour, their conversations interrupted by an increasing number of phone calls, all of which were taped, the callers's voices heard through the recorders, the answering machine delivering Rollins's outgoing message. No calls were answered directly, per orders from Kloss. Many were from the press. Soon, vehicles from the city's media outlets arrived and parked outside, their reporters and crews ready to spring at anyone coming through the Rollinses' door. Kloss called in for uniformed officers to keep them at bay. Kloss's cell phone was busy, too, including a succession of calls from Chief Carter informing him that until the Rollins kidnapping was resolved, it took top priority over any and every other pending case.

"So, what do we do now?" Rollins asked Kloss after they'd settled again at the table, and a fresh supply of coffee had been brewed.

"We wait," Kloss said. "The chief has every spare cop out looking for your daughter. They'll have her picture. They'll do their job, Mr. Rollins. In the meantime, we learn to sit tight."

Chapter 24

Walt Hatcher learned of Samantha Rollins's abduction from Mae. Rearranging the garage had tired him, and he'd fallen asleep on a chaise lounge on their patio.

She came from the kitchen, where she'd been watching TV while seasoning chicken for dinner. He opened his eyes at the sound of her. "Walter," she said, "there's been a kidnapping at the Mall. That lawyer, Rollins, the one who works with Colgate and his campaign. His daughter. Seven years old. It's on the television."

He lowered his feet to the floor and shook his head. "Kidnapping?"

"Yes. Come in and watch. It's all over the news."

He followed her to the kitchen where an anchor on a local channel brought viewers up to date.

". . . and according to Chief of Detectives Willis Carter, a massive search has been launched, using all available manpower. The victim, seven-year-old Samantha Rollins, is the daughter of prominent D.C. attorney Jerrold Rollins, a close advisor and confidant to presidential candidate Robert Colgate. Calls to the Rollins home have not been returned. More on this breaking story."

He lumbered from the kitchen to the stairs, pulling his belt tight.

"Where are you going?" Mae called after him.

"Work. Nobody called me."

"Maybe they—"

His broad back disappeared into the upstairs hall. Ten minutes later he returned, dressed in a suit, a muted two-tone tan dress shirt that didn't match the gray suit, and red tie. He'd never been known as a fashion plate. "I probably won't get back tonight," he told Mae on his way out the door. "I'll call."

She returned to the kitchen and wrapped up the night's dinner fixings to go in the fridge. A TV dinner would do that night.

Hatcher went directly upstairs at Metro and was told that Chief Carter was out. He stepped into the street to dial Jackson's cell, but a half-dozen reporters and a TV crew scotched that plan. Back inside, he found a quiet corner of the main booking room and made the call.

"Jackson."

"Jackson, Hatcher. Where are you?"

"I'm, ah—Mary and I are with the parents."

"Why are *you* with them?"

"Detective Kloss brought us. Look, I can't talk, Hatch. Can I call you later?"

"You can't talk? What the hell do you mean by that? Get your ass down here to Metro."

Hatcher heard a male voice in the background bark, "Can the call, Matt."

The line went dead.

Hatcher swore under his breath and retreated to the locker room, where he splashed tepid water on his face and looked at himself in the old metal mirror, wishing he'd shaved before leaving the house. He sat on a wooden bench and tried to wedge clear thinking into his congested brain. What the hell was Kloss thinking, taking from him his two juniors? It wasn't done that way. You didn't go around raiding other detectives' squads. The department had been going downhill every year, as far as Hatch was concerned, a bunch of pols running things, turning things upside down and making it tough to do your job—to be a cop—to rid the streets of the lice that come out of their nests at night.

A detective came into the room. "Hey, Hatch, you okay?" he asked.

Hatch, who'd been sitting with his head in his hands, looked up. "Yeah, I'm okay." He walked back upstairs, where Carter had now come from his office and conferred with two other white shirts.

Hatcher intruded on their conversation. "You got a minute?" he said.

Carter grimaced. "Not now, Hatch."

"I need to talk to you," Hatcher persisted.

Carter excused himself from the others and led Hatcher into his office, closing the door behind him with some force. "Maybe you haven't heard," the chief said, "but we've got a high-profile kidnapping on our hands."

"Yeah, I heard. That's why I'm here. I call Jackson and he tells me that Kloss pulled him from me—Hall, too—and has them with the parents of the kid. What gives?"

"What gives, Hatch, is that we've got every available cop on this case, and that's the way it'll be until it's resolved."

"Good. So, get Jackson and Hall back here and we'll work it."

Carter shook his head. He was distracted by an administrative officer who entered the office and handed him a file folder.

"You hear what I said?" Hatcher asked after the officer had departed.

Carter sighed. He backed to the side of his desk and perched on its edge. "I talked with Kloss only a few minutes ago," he said. "The parents—you know who they are."

"Yeah, the hotshot attorney, Rollins, Colgate's buddy."

"Right. Kloss says Mr. and Mrs. Rollins have asked that Jackson and Hall remain with them."

"Why, for christsake?"

A tiny smile came to Carter's lips. "Maybe because they've bonded with them, Hatch. It happens."

"Bonded?" he snorted. "That's a laugh."

Carter pushed away from the desk. "I have to go, a joint press conference with the Bureau. Stay around. Check in with Eldridge in missing persons. He'll have something for you to do—*without* Jackson and Hall."

The chief slapped him on the arm and was gone.

Chapter 25

Paul, as he was called, watched television. The kidnapping dominated every news cycle, pushed anything and everything else off the electronic front pages of the cable news channels, and local stations, too. There was little other news to report, each segment rehashing previous ones, talking heads trying desperately to inject fresh insight into the story, to outdo one another, to scoop the competition. One channel had managed to obtain a grainy picture of Samantha from its photo and video morgues and displayed it behind the newscaster's voice-over.

Paul sat up when Governor Bob Colgate's face appeared on the screen, caught by camera crews as he exited his Georgetown home. "I have no comment at this time," he said. "It's a police matter. I will say, however, to whomever did this, you can make it right by returning Samantha safely to her family."

"Have you spoken with the Rollinses?" a reporter shouted.

Colgate ignored the question and climbed into a waiting limousine.

Paul left the TV, put on his ski mask, and opened the door to the bedroom where Greta, as she was called, sat on the bed with Samantha. He motioned with his finger for her to come out of the room.

"Anything new on TV?" Greta asked.

"They just had Colgate on. Big nothing. There's a press conference coming up. The FBI's been brought in."

"No surprise, state lines and all."

"Yeah. No surprise. I hope it stays that way."

"No word from Y-man?"

"No."

"So we sit and do nothing until we hear."

"That's the drill. How's the kid?"

"She's all right. Scared. Keeps asking me why we did this to her."

Paul's grin was crooked. "And you told her, of course."

"I told her it was strictly business, that once the business was over she could go home."

"She eat?"

"Some. I just hope Y-man doesn't let this drag out too long. The Virginia cops will be all over it, too."

"He said two days max."

"I hope he's right. Want me to make dinner?"

"I'll go out and pick up a pizza."

"Go out?"

"Yeah. Nobody knows who we are or what's gone down. I'm in the mood for a pie. Besides, I have to make the call."

The wait continued at the Rollinses' house, too, although pizza wasn't on the menu. Kloss called Metro and instructed someone to pick up Chinese food and deliver it to the house, despite Jerry and Sue's protestations that they weren't hungry. The phone continued to ring incessantly, each time causing everyone to tense. The media's hounding of them intensified.

"Can't we take that damn thing off the hook," Sue said.

"No, ma'am," was Kloss's response.

"I'm sorry," she said. "I wasn't thinking clearly. If the kidnapper calls . . ."

"I understand," the detective assured.

The food arrived. Jerry Rollins picked at a couple of fried dumplings and poured himself bourbon, neat. Sue ate nothing until Mary convinced her that she had to keep up her strength and she settled for brown rice and steamed vegetables. The two females sat together in the kitchen. Sue said little; Mary tried to keep up a conversation to distract Sue, and succeeded for the most part.

"Mr. Rollins," Kloss said, "there's something I want to suggest."

"What's that?"

"It's possible that we won't receive a call tonight from whoever took your daughter. It's been my experience that people in these cases often take their time to make contact. They want to think it out before making the call. Obviously, with this all over TV, the perpetrator knows what's going on here outside the house. They'll be gun-shy and wait until they've figured out how best to reach you."

"But if they don't call, how can we ever know what's happened to Samantha?"

Again, thoughts ran parallel in the room. If the kidnapper was a child molester, a pervert, it was possible that no call would ever be made. He would assault the child and, in all likelihood, kill her. Hopefully, instead, money was the motive. It was the best motive of all, in almost every crime. Money was impersonal. People who kidnapped kids for money weren't interested in harming them. They wanted to be paid, pure and simple, and as long as funds could be delivered without placing them in jeopardy, they'd be content.

Kloss answered his question. "If this is someone with a grudge against you, Mr. Rollins, it's possible that they'll want to make contact away from the house."

"Away?"

"Yes, sir. Your office, or part of the daily routine having to do with your law practice or involvement in the campaign. What do you have scheduled for tomorrow?"

"It's Sunday. I mentioned that I'd canceled a meeting with Governor Colgate this afternoon. I told him I'd try to make time tomorrow."

"All right. What about Monday, Tuesday?"

"My calendar's in my den. I'll get it."

Kloss invited Jackson to join them at the table as they meticulously reviewed Rollins's upcoming schedule. When they were finished, Rollins asked, "Are you suggesting that I leave here and pretend to go about my usual routine?"

"That may be necessary," Kloss said, "depending upon whether we hear from the abductors."

"That doesn't make much sense to me," Rollins said. "Whoever took Samantha will know that the police will be following me at every turn. They wouldn't dare approach me under those circumstances."

"Not necessarily," Kloss countered. What he didn't say was that his gut feeling was that the abduction of Samantha Rollins had something to do with Rollins's position in town, perhaps his close relationship with Robert Colgate. He had nothing to base that on and admitted as much to himself. But the manner in which the girl was taken, the swiftness of it, the smooth execution of what must have been a plan, buttressed his hunch. A child molester wouldn't have been brazen enough to attempt to snatch her on a sunny afternoon on the Mall with thousands of people milling about. No, he decided, this was a professional job. Either the girl had been taken for money—or because the kidnappers wanted something from Rollins besides money.

"Let me ask you a question, Mr. Rollins," Kloss said. "Is it possible that someone has taken Samantha in order to blackmail you, to extort money from you?"

It was more of a snort than a laugh. "I can't imagine

why anyone would want to blackmail me. I have nothing to hide."

"It's not necessarily a matter of having something to hide, sir. I just thought you might have something in your possession that somebody else would want bad enough to use your daughter as a means of getting it."

"I can't think of a thing."

Jackson had sat silently during the exchange. Rollins's coolness in the face of what had occurred was impressive to the young detective. He chalked it up to two things: being a shrewd, hardened attorney, and putting up a front for his wife's sake. But his face changed as Kloss asked his questions. For the first time a modicum of tension crossed it, even nerves. Jackson looked at Kloss to see if the veteran detective had picked up on the same thing. His expression was noncommittal.

As dusk settled over the nation's capital, Kloss took Jackson and Hall aside to say that the Rollinses had asked that they be retained on the case, at least for the near duration. "But I won't need both of you here at the same time. I suggest one of you go home, get a few hours' sleep, pack a bag, and head back."

"You, Mary?" Jackson asked.

"No, Matt, you go ahead. Mrs. Rollins and I are getting along fine. I don't want to leave her."

"Suit yourself," Kloss said.

As Jackson prepared to leave, he said, "Hatcher called a while ago. That was the call I was on when you told me to end it."

Kloss pulled Jackson and Hall into a corner and spoke in low tones. "Matt," he said, "forget about Hatcher. This case takes precedence over everything. I told Chief Carter that the family wanted you and Detective Hall on the case until further notice, and he wholeheartedly agreed. Don't sweat it."

Jackson and Hall looked at each other. "Want anything from the apartment?" he asked her.

"No. I'll pick some things up at my place tomorrow. Get some sleep. This looks like it could go on for a while."

Paul and Greta stood in the living room. He'd removed his maroon sweatshirt and baseball cap, replacing them with a dark blue windbreaker, no hat.

"You have the phone?" she asked.

He pulled a slender cell phone from his jacket pocket. Greta had stolen it from picnickers at the Mall less than an hour before snatching Samantha. Amazing, she'd thought after doing it, how careless people are. The phone was resting in plain view on top of a wicker picnic hamper.

"I'll drive into the District," he said, "and call from there, dump the phone, and head back."

"Take a different route to the city than we took here," she admonished.

"Hey," he said, "I'm not a dummy. Not to worry. I'll hit a pizza parlor on the way back. What you want—pepperoni, sausage?"

"Both. And extra cheese."

"Yeah, extra cheese."

He pulled a black Volkswagen Jetta from a one-car garage at the rear of the property, drove away from the house, and stuck to the speed limit. He was aware of the number of state patrol cars on the roads, and listened to an all-news radio station which reported nothing that concerned him. He crossed the bridge into the District and made his way to the Southwest waterfront, where some of the city's best fish restaurants were located. The parking lot was bustling but he maneuvered the Jetta to a relatively secluded spot alongside the Washington Channel, the body of water that diners feasted their eyes on along with their crabs and lobsters and Chilean sea bass. He turned off the car's lights, got out, and walked to the edge of the channel. The illuminated keypad gave him enough light to dial the number.

"Hello?"

"Mr. Rollins?" he said.

"Yes. Who is this?"

"Your daughter is safe and won't be hurt, provided you do what we tell you to do."

"Let me talk to her," Rollins demanded.

"You'll hear from us again," Paul said. He pushed the OFF button, flung the phone far into the channel, returned to the car, and drove away.

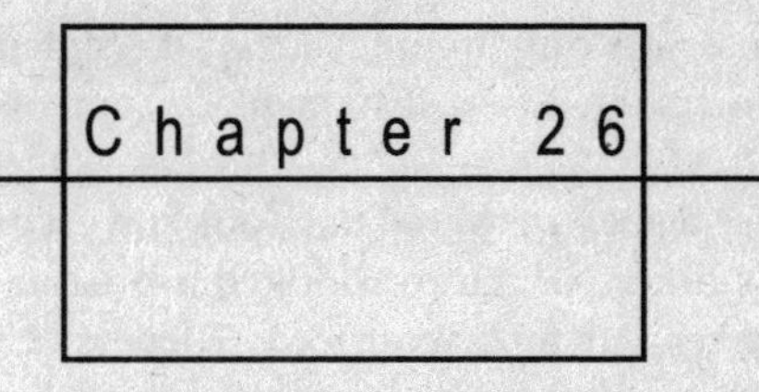

Chapter 26

"This is Governor Colgate."

Mary Hall, who'd been monitoring calls at the Rollins house, had picked up.

"Yes, sir?"

"My wife and I want to visit with Mr. and Mrs. Rollins. I assume that can be arranged."

"I'll check," she said.

Kloss had just returned from home, where he'd picked up a change of clothes and other necessities. "We don't need more of a media circus than we already have," he said.

"I'll tell him no."

Rollins had overheard the exchange. "What if I go there?" he suggested.

"I'd prefer that," said Kloss. "One of my men will drive you."

Rollins got on the line with Colgate. "Bob, it's inconvenient for you to come here. The detective in charge says I can come to your house. Is that okay?"

"I suppose so. Bring Sue with you."

"I'm not sure she'll want to, but I'll ask."

Fifteen minutes later, Rollins sat in the backseat of a marked patrol car. His wife had declined to leave, which he understood. There was something strangely, weirdly comforting being close to the phone on which Samantha's captor might call again. Although Colgate's Georgetown townhouse was only minutes away, it seemed to Rollins as if he'd traveled to a distant place, out of touch and helpless.

A housekeeper answered the door and escorted him to Colgate's office, which overlooked a pristine large yard carefully tended by a team of gardeners. Colgate was dressed casually—jeans, sandals, white button-down shirt he hadn't bothered to tuck in, and a pale yellow cardigan draped over his shoulders. He got up from behind the desk, came to Rollins, and hugged him. "What a bitch," he said. "How you holding up, buddy?"

"All right."

"Sue's not with you?"

"She didn't want to leave the phone. She's there with the detectives."

"Sit down, Jerry. Coffee? Something stronger?"

"Coffee would be fine."

Settled, cups in front of them, Colgate asked whether there had been any progress in finding Samantha.

"Unfortunately, no," Rollins replied. "We received a call last night."

"From the kidnapper?"

"Yes or so he claimed. All he said was that Samantha was okay and that she wouldn't be hurt provided I did what they told me to do."

"That's it?"

"That's it."

"What does he want you to do?"

"I don't know. He didn't say. He said *they'd* be in touch again."

"They'd? There's more than one?"

"Evidently. He said that *we* would be back in touch."

"Did the police trace the call?"

Rollins nodded and sipped his coffee. "The call was made from a cell phone in Southwest, down by those fish restaurants. The number was traced to a couple who said their phone had been stolen yesterday afternoon at the Mall."

"Do you think—?"

"No, they had nothing to do with it, Bob. I don't even know if it was a genuine call or not. The cops say it could be a prankster, a perverted one. I'm hoping they're wrong."

Deborah walked into the room. "Oh, Jerry," she said, going to where he sat and wrapping her arms around his shoulders, "every parent's worst nightmare. I am so sorry. I'm sure that Samantha will be fine."

"We're counting on that," Rollins said.

"Can I do anything?" she asked, "be with Sue?"

"Nothing to be done, thanks. It's a waiting game." He told her what he'd relayed to her husband about the call and the tracing of it. He also filled them in on what Detective Kloss had speculated, that the abductor, or abductors, did not seem to be child molesters. "He thinks it's a professional job," he added.

"Professional?" Colgate mimicked. "What the hell could be professional about it? Money, of course. They're looking for a ransom."

"I don't know, Bob. I'm just telling you what the detective said."

Deborah excused herself. "Please give my love to Sue, Jerry, and call if I can do anything." She kissed his cheek and left.

Colgate picked up the latest edition of *City Paper* from his desk and handed it to Rollins. "Seen this, Jerry?"

"No."

"Page three."

Rollins read Josh Langdon's piece. When he'd finished, he tossed it angrily to the floor.

"Why didn't you tell me you were interviewed?"

"I forgot about it. Just more trash, as I told the reporter."

"It has Pyle's people written all over it."

Colgate leaned forward, his elbows on the desk. "Jerry," he said, "is there anything you're holding back from me?"

"Of course not."

"This prostitute *taped* her clients?"

"That's what Langdon claims in the piece."

Colgate shook his head ruefully and regained his more relaxed pose, leaning far back in his desk chair. "Is it possible that this nasty business with Samantha has something to do with the campaign?"

"I can't imagine how."

Colgate came forward again and fixed him in a hard stare, causing Rollins to wince and turn away.

"We've been close for a long time, Jerry," Colgate said, "a very long time. I trust you like the brother I never had. I'd do anything for you."

"I know that, Bob."

"Feel up to laying some of your solid advice on me about the economic package I'm working on?"

"Frankly, no. You've got some top economists advising you on that subject."

"All guesswork on their part. If they knew what they were talking about, they'd be rich, like stock gurus. Pyle released his economic plans on Friday. More of the same, promises of oversight, keep the tax cuts for the wealthy, let the free market reign. Know what, Jerry? The answer is to pull back on deregulation. Look at the airlines since Reagan deregulated them. It's a mess. A country like this needs a viable commercial aviation system, the way it needs a national standard on clean air and water, education, regulation of the high-rollers on Wall Street. The way I see it . . ."

Rollins listened patiently as Colgate bounced his speech off him. It was a role he'd happily played before, offering reactions to his friend's words, correcting, suggesting changes, pointing out strong points, and urging certain sections, phrases, and lines be cut. This day, however, he wasn't pleased at being put in that position. It occurred to him that Colgate seemed to have forgotten, or pushed aside, Samantha's abduction.

"I have to go, Bob," Rollins said when Colgate took a break.

"Yeah, sure." As though reading Rollins's thoughts, he quickly added, "Deborah and I are with you one hundred percent, buddy. I'll move heaven and earth to help get that precious little girl of yours safely back where she belongs. If you need ransom money, just ask. Count on it."

Colgate walked Rollins to the door and asked if he was going back home.

"I'm going to the office."

Colgate's expression mirrored his surprise.

"The lead detective—his name is Kloss—he's told me to make myself more available in case the kidnappers want to make contact away from the home. They've put a trace on my office phones and are recording all calls there."

"I hope they know what they're doing."

"I have to trust them. The FBI's in on the case, too. A couple of agents are at the house."

The former governor of Maryland and likely next president of the United States watched his friend get into a police cruiser and be driven away, the officer at the wheel navigating the knot of reporters and their vehicles. Colgate felt fulfilled that his friend had sought him out, and that he could offer comfort and succor, real and imagined. Of course, he couldn't know what thought ran through Rollins's head as the police car headed for his office. It was something President Harry Truman had famously said: "If you want a friend in Washington, get a dog!"

As Colgate closed the front door, his wife came up behind him.

"How's he holding up?" she asked.

"Pretty damn good. I think you should prepare a statement about how our friends are in our prayers—you know, how you can relate to a mother whose only child has been callously ripped from her family. Pyle keeps releasing those commercials accusing me of being soft on crime. You can say in your statement that we need to stiffen our laws about crimes against innocent children. Take the lead, get out in front of it. Better coming from you."

They went their separate ways within the house, he to the library where he continued to work on his speech on the economy, she to their bedroom, where she picked up the phone and called Connie.

"I can't believe what's happened to Jerry and Sue," Connie said.

"Jerry just left here," Deborah said. "He's doing okay. Free for lunch?"

"No, but I'll make myself free if you need me."

"Yes, Connie, I need you. Come here. Bob will be away most of the day."

Rollins was dropped off in front of his office building. The cruiser drove off, as instructed, but Rollins knew that it wouldn't be far away, and that officers would be upstairs in his suite. Sophisticated recording devices had been installed in the wee hours of Sunday morning, an ideal time for such surreptitious doings. A plainclothes team had established themselves in a small one-room vacant office adjacent to Rollins's facilities, ready to spring should the abductor visit him there. Kloss had suggested that Rollins spend a few hours at the office, something Rollins often did to catch up on paperwork. "Try to maintain your regular routine," the detective counseled, "within limits."

As he walked into his reception area, one of the detectives told him that a young man had tried to gain access to the suite. "His name's Massie," the detective said. "He said he works here."

"Yes, Brian Massie. Where is he?"

"I don't know," was the detective's reply. "We told him he couldn't enter without clearance."

"Well, I cleared him. How long ago was he here?"

"Twenty minutes, a half hour."

Rollins went to his office and called Massie's cell number. "Brian," he said, "it's Jerry. I'm sorry for the confusion."

"That's okay, Jerry. I certainly understand with everything that's been going on. I thought I'd catch up on some things, that's all."

"Then by all means, come in. Where are you?"

"The Starbucks on the corner, reading the *Post* and sipping a budget-breaking latte."

"Come back, Brian. I'll clear it."

Massie arrived a half hour later and secluded himself in his office while Rollins sat behind his closed door and consulted a list of calls that had come into the house that he intended to answer. He started with members of his staff, thanking them for their hopes and prayers, and for their offers to help. Sue's mother, of course, had called in a panic, and it took a long time to calm her down, and to dissuade her from rushing to the house. She was upset anew this day when he called, but she listened to his reasoning and agreed to stay away and wait by the phone. She had her television on twenty-four hours a day, she told him, which he knew provided her with more questions, and causes for anxiety, than had she left it off. He promised to stay in touch.

After spending the better part of two hours there, with the detectives assigned to him coming and going, he announced he wished to return home. He stopped by Massie's office before leaving.

"You'll be at home tomorrow, Jerry?" Massie said.

"No, I'll be here." He closed the door. "They, the detectives, want me to maintain a relatively normal schedule in case whoever took Samantha wants to make contact away from the house. Whatever meetings are scheduled, my lunch with Testa from Senator Precott's office, everything is to be carried on as though nothing has happened. Caroline has my schedule on her desk."

Massie shook his head. "That'll be tough for you, Jerry," he said. "I'm not sure I could do that."

"I don't have any choice, Brian. It'll be business as usual, if having cops hiding in the next office could ever be normal. I'll see you tomorrow. I've told the detectives that it's all right for you to stay as long as you wish."

The young attorney got up from behind his desk, came to his boss, and wrapped his arms around him. "We're all with you and Sue, Jerry, every inch of the way. You need something, you just ask."

"Thank you, Brian. That means a great deal to me, and I know it will to Sue, too."

A patrol car appeared outside the building and in fifteen minutes Rollins walked through the door of his home, ignoring questions yelled at him by members of the press. By this time, Matt Jackson had returned, carrying a small overnight bag, and Mary Hall had departed for her apartment. Kloss was gone; he was to attend a meeting of the task force established at Metro, but would return in a few hours.

"Anything new?" Rollins asked Jackson.

"No, sir. No calls. Anything happen at your office?"

"No. Where is Mrs. Rollins?"

"Sleeping. Detective Hall convinced her to get some rest. She needs it."

"Good. It's like watching grass grow," Rollins muttered. "Waiting for another call."

Jackson shook his head. "It must be hell for you and your wife," he said. "I can't imagine being in your position."

"You married, Detective?"

"No, sir."

"Been a detective long?"

"About four years."

"Working with Kloss?"

"No, sir. I was assigned to his squad right after I made detective, but was transferred to another unit."

"He seems to have a lot of faith in you and your partner."

"Detective Kloss is a good man," Jackson said. "I've always admired him and was pleased when he asked me to be part of this case."

Rollins fell silent, his gaze at the curtained front window.

"Can I get you anything, sir?" Jackson asked.

"What? No, thank you. Thank you very much."

The FBI agents took Rollins aside to question him further about possible enemies. Jackson strolled into the kitchen, where Detective Garcia, Kloss's second-in-command, drank coffee and chewed on a buttered roll.

"Kloss tells me that you and Hall work for Walt Hatcher," he said absently, using a knife to spread the butter more evenly.

"Right."

"How's he to work for?"

"Hatch?" Jackson was tempted to vent his true feelings, but held back. "He's okay," he said.

Garcia laughed. "That's not what I hear," he said.

"No," Jackson reassured, "he's okay, a little difficult sometimes but—"

"Kloss is high on you."

"I'm happy to hear that."

The roll consumed and the coffee finished, he stood, stretched, and slapped Jackson on the shoulder as he passed his chair. "Hang loose," he said.

"Not much else to do," Jackson said.

Hatcher ended up bunking at Tommy G's Saturday night after consuming too much alcohol and getting into an argument with a man and a woman who were Colgate backers. Hatcher berated them for buying the former governor's liberal line of BS. It became so heated that Tommy Gillette had to pull Hatcher aside and maneuver him into the back room, where he stayed until the couple had left. He reemerged, ordered another drink and slouched at a corner table, brooding over his bourbon and the insults he'd suffered that day.

Chief Carter had effectively pushed him out of the loop, taken his staff away, and reduced him to poring through old missing persons reports on the slim chance that a previous abduction might shed a clue on the Rollins case. He'd seethed for the rest of Saturday, snapping at anyone who approached, left Metro at six and went directly to the restaurant.

The drinks eased his inner turmoil, at least that portion of it caused by the chief's dismissal of him. But there was another level of anxiety that he couldn't shake. He didn't like that Jackson and Hall had been assigned to the kidnapping, didn't like it one bit. The more he drank, the more he conjured scenarios involving them. He'd indicated to the chief that Jackson might be the leak within the department regarding the Rosalie Curzon murder. It was probably true, Hatcher decided. Jackson was like a lot of cops, getting perverted pleasure out of sucking up to the press, feeding them info from inside, jeopardizing cases, and thumbing their noses at the system.

Not only that, Jackson and Hall were probably sleeping together. He'd picked up on subtle clues, the way they looked at each other, knowing that they spent time together off-duty. Mixed race couples upset him. It wasn't the way human beings were supposed to behave, it violated the laws of nature. Every year it seemed there were more and more mixed couples in D.C., flaunting their transgressions and daring anyone to challenge them. Such thoughts turned Hatcher's stomach. Mae said she agreed with him, although she was less vehement about it. He was proud of his kids. They'd followed the rules, *his* rules, and were the better for it. Sure, he'd been a tough father. He'd set the bar high and expected them to reach it. He knew his relationship with them wasn't as smooth as Mae would like it to be, but being liked was never his goal. Being respected, even feared, was more important than winning a popularity contest.

He stayed at his table and avoided the bar for the rest of the evening, becoming more morose with each drink. As the alcohol coursed through his bloodstream and invaded his already addled brain, his thoughts, if that's what they were, shifted to what was really gnawing at him about the kidnapping of Rollins's kid. The guy was a legitimate D.C. big shot, plenty of money and loads of connections, including Robert Colgate. Look how he'd pulled strings to have Jackson and Hall assigned to the case. Only a heavy-duty cat could pull that off. MPD was fawning all over Rollins. Your average Joe wouldn't have a chance in hell of dictating what cops worked their case. He didn't like it that Jackson and Hall now had Rollins's ear, were close to the guy. What were they telling him? What was he telling them?

What was the kidnapper after? Money? Coming up with a ransom wouldn't be difficult for Rollins, who obviously had plenty of money and knew others who did. Men like him traveled in a tight, precious circle of big bucks and influence, pulling strings to get what they wanted even if it meant destroying the country. Greed.

That was the problem, Hatcher mused as he waved his hand over the table to emphasize his point—to whom?—and knocked the empty glass to the floor.

He didn't like Jerrold Rollins. He knew that for certain. He'd seen him once—actually twice, and hadn't liked him on either occasion. From Hatcher's perspective, Rollins was a buttoned-up type, typical lawyer, with narrow eyes, who talked down his nose at people, and through his nose, in a pinched voice that testified to his upbringing and education—Ivy League schools, probably, which wasn't true but supported the image Hatcher had conjured, a typical D.C. wheeler-dealer.

Maybe it was something besides money that the kidnapper wanted. Hatcher's face twisted as that crossed his mind. He motioned to the waitress for another drink.

Tommy had kept an eye on Hatcher throughout the evening, monitoring his foul mood, exacerbated by the drinks.

The waitress asked Tommy whether she should serve him again.

"Yeah. Give him one more, but that's it."

The owner got busy with a large post-theater crowd that arrived, seeing to it that they had what they wanted. It was a lively group. Drinks flowed freely, and conversation was boisterous. After Tommy had handed the check to them, he looked over to where Hatcher sat. His head had come forward and rested on the table, one hand wrapped around his half-empty glass. "Excuse me," Tommy told his customers. He shook Hatcher by the shoulders. "Hey, Hatch, my man, let's go."

Hatcher looked up with glassy eyes.

"You can sleep it off here, pal. You're in no shape to go home."

Hatcher leaned against Tommy and they awkwardly made their way to the back room. Hatcher sat on its edge as Tommy helped him off with his jacket, and undid his tie. He pushed the detective to his back and removed his shoes. “Sleep it off, buddy. The cleaning crew will be around when you wake up. Pleasant dreams.”

They were anything but.

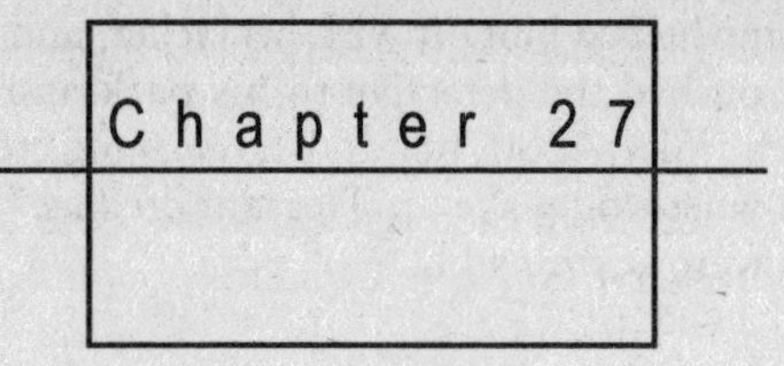

Chapter 27

The decision to send Rollins to his office on Monday had involved input from various law-enforcement entities, including the FBI special agent assigned to head the Bureau's involvement, and members of the MPD task force. Some voiced reservations: "What if the guys behind the snatch are looking to take a shot at the father?" was one raised by a member of the task force.

"Unlikely," Kloss countered. "They're either after money, or something else from him. He's the one who can deliver what they want. Killing him would be counterproductive."

"How are we covering him while he's out and about?" another asked.

That discussion occupied the next half hour. It was eventually decided that Rollins would be shadowed by the two young detectives assigned to the Rollins family, Jackson and Hall. "Rollins is comfortable with them," Kloss explained. "Besides, they're low profile, haven't been in the public eye. And, don't forget, we also have people up at his offices. We position Jackson and Hall somewhere near his building. When he goes out, they trail behind. Make sense?"

It was agreed. When Kloss returned to the home, he filled in Jackson and Hall.

"The officers inside will alert you when Rollins leaves his office. Never let him out of your sight, only don't get too close. Just position yourselves where you can watch for anyone approaching him. Got it?"

"Got it."

"Stay apart from each other," was Kloss's final word. "Always observe him from two different vantage points."

"Okay," Hall said.

"I don't expect anything to come of this, but I want to cover all the bases. Our hands are tied until we hear from the kidnapper again." Kloss suggested to Mary that she dress the next day in tourist clothing. He smiled and said to Matt, "You look like the studious type. Maybe you should play college student—you know, carry a couple of books and a knapsack. Mr. Rollins has a busy day on his calendar, including lunch with a congressional staffer. He's keeping the appointment. They're going to Primi Piatti, on I Street." He consulted his notebook. "They've booked a twelve-thirty table in their sidewalk café. One of you get there earlier and grab a table. Maybe you should do that, Mary. Have lunch and read some tourist guides. Matt, there's another outdoor spot across the street, just a couple of tables in front of a fast-food joint. You hang there. Everybody involved has your cell numbers. Keep 'em on and charged. Any questions?"

"Where do we hang out until lunch?" Jackson asked.

"A white van a half block from the restaurant. It's got an electric company sign on the sides, Colonial Electric. There'll be a command post set up in it. We'll keep in touch with you there. Like I said, nothing may come of this, but without another call, we don't have much of a choice." He handed each of them an envelope. "Spending money," he explained. "Lunch is on MPD."

For the Rollinses, sleep that night was out of the question. They tried to divert their attention from the activity in the house, and the reason for it, by watching television in the bedroom—anything but the news—but everything on the screen was irrelevant, meaningless. Kloss or Garcia monitored news channels on a second set, in the den. The constant ringing of the telephone had lessened to some degree. Rollins handled the personal calls from friends and his professional colleagues, keeping them short to clear the line in the event Samantha's abductors called. They didn't.

"Damn!" Rollins exploded to Kloss at two o'clock Monday morning. "Why haven't we heard anything?"

Kloss had nodded off in a chair. He snapped awake. "I don't know," he said, "but there's nothing we can do but wait. Look, Mr. Rollins, go lie down. Try to sleep. I want you wide awake when you head downtown in the morning."

"I hope you know how much my wife and I appreciate everything you and your people are doing. It's just that—" Rollins collapsed in a chair and sobbed. He hadn't cried since he was a child, and was embarrassed. "I'm sorry," he said.

"Nothing to be sorry about, sir," Kloss said, extending his hand and touching Rollins's shoulder.

"It's just that to think of Samantha out there in the hands of these bastards is too much to bear." He turned to Kloss. "She will be all right, won't she?"

"We'll do everything we possibly can to make sure that she is. Everything!"

Unstated was the reality that no matter what they did, no matter how many cops were on the case, no matter what elaborate plans were put into play, the Rollinses might never see their daughter again.

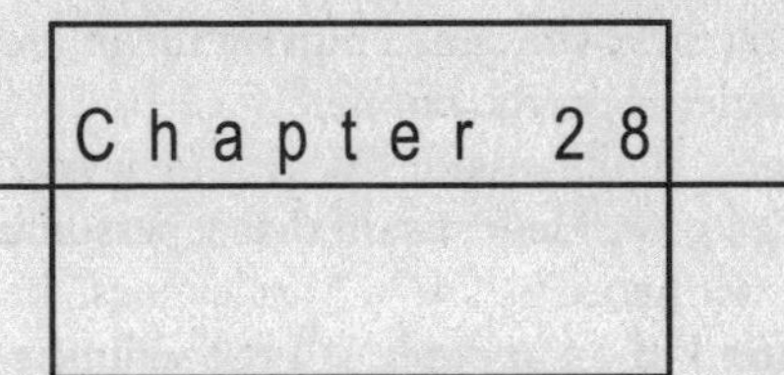

Chapter 28

Rollins's staff was already at work when he arrived on Monday.

"Good morning," he said as he passed them on the way inside.

"Good morning, Jerry," said his secretary, who followed him. "How are you doing?"

"As well as can be expected, I suppose. How was the birthday dinner?"

"It was fine, lots of fun." How typical of him, she thought, to remember such a trivial thing in the midst of his personal travail. "Is there . . . is there anything new on . . . ?"

"On the kidnapping? No."

"I'm sorry. I didn't think you'd be here today, but Brian told me you were coming in, something about keeping a normal schedule."

Rollins shook his head as he slipped out of his blue pin-striped suit jacket and draped it over the back of his chair. "Normal schedule," he said into the air. "Is anything normal anymore? So, what's on the agenda?"

She gave him a rundown of things she thought he might want to look at, and calls to return.

"Thanks, Caroline. You're the best keeper a man could have."

She fought against tearing up and left.

At ten o'clock, she called him on the intercom. "Jerry, Kevin Ziegler is on the phone."

"Ziegler?" Rollins said. "What's *he* want?"

"I don't know. He just said that it was important that he speak with you."

"Tell him I'm on another call but will be off soon."

He hadn't spoken with Ziegler for months. Prior to the launch of the Pyle and Colgate campaigns, they'd occasionally run into each other at social or political events around town, and had shared a table at luncheons and dinners at the National Press Club and other venues at which speakers of interest appeared. He disliked Ziegler, which put him in the mainstream of general feelings about Pyle's puppet-master. At the same time, he recognized the man's intellect and admired his steely resolve to get what he wanted, for his candidate and, by extension, for himself.

Why was he calling? Rollins wondered. Was it to express his concern for what the Rollins family was enduring? He preferred to think that was the case.

He picked up the phone. "Hello, Kevin," he said.

"Jerry. I wasn't sure I'd catch you at the office, considering what's going on. Good God, man, what an ordeal."

"Yes, it's been rough."

"Especially for that lovely wife of yours," Ziegler said. "How is she holding up?"

"She's standing tall. How are you, Kevin?"

"I'm doing just fine. Jerry, I'll get to the point. We have to talk."

"About what?"

"That's better left for when we get together. Are you free for lunch?"

"As a matter of fact, I'm not."

"Can you *make* yourself free for lunch? It's important, Jerry. I realize that everything pales in comparison to your personal ordeal, but there may be something we can do to help in that regard."

Rollins's face twisted into a question mark. What could Kevin possibly mean?

"Jerry," Ziegler said, "the president is deeply concerned about what's happened to you and your daughter. He wants to do everything in his power to get that little girl home safe and sound, and to pull out all the stops to accomplish that. We can discuss the role he might play, along with other things I need to run by you."

"I, ah—all right, Kevin. I'll cancel my lunch. Where would you like to meet?"

"I'll set it up at my club."

"Which one? You belong to a few."

"It isn't a club exactly, Jerry. Sort of a sanctuary from the madness of everyday life in the White House. It's a lovely, secluded country retreat only a few miles into Maryland. I'll come by and pick you up at the office, say at twelve thirty?"

Rollins thought for a moment. Could he agree without running it past the detectives? He knew he couldn't.

"Twelve thirty will be fine, Kevin."

He hung up and pondered what had just transpired. Ziegler's call was unseemly. To have had no contact with him for all these months and then to receive a call out of the blue the day after Samantha's kidnapping was, well, bizarre. President Pyle wanting to help? Absurd. There was nothing he could do. Rollins knew that if he played into such a scenario, anything that came from Pyle and his administration would be spun purely for political posturing and gain, an empty offer to reach across the aisle to his competitor's best friend and chief advisor, in his time of need. The spin machine had always been distasteful to Rollins, but he was as much a part of it as anyone else in D.C.

He called Massie into the office. "Brian, my plans

have changed. I need to cancel my lunch date with Testa from Senator Prescott's office. Would you please call him for me and offer my apologies."

"Sure. Want me to suggest I meet with him?"

"Not a bad idea. You know what it's about."

"Why the change, Jerry?"

"A last-minute thing. I'm having an unchangeable lunch with someone else."

Massie waited to see whether Rollins would elaborate, mention the name of his new lunch date. He didn't.

Rollins's next decision was whether to call Colgate and tell him of the meeting with Ziegler. Until this day, that decision would have been automatic. Colgate would want to know about such a get-together, and Rollins wouldn't have hesitated filling him in. But he decided not to bother. He still carried a sour taste in his mouth from yesterday's meeting, at which Colgate had so callously shifted from Samantha's kidnapping to his upcoming speech on the economy. No, he'd go through with the lunch, and if anything came from it that would impact the campaign, he'd pass it along.

One of the detectives monitoring phones from the vacant adjacent room came in. "Detective Kloss, sir." He handed Rollins a cell phone.

"You've changed your plans," Kloss said.

"You—of course, you heard the conversation," Rollins said. "I was about to let you know."

"I gather from the call that you don't know your destination."

"You know everything I know, Detective. No, I have no idea where we're going. Somewhere in Maryland."

"He's picking you up?"

"Yes. He'll have a car and driver."

"We'll follow."

"I'm sure you will. I'm sorry for the change."

"No problem. I'll assign Jackson and another detective. Ignore them. They'll keep their distance. Detective Hall can stay here with your wife."

"All right."

"Mind a suggestion, Mr. Rollins?"

"Of course not."

"How would you feel about wearing a wire?"

"To the lunch?"

"Yes, sir."

"No, that's out of the question."

"Just a thought. Your caller referred to your daughter."

"It was just a gesture on his part, I'm sure. No, it would be inappropriate to record our conversation during a campaign."

Rollins couldn't see Kloss. Had he, he would have seen the quizzical expression on the detective's face. *Inappropriate to record a conversation during a campaign?* As far as Kloss knew, there was nothing inappropriate during any presidential campaign, especially this one.

"As you wish, sir," Kloss said.

"How is Mrs. Rollins?" Jerry asked.

"She's fine. Doing just fine."

Rollins considered asking to speak with her but decided not to. Better to concentrate on the lunch with Ziegler.

As he waited until it was time to be picked up, he tried to concentrate on legal matters before him, but it proved impossible. His thoughts flew in a dozen directions, never landing long enough to allow focus on any one. He decided he needed to relax, and put a Horace Silver CD on the stereo, a particular favorite of his. As Jerry closed his eyes and allowed the music to soothe his nerves, Brian Massie stopped by Caroline's desk to say he was going out for a smoke.

"When are you going to give up that dreadful habit?" she asked.

"Tomorrow," he replied pleasantly. "Who's Jerry having lunch with?"

"I don't know." She lowered her voice. "He got a call from Kevin Ziegler."

Massie's eyebrows went up. "What's that about?"

"I haven't the slightest idea."

Massie went to the street, lit up, pulled out his cell phone, and placed a call.

"Hello?" a male voice answered.

"It's Brian. He's canceled his lunch date at Primi Piatti."

"We know."

"He might be having lunch with—"

The call was clicked off at the other end.

Caroline received a call at 12:30. "This is Kevin Ziegler," the caller said. "My car is waiting in front for Mr. Rollins."

Rollins had been looking at his office window and saw the black Town Car with darkened windows glide up to the curb. As he strode through the reception area, he said to Massie, who stood by Caroline's desk, "What about your lunch with Testa?"

"He canceled, said he preferred to meet with you, whenever it's convenient."

Rollins rode the elevator to the lobby. As he stepped through the building's revolving glass doors, he looked to his left and saw a sedan parked a few car lengths behind the Town Car. He could make out two faces in the front seat, one of them Detective Matt Jackson.

The rear door to Ziegler's car opened and Rollins got in.

"Hello, Jerry," Ziegler said. "I'm glad you could clear the decks."

Rollins said nothing as the driver pulled away and joined the traffic flow. He glanced over at Ziegler, who sat square in the seat, facing forward. He was a tall, angular man with what could only be described as an unusual face. It had a rubbery quality to it. Large, puffy, red cheeks seemed to sit unnaturally atop the rest of his face, which was basically gaunt. His nose was large and bulbous, his lips so thin as to be almost nonexistent. His hair grew at odd angles, shafts of it pasted against an irregularly shaped skull. He wore a black suit, white shirt, and silver tie. Despite his unconventional looks, he carried himself with the self-confidence of a handsome man, a powerful man sure of who he was and what he expected of others.

"I take it that the car that pulled in behind us contains some of the city's finest," Ziegler said, adding what passed for a knowing laugh.

"It's to be expected," Rollins said.

"Are they doing their job, Jerry?" he asked.

"Yes, I think so. We don't have much choice but to believe that they are."

"Of course. How is Governor Colgate these days?"

"He's fine. The president?"

"As ornery as ever but very much on top of things. He asked me to personally convey his concern about your daughter."

Rollins winced and looked through the tinted side window; it appeared to be nighttime outside.

"You know, Jerry," Ziegler said, never turning to look at his backseat companion, "there are times when we can put politics aside in a time of personal need."

"I'm aware of that, Kevin," Rollins said, shifting position so that he faced Ziegler. "You'll have to excuse me if I have trouble concentrating. There's a lot on my mind."

"No need to explain that, Jerry," Ziegler said. And then he did the inexplicable. He patted Rollins's knee.

Little more was said as they made their way to their destination, a pretty brick house on a tree-lined street of pretty brick houses. This one was on a corner. A plain, white five-foot-high plank fence that appeared to have been recently installed defined the property and created a barrier between it and the adjoining home. Rollins's first thought was that it might be one of Ziegler's private residences. There was no number on the door or fence. The front windows were covered with draperies. A car was parked in the short driveway, nudged up close to the overhead door of the single-car garage. The driver pulled the Town Car behind the other vehicle, allowing its front bumper to gently touch its rear one.

"Your house, Kevin?" Rollins asked as they walked to the front door.

"Mine to use," Ziegler answered. "For special events."

"Is this a special event?" Rollins asked.

"I'm hoping it will be, Jerry."

The door was opened by a young man wearing a suit. Ziegler paused before entering and looked back at the street, where the police vehicle had come to a stop a half block away. "I'd invite them in," Ziegler said, chuckling, "but I'm sure they wouldn't appreciate it."

They passed through a living room, in which two women worked side by side at computer desks, telephone headsets draped over their hairdos. Neither looked up as Ziegler led Rollins into what probably served as a dining room when the house was occupied by normal homeowners. Desks there were also occupied, by a man and a woman. Ziegler opened French doors and stepped into a rear sunroom, in which a table was elaborately set for lunch. A man and a woman wearing short white jackets over black slacks and frilly white shirts stood at attention in a corner.

"Your choice, Jerry," Ziegler said, indicating either of two chairs upholstered in a sunny flowered yellow fabric. The expanse of windows was draped with white muslin from ceiling to floor. The chairs faced each other.

Rollins processed his situation. Each campaign maintained a variety of locations from which to conduct off-site fund-raising and other nitty-gritty tasks away from the centers of attention—in Pyle's case, the White House and his party's "official" headquarters. The Colgate campaign had its own selection of such places. In effect, they were safe houses, although that smacked too much of clandestine activities, the stuff of spy novels. But no matter what they were called, they functioned to allow business to be transacted away from the glare of media and public scrutiny.

"Drink?" Ziegler asked.

"You?"

"I've decided that a glass of wine with lunch prolongs life, Jerry," Ziegler replied. "I admire the French. With all their heavy meals and fatty foods, they still have less coronary disease, not necessarily because the wine they drink is beneficial, but because sipping it prolongs the eating process, allows the digestive tract to more effectively do its job. Join me?"

"Yes."

Ziegler gave the waiter an order for a specific cabernet, and indicated to the waitress that she could serve the soup, which was a delicate crab bisque, accompanied by fresh, hot, small rolls. A simple endive salad followed. Conversation during this portion of the luncheon was limited to the kidnapping of Samantha, direct questions from Ziegler about progress on the case, and repeated expressions of sympathy from him and from President Pyle. Rollins gave cursory answers to the queries about the investigation, denying that they'd heard from the kidnappers, and avoiding any details about how the detectives were proceeding. He was sorry he'd accepted Ziegler's invitation. This was obviously a grandstanding effort to carve some sort of relationship between them that had nothing to do with Samantha, and more to do with the presidential campaign. Though Ziegler's questions about Colgate and how the campaign was progressing were few, and couched as idle curiosity, Rollins wasn't seduced.

"I'm going to have to be getting back soon," Rollins announced after they'd finished the main course, a rack of lamb cooked perfectly pink, baby carrots, and lyonnaise potatoes.

"No dessert? Coffee?"

"Thank you, no. You mentioned when you called, Kevin, that there was something you, or the president, might be able to do concerning Samantha's abduction. If there is something—tangible—I'd like to hear it."

Ziegler sat back and dabbed at his mouth with his napkin. They were alone in the room. The waitstaff had departed, the French doors were tightly closed. Ziegler leaned forward. "I don't mean to insult you, Jerry, but by any chance did your detective friends convince you to wear some sort of recording device?"

Rollins's laugh was involuntary. "No. Of course not."

"Would you mind if I assured myself of that?"

"Yes, I would, as a matter of fact. But here." Rollins stood and opened his jacket, revealing his mid-section. "You *have* insulted me, Kevin," he said, closing the jacket and sitting.

"Just my naturally paranoid nature, I suppose," said Ziegler. "My apologies."

"Just what is it you have to say that shouldn't be recorded for posterity?" Rollins asked, unable to keep the pique from his voice.

"All right," Ziegler said, as though he would continue despite his better judgment. "Someone I know whose name shall not be mentioned here has been contacted by another party, who might be involved in the abduction of your daughter."

The words struck Rollins like a punch. "Say that again," he said.

"There is someone out there, Jerry, who might be able to—how shall I say it?—who might be instrumental in securing your daughter's release."

Rollins sat back and twisted in his chair, threw one leg over the other, waved a hand in front of his face as though to dissipate a cloud that had formed. He looked at Ziegler, who sat stoically, eyes fixed on his lunch guest.

"Who is this person?" Rollins demanded.

"I'm unable to tell you that, Jerry, but does it really matter? Getting Samantha back should be all that counts."

Rollins stood and went to the windows. He could see a garden through the white gauzy drapes, distorted red and yellow and green shapes undulating in the breeze. "What is it you want?" he asked, his back to Ziegler.

"It isn't what *I* want, Jerry, it's what these other people want."

Rollins spun around. "Stop talking about these so-called other people, Kevin. Stop it! Level with me. For God's sake, there's a seven-year-old girl's life at stake. What do you want me to do, call in the detectives sitting outside and make you tell them how to get my daughter back?" It was a threat void of conviction, empty words.

"Sit down, Jerry."

Rollins moved back to the table and slumped in his chair. He felt drained, lifeless.

"Good. You know, Jerry, one of many things I've always admired about you is your intellect, your ability to cut through to the essence of a problem. Yes, I do admire that in a man. I have little patience with those who do not possess that attribute. I'm sure you'll appreciate my exhibiting the same quality. Your detectives would find your claim of my having knowledge of your daughter's whereabouts to be specious, at best. So please, put that thought out of your mind."

"Go on," Rollins said.

"The people to whom I refer inform us that you have in your possession something that could be of great potential interest to the president."

Rollins said nothing.

"I'm sure you know what that is, Jerry."

An uncharacteristic feeling of panic overcame Rollins. He was desperate to run from the room, flee the house, and throw himself into the car with the detectives. He dug his nails into the palms of his hands and looked left and right . . . in search of what? Ziegler watched him dispassionately. When it appeared that a modicum of calm had prevailed, he said, "From what I'm told, Jerry, you have a videotape that our contacts say would be more beneficial to us than to you. True?"

Now, an intense anger returned, replaced Rollins's dread. He extended his hand and pointed an index finger across the table. "My precious daughter has been kidnapped because of a videotape? You bastard. You filthy, rotten bastard!"

"If you can't control yourself, Jerry, we'll end this otherwise pleasant luncheon and I'll have you driven back into town. I won't sit here and be on the receiving end of vile accusations."

"How will these people return Samantha to me?"

"That's something I'll pursue as soon as we part company, Jerry. I'm assured that they're honorable people." He laughed ruefully. "Honor among thieves, and kidnappers, and all that. In other words, I'm assured that they have no desire to harm your daughter, and have every intention of fulfilling their part of the bargain." He paused. "You turn over the tape, and they turn over your daughter. It's really quite that simple."

The reality of his impotency set in heavily, and swiftly, on Rollins.

He nodded.

"Good. There's really no choice, is there?"

"No, there isn't. When. And how?"

"I'll need a day, perhaps two. I know that your phones are monitored by the police, so that form of communication is out of the question. I suggest this: As you know, there is the question of arranging the Miami debate between your Governor Colgate and the president. So many sticking points to be resolved. It's been in the press. I suggest that we make a public display of getting together—say, day after tomorrow, on the pretense of ironing out those sticking points. We'll meet at my office. By then, I'll hopefully have worked out the logistics of your daughter's return, and you can deliver the tape to me. Make sense?"

"What if I decide to not go through with this?" Rollins asked, surprised that he had.

A noncommittal shrug from Ziegler. "In that case, Jerry, the resolution of your daughter's disappearance would be out of my hands. As I say, I don't know these people, nor do I have any control over them, should you make that decision, which, I might add, would be unthinkable."

"All right," Rollins said.

"Splendid. I'll have our people put out a release about our upcoming debate meeting. I assume you'll have no trouble with the good Governor Colgate about arranging such a confab."

"I'll worry about that."

"Good. And Jerry, you do understand that this must never go further than between us—no police, no family discussions, strictly between two professionals who understand and respect each other."

Rollins ignored him and got up from the table. "Can we go?"

"Of course."

"One question, Kevin."

"Yes?"

"How did you know I had the tape?"

Ziegler came up behind Rollins and slapped his hand on his shoulder. "That should be obvious, Jerry. The same person who sold it to you offered it to us first. We dismissed it out-of-hand. He had nothing, simply a promise that he could put his filthy hands on it for a princely sum. We told him to get lost. Obviously, you didn't. Cost a king's ransom?"

Rollins opened the French doors and stepped into the main house, followed by Ziegler. A young man escorted them to the waiting Town Car. The detectives fell in behind, and the trip back into the District was quick and without incident—silence.

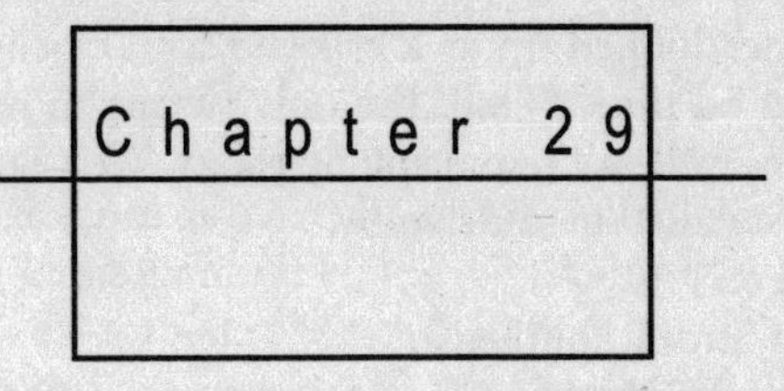

Chapter 29

The cleaning crew at Tommy G's had awakened Hatcher at five Sunday morning, and he'd struggled home, explaining to Mae that he'd pulled an all-night shift because of the Rollins kidnapping. She didn't press, although from the look of him, that all-nighter had included a night of serious drinking at one of his downtown watering holes. He slept most of the morning, and spent the afternoon watching the Nationals–Cubs game on TV. She knew to give him a wide berth on days like this, and busied herself buying plants at a local nursery and arranging them in the small flower garden out back, in which she took considerable pride.

He went to bed early Sunday night and was up Monday at six. He considered calling in sick. With his regular squad assigned elsewhere, he was certain he'd have to spend the day back at Missing Persons, trying to find a link between some long-ago abduction and the Rollins case. But he wasn't comfortable being away from Metro, the center of information about what was going down in the case. Having Jackson and Hall so close to Rollins made his usual sour stomach even worse. Better to be there and stay in the loop, keep tabs on things.

He'd no sooner walked in when Wally, another veteran homicide detective, grabbed him. "Hey, Hatch, where the hell you been?"

Hatcher looked up at a cracked wall clock that kept pretty good time. "Hell, I'm only twenty minutes late."

"Yeah, well, we're pairing up today. We've got a homicide just called in, a drive-by."

"Where?"

"First Street, Southeast."

"Daylight drive-by?"

"Twenty minutes ago. Come on. I've got the car."

They drove to the scene, a rough-and-tumble street beneath the shadow and noise of I-295. After passing a series of taxi companies, auto repair shops, and what seemed an endless succession of battered chain-link fences behind which abandoned vehicles, discarded kitchen appliances, and other trash was heaped, they pulled up in front of a first-floor X-rated video store nestled next to a topless club. Uniformed officers who'd already responded were busy stringing yellow crime scene tape to cordon off the sidewalk directly in front of the shop. A dozen bystanders ringed the action. The marked police cars, lights flashing, had blocked off the street. As Hatcher and Wally approached, they saw the victim sprawled on the sidewalk, facedown, arms akimbo, large rings of blood from multiple wounds where it had seeped into the porous, chipped concrete.

"You ID him?" Hatcher asked one of the uniforms.

"No. We just got here."

"Anybody see it happen?"

"Or admit they did?" Wally added.

The cop pointed to a man standing in the doorway of the porn shop. "You see what went down?" Hatcher asked him.

"He walks outside, a car comes past, slow, very slow, two guys in it, young maybe, I don't know, but two of 'em, and one sticks his hand out and boom, boom, boom, like that, one, two, three, maybe four, and he goes down. Jesus."

"What kind of car?"

A shrug. "Sedan, four doors, I think. Maybe brown, or black. Happened fast."

"You know him?"

"Who?"

"Who the hell do you think I'm talking about? The guy who was in here and who's laying dead on your sidewalk."

"Yeah, I knew him."

"What's his name?"

"Billy."

"Billy? Billy what?"

"McMahon."

"Ooh," Hatcher said, the name immediately registering. "He runs some sort of escort service, right?"

"Yeah. That's what he does."

"He's a friend of yours?"

"Sort of. Not close like, you know?"

"What was he doin' in here this morning?"

"He bought a DVD."

"Porn."

"Adult."

"And he walks out with this DVD, an adult one, and two bananas drive by and take him out. You know why?"

"Why what?"

"You're annoying me, pal. Why somebody wanted him dead."

"I don't know. He was in pretty heavy to some sharks and—"

"Loan sharks?"

"Yeah. He tried to hit me up for some money, but like I told him, business is slow, you know, people getting their stuff off the computers, the Internet, downloading stuff for free. So I told him I couldn't help him, so he gets a little nasty, you know, and starts telling me he knows who his real friends are and—"

"And he walks out, and pop, he's gone."

"Yeah. Scared the hell out of me. This neighborhood's bad, man. Time I got out'a here."

Hatcher grinned and looked around the dingy shop. "Shame. Nice place you've got here."

"You want something, take it."

"I don't watch this garbage. Give one of the officers outside your name, address, phone."

Hatch and Wally spent a few minutes asking onlookers whether anyone could identify the car or the gunmen. There were no takers, nor were any expected. They waited until an ME van pulled up before heading back to Metro.

"You knew the guy?" Wally said.

"Knew of him. Suspect in that hooker murder in Adams Morgan. Ran an escort service she used to work for."

"Anything happening with that, Hatch?"

"No, and nobody cares. Just as well. I'm packing it in, Wally."

"Yeah? You've had enough?"

"More than enough. The minute we get back I'm filing the papers. Already have them filled out. I'll put the house on the market and head south."

"You got a place in Florida, right?"

"Yeah."

"Tough to sell your place with the way the economy's going. Could be on the market, say, months, huh?"

"I don't care. We'll get out of town the minute the pension clears and let some real estate cutie handle things up here. This city's a jungle, Wally. Nothing makes sense anymore."

"I know."

"How much time you got left?"

"A couple'a years. Can't wait. We'll miss you, Hatch."

Hatcher rubbed his eyes and looked out the window

at the passing corner of the D.C. scene. "Yeah," he said, "but I won't miss this place. Not for a minute."

Jackson and the second detective assigned to follow Rollins to his Maryland rendezvous with Kevin Ziegler fell into an easy pace as they trailed Ziegler's Town Car back into the District. Jackson called Kloss at the house, saying that there was nothing to report. He gave the address in Maryland where the two men had met, and said that there hadn't been a sign of them from the minute they entered the house until leaving.

They stopped a few car lengths away from the entrance to Rollins's office building and watched as he got out of the car, lingered for a few moments to exchange parting words with his host, closed the door, and looked back at them before going through the glass revolving doors.

"What's this all about?" Jackson's colleague asked.

"I don't know," Jackson said. "Politics I guess. Ziegler's a big wheel in Pyle's reelection campaign, and Rollins advises Governor Colgate."

"Cutting a deal, huh? Always a deal, even when a kid is missing. Politicians!"

Jackson laughed. "That's a safe assumption."

"They haven't heard again from the kidnappers, Matt?"

"As far as I know."

"What a hell of a thing for the parents to go through."

"Can't imagine anything worse," Jackson responded, "unless . . ."

"Yeah, unless the kid is found dead. I suppose there's always hope."

"Nothing but hope."

Jackson's cell sounded.

"Matt, it's Bob Kloss. Come on back to the house."

When Jackson arrived at the Rollins's Foggy Bottom home, there was heightened tension. The lead FBI special agent looked glumly through a small opening he'd created in a drapery. Sue Rollins sat in a recliner in the living room, feet up, eyes closed. Kloss conferred with a new face from Metro, who'd been sent to spell one of the detectives charged with monitoring the telephone recording devices. Kloss waved Jackson into the dining room, where the equipment was set up, and shut the double doors. "I want you to listen to something," he said. "When Mr. Rollins got the call from Mr. Ziegler about having lunch, Ziegler said something that's bothering me."

"About the kidnapping?"

"Yeah. Not directly, something about the president wanting to help. Listen and tell me what you think. We brought the tape over from his office."

"Can you make yourself free for lunch? It is important, Jerry. I realize that everything pales in comparison to your personal tragedy that's taking place, but there may be something we can do to help in that regard."

Kloss looked to Jackson for a reaction. His blank expression said he didn't have one.

"Then this," Kloss said.

"Jerry, the president is deeply concerned about what's happened to you and your daughter. He wants to do everything in his power to get that little girl home safe and sound, and will pull out all the stops to accomplish that. We can discuss the role he might play, along with other things I need to run by you."

"What 'other things' to run by him?" Kloss said. "And there's something he, Ziegler, can maybe do to help?"

"He's referring to the president," Jackson said.

"Or is he?" Kloss asked. "I mean, what can the president do to bring this to a happy conclusion? Make a speech? Set up some phony photo-op? I don't know, Matt, I just get the feeling that there was maybe more to them getting together than just an empty promise about the president, or politics in general."

They listened to the tape again. This time, Jackson bought in to what Kloss was saying. "Are you suggesting that Ziegler or his people could be involved?" he asked, reluctant to state the unspeakable.

Kloss said nothing.

"Can't be," Jackson offered.

"I agree," said Kloss. "Can't be. But I keep playing this what-if game over in my mind. No one's called, no ransom demands, no further instructions. What did they take the kid for? What's the payoff? Doesn't look like it's money. So, then, what?"

"Something Rollins knows—or has?"

"That's where my mind's going. Look, you and Rollins have gotten pretty close, right?"

"Yeah, he seems to like me. He's been asking a lot about me, you know, why I became a cop, things about my family. We get along okay."

"Good. Stay close to him, see if he gives off any vibes that something's happening we don't know about." Kloss grinned and slapped Jackson on the shoulder. "Put that sociology degree of yours to good use."

"Funny you should say that. Hatcher considers my degree a negative."

Kloss's wince said it all as Mary Hall arrived and joined them. She'd been dispatched to Metro to deliver paperwork from Kloss, and to bring back an assortment of items for the team assigned to the house.

"Interrupting something?" she asked.

"Just talking about your partner's college degree," Kloss said.

"Hatch not appreciating it," Jackson said.

"Oh," she said. "Speaking of that, guess what, Matt?"

His extended hands said *Tell me more.*

"Hatcher has put in for retirement," she said, disguising any sign of glee in her voice.

"You're kidding."

"Would I kid about something like that?" she said. "He filed the papers this afternoon. Oh, and that creep from Beltway Escorts, Billy McMahon? Gunned down this morning in a drive-by in Southeast."

Kloss's eyes looked for an explanation.

"A case we were working on," Jackson said. "The call girl murder in Adams Morgan. The guy was a suspect."

"Not anymore," Kloss said, standing, stretching against a pain somewhere in his lean body, and walking from the dining room to where Sue Rollins was now out of her chair and speaking with a Bureau special agent.

Jackson and Hall huddled in the dining room discussing Hatcher's retirement and what it might mean for them. Once they'd exhausted that topic, Mary asked about Matt's day and his assignment to follow Rollins to his meeting with Kevin Ziegler. He told her what Kloss had said, and paraphrased what had been on the tape the senior detective had played. "It makes sense," Jackson summed up. "They took the girl on Saturday and here it is, the end of Monday. Nothing, just that one call Saturday night saying she was safe and wouldn't be harmed. What do they want? If it were a pedophile, he wouldn't have bothered calling. Something's wrong here."

"Maybe they got cold feet," she suggested, "and are afraid of trying to put a ransom drop in place."

"Maybe, but the abduction was too slick for somebody to chicken out. Kloss wants me to stay close to Rollins, see if I can pick up on anything."

"Good," she said.

"Did you see Hatcher?" Jackson asked.

"No—he caught the McMahon drive-by."

Kloss interrupted to suggest that Jackson go home for a change of clothes. "Rollins says he's leaving his office in a couple of hours and coming here. I'd like you back."

Mary walked Matt to the rear door. "You okay?" she asked.

"Yeah, I'm fine. Hearing about Hatcher is . . . well, it's good news."

"I know. Hurry back."

The waiting game continued in Foggy Bottom that night. The press contingent had thinned out somewhat in front of the house, but there were still plenty of reporters and cameras anxious to catch a glimpse of anyone, anything, to advance the story.

Rollins had arrived at six, followed closely by Jackson's return. Jackson prompted conversation with him when it seemed appropriate, and the grieving father was receptive to those advances. From the young detective's perspective, Rollins's demeanor hadn't changed. He was his usual cool and collected self, with rare moments of annoyance or impatience flaring up. Sue Rollins had settled into an almost fugue state, doing everything by rote, mechanical, without inspiration. Mary Hall stuck close to her, lending a hand in the kitchen or helping her do laundry—a wash in the midst of such personal anguish! There continued to be, of course, various phone calls for both the Rollinses. They handled them with aplomb, keeping them brief, stating the obvious, that the lines had to be kept clear. Everyone understood, of course, yet continued the conversations until Sue or Jerry had to be a little firmer and assure the caller that they appreciated the concern and would certainly let them know if there was anything to report. Sue's mother called regularly and seemed to accept the need to stay away, and to depend upon her daughter and son-in-law for updates. She cried during some of those calls, which made it harder for Sue. But she maintained an even keel and didn't allow her own tears to meld with her mother's.

At eleven, Kloss, whose fatigue was showing, suggested that the Rollinses go to bed.

"What about you?" Jerry said. "You look exhausted."

"I'll be fine on the couch here," Kloss said. "I really doubt whether anyone will call tonight regarding your daughter. We'll handle other calls and say you're resting. You'll accomplish nothing by sitting around with us."

Sue didn't argue. She walked heavily up the stairs and disappeared into the master bedroom. Jackson and Rollins sat at the kitchen table, hands cupped around steaming cups of black coffee.

"How did you enjoy your trip out to Maryland today?" Rollins asked.

"Pretty ride," Jackson said. "You had a meeting."

Rollins nodded.

"I guess with the campaign and all, life marches on."

"Something like that. I met with Kevin Ziegler. He's President Pyle's advisor."

"I know."

"You follow politics, Matt?"

"Best I can."

"Pick a winner yet?"

"I don't know about a winner, sir, but I do intend to vote for Governor Colgate."

"You're not just saying that because you're with me?"

"I wouldn't do that, sir."

"No, I suppose you wouldn't. Mr. Ziegler and I will be meeting again day after tomorrow to iron out details for a debate in Miami."

"I heard about that," Jackson said, pleased that he had kept up with news of the campaign. "Always some sticking points."

"Always. In a way, it's good that these things come up. I don't know how I'd handle this whole mess if it were all I had to think about. I feel bad for Sue in that regard."

"She's a strong woman."

"Very strong."

"Mind if I ask you something, Mr. Rollins?"

"No, and please call me Jerry."

"All right, Jerry. I couldn't help but notice the last time I went out back that you have an impressive machine sitting in the garage."

Jackson's observation brought a wry smile to Rollins's lips. "My baby, my pride and joy."

"I only peeked through the garage window, but . . ."

"Care to see her up close?"

"I'd love that."

The sight of them in the driveway, illuminated by a large halogen lamp over the front of the garage, stirred murmurs from the press, and a few hurled questions, which were ignored. Rollins opened the door and flipped on an interior light.

"That is a beauty," Jackson commented, going to the Porsche and running his hand over its gleaming red surface.

"It's a 2003 nine-eleven," Rollins said. "Three-hundred-eighty horses. She'll get up to one-ninety, if you're crazy enough to do it."

"You ever take it on a track?" Jackson asked.

"No. Sue wouldn't be pleased if I decided to turn race driver. Go ahead, get in."

Jackson slipped behind the black, leather-wrapped wheel. "Like a cockpit," he exclaimed.

"I always feel that way when I'm driving it. My midlife crisis." He laughed.

Jackson climbed out of the car and appreciated the solid "thunk" of the driver's door as he closed it. They left the garage, prompting another chorus from the press, and returned to the house.

"When this is over," Rollins said, "I'll have to take you for a ride in it. Let you drive it."

"That would be great."

Rollins yawned. "I think Detective Kloss was right," he said. "I'm going to join my wife upstairs."

"Good night, sir."

"Good night, Matt. Thank you."

"For what, sir?"

"For being here for us. Somehow, I know this will be over soon and we'll have Samantha back safely."

When Rollins entered the bedroom, Sue hadn't changed into nightclothes. She sat on the bed, her back against the headboard, her feet drawn up, her knees tight against her chest. Rollins placed his arm around her. "Sue," he said.

"What?"

"This will all be over soon. Samantha will be home again."

As she slowly turned to look at him, a torrent of tears flowed from her. She wrapped her arms tightly about him and squeezed as though life itself depended upon it. He allowed her sobbing to abate before gently pushing her away and holding her at arm's length. "Sue," he said, "did you hear me? This will be over soon—everything is going to be all right."

"That's what they keep saying but—"

"It will be, Sue. Trust me, it will be."

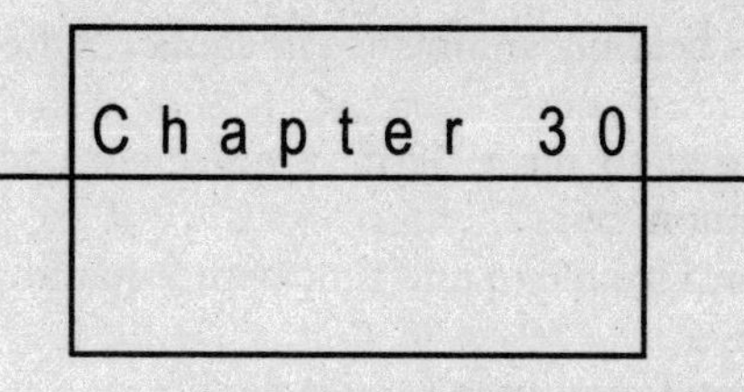

Chapter 30

Paul answered the phone. "It's Y-man," he whispered to Greta.

"We're getting ready to bring this to a conclusion within the next few days. Any questions about the plan to release her?"

"No. When?"

"I'll call again."

Rollins's final phone call before leaving his office the previous night had been to Bob Colgate. He reached him on his cell while en route to a fundraiser.

"It's Jerry, Bob. I wanted to bring you up-to-date on a meeting I had today."

"With Ziegler." There was an edge to Colgate's voice that was all too familiar to Rollins.

"Word gets around," Rollins said.

"Did it ever occur to you to run it past me *before* you meet with someone like Ziegler?"

"It was a last-minute thing, Bob. He seemed anxious to talk and I wanted to hear him out."

Silence on Colgate's end.

"He wants to get together again, day after tomorrow, to try to iron out details for the Miami debate."

"That's nice. You will, of course, consult with me and the staff before committing to anything."

Rollins held his annoyance in check. "Of course," he said.

"We need to meet, Jerry. I never considered you a loose cannon, but—"

"It's hard for me to find time with Samantha's kidnapping and—"

"But you found time for Ziegler."

"I have to go, Bob. I'll call after the second meeting with Ziegler."

As though he'd been struck by a sudden thought, Colgate asked, "How are things going with Samantha? No breaks yet?"

"No, nothing yet, but thanks for asking."

Rollins replaced the phone in its cradle and stared at it. He was well aware, and had been from the earliest days of their friendship, of Colgate's self-centeredness. He'd always excused it as being an integral part of a politician's personality and character. You didn't run for governor of a state, or for president of the United States, without a healthy dose of "me" in your veins. Of course, Colgate had honed a side of him that proclaimed to voters that he was deeply concerned with their personal lives and troubles, and he could turn that faucet on at will. At public gatherings, an aide was never far from his side to remind him that the next person he was about to greet had recently lost a spouse or child, or was going through chemotherapy. *"The man is amazing,"* Rollins had heard more than one person exclaim. *"He's never too busy to remember the troubles I've been having."* Colgate had that ability down to a science and it had held him in good stead throughout his political life.

There were times that Rollins questioned his own willingness to overlook the programmed, ingenuous aspect of his friend Bob Colgate, and to continue to play an important role in his rise to the apex of national politics. He knew the answer, of course. There was something intoxicating about sitting at the right hand of power and being highly valued as a source of wisdom. Too, there were the perks inherent in such a relationship, the invitations to events to which only the cream of Washington's A-list were granted access. A VIP in a city of VIPs. And he didn't kid himself: he'd taken part in enough of his own dubious, even unsavory deals over the years, advocating for clients for whom he had little regard and even less belief in their causes, cases in which his legal acumen, and, yes, his political connections, had prevailed on behalf of those who didn't warrant it, at the expense of those more deserving of justice. He was good at rationalizing those incidents in his life, frequently calling upon the priceless words of others to buttress his self-explanations. His wife, a Shakespearian savant, once offered a sonnet to him when he'd expressed doubts about his chosen life. He recited it aloud on his way home that evening:

> *"Roses have thorns, and silver fountains mud;*
> *Clouds and eclipses stain both moon and sun,*
> *And loathsome canker lives in sweetest bud.*
> *All men make faults."*

On Tuesday morning, the *Washington Post* ran two stories pertaining to Rollins.

A banner over a lengthy article on page one read:

NO BREAKS IN ROLLINS KIDNAPPING:
Lack of Contact by Abductors Concerns Authorities.

Chief Carter had been interviewed for the article. He assured reporters that MPD had pulled out all the stops, and was working in close cooperation with state and local agencies, the FBI, as well as with state police from neighboring states.

Chief Carter had called the house early Monday morning and spoken with Rollins. "I was wondering, Mr. Rollins, if perhaps this might be a good time for you and your wife to make a personal plea to the kidnappers."

"You mean go on television?"

"Yes. There's always the possibility that a direct plea might strike a nerve with one of them."

"I don't think so, Chief."

"You're sure, Mr. Rollins? We can easily set up the taping, or press conference."

"Yes, I'm sure. Mrs. Rollins certainly isn't up to something like that. We had discussed it before you called, and came to the conclusion that it would be inappropriate at this time. But I thank you for the suggestion and for all you and your officers have been doing for us."

Of course, he and Sue had not discussed the possibility of going public and pleading with Samantha's kidnappers. Had they engaged in such a conversation prior to Rollins's meeting with Ziegler, they might have agreed to do it. But now that it appeared likely that arrangements would be made for Samantha's safe return, he wasn't about to do anything to muddy the waters.

The second story that morning was considerably smaller, and was part of a roundup of the day's political news: *Rival Camps to Meet on Miami Debate*. The piece was based upon a press release issued by a Pyle campaign spokesperson. According to it, top Pyle political advisor, Kevin Ziegler, and senior advisor to the Colgate campaign, Jerrold Rollins, had agreed to meet the next day to attempt to iron out differences that stood in the way of a proposed debate in Miami. The spokesman stated, "We're confident that whatever stumbling blocks exist can be surmounted, and that the debate will go forward as planned."

Jackson read both stories, and passed the paper to Mary Hall. They were alone in the kitchen. Mr. and Mrs.

Rollins had been there earlier and invited them to join them for breakfast. After the Rollinses had left, Jackson said to Hall, referring to the newspaper piece, "Looks like he got together with Ziegler for legit reasons after all."

"Seems that way. Did you notice a change in them this morning?"

"The Rollinses? Yeah, I did. More relaxed. She certainly seems to be."

"Why?"

Jackson shrugged. "Maybe it's just a matter of time doing its number. You get numb after a while."

"Did you hear what he said just before they left this morning, that he has renewed confidence that everything will turn out all right?"

"I'm glad he feels that way. It would be hell if he felt otherwise."

"It was almost as though he knows something."

"I don't think so, Mary. Just simple, hopeful optimism."

"He's spending another day in the office?"

"That's the plan."

"It's been three days since she was grabbed. Not another word from whoever has her."

"Seems more like three weeks."

"Are you staying here today?"

"No. Kloss wants me to replace one of the detectives at Rollins's office. You know, stay close to him." He checked his watch. "I'd better get going. Kloss wants me there before Rollins arrives, and I need to swing by Metro on the way." He made sure no one was about to intrude upon them before leaning over and kissing her on the mouth. "I miss you," he said.

"Soon," she said.

"Never soon enough. I'll check in with you later."

As he walked from the house, a reporter yelled, "Hey, when's the family going to make a statement?"

Jackson ignored him, went to a department car parked across the driveway, got in and told the uniformed cop at the wheel to drop him at Metro.

"Anything new?" the cop asked.

"No."

"Know what I figure?"

"What?" Jackson said, not really interested.

"I figure it's some nut who got screwed by the father in a court case. You read about it all the time, some whack-job gets a bad decision and starts shooting at everybody—his lawyer, the judge, anybody."

"As good a theory as any," Jackson said.

"You wait and see," said the cop. "Just wait and see."

Jackson walked into Metro and headed directly for the detectives' section, where Hatcher sat at a table with a couple of other veteran cops.

"Hey, look who's here," Hatcher bellowed. "Solve the kidnapping yet, hot shot?"

"Hello, Hatch," Jackson said, heading for the locker room to retrieve some things he needed from his space. Hatcher followed.

"So, how's it feel to rub elbows with the rich and famous?" the crusty detective asked.

"I don't look at it that way," Jackson said as he found the right numbers on the combination lock.

"Ah, come on, Jackson, sure you do. Guys like you are always sucking up to anybody who can do something for you. Hey, kid, play your cards right and you'll end up running this joint."

Jackson continued to ignore Hatcher, carefully placing items in a small athletic bag.

"Hey, Jackson, I'm talking to you."

"I hear you, Hatch," Jackson said, not turning.

"You really hate my guts, don't you?"

Jackson looked down at the floor and slowly shook his head. "Let's just say that we don't get along, Hatch."

"Jackson, you know why we don't get along, as you put it? We don't get along because you're a piss-poor excuse for a cop. We don't get along because I've forgotten more about being a cop than you'll ever know. You can take all your books and your degrees and shove 'em, pal, because they ain't worth the paper they're printed on."

"You finished with the lecture, Hatch?" Jackson said, slamming closed the locker and spinning the lock with conviction.

"Oh, I'm finished, all right. Maybe you heard. I put in my retirement papers."

"I did hear that. Congratulations."

"Yeah, I figured I'd get out'a here before you filed some dumb charge that I'm a racist or something."

Jackson drew a deep breath. "Enjoy your retirement, Hatch." He moved to walk past but Hatcher stepped in his way.

"I have to go, Hatch. I'm running late."

"Go ahead."

"You're in the way."

Hatcher's grin was crooked, nasty.

"Oh, pardon me, hot shot. Sure, I'll get out of your way, but first let me give you a word of advice."

Jackson knew it was senseless to protest.

"Stay out of *my* way till I'm gone. Got that?"

Hatcher moved aside and Jackson went to the door. He could feel Hatcher's eyes boring into his back. He turned and said, "When you were working vice, Hatch, who were the cops shaking down hookers like Rosalie Curzon and Micki Simmons?"

His question elicited an audible expulsion of air from Hatcher.

Jackson stared at him, awaiting an answer.

"You don't know what the hell you're talking about, Jackson."

"Just asking, Hatch. Somebody was putting the arm on them. No doubt about that."

"They tell you that?"

"Curzon was in no position to tell me anything," Jackson said, "but Simmons—"

"And you take the word of a freakin' whore." Hatcher laughed, too loud and long. "Go crawl back in your hole with the rest of your people, Jackson. Get out'a my sight."

Jackson left the locker room, afraid of what he might do next. There was a time during the confrontation that he thought of the handgun he carried, how easy it would be to pull it out and put an end to the man who'd berated and demeaned him at every turn, the man who caused sleepless nights and fantasies of revenge. He'd never felt that way before about anyone. The thought of using his weapon, even on the criminals he'd pursued, was unpleasant at best. He sometimes wondered whether he'd be able to do it, draw the weapon, aim, and take another person's life. He knew he wasn't alone. He'd heard a few fellow cops express such doubts, always privately, of course, and beyond the earshot of those who would find such reservations unmanly. There were veteran cops who'd never had to draw their weapons during a long career, and were obviously happy that they hadn't needed to.

He stood just outside the locker room, leaned against the wall, and drew deep breaths. He thought of his father's advice on the phone the other night about not allowing someone like Hatcher to drive him from the job he'd coveted since high school. He had to smile. If his father thought that walking away was bad, imagine if his son decided to blow away Hatcher in a locker room at Metro.

Although he was running late, he preceded Rollins to the office by fifteen minutes and was standing in the reception area talking with Caroline when Rollins walked in. They exchanged greetings before Rollins disappeared into his office and closed the door behind him; Jackson joined a second detective in the small, previously unused room, in which recording devices had been installed. There was an issue that had to be resolved before the taping of calls began. Rollins was an attorney, which meant that his conversations with clients were protected under attorney-client privilege. It had been agreed that the detectives monitoring calls would immediately cease recording once they realized it was a client on the line. It wasn't a perfect system, and Rollins had balked initially, but eventually gave in to reason. After all, his daughter's life was at stake. It was also agreed that outgoing calls would not be monitored or taped.

"I wish this thing would get resolved," the second detective said. "I'm getting tired of sitting around."

"Yeah, I know," Jackson said, not offering up the obvious, that much of a detective's life is spent doing just that, sitting or standing around.

"What's he like?" the detective asked, nodding toward Rollins's office, separated from them by a single interior wall.

"Mr. Rollins? He's a nice guy, as far as I can tell. He's cool, a real lawyer, treats those of us assigned to the house pretty good."

"I don't get to see him much. He holes himself up in his office most of the time."

As the day dragged on, Jackson's thoughts kept reverting back to that morning's exchange with Walt Hatcher. He'd done nothing to provoke Hatcher, and was at a loss to explain the older detective's belligerence and combativeness. He came to the conclusion that Hatcher's decision to retire from the force had freed him to vent feelings against Jackson that had been simmering for what seemed forever, going back to his first day on

Hatcher's squad. But that bit of pop psychology didn't salve his feelings about the face-to-face in the locker room. How long did it take for retirement to come through? It couldn't arrive fast enough.

Jackson and his colleague ordered in lunch and ate quietly. It had been a busy morning; they'd logged in fourteen calls, six of which were determined to be from clients. Following lunch, and after checking in with Kloss and Mary at the Rollins house, Jackson went to an unoccupied office and placed a call on his cell phone. Micki Simmons answered.

"It's Matt Jackson," he said. "How are things?"

"Things stink, if you want to know the truth. You tell me I can't leave this lousy city, and I'm not working, so what's good about it? When can I go?"

"It won't be long," Jackson responded, not knowing whether it would be or not. "I thought you'd want to know that your former employer, Billy McMahon, was gunned down yesterday."

"He's dead?"

"Yeah, he's dead."

"Maybe there's justice after all."

"Micki, I need to talk to you."

"You always say you need to talk to me."

"I need for you to be honest with me."

"I have been."

"Maybe you've been honest, but not always forthcoming."

She didn't respond; he could hear her breathing into the phone.

"I have to know, Micki, the names of the cops who were shaking down you and Rosalie."

"I'm not stupid."

"Micki, I'm calling from my cell phone. I've never lied to you." (*Well, almost never,* he thought). "Your friend

Rosalie is dead, and I want to know who killed her. Don't you?"

"Sure, but not if it means I end up the same way."

"You won't, Micki. Whatever you tell me stays with me, like in Las Vegas."

"I can take that to the bank?"

He smiled. He'd thought of using that cliché but had fought the urge. "Yeah, you can take it to the bank. You want to meet somewhere?"

He'd hoped she'd give him the information on the phone. Shaking free of Kloss, Rollins, and the kidnapping case wouldn't be easy. But he decided he would work it out, *had* to work it out.

"I'm not sure when I can get free. I'm working on a big case and—"

"The kid who went missing?"

"Right. Look, I'll meet anyplace you say. Name it. The Silver Veil? Dinner's on me. Oh, right, you don't like that place."

"Too many bad memories."

"All right. You pick the place."

"What time?"

"I'll call you back within the hour."

"Hey, Matt."

Her familiar tone pleased him. "What?"

"I do this for you, you do something for me."

"Quid pro quo."

"Whatever that means. I meet and tell you who the cops were, and you let me go home. I want to go home, Matt."

He went through a fast series of mental calculations. Could he promise her what she wanted? He decided that he could, and would.

"It's a deal," he said.

"Great," she said. "What did you call it?"

"Oh, quid pro quo. It's Latin."

"A cop who speaks Latin," she said. "I'm impressed." She ended the call.

Jackson called Kloss. "Detective, I was wondering if I could steal a couple of hours tonight around dinnertime."

"Got a date?"

He thought of Mary. "No, but I'd like to follow up on something. It has to do with a case I was working before joining the Rollins case."

"Sure. Mr. Rollins informs us that he intends to be home by six. Does that work for you?"

"Perfect. I'll be back to the house by eight. Thanks."

The day dragged on slowly, minutes seeming to be hours. But at three, the relative peace was shattered when Rollins came to the reception area to tell Caroline that Governor Colgate's wife, Deborah Colgate, would be stopping by the office at four. This set into motion a series of events as the staff prepared for her visit. Two Secret Service agents arrived to check out the offices. They were surprised that Jackson and his partner were there, and posed a series of questions before clearing them. All staff members were vetted, too.

"Where will you meet with her?" Rollins was asked.

"In my office."

Rollins's office was swept with a handheld device.

After the Secret Service had departed, Rollins instructed Caroline that he and Mrs. Colgate were not to be disturbed. "Please see that everyone understands that," he added to his secretary of many years.

Jackson called Micki Simmons back and told her that they'd meet at six thirty.

At 3:45, a call came in from Kevin Ziegler. Jackson and his partner listened, and the digital recorder went into action.

"Just nailing down tomorrow, Jerry," Ziegler said. "My office, ten A.M.?"

"I'll be there."

"I know this isn't easy, Jerry, but—"

"Ten at your office," Rollins said sharply, and hung up.

"Sounds like he didn't want to talk," Jackson's colleague commented.

"Yeah, sure sounds that way."

Deborah Colgate, accompanied by her two Secret Service agents, arrived precisely at four and was immediately ushered into Rollins's office, the agents occupying chairs in the reception area.

"Love to hear what's going on in there," the detective with Jackson said.

"So would I," Jackson agreed.

"Who do you figure will win in November?"

"Haven't given it much thought," Jackson said.

"Looks like Colgate's a shoo-in, despite all his baggage."

"You never know," was Jackson's reply. "You just never know."

Chapter 31

For reasons he couldn't explain even to himself, Rollins felt the need to stage his office for Deborah's arrival. The external surroundings would do nothing to mitigate what he intended to say, but he went about the task nonetheless. The blinds and drapes were tightly closed. He pulled a comfortable armchair to the side of his desk, and placed a floor lamp at its side. Two desk lamps added additional lighting. He selected what he considered a soothing jazz CD, a selection of ballads by the Canadian pianist Oliver Jones. He kept the door closed, but Caroline had a brief glance into the room and found its artificial ambiance to be strange, almost amusing. If she didn't know her boss better, she would have thought that he was planning a seduction.

He'd debated where to hold the meeting. His initial idea was to choose somewhere far away from the District, perhaps a secluded inn like the King's Contrivance, where they'd rendezvoused before. He'd also considered a secluded park, a bench beneath graceful trees, where his words would be softened by singing birds and gentle breezes. Neither venue held up to further scrutiny. With the press following their every move, although for different reasons—she as the wife of a presidential candidate, he as the tragic father of an abducted daughter—meeting in such intimate surroundings would surely feed already voracious media appetites.

It had to be the office, he decided. That put it on a formal, businesslike footing, two people professionally intertwined getting together to discuss campaign issues, fine-tuning talking points, and plotting strategy, all perfectly within the realm of their acknowledged relationship. And in a sense, that's exactly what it was.

Caroline called Rollins to announce Deborah's arrival and he went to where Deb waited. "I'm so glad you could come," he told her, taking her hand and whisking her into the office. "Hold all my calls," he told Caroline. Brian Massie lingered in the doorway to his office and watched his boss greet the new presumptive first lady. It was time to go outside for a cigarette, and to make a call.

"What's this all about, Jerry?" Deborah asked the minute the door was closed. "I canceled two appointments to be here."

"I appreciate that, Deb. Believe me, I wouldn't have asked you to come if I didn't consider it urgent."

"Urgent?" she said. "Could you turn off that music?"

"I thought—"

"I'm not in the mood for romantic ballads."

He did as she'd asked, and came to where she stood in the center of the room. "Better?" he said.

"Yes. Thank you."

"Sit down, Deb." He indicated the chair next to his desk.

She remained standing. "Jerry, what's wrong? What's happened? Is it Samantha?"

"No. Please, sit."

"I spoke with Sue today," she said, taking the chair.

"After I called you?"

"No, before. She sounded good, strong, said she was certain that Sammy would be back soon. God, I admire that sort of faith. I'm afraid I couldn't muster it under such dire circumstances."

"We never know what we're capable of, Deb, until

we're faced with adversity. Sue is a strong person. I share her confidence about Samantha."

She exhaled a stream of air and adjusted herself in the chair. "So, this is not about Sammy," she said. "What *is* it about?"

Rollins touched her shoulder as he walked past and took his seat behind the desk. He rolled forward so that his knees came closer to hers. "I said we had to get together, Deb, because of something I've recently learned."

"Go on."

He glanced up at the James Vann painting, behind which the wall safe was situated, before responding. "I'm sure you know that I'd move heaven and earth for you and Bob in this campaign."

"And Bob has always appreciated it."

"You? Have you appreciated it?"

She cocked her head as though to say she considered it a strange question.

"It's important to me, Deb, that you understand how much you and Bob mean to me."

Now she turned her head right and left. "Why do I get the feeling that I'm being set up for a fall, Jerry?"

He ignored the comment and forged ahead with what was a semblance of the speech he'd been running over and over since deciding to meet—the words to use, the tone to cushion the blow, the preamble, creating a relaxing atmosphere, all the tools he used when confronting an adversary in the courtroom.

"The problem, Deb, is that in this dirty game of national politics, there are some things that take on their own life, that *happen*, no matter how hard we try to head them off."

"Thanks for trying to let me down easy, Jerry," she said, reaching and patting his knee. "But I'm a big girl. I've taken a few blows and I'm still standing. Swing away."

"Okay." He sat back and searched the ceiling for the right way to phrase what he was about to say. There wasn't one. "Deb, I've learned through sources that there exists a videotape that can be extremely damaging to Bob's campaign."

Her placid expression didn't indicate shock. It was void of any emotion. Had she even heard him? She had. "A videotape?" she said.

"Yes."

"Of Bob?"

He hesitated. "Yes," he said.

He allowed her to process what she'd heard. The room was still, silent, threatening.

"That tape that was mentioned in *City Paper*?" she asked, her voice soft and lacking strength.

The question took him by surprise. He'd forgotten about the article that had hinted at such a tape existing, and that mentioned rumors linking her husband to the slain call girl in Adams Morgan. "Trash," had been his reply to the reporter. If only that were so.

"I wouldn't give that article any credence, Deb," he said, glad that the subject had been changed, if only for the moment.

"I'm not," she said. "I don't give credence to anything in the media when it comes to politics. But now *you* say such a tape exists."

"I'm afraid so."

"How? Who has it?"

"I don't know the specific answers to those questions, Deb. I wish I did." Another guilty glance at the painting hiding the wall safe. "What I do know is that the tape has surfaced and is likely to be used against Bob, and you, in the campaign." He got up and walked to the window, wishing he could look outside through the drapes and blinds. "The Pyle people have the tape," he said, his back still to her.

When she didn't respond, he turned, and saw that she was hunched over, her arms wrapped around herself. He came up behind her and placed his hands on her shoulders, kneaded them with tenderness. "I'm sorry," he said. "If there were anything I could have done to stave this off, I would have."

He wanted her to leave now. He hadn't been sure that he could lie with such conviction and without remorse, but he had. He wanted to say that the only thing that could have caused him to turn over the tape to the Pyle campaign was the life of his daughter, to save her, to put an end to the nightmare he and Sue had been dealing with since Saturday. But he knew, had known from the moment he made the decision, that while the predicament in which he'd found himself and the resulting decision would be understood—what parent wouldn't make this choice?—he couldn't bring himself to express it. He couldn't face her with that truth.

She straightened. "Have you seen the tape?" she asked absently.

"Seen it? No."

He had seen it, of course, had watched it more than once, alone in his darkened office, the flickering images casting macabre shafts of red and yellow and orange light over the room, and over him. He'd felt sick the first time he'd watched, and had wondered whether he would need to run to the bathroom to vomit. The impact of the second viewing was no less potent than the first.

"But you know what's on it," she said.

"Only what I've been told."

"And what have you been told?"

"That it places Bob in a compromising position with a call girl."

"It was taped?"

"Yes. The call girl taped it."

Rage crossed her face. She clenched her fists and let

out a stream of four-letter words, then ended with, "How could he have been so stupid, so careless?"

"I don't have an answer for that, Deb," he said, retaking his seat. "Look, I'm meeting with Kevin Ziegler tomorrow about the Miami debate. I'll try to convince him that to make use of the tape would bring politics down to a new level, down into the gutter. I don't have any illusions, though. Pyle's campaign will never directly claim responsibility for the tape's release, but with the Internet and blogs and out-of-control surrogates, it's easy to let someone else claim the . . . responsibility."

"This was the call girl who was murdered," Deborah said.

"Yes."

Her thoughts were as visible as though written in a cartoon balloon above her head. Had her husband, candidate for the most powerful office in the world, killed the prostitute? He wanted to dissuade her of that possibility, but couldn't. Instead, he said, "I've told you about this, Deb, to give you a heads-up, no surprises, no blindsiding. You had to know."

"Does Bob know?"

"I haven't told him, but I will. Unless, of course . . ."

"Unless I tell him," she said. "No, I won't tell him, Jerry. He doesn't deserve that from me."

"I understand how you feel, Deb. I'll find the right time, maybe after I meet with Ziegler tomorrow."

"I don't care," she said. The anger returned. "God, I detest him. He couldn't be content with bedding down his bimbos in the privacy of a hotel room, could he? Having women fall at his feet wasn't enough, was it? No, he had to go pay some common whore." She spun around to face Rollins, and expressed what she'd been thinking. "Did he kill that girl, Jerry?" She said it through bitter tears that had mascara running down her cheeks.

"Don't go there, Deb. This is bad enough without adding murder to it."

He fetched a Kleenex from his desk and handed it to her. "Try to pull yourself together, Deb. If the tape does surface, it hopefully won't be for a while. I'll see what I can accomplish with Ziegler tomorrow. In the meantime, I hope you realize that this hasn't been easy for me, having to break this sort of bad news to you."

She nodded. "You're in the midst of your own nightmare, Jerry, and had to deal with this, too."

"I'm sure Sue and I will have Samantha back home soon. As for the tape, let's just hope that reason will prevail."

That prompted the first smile, actually a laugh, from her since arriving. "Reason prevail? In a presidential campaign? And the earth is flat. Do I look a fright, Jerry?"

"Go freshen up," he suggested, pointing to the private bath off his office.

He opened the drapes and blinds and moved her chair and the floor lamp back to their original positions. He was seated behind his desk when she emerged. He rose and embraced her, held her at arm's length, and said, "You look fine."

"Thanks. I hope Sammy's back soon."

"I'm counting on it."

He escorted her to the reception area, where the Secret Service agents jumped to their feet. Deborah flashed a smile at members of Rollins's staff who happened to be there. "Good seeing you," she said sprightly as she and the agents entered the elevator.

Rollins returned to his office, with Caroline at his heels. "Good meeting?" she asked.

"Yes, it went well. Anything important happen?"

She laughed. "Mr. Scraggs called to ask whether you'd found a publisher yet for his book."

"And you told him . . . ?"

"I told him you were tied up all day but would get back to him tomorrow." She shook her head.

"What?" he asked.

"He never even asked about your daughter."

"Some people are just too into themselves, Caroline."

Especially in Washington, D.C., she thought as she returned to her desk.

At six, Rollins announced that he was leaving for the day. "Coming with me, Matt?"

"I'll be by a little later," Jackson said. "Detective Kloss gave me a couple of hours off for dinner."

"Good for you. Enjoy it. I know that this probably has eaten into your life in a big way."

They went their separate ways, Jackson to meet with Micki Simmons, Rollins to his Foggy Bottom home. As he turned into his street, a bizarre thought came to him: *Does self-loathing emit an odor that others can smell?*

Chapter 32

"Your partner's taking a couple hours off tonight for dinner," Kloss told Mary Hall.

She was surprised, and expressed it.

"Something about a case he'd been working on."

Mary went to the back porch and used her cell to call Jackson. "What are you up to?" she asked.

"I was going to fill you in," he said, wishing he already had. "I had a run-in with Hatcher this morning at Metro. I asked him about when he worked vice, and he blew. I can't shake this feeling that those days have something to do with the Curzon murder."

"Kloss said you're taking time for dinner."

"Right, only I'm not sure it'll include eating. I got hold of Micki Simmons and suggested we meet at the Silver Veil, but she nixed it. She wants to meet at Montrose Park, next to Dumbarton Oaks."

"Why there?"

"Beats me, only she sounded upset. No, scared is more like it. I don't care where we meet as long as she comes through with the names of the cops who shook Rosalie and her down." When Mary didn't say anything, he said, "You there?"

"Yes, I'm here. She's agreed to give you those names?"

"Uh-huh."

"Matt, we worked the Curzon case together. I feel like I'm being pushed aside all of a sudden."

"Come on, Mary, you know that's not true. I would have suggested that you come with me but I think the two of us might make her nervous. Besides, I don't think Kloss would want both of us away from the house."

She knew he was right, which didn't mitigate her feeling of being left out. "What happened with Hatcher?" she asked.

"He got belligerent, the usual, only he was more physical this time. The guy is going off the deep end, I think."

"Stay away from him, Matt."

"Oh, I intend to. Believe me, I intend to. I'll be back at the house by eight."

"I'll be here. Take care."

He arrived at the small, quiet Georgetown leafy refuge a few minutes before six thirty and walked down Lovers Lane, a cobblestone path on its western edge that separated the park from the much larger and more famous Dumbarton Oaks. It was a pristine evening; the lack of people in the park was surprising. The tennis courts were occupied, however. He'd always meant to take up the game, but never got around to it.

Micki was alone, seated on a bench. She was dressed all in black—slacks, sweater, shoes. She didn't acknowledge him as he sat next to her.

"Thanks for coming," he said.

Her response was not what he expected. "You bastard," she said. "You lousy, lying bastard."

"Hey, back off. What'd I do to deserve that?"

"You promised you wouldn't mention me to anybody."

"Right. I didn't."

"Sure," she said. "So how come your cop buddy pays me a visit this afternoon?"

"What cop buddy?"

"Hatcher, that's who."

"Hatcher? He came to see you? Today?"

"Oh, he sure did. He told me that if I ever opened my mouth I'd end up like Rosalie."

"Whew!" was all Jackson could manage.

Her anger was palpable. She sat so that a quarter of her back was to him, one leg crossed over the other, the dangling foot pumping up and down. Jackson's mind raced back to his locker room encounter with Hatcher. Had he inadvertently blurted out her name? He didn't think so. At least he didn't remember doing it. But he must have. Either that, or Hatcher assumed from his question about his days on the vice squad that it had to have been Micki who prompted it. Hatcher knew that Jackson and Hall had spoken with her about the Curzon murder, and having interviewed her at his apartment had prompted a snide remark. But he decided that how Hatcher knew to pay a visit to Micki wasn't the issue, at least not at the moment. What *was* important was that he'd been right in his belief, unsupported by any facts, that Hatcher had shaken down Micki and Rosalie.

"Look," Jackson said, "if I did something to cause Hatcher to threaten you, I'm sorry."

" 'I'm sorry,' " she mimicked. "That's swell. The guy's capable of anything."

Jackson made sure that no one was near. He moved closer and said, "I'll make this up to you, Micki. I promise. Okay, so Hatcher has threatened you, and he was one of the cops who shook you and Rosalie down. Who were the other cops?"

"It doesn't matter. He's gone."

"From the force?"

"Yeah. I heard he retired, probably with a fat pension, to go with the money he squeezed out of me and the other girls."

"What was his name?"

"Vazquez. And when Hatcher was transferred from

vice, another cop took his place, a Russian name, or something that sounds Russian, I don't remember."

"They don't matter for the moment," he said.

"Jesus, when I saw him arrive I—"

"Hatcher."

"Yeah, Hatcher. When he showed up, it was like going back in time. I thought I was through with him and his kind."

"He said you'd end up like Rosalie if you talked to anyone?"

"You got it." Now she faced him. "Look, I'm sorry if I took it out on you when you arrived. I wouldn't be here if I didn't trust you. It's just that we make a date and then *he* shows up."

"I appreciate your trust, Micki. The last time we spoke—I was with my partner, Detective Hall, remember?—I asked whether you'd told anyone about the tapes Rosalie had recorded of some of her clients. You said you had."

"What does it matter?"

"It matters a lot, Micki. I asked whether you'd told any of the cops. I think you said that you probably had told one of them. Was it Hatcher?"

"This is getting in too deep for me," she replied.

"Was it Hatcher?" he repeated.

"Hatcher knew about them," she said.

"Why did you tell him?"

"I don't know. Sometimes he could be, well, friendly when he was collecting his payoff, joke around."

"He ever put the make on you in place of cash?"

She laughed. "Hatcher? No. It was all money with him. He had a whole spiel to go with it. You know, coming up with reasons for taking payoffs—keeping us safe, helping us run our businesses. He used to say that if a john ever gave us trouble we should call him and he'd straighten him out."

"The patron saint of escorts," Matt quipped.

She grunted.

"How did it happen that you told him about Rosalie's tapes?" he asked.

"I don't know. No, I do know. It wasn't me, now that I think of it. We—Rosie and me—we used to meet him for the payoffs at that greasy spoon owned by a friend of his, Joe Yankavich."

"Joe's Bar and Grille, in Adams Morgan."

"Yeah. Joe's a slob but he's okay. He was always good to us. Hatcher had him on his payroll, too. Maybe he still does."

Jackson thought of Kahil, owner of the Silver Veil, who admitted to being shaken down. Hatcher?

"Rosie was in a funny mood that night," Micki continued. "She sometimes had a little trouble with the booze, just now and then. She'd get a snoot full and start talking—you know, gossip kind of things, funny stories about some of her johns."

"And she was in that mood the night you were with Hatcher?"

"Yeah. I started to get uncomfortable. I mean, talking about your johns is a no-no. Breaks the rules."

"Go on."

"So, Rosie keeps drinking, and Hatcher is egging her on, buying the drinks, being buddy-buddy, even after we'd handed over that week's payoff. At one point, Hatcher starts talking politics. He's a right-winger, right of . . ."

"Attila, the Hun," Jackson filled in.

"I guess. So Rosie says that liberals are lousy lovers. Hatcher says he figures, but challenges her to back it up."

"And she did."

A nod this time, then a sad shaking of the head. "The minute she mentioned Colgate's name, I wanted to crawl under the table."

"Wait a minute. She specifically mentioned Governor Colgate as one of her johns?"

"She sure did."

"What was Hatcher's reaction?"

"Oh, he thought it was hysterical. He kept telling her she was full of it, that she didn't have any clients like Colgate."

"To keep her talking."

"Right. He told her to prove it."

"And she mentioned the tapes."

"Yeah."

Jackson swatted away a mosquito. "Did the topic ever come up again?"

"Not like that. He asked me about it once, whether I knew if Rosie really had tapes of clients."

"You confirmed it?"

"I didn't want to."

"But you did."

She started to cry. "Damn it," she said, wiping her eyes with her knuckles. "Was she killed for those tapes?"

"I don't know," he said. "I really don't know. But I intend to find out."

Chapter 33

Jackson couldn't wait to get back to the Rollins house to share with Mary what he'd learned from Micki. He arrived a little before eight and found her in the kitchen, doing dinner dishes with Sue Rollins. Her raised eyebrows said she wanted to hear about the meeting. He winked and raised his index finger; *We'll get to that,* the gesture said.

Jerry Rollins was in the living room with the lead FBI special agent and Detective Bob Kloss.

"Enjoy your dinner?" Kloss asked.

"Oh, yeah, I did. Thanks for the time off. Nothing new here?"

"Afraid not. Mr. Rollins is reconsidering putting out a personal plea from him and his wife, maybe tomorrow or the day after."

"Sounds like a good idea," Jackson said. "Am I back at the office with Mr. Rollins tomorrow?"

"Afraid you're stuck with me again," Rollins said pleasantly, "but I won't be there for much of the day. Meetings."

With Kevin Ziegler, Jackson thought.

Mary eventually joined them.

"Mr. Rollins showed me his pride and joy in the garage," Jackson told her. "He's got a beautiful Porsche out there."

"Show her," Rollins said.

"Want to see it?" Jackson asked.

Mary had no interest in cars, but realized that he was using it as an excuse to get away from the others. "Sure," she said. "Love to."

Rollins escorted them to the kitchen, where he pulled the car's keys from a rack. "Start her up," he told Jackson. "She really hums."

Their appearance in the drive brought forth the usual couple of shouted questions from encamped reporters, which they ignored. Jackson turned on the garage's interior lights and closed the door.

"Okay," she said, "it's a nice car. Now, what happened with Micki Simmons?"

"Lots," he said, "but I'll try and whittle it down. I must have let slip her name when I confronted Hatcher today in the locker room at Metro. Know what he does? He visits Micki this afternoon and threatens her, says that if she talks she'll end up like Rosalie Curzon."

"Talks about what?"

"About him shaking down Micki and Rosalie and who knows how many other hookers. That's number one. He was getting protection money from them. Here's number two: He knew about the tapes."

"How?"

"Rosalie told him. She got drunk one night at Joe's Bar and Grille where he used to meet them for his payoffs. Looks like the owner, Yankavich, was on Hatcher's payroll, too. That explains why he hasn't written up Yankavich as a suspect. Anyway, Rosalie lets spill that she taped some of her clients."

"He knew about the tapes? When we were at the crime scene he acted like finding them was a big surprise."

"He put on a good show. Not only did he know about the tapes, he knew that one of them contained footage of Rosalie with Governor Colgate."

"Come on."

"I'm serious."

"So the rumors about Colgate and Rosalie are true."

"Evidently."

"And Hatcher knew about it."

"Yes."

"Does that mean he's the one who took the tapes from her apartment?"

"I'd say it's a good possibility."

"Which also means it's a possibility that he killed her to get them."

"Can't be ruled out."

"What about Micki Simmons? She can testify to what she told you."

He shook his head and absently ran his hand over the Porsche's fender. "She told me she'd never testify, and I understand. Besides, what can she testify to, and who'll believe her? She's an acknowledged prostitute. All she can claim is that Hatcher was shaking her down—which he'll deny, it was all cash, no paper trail—and that he knew about the tapes, including the one on which Colgate stars—which he'll also deny. It all comes down to he said, she said, and that means zilch. Right now, the worst charge that could be brought against him is through Internal Affairs about the shakedowns. Know what'll happen with that? He's retiring, probably on a fast track. They'll throw him a going-away party, he'll get his pension, and it'll be swept under the rug. Like I said, I told Micki she could leave the city. Hatcher's visit really shook her."

"But MPD can't sweep Hatcher under the rug if he killed Rosalie for the tapes."

"There's nothing to place him there that night, Mary, no witnesses, no forensics. If he'd actually been there earlier in the evening and killed her, he put on one hell of an act for us. He'd have to have grabbed the tapes, left, come back to Metro or stopped someplace else first to wash off any signs of the struggle, and then catch the case a few hours later and show up as the lead investigator. Perfect, actually, from his perspective. He ends up in charge of his own murder investigation."

She grabbed his arm. "We have to go to IA, Matt."

"No, we have to go higher, to Chief Carter."

She agreed.

"In the meantime, I want to stay close to Rollins until the kidnapping is resolved. If Colgate knew that he'd been taped in bed with Curzon—and there's a good possibility that he did, based upon the rumors floating around—the person he would have confided in would be Rollins, his close friend and advisor. The big question right now is that if Hatcher had the tapes, what did he do with them?"

"Sold them?"

"To who? They're damaging to Colgate, so it's the Pyle people who would benefit from having them."

"But wouldn't they have used them by now in the campaign?"

"You'd think so. Then again, maybe they don't have them—yet."

Rollins walked into the garage. "Well, what do you think?" he asked Mary, pointing with pride at the Porsche.

"It's beautiful."

He took the keys from Jackson, slid behind the wheel, and started the engine. A smile crossed his face and he looked up at them. "Is that perfection?" he said. "I love perfection."

Jackson and Hall looked at each other, each thinking the same thing: To be sitting behind the wheel of a fancy sports car and soaking up pleasure from the sound of its engine was incongruous, considering the larger picture.

Rollins turned off the ignition, got out, and led them back to the house. Small talk occupied the rest of the evening, and very little of that. After watching TV—the kidnapping was still in the news but had dropped down in order of importance—the Rollinses went upstairs, leaving the detectives and special agents to fend for themselves—napping, watching a cop show on TV, reading. Mary fell asleep in a recliner and Jackson covered her with a multicolored patchwork throw from the couch.

The waiting was taking its toll on everyone. Whoever abducted Samantha had done a clean, professional job. There had been calls to MPD from people with theories, and some who claimed to have seen something strange going on in their neighborhood. Those calls were followed up, of course, but nothing tangible came from them. The lack of contact from the kidnappers was the most unsettling of all. According to Kloss, who'd participated in other abduction investigations, not receiving a call for such an extended length of time was highly unusual. He'd pointed out to Jackson that of the approximately 800,000 children abducted each year in the United States, less than ten percent were taken by strangers with no connection whatsoever to the family of the child. The Rollins kidnapping clearly fell into that category. Those who picked the child up and swept her away from the fringe of the Mall were pros, with no axes to grind with the Rollins family, no grudges being played out, no questions of paternity or creating a wedge in a family dispute. No, these abductors were after something tangible, presumably money—or something else. The question was, what was it they wanted? There was no way of knowing without a phone call from them, or a note. Or a mistake.

The tapes?

Jackson couldn't shake that possibility from his mind.

He sat alone in the kitchen and mulled over his conversation with Micki Simmons. He liked her and was sympathetic to her situation, no matter that it had been self-generated. It was Rosalie Curzon with whom he had trouble mustering sympathy. Deciding to videotape some of her trysts with men, primarily those with high profiles in D.C., had been a shabby and certainly foolhardy thing to do, and had probably led to her murder. He admired Micki for adhering to the prostitute's so-called code of honor, maintaining the secrecy of customers. It didn't make prostitution more honorable, but there was, at once, a certain kind of honor in even considering a code of conduct in a distinctly dishonorable, albeit ancient profession.

He used the downstairs guest bathroom to brush his teeth, stripped down to his shorts and T-shirt, and climbed into one of two single beds in the guestroom, where he quickly fell asleep, his final thoughts of himself behind the wheel of Rollins's Porsche, Mary in the passenger seat, racing through a fall countryside, the top down, the sweet roar of the engine bringing wide smiles to both of them. It was a pleasant way to end a distinctly unpleasant day.

Chapter 34

As was by now their custom, Jackson preceded Rollins to his office the next morning and was with the second detective in the reception area when Rollins arrived. The attorney and confidant to the high-and-mighty was grim-faced as he walked past them, grunting a greeting, and closed his office door behind him.

Caroline raised her eyebrows. "A good morning to stay clear," she commented, returning to her chores.

At quarter of ten, Rollins left, carrying his briefcase. He stopped at Caroline's desk to say he'd be meeting with Kevin Ziegler at his office, but he expected to be back by noon.

Rollins took a taxi to the Eisenhower Executive Office Building, separated from the White House's West Wing by a narrow street. Many of the administration's offices were located there, as was the vice president's ceremonial second office. Richard Nixon had made more daily use of it than any other VP. Built between 1871 and 1888, the imposing building held a rich history in a city of rich histories. It took up an entire city block, and had been the site of the nation's first televised press conference. Top political advisors to presidents maintained their working offices there, although much of their time was spent in the West Wing, where they could be in closer proximity to their clients-in-chief.

After being cleared, Rollins was escorted to Ziegler's

office, a large, airy room with tall windows that afforded an unhindered view of the West Wing of the White House, a fitting perch from which to look down on his presidential protégé to make sure he didn't do something stupid and stray from the Ziegler political Bible.

"Sit down, Jerry," Ziegler said, indicating one of two matching blue leather club chairs on either side of a small, round table. "Thank you for being on time."

Rollins placed his briefcase on the floor next to him. He kept his leg in touch with it, as though expecting a hand to reach in and steal it at any moment. His emotions had run the gamut since his initial meeting with Ziegler and his decision. This day, at this moment, anger prevailed, anger at Ziegler and at himself, at Washington, and at Bob Colgate, at the sewer into which politics had sunk, and at the world in general and his place in it. It took all the restraint he possessed that morning to keep from erupting, from lashing out at Ziegler verbally and physically.

"I know this is unpleasant for you, Jerry," Ziegler said, a perpetual small smile on his lips, "but life takes funny turns."

"I find nothing funny about it," Rollins said.

"Poor choice of words on my part," Ziegler said. "Of course, you've brought what we discussed."

"Yes." Rollins reached down, opened his briefcase, removed the envelope and placed it on the table. Ziegler looked at it, a quizzical expression on his malleable face. "What do you figure the cost of a couple of videotapes is, Jerry?" he asked.

"I wouldn't know."

"Surely not much. How much did you pay for them?"

"I don't see where that's relevant."

"Just curious. They were brought to us first. I told you that."

Rollins sat up a little straighter. He'd wondered why

the tapes hadn't been offered to the Pyle campaign. It was only logical. "Why didn't you buy them?" he asked.

"Because there wasn't anything tangible to buy. We were told that the tapes existed but weren't provided with specifics. We decided it was a ploy, a scam, and told the seller to get lost."

That hadn't been the case with Rollins. He'd been offered the opportunity to actually view the tapes before committing to buying them, and had taken the seller up on that opportunity. He was stunned, of course, at what they contained, but kept his feelings to himself. "How much?" he'd asked.

"A quarter mil," was the answer.

"How do I know you haven't made copies of them?" he asked.

"You'll have to take my word for it," the seller replied, grinning. "I didn't make copies. I don't play games. We have a deal?"

"It will take me a few days to arrange for the money."

The seller put the tapes back in the shopping bag he carried and told Rollins to call when he had the money.

"I don't want to see you again," Rollins had said. "Can we arrange to have the tapes and the money exchanged without actually meeting?"

"Sure. I'll tell you where to come. But don't let this drag on too long, huh? You're not the only game in town." Another grin. "Nice meeting you."

Rollins manipulated campaign funds under his control—there was so much money, and so little oversight, that coming up with $250,000 and hiding it under miscellaneous expenses wasn't difficult. He called the seller and it was agreed that the tapes would be left at a designated spot, and where Rollins could deposit an envelope containing the cash. It went smoothly, and Rollins had not heard from the seller again, to his relief.

* * *

"I do have something to ask of you, Kevin," Rollins said.

"If I can."

"As you know, there are two embarrassing episodes on the tapes. I suppose you can call them 'episodes.' While one will suit your purposes, to use the other will smack of nothing but the vilest of motives."

"I understand what you're saying, Jerry, and you may be surprised that I totally agree with you."

"Good. Now, my daughter."

"Before we get to the specifics of that, Jerry, you must understand that her abduction had nothing to do with me, our campaign, or the president and his people."

"I don't believe you, Kevin, but that's irrelevant. I've delivered the tapes. I want my daughter back and I want her back now."

"Of course. But you do understand that for you to sit here and think of me as being even remotely capable of such a heinous act is saddening. I've always known you as a man who could compartmentalize the personal from the professional. You and I are both professionals, Jerry. Neither of us have within us the level of evil necessary to use an innocent child to achieve political advantage."

Rollins sighed. He didn't want to hear this sort of self-serving lecture, this blatantly dishonest attempt to salve Ziegler's conscience. Not that it was surprising. The Pyle machine had set the standard for lying away its misdeeds, a callous economic policy leaving millions behind, disastrous foreign incursions sold to the American public through out-and-out falsehoods, abject corruption in myriad agencies and departments, a litany of disasters that would seem to ensure a one-term presidency. Ziegler's disavowal of having knowledge of the plan to kidnap Samantha in order to obtain the tapes was business as usual.

"My daughter's return, Kevin. These people you say are behind it, when will they return her?"

"It is my understanding, Jerry, that she will be back in your loving arms tonight. I have been told through these other parties—and I emphasize that I do not know their identities—that you are to tell no one of her imminent release, not the police, not your lovely wife, no one. You are to be by your phone tonight. That's all I can tell you, because that is all I know."

Rollins grabbed his briefcase from the floor, stood, and walked to the door. He paused, his hand on the knob, turned, and asked, "How did you know that I had the tapes, Kevin?"

"How else, Jerry. The person who sold them to you was quite forthcoming with us. Enjoy your reunion with your daughter, Jerry. And forget this ever happened. It didn't."

Rollins returned to his office and announced that he was leaving for the day and could be reached at home. No one questioned him, although Caroline was tempted. He seldom took part of a day off. Of course, these were different times. Perhaps he needed to be close to Sue as the days dragged on without word or sign of Samantha. It was good, she decided, that he gave in to what must be exhausting and unending mental anguish. As he was leaving, she did mention that Mr. Scraggs had called to ask the status of his book proposal.

"Did he ask about Samantha?" Rollins asked.

"No, he didn't."

"Call him back and say that I have been unable to find a publisher and no longer wish to represent his book. Send his ridiculous proposal back to him. Call me if you need me."

"Yes, sir," Caroline said, smiling.

When Jackson was told that Rollins had left for the day, he called Kloss, who instructed him to return to the house. The afternoon was spent as all afternoons were—waiting for a fateful phone call that never came. Jackson observed that Rollins seemed unusually tense. He did a lot of pacing. When he wasn't in motion, he sat close to the phone in the living room, staring at it as though to will it into action. Afternoon turned to dusk and early evening.

"When will it end?" Sue asked at one point.

No one had an answer, except perhaps her husband, and he was mute.

Chapter 35

The call from Y-man came at 7:30 that night. The man who answered to "Paul" took it.

"Time to move," Y-man said. "Deliver her."

"All right."

"You're sure of every detail?"

"Of course."

"Good."

"What about the money?"

"It will be at the planned place at midnight, provided everything goes as planned on your end."

"It will."

The click in Paul's ear was loud and final.

Greta had been with Paul when he took the call. He told her to prepare Samantha to leave. Greta slipped on her homemade mask before entering Samantha's room. "Hi, honey," she said in her nicely modulated voice. "I have good news for you."

Samantha was sitting up in her bed. Her ankles were fastened together with tape. A tray containing the remnants of her dinner—a hot dog in a bun, cole slaw, potato salad, and a black-and-white milk shake purchased by Greta from a luncheonette and deli a few miles away—rested next to her.

Greta joined her on the bed and placed her hand on the girl's bare knee. "You're going home, honey," she said.

Samantha squirmed to face her captor. "I am? When?"

"Tonight."

Samantha cried. Greta pulled her close and massaged her slender back. "There's no need to cry, honey," she said, "but I understand. Tears of happiness." She held the child at arm's length. "Now," she said, "there are a few things I have to say, and you have to promise to listen to me closely. Okay?"

Samantha wiped her eyes with her hands and nodded.

"First of all, do you agree that we've never hurt you? Oh, I know, the tape we use hurts a little when we pull it off, but we never hit you, do we?"

Samantha agreed that they hadn't.

"We never beat you. Right?"

A nod.

"And we fed you good. I ran out many times to buy you what you said you liked, didn't I?"

"Yes."

"It's important that you know this, Samantha. When you get home, lots of people will ask you lots of questions about how you were treated. I just want you to be honest when you answer them."

"I will."

"Good. And I also hope you realize that this was just business. We have nothing personal against you or your family. The business had to be finished before we could take you home."

"Okay."

Greta stood. "All right, my little friend, I'm going to take the tape off your ankles, but you'll have to wear something over your eyes. I won't use tape, provided you promise not to try to remove what I put there. Promise?"

"I promise."

"Good. You're not only a very pretty young lady, you're very smart."

A half hour later, Greta sat in the back of the tan four-door sedan with the blindfolded Samantha. Paul drove.

They meandered toward the District, obeying all traffic signals and speed limits. Eventually, they turned onto Fourth Street, SE, and pulled to the curb, four blocks from the U.S. Capitol. It had started to rain hard during their trip, which pleased them. Fewer people on the streets.

"We're almost there, honey," Greta said. "Now, this is when you really have to listen to me and do everything I say. Understand?"

"I think so."

"Oh, no, sweetheart, you have to do *exactly* what I say."

"All right."

"When I take off your blindfold and let you out, you have to promise not to look back at us. Promise?"

"Yes."

"Say 'I promise.' "

"I promise."

"We'll be right in front of a very nice church. You are to walk into the church—no looking back—and sit down in a pew. You know what a pew is?"

Samantha nodded.

"I want you to sit there for five minutes. You can count to five minutes, can't you?"

"Yes."

"After five minutes, you can use this." She placed a stolen cell phone in the girl's hands. "This is a simple cell phone. It's all charged up. You know how to use a cell phone, I'm sure. All kids your age know how. After five minutes, you can use it to call your parents and tell them to come pick you up. The church is called the Capitol Hill Presbyterian Church. It's on Fourth Street and Independence Avenue. That's in the Southeast section of the city. Can you remember that?"

Samantha affirmed that she could, but Greta had her recite what she'd been told, which she did perfectly.

"All right. Ready?"

"Yes." Samantha started to cry again.

"No tears," Greta said, "or we won't be able to let you go."

The girl drew in a deep breath and brought herself under control.

"You're a very good girl, Samantha," Greta said. She kissed the girl's cheek as Paul pulled directly in front of the church. There was no one on the street. Greta opened the door, turned Samantha so that she faced away from her, pulled off her blindfold, and gave her a nudge out the door.

"Go!" Greta said.

Paul waited a few seconds to be sure that the girl did as she'd been told, walked directly to the church's front doors without even a glance back.

Jackson, Hall, another detective, and two FBI special agents were stationed in various parts of the Rollins house. Kloss had returned to headquarters for yet another briefing on what steps might be taken next. Jerry sat near the phone, his attention ostensibly on a magazine. His wife had been upstairs napping, but had just returned to the living room when the phone rang. Jerry had gone to the kitchen for a glass of water, leaving the phone for Sue to pick up. "Hello?"

All eyes were on her as she gasped, "Oh, my God!"

"What is it?" Jerry said, racing from the kitchen.

"It's Samantha," Sue said.

The hand holding the phone trembled uncontrollably and Jerry grabbed it from her. "Samantha?" he said. He turned to others. "It's her! It's Samantha. Where are you, honey? Are you all right?"

Jackson picked up an extension and listened as the girl, sounding remarkably calm, recited where she was.

"Let's go," Jackson said.

A marked patrol car parked in front of the house led

the procession of vehicles, its siren wailing and lights flashing. Jackson, Hall, and Jerry and Sue Rollins piled into Jackson's unmarked sedan and followed. A call was put out for other units to rendezvous at the church. The media camped on the street was taken by surprise but managed to dispatch a few vehicles in an attempt to catch up with the police. By the time Jackson pulled to a screeching stop at the church's entrance, three other police cars had arrived, their uniformed occupants fanning out along the sidewalk. Despite the heavy rain, the scene had attracted a sizable number of onlookers, who were kept at bay by the first officers to arrive.

The Rollinses, Jackson, and Hall raced up the steps and into the church's interior. It took a second to acclimate to the dim lighting, but when they did, they saw Samantha seated in a pew off to the left. She seemed oblivious at first to their arrival, as though in shock, afraid to look anywhere but straight ahead. But the sound of her name from her mother broke the spell. She turned as Jerry reached her and scooped her up in his arms. Sue wrapped her arms around them and they held the embrace for what seemed an eternity to Jackson and Hall, who watched the reunion with wide smiles, and tears.

"Let's get her back to the house," Jackson suggested.

It took some navigating to move vehicles and people who clogged the street to allow the car driven by Jackson, and containing Mary Hall and the Rollins family, to make its way back to Foggy Bottom and into the dry sanctuary of the Rollins home. Rollins had started trying to elicit from his daughter details of her captivity, but Jackson suggested they wait until reaching the house.

"You're right," Rollins said. "This isn't the time."

Kloss had heard the news and was there when they arrived. He took Jackson aside and asked what had brought about the release.

"I don't know," Jackson said. "It was the girl who

called from the church. She said where she was, right down to the address and quadrant. She was calm. Whoever dropped her there had obviously briefed her pretty good."

"What did she call on?"

Jackson handed him the plastic bag in which he'd dropped the cell phone Samantha had given him.

"Hers?"

"I don't know. I didn't want to question her until you arrived."

"I want to put her to bed," Sue announced. "She looks exhausted."

"Just hold up a second," Kloss suggested. He took Jerry Rollins aside. "I'd like to ask her some questions," he said.

"Now?" Rollins replied, incredulous. "She's been through a hellish ordeal. Can't it wait?"

"I understand your concern, Mr. Rollins, but I'd like to get from her anything she remembers while it's fresh in her mind. It's important, sir. You and Mrs. Rollins can be with her, and I promise I won't prolong it longer than necessary."

"All right, but keep it short."

Kloss, Jackson, Hall, and one of the FBI men sat with Samantha in the living room. She was huddled on the couch, between her mother and father, Sue's arm firmly surrounding her as though the questions might come as physical blows.

"You're quite a brave young lady," Kloss began. "We're all very proud of you."

Samantha looked up at her mother and smiled shyly.

"What can you tell us about the people who took you?" Kloss asked.

A puzzled frown crossed the girl's face. She shrugged. "I don't know," she said quietly. "There was a man and woman."

"Did you see them?"

She shook her head. "They wore things over their faces."

"Uh-huh. Masks. Just over their eyes?"

"No. Their whole faces, like ski masks."

"Did they call each other by name?"

"Once I heard him call her 'Greta.' "

"Okay. What about Greta?"

"She was nice to me. She had a nice voice, and she bought me food I liked."

"That's good to hear," Kloss said. "Do you remember how far you drove the day they took you from the Mall?"

"I don't remember. It was a long time."

"A long drive," Kloss said. "You have no idea where they kept you, whether it was in a big building or a house?"

"A house. I had a small room with a bed." Then, as though remembering something she was supposed to say, she said, "They never hurt me, never hit me. They were nice to me."

Sue broke down. "I'm sorry, but this is all so difficult."

"I understand, ma'am," Kloss said. "Only a few more minutes, Samantha. Did they say anything that might help us know who they were or what they wanted? Did they say anything about why they took you?"

"They said it was for business," she replied. "They said that they were going to let me go because the business was over."

"Business? Did they say what sort of business?"

"No." She turned to her mother. "Mommy, I'm so tired."

"Please," Jerry Rollins said.

"Of course," Kloss said. "Get her to bed. We'll talk more when she's rested."

As Mr. and Mrs. Rollins started up the stairs with

their daughter, Kloss called after them, "Mr. Rollins, I'd like time with you once she's tucked in."

Kloss took Jackson and Hall aside. "What do you figure happened?" he asked. "They hold the kid for days, then drop her at a church with a cell phone to call home. No ransom demands, no nothing, just some vague comment about business being done."

Matt and Mary looked at each other before Jackson said, "I don't know for sure what's going down, Detective, but I have a few ideas."

"Lay 'em on me," said Kloss. "I'm all ears."

Chapter 36

With Hall at his side, Jackson related to Kloss everything he'd learned about the tapes and his suspicions about Walt Hatcher's involvement with them and with Rosalie Curzon. Kloss listened without interrupting. When Jackson finished, Kloss summed up for himself what he'd heard.

"You say that Hatcher was shaking down the murder victim and others," he said. "Hatcher knew of the existence of the tapes, and that Governor Colgate was caught on one of them. And Hatcher threatened this other call girl, the Simmons woman, that if she talked she'd end up like her friend, Ms. Curzon?"

Jackson affirmed.

"You know, Matt, accusing a fellow officer of committing a crime carries with it an extra weight. Hatcher has had a long career with MPD, and plenty of decorations. You'd better be sure of your facts."

"We are."

"And you think Mr. Rollins might have used the tapes as ransom to get his daughter back."

"I don't know that," Jackson quickly said, "but considering the unusual circumstances of her return, it's a possibility."

"If you're right, Rollins put himself in one hell of a dilemma. What do you think, that Hatcher ended up with the tapes and passed them along to Rollins?"

"I doubt if he passed them along," Jackson said. "Sold them, is more like it."

"Which put Rollins between that classic rock and a hard place. Turn over those tapes to save your daughter and in the process sink your best friend's chances of winning the White House."

"Really no choice when it comes down to it," Mary offered.

"No, I suppose not," Kloss agreed. "I think we need a serious talk with Mr. Rollins when he comes down."

Other officers had packed up the monitoring gear and their personal belongings, and departed, leaving Kloss, Jackson, and Hall to question Rollins. Kloss took the lead, while Jackson and Hall sat quietly across the dining room table. They were impressed with Kloss's approach. There wasn't a hint from the wily detective that he knew anything of the tapes that might have led to Samantha's release. He was gentle, yet firm, a skilled interviewer.

"Obviously, Mr. Rollins," Kloss said, "there's been a happy ending to this unfortunate event."

"Thank God," Rollins said.

"Your daughter seems fine. I'm sure you and Mrs. Rollins were pleased to hear her say that she hadn't been mistreated."

"Something else to be thankful for."

"Detectives Jackson, Hall, and I have been trying to come up with a rationale for them releasing Samantha at this particular time. Your daughter mentioned that her captors talked about some sort of business having to be concluded before they could return her."

"Yes."

"Do you have any idea what they meant by that, what sort of business they were referring to?"

"I haven't the slightest idea," Rollins replied.

"I'm sure you can understand, sir, the reason for our

confusion. We've felt all along that the abduction was a professional job. The way they arranged for her release—no further phone calls from them, dropping her off at a safe haven like a church, and providing her with a cell phone to call you—only reinforces that belief. The question is, *why*?"

"Isn't it enough that Samantha is now safe at home?" Rollins said.

"That's certainly important," said Kloss, "and we share your relief. But that doesn't end it. A kidnapping has occurred, and we have an obligation to find and prosecute those behind it. It isn't over for us."

Rollins was having trouble disguising his annoyance at this line of questioning. To an extent, Jackson understood. The family nightmare was over. Time to get on with their lives, regardless of the police's need to press forward with the investigation. But he was also very much in tune with Kloss's responsibilities.

Rollins thought for a moment before responding. "Look," he said, "I fully understand that you have a job to do, and I assure you that I'll cooperate in any way I can. But I'm as baffled as you are why Samantha was taken, and why she was allowed to return home. As for this vague mention of some sort of 'business,' only the kidnappers know what they meant."

"Hopefully," Kloss said, "we'll come up with an answer to that question. In the meantime—"

Kloss's radio sounded. He listened, made a few notes, and ended the call. "I have to go," he said. "We've got a hostage situation, an estranged father holding one of his kids." He said to Jackson and Hall, "Why don't you continue this debriefing of Mr. Rollins. I'll be back in touch."

Jackson walked outside with Kloss. "What about Hatcher?" Jackson asked.

"Yes, what about Hatcher?" the senior detective replied. "You and Hall finish up with Rollins and head on home. I have your numbers. I'll call when this hostage situation is resolved and we'll discuss it."

Jackson rejoined Hall and Rollins. "I was just telling Detective Hall how much I resent this line of questioning," Rollins said after Jackson had retaken his seat. "It sounds as though I'm being accused of being involved in some sort of nefarious deal with the kidnappers."

"No one is accusing you of anything, Mr. Rollins," Jackson said. "But you will admit that the circumstances surrounding the abduction and return of your daughter raise the sort of questions Detective Kloss was asking."

"Sorry," Rollins said, "but your professional obligations don't give you the right to cast aspersions on me or my family. As far as Sue and I are concerned, the matter is over, closed, a nasty nightmare put behind us."

Jackson and Hall said nothing. Rollins stood and stretched. "If you'll excuse me," he said.

"One other thing, sir," Jackson said.

"Yes?"

"There have been these rumors about videotapes on which Governor Colgate might have been captured with the murdered call girl."

His words stopped Rollins as he was on his way out of the room. He turned and glared at Jackson. "Are you suggesting that—?"

"I'm just asking, sir, that's all. I realize it's a rumor but—"

"A salacious, baseless one."

"Even so, sir," Hall said, realizing her partner, and lover, had stepped into a minefield, "it's an avenue that we can't ignore."

Rollins's small smile wasn't convincing. "Somehow," he said, "I didn't think that rumors like that would be given credence by bright, young officers like you."

Jackson wanted to further explain, using what he knew about Hatcher and the tapes to make his case. He thought

Mary Hall might be about to go in that direction and headed her off with a look. He was also aware that Rollins's demeanor had changed. A nerve had been struck. Rollins seemed to be caught in a vortex of conflicting messages, unsure of what to say, or do, next.

When Rollins said nothing, Jackson said, "The tapes might represent just a rumor, Mr. Rollins, but we have to follow up on them as a possible motive in your daughter's kidnapping. I'm sorry, but that's the way it is."

Rollins left the room and went upstairs, leaving Jackson and Hall to pack up. As they gathered their things, Mr. and Mrs. Rollins appeared. "I just want to thank you for everything you've done," Sue said. She hugged Mary and kissed Jackson's cheek. "It's good to know that the city and its law-abiding citizens have fine young people like you working on our behalf."

"I thought I'd take a ride," Jerry Rollins said, "rev up the monster out in the garage. Take a spin with me?" he asked Jackson.

"I don't know, I—"

"Oh, come on, I know you're dying to. I need to get out now that this ordeal is over. I'll drop you wherever you want."

"Go ahead," Mary said to Matt. "Do you good. We'll catch up later."

"Sure?"

"Jerry and his toy," Sue said without malice. "Just as long as he doesn't wrap himself around a pole."

Jackson laughed. "Any danger of that, Mr. Rollins?"

"No, and it's Jerry. Remember?"

"Sure, Jerry, I'd love to."

As Rollins fetched his driving gloves and Sue disappeared into the kitchen, Mary said to Matt, "I'll grab some things at home and go to your apartment."

Once it became evident that there would be no statement that night from the Rollinses, much of the media had abandoned their stakeout in front of the house. The few who remained were taken by surprise as Rollins, with Jackson in the passenger seat, backed the Porsche from the garage, turned, and roared onto the street, tires screeching.

"Where's he going?" a reporter asked a colleague who was getting ready to leave.

"Beats me. Who's the guy with him?"

"That cop who's been here from the git-go."

"We follow?"

"Nah. I just caught that hostage situation. See ya."

The rain that had pelted the city earlier in the evening had stopped, the clouds breaking to allow a three-quarter moon and a smattering of stars to become visible. Rollins drove fast, glancing occasionally in the rearview mirror to be sure no one, especially media, was following.

"Slow down," Jackson said.

"Nervous, Matt? She really performs," he said to Jackson over the rush of air and the engine's fine-tuned hum.

"Sure does," Jackson agreed. "But I'd appreciate it if you'd drive slower."

Rollins laughed and maintained his excessive speed.

"Where are we heading?" Jackson asked.

"One of my favorite spots."

"Where's that?"

"Out by the airport."

Rollins sharply turned off into what Jackson recognized as West Potomac Park, a spit of land between the Potomac River and the Tidal Basin. As Rollins maneuvered into a parking spot away from a few other cars, a jet aircraft departing from Reagan National Airport thundered above; Jackson had the impression that he could almost reach up and touch its underbelly. Rollins turned off the ignition, sat back, sighed, and closed his eyes. Jackson didn't say anything to disturb his reverie. Another jet broke the silence, awakening Rollins. "Like to fly, Matt?" he asked.

"Always a little nervous."

"I love it. I wanted to take flying lessons but never got around to it. You know, business and family getting in the way."

"Must be fun flying your own plane."

"I'll never know. I sometimes come out here just to enjoy the takeoffs. Of course, it depends on which runway is being used. Planes always take off and land into the wind. Did you know that?"

"No."

"It takes such power to lift one of those planes off the ground. Such power."

Jackson agreed, and wondered why they were there.

"I'm always curious why people pursue certain careers. Why did you become a cop, Matt?"

Matt laughed. "I've been asking myself that same question a lot lately."

"Disillusioned?"

"Sometimes."

"I imagine you became a cop because you were going to do something good, get the bad guys off the streets, make society better. Am I right?"

"Something like that."

"We all come into our chosen professions with lofty ideals. I know I did."

"The law?"

"That, and politics. You know, Matt, politics in its purest sense is a noble profession. It has the power to change things for the better, cure social ills, promote a peaceful world, lift men's spirits."

Rollins glanced at the detective, who sat passively, waiting for more.

"The problem is that idealism too often gives way to

cynicism. The power that can be used for the good soon corrupts the idealist. Reality sets in, and you either adapt or find another calling."

"I'm sure you're right, Jerry, but I'm not sure why you're telling me this."

His words were snuffed out by another takeoff, this one seeming even lower than previous jets. Rollins looked to where the few other people in the park were intent upon watching the planes. "You see the same people out here all the time, Matt. It's a perfect place to see raw power in action."

Jackson didn't know how much longer he had with Rollins. The man obviously had something profound on his mind and was trying to express it—for what purpose, Jackson could only guess. Guess? He decided to push it.

"What about those tapes, Jerry?" he asked, not sure whether the question would elicit an angry response, or open up the conversation. He was pleasantly surprised.

"All right," Rollins said, "let's say such tapes existed, and that they played a part in Samantha's kidnapping and return. I'm not saying they did, but let's accept it as a hypothetical for this conversation. Fair enough?"

"Fair enough."

"I said before that politics in its purest sense is a positive thing, but that it can turn ugly, the way a war can turn ugly for either side. And let's face it, politics is war. People may not want to accept that, but it's the truth, and like any war things are done to hurt the enemy. Am I making sense?"

"I don't know," Jackson said. "What I *do* know is that a woman, a prostitute, was murdered, the same woman who taped clients, including some well-known people."

"And it's your job to find that murderer."

"Exactly."

"And you further think that murderer might be the next president of the United States."

Rollins introducing Governor Robert Colgate so directly into the conversation threw Matt off guard. And it was at that moment that he decided he didn't care about the tapes as a tool in the political war Rollins referenced. It didn't matter whether Colgate or Pyle occupied the White House next January. Nothing really mattered except Walt Hatcher and the conclusion Matt had come to regarding his involvement in the Rosalie Curzon murder.

"Did you buy those tapes from a detective?" he asked bluntly.

Rollins didn't answer.

"A detective named Hatcher, Walter Hatcher?"

Another jet snuffed out Rollins's response.

"You know more than you let on," Rollins said when the jet's engine noise had faded. "I'm impressed."

"Was it Hatcher?"

Rollins bit his lip.

"If it was," Jackson said, "it was Hatcher who killed the woman for the tapes. I want to nail him, and I'm sure you don't want to see a murderer go free."

"What I want, Matt, is *why* Samantha was kidnapped put to rest," Rollins said.

"I can't promise that," he said. "We'll try to identify and prosecute those who took her, of course. Personally, I really don't care as much about the tapes, Jerry, or why you bought them or where they've ended up. But I do care about seeing a murderer prosecuted and punished. It must have occurred to you when Hatcher brought them to you that he might have killed in order to get them. The murder of the call girl was in the papers."

Rollins started the car. He waited for another aircraft to pass over before turning to Jackson and saying, "Go get your murderer, Matt, but leave me out of it."

"I'm not sure I can. His selling you the tapes confirms that he took them."

"And I'll deny having ever had this conversation with

you. It's like politics, Matt. You give some, you take some. You negotiate and hope you end up with the better end of the deal. I intend to be sure that I do. Where would you like me to drop you off?"

"My apartment. It's in Adams Morgan."

Despite Jackson's pleas for Rollins to drive at a saner speed, the attorney floored the Porsche as he headed for Jackson's neighborhood. As he sped by an intersection, Jackson spotted the patrol car parked at the corner. The officer turned on his flashing lights and siren and swung in behind the Porsche. Rollins saw him and pulled to the curb.

The tall, burly officer swaggered up to Rollins. "License and registration," he demanded.

Rollins obliged. As he did, Jackson withdrew his gold detective's badge and displayed it.

"What's going on here?" the patrolman asked.

"Mr. Rollins and I have been investigating a crime," Jackson explained.

"That doesn't give him the right to drive like a maniac."

"You're right," Jackson said.

The cop squinted at Rollins's license, then at the man. "You're the Rollins whose daughter was kidnapped," he said.

"Yes."

He handed the license and registration back to Rollins. "Glad you got your kid back, Mr. Rollins," he said. "But take it easy or you'll end up a vehicular homicide."

"Thank you, Officer."

The cop cast a final, quizzical look at Jackson before returning to his vehicle.

"Thanks," Rollins said.

The Porsche attracted attention from passersby when Rollins pulled to the curb in front of Matt's apartment building.

"You're a nice young man," Rollins said, "and I sense that you're still an idealist. Don't lose that, Matt. Once you do, you can never get it back. Say hello to your lovely fellow detective, Detective Hall. I get the feeling there's more between you than simply being cops."

Jackson got out of the car. He leaned back in and said, "Slow down, Mr. Rollins."

Rollins flipped a crisp salute and drove off, racing the engine as punctuation to the power he'd obviously craved, and had lost forever.

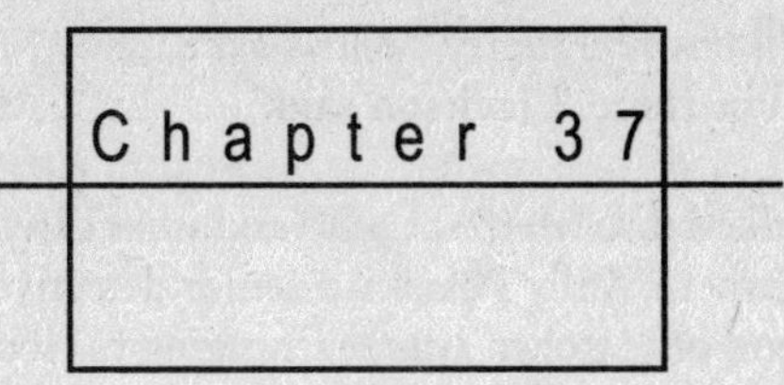

Chapter 37

At eleven that night, Matt Jackson and Mary Hall sat in front of the television set in his apartment, watching the news. It was reported that the hostage situation had been peacefully resolved, and Detective Bob Kloss was interviewed.

"The estranged father was distraught over the way a court hearing had gone," he said into the camera. "The child is okay, the father is in custody."

A half hour later, the phone rang. It was Kloss.

"Congratulations on resolving the hostage crisis," Jackson said.

"Thanks. It wasn't hard. The guy was upset, that's all, went off the deep end. Look, Matt, I said I'd call about Hatcher. Anything useful come out of your debriefing with Mr. Rollins?"

"I'd say so. Hatcher sold him the tapes taken from the murdered call girl."

"Rollins confirmed that?"

"He won't go on the record and he didn't use those exact words, but yes, he confirmed it. Gave me a lecture on the reality of politics. I feel bad for the guy. He might be going off the deep end, too."

"I called Chief Carter at home," Kloss said.

"And?"

"He wants to meet with us tomorrow morning at ten."

Jackson told Hall what Kloss had just said.

"You'll both be there?" Kloss asked.

"We'll be there," Jackson said.

They walked into Metro at 8:30 and went directly to their lockers, where Wally Pulaski, a senior detective and long-time friend of Hatcher, was rearranging his locker.

"You guys are off the Rollins case now?" he asked.

"Looks like it," Mary answered.

"You're back with Hatch?"

"We haven't been told," Jackson said.

"He's not coming in today," Pulaski said. "Called in sick."

"Sorry to hear that," Mary said. "He hasn't been feeling good lately."

"Yeah, I know," said Wally.

"I'm sure they'll give us something to do until Hatch comes back," Jackson mused aloud.

"Let me ask you something," Pulaski said. "Are you two out to make some kind of trouble for Hatch?"

"Of course not," Mary said. "Why would you think that?"

"Word gets around, you know. Scuttlebutt. He put in his papers, you know."

"So I heard," said Jackson.

"Be a shame to make trouble for a good cop who's about to retire. Wouldn't go down good with the others."

"I'll keep that in mind," Jackson said, anxious to leave. "Have a good one, Wally."

"Yeah, you, too."

They secluded themselves in the records room until it was time to go to Chief Carter's office. Jackson was sure it was his imagination, but he felt that other cops were looking at him and Mary in an accusatory way. Did people know that they and Kloss were scheduled to meet with the chief? More important, did they know *why*? One thing was certain. They were about to put into motion a course of action with serious ramifications, one that couldn't be called back once initiated.

He'd had moments after agreeing to meet with Kloss and Chief Carter that he'd wondered whether he should simply resign, go home to Chicago, and let Hatcher retire and sail away into the sunset, allow him to reap the rewards of his years on the force and get away with years of shaking down hookers and restaurant owners, and of murder. It certainly would have been simpler. He wasn't disillusioned about what this move would mean to his career with the Washington MPD.

Wally Pulaski's words stayed with him as he and Hall went upstairs to where Kloss waited outside Carter's office. They joined him on the wooden bench. A passing detective stopped and asked, "You seeing the chief?"

"Yeah," Kloss said.

"What's up?"

"Just routine," Kloss replied.

The detective looked at him skeptically but continued on his way.

"Know what you're going to say?" Kloss asked Jackson in a low voice.

"The same things I told you," was Jackson's reply.

"There's not much to back it up," Kloss commented.

"I know," Jackson agreed. "But there should be enough to at least bring Hatcher in for questioning."

"Carter will probably send your charges about Hatcher shaking down people to IA," Kloss said.

"What about the murder of Rosalie Curzon?"

Kloss shrugged. "Remember," he said, "I'm in your corner. But Walt Hatcher has a long career with Metro, and did plenty of good work over those years. But a crooked cop spoils the broth for all of us. If he's done what you say he's done, I want him strung up as much as you do."

"I'm not looking to string anybody up," Jackson said.

"Carter's bound to ask about your relationship with Hatcher, whether you're here carrying a grudge."

"That's not the case."

"I'm glad to hear that, Matt."

Was it the case? Matt wondered silently. Had he been looking for something to hang on Hatcher in retribution for the abuse and racial slurs he'd suffered? He didn't think so. At least he'd convinced himself that he would be sitting there no matter who it involved. Kloss was right. One bad cop cast a shadow over every good one. He thought of Manfredi. Nothing more had been said about his having been one of Rosalie Curzon's johns.

Was Matt being naïve in thinking he could single-handedly clean up a sprawling agency like the Washington MPD, the white knight on horseback riding in to rid the city of its dishonest cops? And was he about to paint the majority of good cops with the broad brush of Hatcher's misdeeds?

He was deep into these thoughts when the door opened and they were ushered into Carter's office, where the chief of detectives was joined by the ranking member of Internal Affairs and the deputy chief of police.

Forty-five minutes later, the three detectives emerged. They walked quickly downstairs and outside to the parking lot, where they could talk freely.

"I didn't think it would happen so fast," Hall said.

"Frankly, I didn't either," said Kloss. "You made a solid presentation, Matt."

"I was just happy that he listened. He really listened. I expected him to pass it off, call for some internal committee to study it."

"You've been in D.C. too long," Kloss said, slapping Jackson on the back. "Too many committees and too little action."

"But not in this case," Mary said.

Carter and the other brass had shown intense interest

in everything Jackson had said during the meeting, particularly the possibility that Hatcher had murdered Rosalie Curzon. The deputy chief referenced the rumors linking Governor Colgate to the slain call girl, some of which went as far as speculating whether her murder had anything to do with the former governor's paid liaisons with her. At one point, he commented, "If Hatcher killed her and it can be proven, it would go a long way to dispelling those rumors. And let's face it, Colgate's likely to end up the next president. I'm sure he'd appreciate our taking that heat off him."

Clearing Colgate by linking Hatcher to the murder was good politics.

The IA and deputy chief of police were the first to leave the meeting, and it was left for Carter to take whatever action he considered appropriate. He announced to Kloss, Jackson, and Hall: "I understand that Hatcher took a sick day," he said. "I'll call him and suggest he come in to meet with me. If he refuses, we'll go get him. I'll give him until three."

Kloss settled in, writing reports of his successful hostage negotiation the night before, while Jackson and Hall were instructed to stay away from Metro until called. They browsed shops in Georgetown and took out sandwiches and drinks from Booeymonger, which they enjoyed on a bench in a pocket park near Dumbarton Oaks. They'd said little during this mandated exile from headquarters, focusing on trinkets and clothing in store windows, and Georgetown's passing parade of tourists and locals who crowded the sidewalks. Jackson's cell phone rang at 2:30. He listened, ended the call, and said to Mary, "Time to go."

The small force of police assigned to go to Walt Hatcher's house and bring him into Metro left in two unmarked cars. Accompanying Jackson and Hall were Kloss, two detectives from Internal Affairs, and two additional detectives, who'd been recruited from the Crimes Against Persons division. One of the IA officers was in charge. Prior to leaving, he said, "We want to do this with a minimum of fuss and fanfare. Chief Carter called Hatcher, but he declined to come in on his own. He knows something's up and might give us a hard time, but I don't anticipate a need for force. If it proves necessary, do it quick and clean. Let's roll."

Jackson had often wondered where Hatcher lived, the sort of house, whether he was meticulous in keeping up his property or someone who tended to let things slide. He'd never met Hatcher's wife, Mae, and tried to picture the sort of woman who would be married to a man like Hatcher. Was he as difficult at home as he was at work? From what Jackson knew, Hatcher and his wife had been married for a long time. A few detectives who socialized with them talked of what a sweet woman she was—"She'd have to be to put up with Hatch," they joked—and lauded her cooking. Hopefully, their arrival at the house wouldn't be too traumatic for her. Maybe she wouldn't be home, he mused. That would be good.

The narrow, suburban street on which the Hatchers lived was quiet at 3:30 in the afternoon. Jackson looked left and right as they proceeded down it and saw no one. He was grateful for that. As much as he personally disliked Hatcher, he wasn't anxious to contribute to a public humiliation of the man.

The pleasant solitude of the street changed, however, as they approached Hatcher's address. A local ambulance was parked in the driveway.

"What's that about?" Kloss wondered aloud.

The two police cars came to a halt at the curb and everyone exited the vehicles. They stood in a group and surveyed the scene. There was no sign of anyone. Then the front door opened and a woman came out, accompanied by two EMTs dressed in white. Kloss led the police contingent to them.

"Mrs. Hatcher?" he asked.

She seemed startled by his words. "Yes?" she said.

"I'm Detective Kloss, ma'am. Is someone ill here?"

"My husband. He's . . ."

"We tried to reason with him," one of the EMTs said, "but he won't listen."

"What's wrong with him?" Kloss asked.

"Stroke, heart attack," the second EMT replied. "He needs to get to a hospital."

"Where is he?" the IA officer asked.

"He's in the back of the house," Mae responded. It was obvious she'd been crying. "I called nine-one-one when he started acting funny. He got a call from his friend, Wally—they work together—and after that his face looked sort of strange and he had trouble breathing. I pleaded with him but he won't listen. He can be so stubborn."

"He's back there alone?" Kloss asked.

"Yes. He . . ."

Kloss cocked his head. "He what?"

"He has his gun."

The IA cop took a fast look at the property. "You can get to the back around both ends of the house?" he asked.

"Yes. Why are you all here?"

"We just have to ask your husband a few questions, that's all," IA replied.

"Is that why Chief Carter called?" she asked.

Her question was ignored as the IA instructed two of the detectives to approach the rear of the house from one direction, while the others came at it from the other.

"Let me talk to him," Mary Hall said.

"He's armed," Kloss said.

"Let me try," she said. "I'll watch myself."

"No," Jackson said.

Mary headed for the side lawn that separated the house from the neighbor's home. Jackson followed closely, with Kloss and the IA not far behind.

"He's in a bad way," Jackson told her. "He's liable to do anything."

They reached the corner of the house and paused. "Hatch?" Mary called. "It's Mary Hall. Feel like company?"

There was no response.

Her second call also went unanswered.

She took a few steps forward, which allowed her to peer around the house and into the backyard. "Hi, Hatch," she said, further separating herself from the others.

Hatcher was seated in a green metal outdoor chair with a colorful yellow-and-blue cushion. Jackson moved closer so he, too, could see. The veteran cop wore khaki knee-length shorts on this warm day, a multi-colored Hawaiian shirt open to the navel, exposing his sizable gut, and sandals. But it wasn't his clothing that captured their attention. The left side of his face had slid down slightly, like heated paraffin. His left eye was rendered larger than usual, and the corner of his lips had parted into a crooked smile. And he held his department-issued Glock automatic.

"Well, look who's here," he said in a raspy voice. "Little Miss Sunshine. Your Oreo-cookie friend with you?"

Jackson stood up to Hatcher. "Yeah, I'm here, Hatch. You look like you could use some help."

"No, I don't need any help, especially from a punk like you."

Jackson let it pass and said, "Hatch, your wife's out front with the EMTs. They want to get you to a hospital. That's what's important, to get you well."

"You think I buy that?" Hatcher snarled, shifting in

the chair and groaning, his free hand going to his forehead.

"Your wife's worried," Mary said. "She wants you to get help."

Jackson noticed that a neighbor now stood in his yard watching what transpired.

"What do you say, Hatch?" Jackson said, taking a few tentative steps toward Hatcher.

Hatcher raised the Glock and pointed it at Jackson. "You come any closer, punk, and you're dead meat." His words were slurred; drool came from the sagging corner of his mouth.

Jackson raised his hands in mock defense, and backed away. "Okay," he said. "Take it easy. Nobody's here to hurt you. We just want you to get medical help and—"

"And take away everything I've worked for," Hatcher said. He waved the Glock in a circle, slumped back, and again pressed fingertips to his forehead and temple. Jackson thought he might be able to move on the hulking detective, but Hatch quickly straightened in the chair and raised the weapon again, this time to his mouth.

"That's no answer, Hatch," Mary said, unable to keep the panic from her voice. "Don't do it!"

Kloss and the IA stood behind Jackson and Hall, sharing in their helplessness. They watched as Hatcher, the Glock still pressed against his mouth, pulled himself up to full height in the chair. Then he went into a spasm, his right hand, which held the gun, going into gyrations, his finger involuntarily pulling on the trigger, one shot after the other, nine in all, sprayed over the yard. Jackson and the others ducked as one of the bullets passed over them. The neighbor threw himself on the ground. As Hatcher went into a tremor, the Glock flew from his hand and landed on the stone patio with a metallic thud.

The EMTs, who'd been just out of Hatcher's sight, rushed around the corner of the house and immediately went to work on him. He struggled against them. "He's like a damn bull," an EMT said as he and his partner tried to restrain the big detective. Jackson and the IA went to their aid, and between them they managed to contain him and deliver sedation through a well-placed shot in his arm.

He was still now, his chest heaving, his mouth more fully open.

"Where are you taking him?" Kloss asked an EMT. He was given the name of the nearest hospital.

"We'll have people assigned to his room," the IA said.

Hatcher was loaded into the back of the ambulance. A distraught Mae Hatcher stood and watched.

"Hopefully he'll be okay," Jackson said, putting his arm around the woman. "If you'd like, we'll drive you to the hospital."

Which they did.

Detective Walter Hatcher died that night in the hospital. He never regained consciousness. An autopsy was ordered.

Chapter 38

Walt Hatcher's obituary was short. It referred to him as a decorated veteran police officer who was within months of retirement. He left behind a wife, Mae, three children, and four grandchildren. The cause of death was a cerebral hemorrhage.

Within the MPD, the account of his passing, enhanced by rampant speculation, was less succinct. Everyone knew that a team had been dispatched to bring Hatcher in for questioning about a number of charges, including the shaking down of local businesses, extortion, suspicion of murder—and more important, that Jackson and Hall had been behind it.

They were assigned to temporary desk duty until a suitable permanent assignment could be determined. They weren't blind to the reason for being chained to a desk and kept out of the mainstream. A strong current of distrust swept through detectives loyal to Hatcher. Hall and Jackson were shunned by those cops, some of whom made it clear to Chief Carter that they would not welcome having either detective assigned to work with them.

Three days after Hatcher's death, Jackson found the word "traitor" scrawled on his locker door. Later that day, Mary's locker was defaced with the crude drawing of a rat. They complained to Carter about it and were told to let some time pass. "They'll get over it," he counseled.

"Keep your noses clean and things will straighten themselves out."

But while this pervasive, oppressive atmosphere pressed down on two young detectives within the walls of MPD, the fallout from Hatcher's death reached far beyond Indiana Avenue.

The first news of the existence of salacious tapes was floated by a lower-level member of President Burton Pyle's campaign staff, who confided in a political blogger on the campaign's payroll. He reported it on his daily blog, careful to issue the disclaimer that he personally had not seen the videotapes but had received word of them from "a trusted source within Washington political circles." He characterized the tapes—"as described to him"—as an X-rated encounter between former governor of Maryland and presidential hopeful Robert Colgate, and a paid escort, Rosalie Curzon, and the blog ended, almost as a throwaway, that she'd been the victim of a brutal murder.

This was, of course, picked up by other bloggers; within 24 hours, a single mushroom had exploded into a field of them, prompting Colgate to summon Rollins to a late-night meeting at a room in the Willard Hotel.

"I can't believe this," Colgate said after they'd shucked their suit jackets, loosened their ties, and poured bourbon over ice. Only a few table and floor lamps cast light over the suite's expansive living room, rendered darker by the mood. Rollins noted that Colgate looked as though he hadn't slept much, which was true. While presidents were known to age while in office, Colgate was visibly growing older before even attaining the post. His normally flushed complexion was wan, the cheeks sagging where once his boyish expression had masked his age.

Rollins had dreaded the meeting but couldn't see a

way out of it. Since the kidnapping and the events surrounding it, he'd wanted nothing more than to bow out of the campaign, tidy up affairs at his office, and take the trip to Hawaii he'd promised Sue and Samantha, maybe never to come back. But that was out of the question. He was in D.C., and as long as he was, he knew he had to play the game.

"Believe it or not, Bob, it's obviously out there."

"Is it? Just because some damn blogger says it is doesn't make it so."

"I understand what you're saying, but I don't think we have any other choice than to treat it as reality."

"Reality?"

"In the sense that if such tapes do exist, they'll start showing up on YouTube and the Drudge Report and every other sleazy video site."

"God, how could this be happening?"

Rollins exhaled and tasted his drink. He'd read Hatcher's obit and realized its ramifications. The detective had been the one person who could clear Colgate of any charges that he'd killed the call girl, and the man had taken that knowledge to his grave. Although Jackson had speculated that Hatcher had been Rosalie Curzon's killer, that's all it was, speculation. No one had publicly accused Hatcher, nor, Rollins was sure, were posthumous charges likely to be filed.

But any conjecture about the murder was almost irrelevant from a political perspective. That would float in the air for a while and then fade into the ether. Even someone as crass as Burton Pyle and his people wouldn't level that charge. What was crucially, perhaps terminally, damaging to Colgate's chances for the White House was that he'd paid for sexual services and was captured in the act on videotape. All the talk about Colgate's extramarital affairs would rise above gossip and be there in garish living color for a nation to witness.

"So what you're saying," Colgate muttered, "is that you believe I got caught on tape with some hooker."

Rollins shrugged but realized it was an inadequate response. "I have to assume that it's true," he managed. "Is it true?"

"All right. It's true. But who the hell would ever think that a hooker was taping her johns? It only happened once, Jerry, and I'm taking a big chance in confiding that in you."

"Have you spoken with Deborah about it?" Rollins asked.

"No, and she's the real problem. I can ride out the political fallout, but I don't know how to finesse this with her."

Maybe you can't ride it out politically, Rollins thought. *As for finessing it with Deborah . . .*

"I need answers, Jerry," Colgate continued.

You needed to control your libido, was what Rollins was thinking. *You should have thought of your wife when you made your date with the hooker.*

"This is outrageous," Colgate said. "People can go around making tapes of other people in private moments and turn them into freak shows on somebody's website?"

"Unfortunately, Bob, that's today's reality, and there's nothing to be gained by denying it's happening."

"You met with Ziegler."

Rollins's stomach dropped. Did Colgate suspect something?

"Right," he said. "We couldn't reach an agreement on the Miami debate."

"But maybe you can cut a deal with him. Hell, if those tapes go public, there's no question who's behind it. How did Pyle's people get hold of them? That's what I'd like to know. What did this hooker do, sell them to Pyle and his thugs?" His eyes suddenly brightened. "Maybe Pyle's people learned about the tapes and killed her to get their hands on them. Can we counter this thing by floating that possibility? We've got journalists we control."

"That's not a good idea, Bob. Frankly, I don't see any recourse but to wait until the tapes show up—and they may not—and face the storm head-on."

"That's the best you can do?" Colgate asked.

"I didn't put you in this position, Bob," Rollins said, realizing how easy it was to lie to one of his best friends, a man who depended on him in a most profound way. "By the way, Samantha seems to have weathered her ordeal nicely, no nightmares, no evidence of having been traumatized."

"That's good. Glad to hear it."

"Just thought you'd want to know."

Silence permeated the room.

"Any ideas about how to smooth this over with Deb?"

"No. And don't ask me to speak with her, Bob." Rollins got up to leave. "Let's see how this plays out," he said, heading for the door. "You've weathered some blows before. I'm sure you'll weather this one."

He left Colgate sitting in a chair near the window, his chin drawn down, his eyes staring straight ahead as though Rollins, as though no one, had been there. No matter how many loyal supporters were on hand to buoy his spirits, no matter what advice the collective genius of his close advisors could offer, the crowds at campaign stops, the media attention to his policies and visions for the nation's future, he was at this hour a man alone.

Rollins didn't envy him, any more than he envied himself.

Chapter 39

The rumor that the tapes existed was bad news enough for the Colgate campaign, but it paled in comparison to the public exhibition.

That happened two days later, on a popular video site. Only an abbreviated portion of one tape was shown. The male and female bodies were electronically blurred, although there was no doubt that they were naked. Colgate's face was also partially obscured, except for a few brief seconds during which no one would mistake him for someone else.

He was on the first day of a two-day campaign swing through the South when the tape first aired. He immediately canceled his few remaining appearances and flew back to Washington on a private jet, going directly to a suite in the Willard. Facing Deborah at that moment was too painful to contemplate. He knew, of course, that he was only postponing the inevitable, but felt he needed time to collect his thoughts in preparation for what was certain to be a nasty confrontation.

He gathered around him some of his top staff, but they had little to do. He secluded himself in the suite's bedroom for most of his first day back, leaving them to chatter with one another in hushed tones about what this meant to his candidacy—and by extension, their jobs.

He summoned the courage to call Deborah late in the afternoon but was told by their housekeeper of many years that Mrs. Colgate wasn't taking any calls.

"This is her husband, damn it!" Colgate exploded. "I'm not the press."

He was put on hold until the housekeeper returned with the message, "I am so sorry, sir, but Mrs. Colgate—"

He slammed down the phone.

He had better luck reaching Rollins on the attorney's cell phone.

"Have you seen it?" Colgate asked.

"No, but I'm told it's on some website."

"I'm at the Willard with the staff. I need you here, Jerry."

Rollins's hesitancy wasn't lost on Colgate. "I'll be free by six," he finally said. "I'll come then."

Rollins arrived on time. Food was sent up to the suite, and the staff engaged in a spirited discussion of how to best combat the release of the tape. Rollins took part in the brainstorming but his heart wasn't in it. He wanted to be somewhere else far away from this blaze that he'd ignited.

He'd worked hard since the day he turned over the tapes to Ziegler, to excuse his actions to himself. What was a man to do? His daughter's life was at stake. That trumped anything and everything. There were times when he considered admitting to Colgate that he'd been behind the release of the tapes to Pyle's people. After all, he'd bought those tapes from the rogue cop named Hatcher to protect Colgate and his candidacy, and had taken comfort in the fact that his actions were well meaning. He'd intended to destroy them from the moment they came into his possession but had never gotten around to it. Or had he wanted, at some psychological level, to keep them? Shades of Nixon and the eighteen-minute tape.

Once Samantha had disappeared, though, all bets were off. How could any thinking, caring person question his decision?

Colgate listened to the variety of suggestions offered by the staff. When the ideas had been exhausted, he said, "Facing it head-on is the only way." He turned to Rollins. "You agree, Jerry?"

Rollins nodded. "I see no other approach," he said.

Most of the staff eventually drifted from the hotel, leaving Colgate, Rollins, and a press aide to field calls from media that had tracked down the candidate. Colgate and Rollins went into the bedroom and closed the door.

"I've been trying to reach Deb. She's laying low. Can't blame her. I'm going to the house. I want you to come with me."

"I won't do that, Bob."

"I don't believe I'm hearing this."

"This is between you and Deb," Rollins said. "There's no role I can play that would possibly help."

"I need a buffer, Jerry. Deb has always respected you. You two have been close for a long time."

Rollins read more into that statement than Colgate intended.

"No," Rollins said. "You and Deb have to work this out. You have a marriage to salvage, as well as a campaign. I work on your campaign. Your marriage isn't in my job description."

Colgate stayed in the suite until nine, when he announced to the press aide that he was leaving and could be reached at home. She briefed him on the calls from the press—there were forty-seven of them—and asked whether he had decided to address the media.

"That depends," he said.

"The hotel says that there's a slew of them downstairs," she said.

He called the hotel manager and asked that an alternative exit be arranged. Twenty minutes later, he was escorted from the suite by hotel executives and the Secret Service agents who'd been camped outside his door. They led him through the inner recesses of the Willard to a rear door used by deliverymen.

There was no escaping the reporters in front of his Georgetown townhouse, however. Uniformed police dispatched to maintain order cleared a path for Colgate as he ignored the chorus of questions hurled at him, bounded up the steps, and used his key to open the front door, shutting out the cacophony behind him.

The housekeeper heard his arrival and came to the foyer.

"Where's Mrs. Colgate?" he asked.

The housekeeper fought back tears. "Upstairs, sir."

"What's wrong?" Colgate asked.

She shook her head and ran from the foyer.

He approached the stairs and looked up. The landing was dark, but light from the master bedroom seeped through the door, which was slightly ajar. He walked up slowly, his legs heavy, his breath shallow. He paused at the top. "Deb?" he called. There was no response. He went to the door and pushed it fully open. Deborah sat in a wing chair by the window, an empty glass next to her. His eyes shifted to her designer luggage, which was nestled together at the foot of the bed.

"Hi," he said, stepping into the room.

She was mum.

He crossed the room and took the matching chair. "I came back early," he said.

"I heard."

"I know what you must be thinking, Deb, but—"

She held up her hand. "I don't want to hear it, Bob. Please, I don't want to hear it from you."

"Is there someone else you'd rather hear it from? The press?"

She dropped her hand and turned away.

He reached for her knee. She remained motionless.

He looked at the luggage. "You have an appearance scheduled?" he asked.

"No."

She abruptly stood and walked to another window. "I'm leaving," she said.

"What are you talking about?"

"I'm leaving, Bob. I'm leaving the marriage and the campaign."

"Oh, now, wait a minute," he said. "I know this is rough, but we can get through it. We have to get through it, and we can only do that together, as a team. We've come so far that to—"

"Shut up!" she snapped, now facing him. "Do you really think I'd continue with this farce?"

"It's anything but, babe," he said, closing the gap between them but having the good sense to not close it all the way. "We knew going into this that it would be tough, dirty, slime tossed at us. Pyle and his people are ruthless, Deb. That's all this is, Pyle and his people throwing the kitchen sink at us, character assassination, gutter politics. We can overcome it. I know we can. The voters don't give a damn about sexual slurs and innuendos. What they do care about are the issues, the economy, this immoral war Pyle got us into through lies. Health care, college tuition, gas prices—those are the bread-and-butter issues that hit them in the pocketbook."

"Is that all this is, Bob, sexual slurs and innuendo?"

"You bet that's all it is, Deb. Look, we can ride this out, provided we act as one. We can set up something on TV, a prime-time interview, go straight to the American people. Believe me, I know how to spin this—and it *will* work."

Her voice was as hard as her face. "No, Bob," she said, "*we* will not go directly to the American people.

Do you really think that I'll be at your side like those other pathetic women who stand by their men, aging by the minute, looking adoringly at their philandering husbands while inside they're seething with rage and loathing? No, Bob, you won't get that kind of performance from me. You're on your own."

She went into the bathroom and closed the door, leaving him to ponder what she'd just said and to contemplate his next move. Surely she couldn't mean it. You didn't just walk away from becoming the most powerful woman in the land.

"Deb?" he called.

Her driver appeared at the bedroom door.

"What do you want?" Colgate said.

"Mrs. Colgate's luggage," he replied meekly.

"She won't be needing it."

Deborah came into the room. "Thank you, Joe," she said. "I'll be down in a minute. You can take the bags."

The driver wrestled the luggage from the room and into the hallway. Colgate followed him and slammed the door, turned and faced his wife. "This is insanity," he said. "You're overwrought, and I can understand that, but you don't just toss away years of working together to reach the goal we've had our eyes on. Please, sit down and let's discuss this like two rational people, the way we've always done when we've faced a problem."

She ignored him as she checked herself in a full-length mirror. She wore one of his favorite outfits, a smart teal pants suit and tailored white blouse, not unlike a man's tux shirt. She was always attractive, he thought, but at this moment she was stunningly beautiful.

"One last thing, Bob," she said. "I don't want you to be blindsided. A second tape might show up on YouTube, or some other video blog site."

"A second tape? What are you talking about?"

"A tape of me with your whore."

"What kind of crazy talk is that?"

"I knew about Ms. Curzon, Bob, knew that you'd had sessions with her. Meeting her at hotels was at least prudent, but going to her place was so stupid."

"How did you know?"

"You assume everyone around you is loyal. Your ego doesn't allow any room to think that maybe there are people who find your behavior to be shabby, people who have some feelings for me. I called Ms. Curzon and made a date, just like you did."

"I can't believe I'm hearing this," he said.

"Oh, you'd better believe it, Bob. It's true."

"And you . . . ?"

"That's right. I went there. I wanted to see what it was that attracted you to her, what she had that I didn't. I intended to go through with the reason I was there, to have sex with her, but I chickened out halfway through. It wouldn't have been my first lesbian experience. Connie and I tried it in college, just an experiment, just once, but it didn't do much for either of us."

"This is insanity," he said, no energy behind his words.

"The point is, Bob, don't be shocked if Ms. Curzon caught me on tape, too." She forced a rueful laugh. "Quite a pair we make, huh? We can always find new careers in the porn movie business."

She went to the door and opened it, turned, and said, "You probably don't believe this, but I hope you win the White House, Bob. Pyle has been a disgrace as president. You'll make a much better one."

He sat stunned for a minute before going to the second-floor landing and looking down to where she spoke with the Secret Service agents assigned to her. "I won't be needing you anymore," she said. "I'll no longer be campaigning. Thank you for everything you've done."

She stepped through the door while the lead agent used his radio to report this unexpected turn of events.

Colgate heard a car start and pull away, followed by a chorus of shouts from the press. The agent looked up at Colgate as though asking what his next move was.

He heard nothing from Colgate, who walked back into the bedroom and shut the door.

Chapter 40

Robert Colgate, former governor of Maryland and candidate for the president of the United States, was interviewed in prime time by Barbara Walters.

"Although you aren't legally divorced yet," Walters said during the interview, "you will go into the White House if elected in November as a bachelor, the first since James Buchanan. Buchanan never married, but do you expect to marry while in office, the way Presidents Tyler and Cleveland did?"

"That's impossible to say, Barbara," he replied, "but I wouldn't rule it out." His smile was charming, as it was throughout the interview.

"Do you think being a separated and soon-to-be-divorced man will hurt your chances to win in November?"

"It didn't hurt Ronald Reagan," he responded. "He was the first divorced man to win the presidency, and I intend to be the second."

Questions about the tape on which he was captured with a prostitute were nimbly skirted and quickly turned to what he intended to say about his policies versus those of his opponent. "I'm a human being," he said, "one who had a momentary human weakness. But what's important to the American people is that they have a president who understands their concerns and needs, a president who . . ."

Pyle's surrogates wasted no time, of course, in jumping on the bandwagon and piling it on. They made the rounds of talk shows, denouncing Colgate for being a brazen philanderer and law-breaker. "Is this the sort of man the American people want to lead them through these perilous times?" they asked, always adding, "Our hearts go out to the family of Governor Colgate at a time like this."

Conservative spiritual leaders were also quick to chime in from their pulpits, delivering fiery sermons bemoaning the lack of moral values in the nation and calling for a cleansing of America's soul.

Naturally, the fact that the woman in the tape, an acknowledged prostitute, had been murdered came up tangentially, but no one attempted to create a direct link between Colgate and the crime except for a rabid publisher of a right-wing newspaper, who demanded that the Washington MPD conduct a thorough investigation. "We've had a variety of scoundrels in the White House," he editorialized, "but having a murderer place his hand on the Holy Bible and swear to uphold the Constitution would be a first, as well as a travesty."

Many Americans followed the tale of the tape, but eventually even those with the most prurient interests tired of seeing it and returned to their less real reality shows.

Although overt harassment at MPD of Jackson and Hall had abated by October, he announced to her that he was resigning from MPD to return to pursue an advanced degree at the University of Chicago. She tried to dissuade him but knew his mind was made up.

"I don't think I was ever cut out to be a cop," he said.

"I think you were a great cop," she said. "I'll miss you."

"I'd like you to meet my folks," he said. "You'd like them."

"I'm sure I will. Just say the word and I'll be there."

As Election Day approached, polls showed that Colgate trailed Pyle. Although the tape's importance had faded, Pyle's people worked hard to keep it front-and-center, and succeeded to some extent with sympathetic bloggers and talk show hosts. Jerry Rollins continued to advise the Colgate campaign but found his importance waning as the days went by. His role abruptly ended on a rainy Sunday afternoon when the Porsche he was driving slammed into a bridge abutment. Police estimated he was traveling at close to 100 miles an hour. His obituary was long and glowing, a fitting tribute to one of Washington's most influential power brokers. Although the insurance company that had written his multi-million dollar life insurance policy initially questioned whether it was an accident or a deliberate crash, they eventually, albeit reluctantly, paid up.

Mae Hatcher sold the house in which she and her husband, Walter, had spent so many years together and in which they brought up their children. While cleaning out the garage in preparation for the move to Florida, she discovered $250,000 in cash hidden behind old tires, oil cans, and other paraphernalia. There was a moment when she considered reporting it to someone, but quickly scotched that idea. Her husband's frugality had paid off. He'd always provided for them when he was alive, and had done the same after his death. She said a silent prayer in praise of him right there in the garage, and took the cash on the drive to her new life.

And on the November Wednesday after Election Day, headlines proclaimed:

Colgate Bests Pyle in Squeaker
Challenger Closes Gap in the Final Days